SIGRID AND ELYN

EDALE LANE

PAST AND PROLOGUE PRESS

CONTENTS

Sigrid and Elyn: A Tale from Norvegr

By Edale Lane

Published by Past and Prologue Press

Edited by Melodie Romeo

Cover art by Enggar Adirasa

First Edition September 2022

Printed in the United States of America

Created with Vellum

✿ Created with Vellum

ACKNOWLEDGMENTS

A special word of thanks to my beta readers, Sarah Tubbs, Kris Walls, Rowan Liddell, and Debbie Fahlman, for their time and ideas. Added thanks to Laure Dherbécourt for proofreading and Johanna White for scouring through every word with me. I also wish to recognize my production team of J. Scott Coatsworth, Stephen Zimmer, and artist Enggar Adirasa. And I will not forget to say thank you to my newly formed team of ARC readers and promoters—thank you so much for your support! Also, after the epilogue you will find helpful notes, pronunciations, and definitions of terms, so if anything tries to confuse you, just flip to the endnotes.

TRIGGER WARNINGS

This is a Viking action novel, but for readers who may not be certain what that entails, please be advised there will be battle violence, slavery was a part of life, and characters will die in this book. There is an additional content warning for the memory of a rape which occurred before the series of events in this story begin.

CHAPTER 1

In the year 649 C.E., west coastal area of a land known as Norvegr

"Shield wall!" Sigurd's commanding voice cut through the clamor of approaching hoofbeats and swells breaking against the rocks of the fjord below the gently sloping meadow. The lea reserved for sheep, goats, and cattle to graze upon had become hotly contested soil that would soon soak up the blood of once peaceful neighbors.

In an instant, Sigrid pressed her shoulder to his, their shields locking, long shafted spears in their right hands. Rangvoldr and Gunnlief held to either side of the twins who formed the center of the line while more round shields rippled down a row twelve across and three deep, like the wings of black and yellow magpies. With a shout, they defied the attacking army of Firdafylke.

Under the colors of red and black, their flag bearing the image of the serpent, warriors from the north dismounted their steeds and raced to form their own shield wall. Sigrid could not make out the faces of individuals from behind the hedge of shields, but it was just as well. These men were no longer their friends, though why King Tortryggr the Navigator would have sanctioned such an attack was beyond her understanding. Diplomacy would have to wait. Today she and her brother's forces must defeat this band and send them fleeing to the safety of their walled towns.

Sigurd, who was taller by two inches, peeked over the iron rim of his wooden rönd. "Where is Jarl Njord, hiding behind his mother's skirts? Ah, there you are on your horse, using your men as a shield!"

"Jarl Sigurd Olafsson!" he yelled in reply. "Is that you? I thought you still suckled at your mother's tits! I hear Sigrid can best you on her worst day."

Sigrid's brother shot her a grin. "She can wipe her ass with your entire army on her worst day! Go home, Njord," Sigurd advised in a serious tone. "Why should we kill each other?"

"Because your King Grimolf the Wolf is a greedy bastard." Njord's manner was no longer teasing, but rife with anger. "Attack!"

The group of warriors with the red and black shields rushed across the field, holding their formation as tight as they could.

"To the fore!" Sigrid cried out, and her line advanced as one soldier, shield wall knit with spears extended like narwhal horns. She and her brother wore silver-plated iron broe helmets with chinstraps and cheek guards, but because of their expense, most of their fighting men had none. Being a jarl's children also afforded them better armor and weapons. Sigrid donned spaulders and a breastplate over her padded gambeson with a thick leather belt and bracers casing her forearms and shins. Sigurd's lamellar armor of metal squares sewn into a tunic covered his gambeson, adding to the buffer his iron-bar bracers and greaves granted. Armed with a spear, Ulfberht sword, bearded ax, and long knife, each twin epitomized a Norse champion. Though only twenty-six years old, they had already carved out reputations and stories were told of them throughout the fylkes, the small independent kingdoms of Norvegr.

Each time she engaged in battle, Sigrid's energy raced, and this was no exception. Sweat formed at the edge of her blonde hair under the leather lining of her helm and trickled past sky-blue eyes, over high cheekbones, and down a firm chin to dampen her throat. With her left forearm bracing her rönd and her spear gripped firmly in her right hand, the front line of the push crashed into the oncoming infantry with tremendous force, sending a jarring wave through her body. She pulled back her lance and thrust it forward, sneaking peeks between, below, or above her shield for aim. The second and third rows of fighters raised their shields up and over, creating a turtle-shell effect which discouraged attackers from attempting to jump over them to assault their rear. This did not mean they didn't try.

A lanky fellow from the enemy lines climbed onto steps formed from shields and lunged forward with a mighty leap, an ax in each hand, but a man on their third row pushed up with his twelve-inch sharpened iron blade affixed to his eight-foot-long ash stave, impaling him through the middle. Sigrid heard a moaning thud as his body crashed to the ground but could not afford to look back. An assailant's spear point glanced off the edge of her greave and Gunnlief to her right stomped on it, breaking tip from shaft.

For several minutes, each side pressed ahead, digging in with their heels, exerting their muscles to force forward momentum. Someone to the left of Rangvoldr's position fell to an injury, but a warrior from the second row immediately filled the void. Every muscle strained with adrenaline-driven intensity as Sigrid gained a few inches of earth, remaining yoked with Sigurd. Grunts and power-invoking yells emanated from both small armies of roughly forty fighting men each until at last, a hole broke in the center of their opponent's line, causing Sigrid and Sigurd to all but stumble through.

In an instant, the twins were back-to-back as single combat ensued between members of the opposing forces. With complete confidence in her brother, Sigrid focused her attention on the foe in front of her, a stout but shorter man, with a wiry brown beard and half-shaven head. Dirt and blood speckled a face only a mother could love. She blocked his ax with her shield and thrust her spear at him. He sidestepped her jab and brought his weapon down toward her shaft, but she pulled it back and lunged ahead, leading with her rönd while his ax head was down. Ramming him with her yellow shield adorned with twin black ravens knocked him back, and she drove her spear forward, wounding him in his left side.

She yanked her spear tip free of his torso and the man doubled over, clasping a hand to his issue of blood, but to his credit, remained on his feet. All the same, he was of no concern and Sigrid turned her attention to the next combatant. This blond warrior's hair whipped loosely about the sparsely bearded face of a youth. She never liked to kill women or boys in a battle and couldn't recall having done so in the past. Drawing on her skill to maim rather than destroy, Sigrid bent to lay her spear on the ground, pulling the long knife from her boot with the same motion. She briefly stepped away from Sigurd to block the youth's ax swing. She whirled around him, reaching low and cut his hamstrings on peasant legs that bore no protection beyond woolen trousers. It would take him out of the fight and perhaps save his life.

In an instant, Sigrid was once again at her brother's back. With no one swinging a weapon at her head, she took a moment to scan the battlefield. There was Njord on his steed directing his troops from a distance, like a coward. Autumn leaf hair hung in braids beneath his silver helmet, which without a chainmail veil or cheek guards showed off his groomed mustache and sideburns with a smooth, shaved chin. His armor was even more elaborate than hers or Sigurd's, as well as remaining clean and unmarred from steel or iron blades. The sight of him filled her with contempt.

"Jarl Njord, your cock is so tiny—how can your woman find it?" She jeered, hoping to draw him into the fray, but he may not have heard her over the tumult as he did not so much as flinch.

Turning away from him with disgust, her gaze fell upon a singular vision, and Sigrid froze, fixed on the form of a compelling shieldmaiden with hair of flame and a body that made her loins tighten. *"Tis but the heat of combat that fuels this lust,* she reasoned as adrenaline rushed through her. The woman wore only a gray tunic and trousers covered by a mud-brown gambeson, but she wielded a sword and rönd with precision and power. She stood her own against one of Sigrid's fighters and had already bloodied him. Sigrid did not wish her ally ill, but a fierce sense of desire for this fair warrior to survive the battle was so prevailing she could not deny it.

Sigrid was so mesmerized by the image of one of Odin's Valkyries she almost didn't raise her shield in time. Blocking the enemy's attack, she drew her sword and traded a few blows with him before the tip of her blade slashed his neck. He collapsed to the ground with a dozen other fallen, yet under the darkening clouds of the sky, the hostilities raged on.

After defeating her next two opponents, Sigrid spun to realize she stood toe to toe with the red-haired shieldmaiden who swung a sword at her. Sigrid blocked with her rönd and replied with her blade. She wanted to speak to the woman, but what could she say? This valiant female fought on the side of her enemies, of a king who had broken a long-standing truce by sending soldiers to cross the border and attack them.

Up close, she was even more beautiful, as if she had fallen from Ásgarðr and the hall of the gods. But there was determination in the jade green eyes which met hers, and though she did not stand as tall, the woman's robust arms and shoulders matched her own strength. She pushed off Sigrid and resumed her stance but hesitated to mount another assault. *Is she as thrown off balance as I am? Stop this, Sigrid! You lead this army. You cannot shy away from a fight because you face a heavenly shieldmaiden.*

Sigrid spun her sword and began placing her feet with deliberation as she initiated a measured advance, never taking her gaze from the one gleaming at her from a staff's distance away. Their swords clashed, sending sparks to the moist ground below as the two circled, trading blows intended to strike steel or wood, rather than flesh.

"What are you planning to do?" she heard Sigurd's voice cut through the din of battle. "Invite her to dance at the next feast in our great hall?"

At once, Sigrid spied a spear flying at them out of the corner of her eye. There was no time to think, only react. She reached out and grabbed a handful of her foe's tunic above her gambeson and pulled her into herself, their shields clanging together. The lance sailed through the space her opponent had occupied less than an instant ago, striking the ground several yards past them. The red-haired warrior looked as shocked as Sigrid, who immediately released her garment, taking a step to the rear and readying her sword.

The women's steel struck again, and they both pushed into the blow, drawing near to each other a second time. Sigrid felt as if she was once more in the shield wall as the woman with stronger curves dug in to push her back, but Sigrid held firm.

"Why does King Tortryggr send you to attack us?" Sigrid wanted to ask her name, her rank, why she'd never seen her before, but this question made more sense, given the circumstances.

"What do you mean?" shot her heated retort. "You attacked us first!"

Now anger and insult flashed in those gemstone eyes, but only for a second before streaks of lightning split the sky. Sigrid had not noticed, but the day had darkened as if unto night and an icy wind whipped off the fjord. Great rolls of thunder crescendoed into a mighty crack and the firmament opened up.

The fighting waned as warriors raised wary glances upward. A white bolt of lightning accompanied by a deafening roar struck the ground nearby and Sigrid felt tiny fingers of electric current shoot up from her boots through the blood in her veins.

"Thor strikes his hammer!" roared a warrior of Firdafylke. He backed away from Sigurd with dread, glancing up at the bright chains that rattled overhead.

"Call this off, Sigurd!" Gunnlief insisted. "Thor is angry with us!"

"What say you, Njord?" Sigurd yelled through the mounting storm. "Must we do battle with the gods and each other? Pull back your warriors. Let's settle this another day."

As driving rain drenched the red-haired shieldmaiden, her clothing sticking tight to her skin left little to the imagination; it was a vision Sigrid would carry home with her. She took a backward step, and her opponent nodded to her.

"Why did you save me from the spear?" she asked, drawing Sigrid's attention away from Njord's consent to cease combat.

Sliding her sword back into its scabbard, she picked up her lance from where she had left it on the grass. "Why would I wish to see such a worthy opponent done in by a random spear hurled by someone other than me? It was not your day to die, shieldmaiden," she declared, and turned to trot after her brother and their crew under the fury of the deluge.

CHAPTER 2

That night in the village of Kaldrlogr, Firdafylke

$\mathcal{E}$ lyn sat at a long pine table in the dry warmth of Jarl Njord's great hall, drinking mead and recounting the events of the day with her fellow warriors. A huge firepit, torches, and candles lit the spacious banquet hall where the jarl would mete out justice and settle arguments as well as entertain. Banners of Firdafylke, a black serpent bent in the center of a red flag, hung on the walls along with shields, wood carvings, and multicolored tapestries. The chamber was abuzz with excitement and Elyn was eager to be an integral part of the celebration.

"The gods intervened on our behalf," announced her cousin Geir, who was seated to her right. The young man with curly brown hair wiped a hand down his meager beard to rid it of spilled mead. "Thor struck his hammer to send the rabbits of Svithjod scampering away before too many of our men were maimed or killed."

"Nay!" disputed Ingvar, Elyn's youthful blond friend, sitting to her left. He slammed his fist on the table, rattling the cups. "We were winning the battle. 'Twas our enemies to the south who received the benefit."

"It may be true we were prevailing," Geir conceded, "but to claim Thor came to the rescue of our enemies would mean we were in the wrong. That cannot be!"

Friend and cousin, both close to Elyn's age, turned to her to settle their dispute.

7

"What say you, Elyn?" Ingvar asked. "I saw you cut a path through our foes, even take on Sigrid the Valiant and live to tell of it!" Both men raised their mugs of mead, reaching around her to clank them together with broad, bright smiles.

"Skol!" They cheered, and Elyn lifted her goblet to meet their toast.

Thoughts raced through her mind in an instant. She had been hearing tales of the famous twins Sigurd and Sigrid since before she became a woman, when she still lived in the safety of her own home with her farmer parents, and still the tall blonde warrior had appeared young. Thor had struck his hammer only after the two of them had become locked in combat. Sigrid was strong, as the stories said, and as skilled as any man, yet she had pulled her from the path of a flying spear. Why?

Elyn had pictured a woman who was larger than life, as savage as Fenrir the wolf, as fearsome and deadly as Hel, Queen of Helheim, and as wise as the three Norns. People spoke of Jarls Sigurd and Sigrid as if they were the embodiment of Freyr and Freya, twin children of the god Njord, ruler of Vanir. Freya, a goddess of war, shared soldiers fallen in battle with Odin, and many prayed and sacrificed to her as well as Odin, for they did not know whose hall they may spend eternity in.

But Sigrid did not fly, nor did she wield a flaming sword, nor did her gaze cause Elyn to turn to stone, though she wondered if those sky-blue eyes had cast a spell over her. Sigrid was tall, with flowing blonde hair, powerful lean muscles, and a singular will, but all in all, she looked like a normal human female, one whose nearness had roused Elyn's senses in a way she had not experienced before. She liked Ingvar, who was respectful to her and treated her as an equal. A few times, when they were both quite drunk, she had even lain with him, though she didn't remember much of the experience. She would notice a beautiful woman walking in town or at a banquet hall, for sure, but they had not stolen her breath. *It was because of so many legends you have heard of her, that is all. You've never met anyone famous before. She is probably a mean tyrant who beats her slaves and slaughters lovers who disappoint her in bed.* And yet, she had pulled Elyn close to save her life. It was too much to process.

Answering her comrades in arms, Elyn said, "Perhaps Thor intervened for all our sakes. Mayhap it was not our day to die."

Geir and Ingvar laughed and downed their cups. Then her cousin expressed his admiration. "You are a wise and discerning woman, Elyn, and will make a man a fine wife one day, eh, Ingvar?" he added with a wink. "You know how to smooth over an argument so everyone can see himself as right in his own estimation."

A blush rose in Elyn's cheeks at his praise and Ingvar had just opened his mouth to reply when an angry voice bellowed, "What in the name of all the gods do you think you are doing sitting at table with the warriors of Firdafylke, girl? Get up and go help the women serve the feast, as is your place!"

Elyn cringed as the pang of a familiar dread dampened her celebration. Her gaze snapped up to the fiery darts shooting from hooded ice-blue eyes, as the man's thin lips pulled down, parting for the jagged teeth of a sneering scowl. Her Uncle Unnulf kept his brawny arms despite the pudge which had formed around his belly. Dressed in an embroidered red tunic with his ash-brown and gray hair combed back and his beard trimmed, the man who had taken her in never let her forget the "kindness" he had done for her. The back of his hand and the length of his belt had reminded her often enough. She supposed it wasn't entirely her fault, as he treated his wife much the same way.

"But Father." Geir rose to her defense. "Elyn fought with the warriors today, side by side with us, wounding and slaying our enemies without receiving a scratch. She brings great luck and deserves—"

"Shut your mouth, whelp, before I knock those ivories right out of it!" Unnulf straightened, placing fists on his hips. "When you think you can best me, boy, you may have your say, but I am chief of our household, not you."

Elyn's heart sank. She wanted to blast back with, "Where were you when the fighting men took the field?" but she didn't dare. He exercised authority over her as long as she remained in his household.

"Yes, sir." She lowered her chin and rose from the table. "If you will excuse me, Geir, Ingvar, I must attend to my duties."

Everyone had changed out of their soaking wet, torn, and bloodied battle attire and dressed for the Jarl's banquet, including Elyn, who wore a simple tan and cream dress similar to most village women's. As she scurried off to assist the others prepare and serve the meal, she recalled the fateful day which had altered her life forever.

Six years ago, when Elyn was only twelve and lived on a farm with her parents and siblings, raiders from the kingdom of Raumsdal to the north poured into their fjord, pillaging farms that lay in the valley and steppes beneath the mountains. They came at harvesting season as Elyn recalled she was winnowing grain with her mother when they were attacked. Her father and brothers were cut down in the field where they labored and she and her mother were dragged into their hut, where the warriors descended on them like rutting swine.

But Elyn had fought back. She caught hold of a branch of firewood and clubbed her foul attacker in the head with it, stunning him enough she could break free. Scrambling to her feet, she had scooped up a kitchen knife. The fat, hairy Northman with a fur vest grinned at her and swatted the knife from her hand, so she grabbed an iron cooking pot and flailed at him with it. She would never forget his broad nose, the gap between his teeth, or the lusty gleam in his two-toned eyes.

Frightened but fiercely determined, she had continued to defy him even as he took her, overpowering her blows with his bulk. She remembered his rancid body odor and the pain that tore through her womanhood at his penetration. Then she had felt a jolt and blood dripped from his shocked mouth before her Uncle Unnulf and cousin Geir pulled his lifeless corpse off her. They had come! All the neighbors had come to their defense. Geir, who was little more than a lad, reached his hand down and she clasped it, allowing him to yank her to her feet. She recalled being embarrassed by the fresh blood staining her skirt. She had rushed into her uncle's arms and hugged him, crying into his shoulder, but he had brushed her aside. "We cannot tarry, child," he had said.

"Mother!" Elyn could never forget the sickening blade which pierced her heart the instant she spied her mother's lifeless body on the floor of their hut. Cruel bruises encircled her neck, but at least the man who had put them there lay slain beside her.

"There is no time to mourn," Uncle Unnulf decreed. "Come now."

Elyn was shaken to the core, and he was demanding she leave at once. In retrospect, she understood why. There were more raiders about, more families who needed protecting, not to mention the stores of grain which were to see them through the long, harsh winter. But leaving her mother, recognized far and wide for her beautiful red hair and charming disposition, was unthinkable. Elyn had wrenched out of her uncle's grasp and raced to kneel beside the greatest security she had ever known, realizing she had already crossed over. "Freya, keep my mother," she had prayed. Sensing her uncle's hand shoot toward her, she snatched the one thing she could to remember her by—a silver raven cloak pin.

With the memento clutched tightly in her fist and tears streaming down her face, she allowed her cousin Geir to take charge of her while Unnulf joined the other fighting men to chase away the intruders. Out of a sense of duty to his slain half-brother, Unnulf had received Elyn into his household, for which his wife Liv and daughter Frigga were exceedingly glad. There was always so much work to be done, and they welcomed another set of hands. However, while Liv, Frigga, and Geir thought of her as an addition to the family, Unnulf regarded Elyn as a servant, one step above a slave, but still his to command as he deemed fit. Because they were blood kin, he never took her to his bed, but he found a variety of other ways to use and abuse her. She recognized the fact she owed her life to him and was grateful; she would have been more grateful, obedient, and served him with her whole heart had he only been kind to her. Perhaps he knew no other way to behave.

When Njord's wife Hilda heard of how Elyn had fought against her attackers, she had invited her to join other young women in training as shieldmaidens, and her uncle allowed it because to refuse would make him look bad with the jarl. She had excelled in skill and tactics, and as she grew, developed strength to match her daring. By the time she was sixteen, she was being brought on voyages, hunts, and retaliatory raids against the blue shields of Raumsdal. At first, her job was to stay in the background guarding the men's rear and only step into the shield wall to replace one who had fallen, but her talent and ferocity made a place for her among the elite. Fighting granted Elyn an outlet for bottled up emotions and an arena in which to excel when all Unnulf did was berate her as a worthless mouth to feed. She mourned, cut her hair, and rent her garments in her sixteenth winter when Hilda died of a fever, but now her flowing strands had grown back.

Elyn joined the other women in passing out platters of steaming food and refilling the mead bowl men dipped their cups and horns into, while musicians strummed lyres, tapped drums, and blew melodies on their flutes. Laughter and cheerful voices filled the hall while the aroma of roasted venison, lentil soup, fresh bread, and sweet mead mingled with smoke from the firepit and perfume.

"We are saving your seat," Ingvar told her when she set a dish before him and Geir. "You should join us soon, right?"

"I would like to." Elyn smiled back at his kind expression.

She returned with a tray of bread for the Jarl's table. "My lord," she bade him with a bow of her head.

11

As she was walking away, Njord spoke to her. "Elyn, is that you?"

Pivoting to see what he wanted, she answered, "Yes, my lord. Is there something else you require?"

"Indeed!" The jarl raised his hands to quiet the room, and the attention turned to him. He was young to rule a jarldom in his mid-thirties, and not bad to look upon. The short cap of his sleeves allowed the bands and swirls of his warrior tattoos to show along his ripped muscles. Sigurd and Sigrid had taunted him for leading from the rear, but Njord was a powerful fighter in single combat, which is how he won his seat from the fat drunkard he replaced. He just did not wish to put himself in danger lest he be killed before he could rise to power as King of Firdafylke.

"Why are you serving when you should be sitting with our honored guests tonight?" he asked. "Did you not all hear of Elyn's exploits on the battlefield today? She is a worthy shieldmaiden who is as lovely as she is deadly. Come and sit at my table," he insisted. "Allow me to raise my cup to you."

Elyn was stunned, not knowing what to say. The jarl had never invited her to his table before. Then again, he had not seen her fight against a real foe until that day. Pleased her skill had caught his eye, she smiled and nodded. "Thank you, my lord. I am honored to accept your hospitality." The hall cheered as two men scooted over to make a place for her on their bench and offered her food.

"Tell me, Elyn, when did you become so grown up?" he asked as he admired her with earthy brown eyes.

"I don't know, my lord," she replied, flattered, but uneasy under his scrutiny. "I suppose when you were not looking."

Her response drew laughs from all who heard it, and the musicians started to play again.

THE HOUR WAS late when warriors passed out from weariness or drink. A few coupled up with a woman in attendance, while some others bade farewell and stumbled out into the cool early summer night. Geir sat in a corner with the blacksmith's daughter when Uncle Unnulf took Elyn's arm to walk her home. He thanked Njord for the meal and entertainment with profuse words of praise and unabashed flattery, then led her away from the jarl's compound, through his gates under a starry sky since the storm had blown past, and headed for their house in the village.

"It is a good thing you pleased Jarl Njord tonight," he said in a more pleasant tone than usual. "I hear he has become lonely and weary of casual women, and he may seek a new wife. How wonderful it would be if he were to choose you."

An icy chill ran down Elyn's spine, but it was not from the wind. She could practically hear his brain plotting how he could rise in station if his niece became the jarl's wife. Women of Norvegr were allowed a say in their marriages and could not be forced to wed against their will. However, she also knew her uncle and how he could manipulate and coerce, how he may punish her or other members of the family if she refused his directive. But she did not want to marry Njord for so many reasons, none of which she could articulate to Unnulf.

"If I must marry, why can't it be to Ingvar?" she asked in a still, small voice. "He is my friend."

Uncle Unnulf scoffed and waved an impatient arm in the air. "He is only a boy Geir's age, the son of a poor farmer. He has nothing to offer us. The jarl, on the other hand…" He turned a judgmental glare on her. "What is wrong with you, Elyn? Jarl Njord could be king one day. Do you not care about Liv and myself? Do you not care if we go cold and hungry all winter? Have you no ambition for a better life? I swear, girl, you have always been odd. You are eighteen, and most women your age already have a first child. I haven't sent you off to marry before now only because the Völva told me…" He became suddenly quiet, as if he had not intended to reveal the knowledge.

"The Völva told you what, Uncle?" Elyn's curiosity had been peaked.

He scowled and shook his head. "Nothing. It is none of your concern."

"If there is a prophecy about me, then–"

"Who said anything about a prophecy!" he snapped as he marched along the path. "Leave it be."

Elyn was not eager to incur more of her uncle's displeasure, so she did not pursue the matter. However, her mind raced with possibilities of what the seer might have told him and why he wished the words to remain hidden from her.

CHAPTER 3

That night in the village of Gnóttdalr, Svithjod

"I have your bath hot just the way you like it." Sveina greeted her mistress with a smile.

"Thank you, Sveina." Sigrid closed the door to her private chamber and crossed to the wooden tub filled with steaming water.

"I will unfasten your armor, my lady," offered the slender woman with wheat-blonde hair arranged in a mix of braids and loose strands. She wore the simple garb of a slave but bore no marks or identifying bands.

Sigrid allowed Sveina to unbuckle her spaulders and breastplate and lift them from her shoulders before she pealed out of her gambeson, boots, and trousers. "I wish we had a hot spring like King Grimolf in Sochabrot. Then you wouldn't have to heat stones for the water and hang buckets over the firepit."

Sveina assisted the toned warrior into her bath. "I do not mind, Jarl Sigrid. It is my pleasure to serve you."

"This feels divine," Sigrid sighed as she slid to recline at the bottom of the tub. "It is good to be home after a day such as this."

"A messenger arrived saying you chased the Firdafylkers away like field mice." Sveina's familiar, soothing voice was as a balm, but it was her talented fingers and smooth skin Sigrid always craved after combat. "That is how I knew to heat the water."

With a cloth in one hand and soap in the other, Sveina bathed her mistress, every stroke a caress as the relaxing warmth of the elixir relieved aching muscles. "It was the gods who chased us all from the fray this day," she admitted as she closed her eyes.

Although it was her thrall Sveina's hands gliding over her flesh, Sigrid's mind brought forth the image of the red-haired shieldmaiden. She recalled how she felt when only mere inches of wood stood between them. *Something must be wrong with me.* She frowned at the realization an enemy made her feel more passionate longing than the woman who had served her for years. The relaxing motion of Sveina's fingers massaging her scalp, working the soap through her hair, was as pleasing as ever, so why did her thoughts dwell on the flame-haired female from Firdafylke?

"I am just thankful my prayers were answered," Sveina offered in satisfaction. "Neither you nor Jarl Sigurd were harmed."

Sigrid caught Sveina's hand and placed a kiss on her palm. "I appreciate your prayers, sweet Sveina. How was Mother while we were gone?"

Sveina shook her head. "She has not been herself since..."

"I know," Sigrid sighed. "Has it been a moon already?"

"Yes, my lady." Sigrid's loins tightened when Sveina rubbed the washcloth between her legs. "I still weep for your father some days, but let us not speak of sadness tonight. We have only an hour before you should join your brother in the great hall to receive your guests and celebrate your victory. And before you dispute me..." Sveina had the most marvelous knack of being able to anticipate anything Sigrid would say, do, or request.

Sigrid lifted her eyes to meet the green-brown hazel of her servant's. A smile pulled at the corner of Sveina's lush lips. "Any battle which does not end in total defeat is a victory." She brushed a kiss to Sigrid's cheek and gathered a linen bath sheet, holding it wide for the lady jarl.

Stepping out, as wet as she had been in the downpour but so much warmer and more comforted, Sigrid let Sveina wrap it around her to absorb the droplets. "An hour you say?" Sigrid's brow rose along with her expectations.

"Only if that is enough time for you," Sveina replied in a coy, flirtatious tone. "I know how you are when you return energized from fighting. If Jarl Sigurd must wait a few extra minutes, it will only serve to teach him patience."

And this is why she treasured the captive her father had brought back from Skåne and given to her to be her attendant when she was fifteen.

Sveina had been included along with others returned as slaves when hostilities broke out between the Norvegr traders and the local Danes. It had taken time for Sigrid to adjust to having a servant and for the girl to being one, but by the summer Sigrid turned eighteen, they had their dynamic running like a well-bred racehorse. At that age, Sigrid realized she preferred a feminine touch to a man's, and being the jarl's daughter, her fame announced through the land after the success of Sigurd's and her initial voyage east around the peninsula, she could do whatever pleased her. Sigrid had been overjoyed when Sveina responded positively the first time she had kissed her. She never made demands of her lady-in-waiting, for it is how she viewed Sveina rather than as property, but the girl, then young woman, and now grown woman had always been eager to please her. It had been a tremendous relief for Sigrid to learn she was not such an oddity after all, that other women enjoyed the same kind of pleasures she did. But aside from experimentation and the occasional request for a threesome, she had not found anyone else who wished to forgo marriage for the prospect of spending her life with another woman. If Sveina was not bound to Sigrid, would she leave her bed for a man's?

Sveina led Sigrid to the grand sleigh-bed with its carved header and footboard, its down-stuffed mattress laid upon tightly strung ropes spread with clean linen sheets. Despite everything Sveina did for her, nothing had prepared her for the response her body and heart produced at the sight of the beautiful shieldmaiden she had met that day. Mayhap she loved Sveina the way Sigurd had loved several young women and yet been unable to choose one to wed, as a placeholder while awaiting someone special to appear. The thought disgusted Sigrid. *Certainly I am not so shallow.* But she comprehended there was no future in this relationship. As fond as she was of Sveina, no fire burned in her heart for the woman.

Dropping the bath sheet, Sigrid fell into bed with the lovely servant who took pleasing her mistress to a whole other level.

AN HOUR LATER, a clean and refreshed Sigrid attired in green and gold silks sat beside her twin in the center of the longest table in their great hall, which lay at the opposite end of the longhouse from the family's sleeping quarters. Its lofty raftered roof, plank walls adorned with tapestries, and lit by candle wheels hanging from the beams, rivaled any residence in Norvegr. Straw had been scattered across the pine slat floor to absorb moisture and two enormous gray-brindle Cu dogs reclined near their master and mistress, lazily awaiting their moment to scarf up crumbs and morsels when they fell.

Sigurd raised his goblet of ale, catching the attention of the chamber. "Tonight is more than a celebration of a successful confrontation with our disagreeable neighbors," he declared with cheer.

"Our brother, Odo, has returned from his first command of a trading ship with silver, silk, and spices," Sigrid continued in a resounding voice.

"Which he received in exchange for our honey, furs, and ivory," Sigurd concluded, shifting his beaming gaze from twenty-one-year-old Odo, who sat at his left, to Sigrid on his right.

"To Odo!" the twins cheered in unison.

"Skol!" called out the men and women who filled the hall.

Sigrid and Sigurd appeared to have been chiseled from a singular hunk of granite and anyone could spot the striking resemblance they carried to each other. Sigrid's honey blonde hair and sky-blue eyes were the same as her brother's, while Sigurd's high cheekbones, straight nose, and noble chin mirrored his sister's. They each bore an identical sequence of line and swirl tattoos on their upper arms and they both exuded equivalent commanding presences. People often joked if not for Sigurd's beard, nobody could tell them apart.

"We are so proud of Odo," their mother, Gudred, cooed from her seat on Sigrid's other side. "And so grateful he has returned to us safely." Sigrid noticed she looked better than she had in a while. She had brushed and adorned her nut-brown hair and her dark blue eyes were without gloomy circles under them for a change. Losing Olaf to a cowardly snake was almost more than Gudred could bear, but Sigrid presumed having her younger son home had raised her spirits.

"I should have arrived sooner to aid our warriors in the skirmish against the Firdafylke invaders." Rather than cheer, Odo's expression was as sour as a man who was last to the ale barrel and found it empty. "Better yet," he added in a quiet grumble only the family could hear, "I should have been here when Papa was murdered. Mayhap my presence would have made a difference."

"Do not think such things," Sigurd commanded him in a gentle rebuke. "We were here, and it made no matter. Let us enjoy a feast, little brother, for I fear war is on the horizon."

Sveina set platters before the jarls' family and Sigrid met her gaze with a warm smile. Other servants passed out dishes of fish, rabbit, greens, fruit, cheese, bread, and sops while a whole hog occupied a spit over the firepit in the center of the hall. Asmond, another household thrall, carved tender pork portions which practically fell off the bone onto the platter he filled. The aromas were pleasing to Sigrid, as well as the company, but her heart remained troubled with suspicion. *Could someone here have conspired to murder my father? Did one of them drive in the knife?*

"Standing in the shield wall is not the only way to serve our people." Jarl Siegfried Strongarm had accepted the twins' invitation to attend this evening and sat with his attractive younger sister, Birgitta. His rusty, wiry beard stood in contrast to the tawny brown hair which fell to his shoulders. "Odo's trading expedition has increased our resources and spread our reputation and he is to be commended." The visiting jarl raised his goblet, and everyone drank with him.

"And let us not forget our comrades who feast in Valhalla tonight," Sigrid reminded the crowd. "Remember their names. Leiknir," she hailed to begin the list.

"Harald," Rangvoldr stated.

"Gorm Thorkellsson," called a warrior.

"Snorri Lockjaw."

Sigurd added, "Runar Long Beard was badly injured, but as of earlier this evening, he still lives. I will visit his hut tomorrow. We shall all offer prayers for him. Our friends fought without fear because they all knew as we do the day of their death is decreed by the gods. We all have a time to be born and a time to die; it is what we do in between that counts. A man who dies well shall receive his reward while a coward will be barred entry to Odin's dining hall. To the fallen."

He raised his goblet and all present joined him. "Skol!"

With the solemn moment past, everyone resumed eating, drinking, and conversing.

"Tell us the truth, Sigurd," Siegfried bade when he had drained his cup. "Bards come to my hall and sing of the time you bridled a whale and rode upon its back across the sea. I wish to hear the story from your lips."

Sigurd laughed and waved a hand. "A gross exaggeration." Every ear of the warriors and women tuned to hear his words. "I merely put a bit in the creature's mouth; 'twas Sigrid who was fool enough to leap onto the giant's back and guide it through the waves!"

Laughs and cheers thundered through the spacious hall, and Sigrid blushed. Her brother prodded her with his elbow while she worked to swallow the food she chewed. "We were on a whale hunt," she explained. "Sigurd and Rangvoldr had pierced the whale's hide with darts trailing ropes tied to sealskin bladders and our ship followed until it tired and slowed. It wasn't safe to bring the longboat close enough to the enormous creature for someone to strike the killing blow, so I jumped onto its back, ran up to the right spot, and drove my harpoon into its heart. There was not much 'riding through the waves', but I suppose one may construe it as fool-hearty."

"Nay!" Siegfried's honey eyes shone at her from across the room as he engaged in a jovial laugh. "Your fearless courage is an inspiration to all, noble Sigrid. 'Tis why you are called 'the Valiant'. And I hear your whole band fought well today. I salute you!" He raised his cup again, and the people drank.

"Let us have music," Sigurd proposed, and the musicians began to play.

As they enjoyed the feast, Sigrid passed a discerning gaze over all in attendance, suspicion rising in her at every face. Across from her family sat their closest friends. Gunnlief laughed at something Sigurd had said. The good-humored farmer, as tall and brawny as her brother, shaved his ginger hair above his ears and kept the length of it wound in a plait over his crown, spilling to his back. He arranged his wide beard in three small braids hanging from his chin. Brenn, his fair-haired wife, had left their two young boys at home with their grandmother so she could celebrate with Gunnlief. Sigrid had known them all her life, but could they be trusted now?

Rangvoldr the Black, Sigurd's devoted comrade, challenged him to arm wrestle.

"Again?" Sigurd laughed.

"We'll make it interesting with a wager," Rangvoldr suggested. He was called "the Black" because of his unusual ebony mane and beard. Most inhabitants of Norvegr had sun-touched or brown hair with a few red hues thrown in for good measure, however raven-black like Rangvoldr's was rare. But was his heart as true as it seemed?

Each of their tenant farmers, village fishers, and fighting men, all the weavers and crafters, carpenters and herders, every brewer and potter smiled, ate, and seemed at ease, none bearing a guilty aspect, but any of them could be a traitor.

As she studied faces of the guests, Sigrid noticed Birgitta and Sigurd exchanging glances and smiles, while Siegfried's oldest son could not tear his attention from Girrid, Sigrid's little sister. Her thoughts turned again to the red-haired shieldmaiden as she wondered who she was, what she was like, and if she would ever see her again. Presently, as if he had read her mind, which was indeed a strong possibility, Sigurd leaned into whisper into her ear.

"No red-haired warrior woman here for your pleasure tonight, Sigrid."

She blushed. "Birgitta has her eyes on you as much as yours are on her. When are you going to speak to her? Why don't you ask her to dance?"

"I'll talk to her, but first you and I need a conference with Jarl Siegfried."

Sigrid nodded her agreement, and they rose in unison. Sigurd waved to the visiting jarl. "Esteemed Siegfried, would you join us?" As they made their way to a small table in a corner, he turned to her with a serious expression. "And if it turns out the woman of Firdafylke was involved in Father's murder?"

With a tone as icy as winter, Sigrid answered, "Then I will remove her head from her body with one stroke of my blade."

CHAPTER 4

"*T*hank you for coming, neighbor and friend," Sigurd bade to Siegfried as he joined the twins at the small table away from the festivities.

"I am your neighbor and friend, and as I mourned Olaf's passing, I wish to see the two of you succeed."

"Do you think it too odd of an arrangement for us to share rule over this fylke?" Sigrid asked in honest concern. "Some men have grumbled about my inclusion as joint-jarl with my brother."

Siegfried shrugged. "Some people will always grumble, whatever their excuse. King Grimolf accepts you and that is all that matters. Now, what is going on with Firdafylke?"

"I wish we knew." Sigurd ran a hand through his hair, pushing it away from his face.

"They sent a challenge claiming we had raided some of their farms and slaughtered their livestock, burned houses, killed tenants," Sigrid picked up the narrative.

"Which we did not," her twin confirmed. "It was Firdafylke who plundered our farms. The battle was undecided when the gods intervened to stop it."

"I have met King Tortryggr the Navigator," the older Siegfried stated. "I found him to be a fair man of excellent reputation, but he is getting along in years. His beard is snowy white, and he no longer rides into combat. It is possible some of his jarls are acting without his consent."

"Doesn't he have a son who commands his armies?" Sigrid inquired. "And why should they turn against us after we supported them in their war with Raumsdal several years ago?"

"Who knows what treachery lies in men's hearts?" Siegfried responded.

Who indeed? But Sigrid's thoughts were more focused on the treachery which killed her father than the current conflict with Firdafylke... unless they were related. *Could they be? But in what way?*

"Perhaps we should seek advice from a Völva," Sigrid suggested. "Surely the gods know."

"The gods have been tight-lipped with their secrets of late," Sigurd responded with a sigh. "But it would not hurt to ask. Siegfried, keep a close watch over your farms and ships, as your land borders ours. If raiders of Firdafylke strike, they could hit you as easily as us. Jarl Njord was with the warriors today. What do you know of him?"

Siegfried frowned and scratched his beard. "I have not met Jarl Njord in person, but I've heard stories about him. He was not born a jarl's son but killed his predecessor in a duel to gain power. They say he uses strategy and politics along with his sword to advance his position. One may even suspect he has his eye on Tortryggr's crown, and to get back to your question, Sigrid, yes, the king has a capable son, Erling, but only the one, as his other sons were killed in battle or at sea."

"Which would mean Njord only needs to defeat Erling to become ruler of Firdafylke," Sigurd mused. "Still, why deplete his forces in a useless quarrel with us? It makes no sense."

"You may depend on our aid, Jarl Siegfried," Sigrid declared. "Can we count on yours?"

"Without hesitation," he avowed.

"One more thing." Sigrid's expression brightened, and she cast a gaze over her shoulder to where the fair Birgitta sat. "Introduce Sigurd here to your younger sister."

Siegfried laughed as the three rose from their seats. He reached for Sigurd's hand, and they clasped wrists in comradery. "It would be my pleasure."

"You just wait, Sigrid!" her brother teased from behind reddened cheeks.

"Someone has to give you a kick in the ass," she grinned.

While Sigurd went with Siegfried to be introduced to Birgitta, Sigrid left the great hall to take a walk to the yard house, a small structure out back for relieving oneself. She ran across Gudred as she returned.

"I am happy to see you looking well this evening, Mother."

Gudred peered up at her. "I would be happier if you spent more time entertaining Jarl Siegfried than brooding and making eyes with your slave girl. Are you aware people talk about you?"

Sigrid crossed her arms over her breast and cocked her head at her mother. "Let them express their grievances to my face. What I do is of no concern to anyone."

"I know, child, but we ever only have the illusion of privacy," Gudred explained. "Everyone knows everyone else's affairs."

"And yet no one saw or heard a thing the night Papa was killed." Seeing the shadow of grief cloud her mother's expression, Sigrid regretted her comment. "I'm sorry, Mother. Sigurd and I will find the culprit and punish him; on that you have my word."

Gudred sighed, shook her head, then lifted her gaze to Sigrid's once more. "No one cares if you like women," she said with concern. "It is that you do not also entertain men. It is because you refuse to take a husband. Look at Jarl Siegfried—"

"You know why I do not marry." This topic came up several times a year, though thankfully her mother did not badger her with it too often. "Why would I want a husband to rule over me, to usurp my power and authority, to order me about like his thrall? Father esteemed Sigurd and I equally. He set forth in his will my brother and I should succeed him as jarls, to administer his lands wisely and fairly, not Sigurd and whatever man could seduce me into a marriage contract. I will not allow a situation which could cause strife for Sigurd, and you of all people must see the potential for disaster. I do not even trust Rangvoldr, his best friend. With Father gone, all one need do is marry me and kill my brother. Who would share power with Sigurd but me? Who can he entrust at his back but me?"

"You have said this before, and I understand to an extent. But if the two of you allied with Jarl Siegfried, with you as his lawful wife, our families would have the largest holdings in the kingdom aside from King Grimolf. You would have more ships to command, more farmland and cattle, and you could have children. Don't you ever think of it? Who will you have to pass your title to?"

Sigrid responded with an impatient frown. "Even you do not consider me Sigurd's equal. Why not pester him with talk of marriage and children? Do you worry about the women he sleeps with or the fact he does not have an heir? Yes, we made a pledge with Siegfried tonight, and I feel certain he will stand with us against outsiders, but there is no way to ensure he would not break faith with Sigurd in the future and I do not wish to be forced to choose between loyalty to a husband and to my brother." She thought, but did not say, *And what if he is jealous and will not allow me to keep Sveina? I barely know the man and he is ten years my elder with children by his first wife.*

Gudred pursed her lips in displeasure. "You will do exactly as you please, as you have always done. Your father indulged you too much when you were younger. Look at your reflection, daughter—you are a woman, not a man, despite what feats you can perform or exploits you count to your credit. Sometimes I think the gods made a mistake, or maybe it was my fault something went wrong in my womb, and I should have brought forth twin sons. I tried to interest you in girls' activities, but you only wished to play with Sigurd and his friends. I wish Olaf had never allowed you to train to be a shieldmaiden, and never allowed you to join in his voyages." She lowered her head, not able to meet Sigrid's gaze.

"Father understood. You do not keep your best racehorse in the stable just because it is a mare. People may talk, and countless do not understand, but they respect me and acknowledge the role I play," Sigrid explained. "I can be many things to many people, but I cannot be less than I am. The Valkyries are women. Freya, goddess of war, is a woman. The sagas and stories of our ancestors speak of mighty female heroes of the past. Would you deny me a destiny which rivals theirs simply to be 'normal'? You have Girrid. See if Jarl Siegfried wishes to marry her."

Without awaiting a response, Sigrid paced back into the longhouse. Some of the guests had gone home but others still sat around the tables drinking, telling stories, placing wagers on throws of the dice, or playing a game of Hnefatafl. Sveina, Asmund, and the other servants cleared the tables, putting away leftover food that could not be wasted and washing the dishes in a corner of the room. A pretty young woman flirted with Odo and Girrid had joined Sigurd visiting with Siegfried's family.

"Good evening, Sigrid," Gunnlief bade her as he and Brenn headed for the exit. "We had a wonderful time as always, but we need to be getting home."

24

"We have a cow expecting a calf any day now," Brenn shared with excitement. It struck Sigrid how short the woman her age was as her head just reached her husband's shoulder. "And tomorrow we must rise early to get all our chores done. Summer is beginning and we have much work."

"I will come out to check on you and your cow in the morning," Sigrid said with a friendly smile. "Odo brought back a new farming implement I want you to try. If you think it works well, we'll have more of them made."

"Thank you," Gunnlief responded as he wrapped an arm around Brenn. "Olaf's fylke prospers more than others because you and Sigurd actively engage with your tenants and villagers rather than sit behind your palisade and issue orders. Do not be troubled, Sigrid; the people love you."

She granted him an appreciative nod, and Brenn pushed up on her toes to press her cheek to Sigrid's. "And we loved your father," she assured her. "The rot will be dug out soon—I know it will. If you need anything..."

"Thank you," Sigrid responded, and gave Brenn a brief hug. "For being our friends."

Sigrid watched them leave, hoping all was as it seemed and none of their people were involved, until she perceived Rangvoldr step behind her and hover over her shoulder. She recognized his gait with the slight limp he earned in battle three years ago. When she turned to him, she smelled how alcohol overpowered even the scent of wood-smoke which clung to him. His glazed eyes beamed at her. "We had a good day, did we not?" His speech was slurred, but he did not sway too much.

Smiling, she nodded. "We did. Let me help you find your sleeping bench."

Rangvoldr slung an arm over Sigrid's shoulder and leaned on her while she walked him to the long, broad benches that lined the walls of the great hall. This was where warriors and servants slept, along with visitors who needed to spend the night. He sat on a fur throw with a pillow and woolen blanket nearby. Grabbing Sigrid's hand, he pulled her down beside him.

"Won't you lie with me tonight?" he asked with a loopy grin and heavy lids.

"No, Rangvoldr," she replied with gentle humor. "Not tonight. You will fall asleep and miss all the excitement."

"Ah, come on, Sigrid," he pleaded. "You can even bring Sveina. It'll be fun. I'm Sigurd's closest friend; we should be together."

She eased his head down onto the pillow and covered him with the blanket. "You sleep now," she instructed. "Mayhap I'll let you spar with me tomorrow." She kissed his cheek and prayed he was as he claimed, her brother's most devoted ally.

With a glance around the room, she spotted Sveina. One of the drunk warriors was putting his hands on her. That simply would not do. Sigrid marched over to them. "Skelkollr, shall I tell your wife how you behaved here tonight?"

He jumped at her voice and lifted empty palms. "I was only looking," he declared innocently.

"So that's what they are calling it these days," she chided. Skelkollr was an older fighter who had served her father for many years. Surely he was innocent where murder was concerned, wasn't he?

"Don't tell Hilda. Shhhh." He placed a shaky finger to his lips. "She doesn't like it when I look at other women. She's liable to wallop me good!"

Sigrid shook her head, trying to suppress a smile. "I won't mention it as long as you quit looking," she promised, poking her forefinger into his chest. "Now, off home you go."

Turning her attention to Sveina, she narrowed her brows. "Men know better than to touch you, don't they? I mean, they don't ever—"

"Oh, no, my lady!" Sveina's brows shot up. "They understand I belong to you and treat me with respect. Skelkollr had too much ale, is all."

"And you would tell me if anyone were to act unseemly toward you?" Sveina nodded. "Of course, it is different if it is something you want," Sigrid added in hesitation, not truly caring for Sveina to answer. "Would you like to share my bed tonight, just to keep me company?" she asked in a hush. "It would be more comfortable than a bench."

"As always, you are so kind to consider me, Jarl Sigrid. May I join you when we are finished cleaning? I don't want the others to think you play favorites."

Sigrid brushed back a lock of Sveina's hair, then trailed her fingers down her cheek. "I may be asleep by then, but please join me. And everyone already knows you are my favorite." With a grin and a wink, Sigrid departed the lulling, half-empty hall for some much-needed rest.

In the night, beset by nightmares of faceless assassins interwoven with rapturous visions of a beautiful flame-haired Valkyrie, Sigrid found comfort by wrapping tender Sveina in her strong arms. But somehow, the valiant warrior sensed everything was about to change.

CHAPTER 5

Kaldrlogr, Firdafylke, a few days later

*E*lyn sat on a round three-legged stool working beside her Aunt Liv at the loom positioned along the back wall of her uncle's house. Each tightened the next thread on her side of the frame, pushing the weave snug with a double-ended pin-beater carved from the long bone of a reindeer. The vertical threads were tied to small stone wheels that dangled from the warp-weighted loom, which held the warp in place while still allowing the weavers the ability to manipulate the threads. Some women used weights of iron or fired clay at the ends of their fibers, but these had been passed down through Liv's family for generations. They did not rust like iron or have the chance of breaking like clay, so everyone considered them to be the highest quality. Only the poorest huts did not have a loom, as weaving cloth was an essential part of women's work, even for a shieldmaiden. Elyn had always been required to complete her household chores before being allowed the privilege of training or sparring with the jarl's warriors.

Daylight blazed through narrow cracks in the walls, and the hut's door remained open. The central hearth burned low, the embers preserved to stir up to cook the evening meal as the longer, warm days did not require the fire for light or heat. The steeply pitched roof extended several feet beyond the doorway to discourage snow from piling up to block the exit and also creating a transition space for removing wet outer garments before entering. The eaves stretched almost to the ground, facilitating rain and snow run-off and added insulation to the rough-hewn planks which acted as siding on the pole construction. Sod and moss sprouted on their roof and a few roots straggled through gaps in the wood to dangle from the tall peak. The small smoke hole had to be unplugged at least once a year as grass would grow over it. Some people, especially in the village, discouraged the turf, which spotted most farmhouses, but it kept the house warmer in the winter and cooler in the summer, even if it required more maintenance. Elyn recalled many a time when she and Geir would toss a goat or two up there to nibble it down.

Pegs and wooden boxes for clothes and shoes flanked the doorway for easy access and long sleeping benches piled with furs, blankets, and pillows lined the low sides of the slanted roof-wall. Not all commoners had furniture, but Unnulf was a carpenter, among other endeavors. He had crafted a table for working on, preparing and serving meals, or for playing games during the deep dark of winter. Baskets and buckets, some containing foodstuffs, tools, or water, hung from the rafters or hooks overhead while the waste bucket occupied a spot near the door for convenience and to mitigate odors.

The centerpiece of the home was the stone-lined hearth, serving many purposes. Unnulf had erected a pole frame around it with an iron hook to hold a kettle and an iron spit for roasting meat. Firewood was stacked at one end of the rectangular firepit while cooking pots and utensils rested on a low stone platform at the other. While the longhouses of jarls and kings boasted wood-planked or slate floors, theirs, like most commoners, was only packed dirt.

Elyn had been enjoying pleasant conversation with Liv, who bubbled on about her daughter Frigga's pregnancy, when Uncle Unnulf burst through the door, casting a damper on their mood. "Will you ever finish that cloth?" were the first words out of his mouth. "I need a new tunic and it won't hurt for Geir to have one as well."

"You want it to be of high quality, do you not?" Liv replied with a question of her own. "This cloth should be finished within the week, and then it can be cut and sewn into a tunic for one of you."

"Then we will start on another," Elyn concluded. "We still have to take care of the garden, the chickens and goats, bake the bread, prepare the meals—"

"All you women do is complain!" he snapped. "Who built this house?

Did you chop the trees and plane the timbers? Don't talk to me about work. Now, Elyn, Jarl Njord has invited us to visit in his great hall tomorrow night. You will make yourself as attractive as possible and you will be agreeable and converse with humility. Is that clear?"

Elyn blinked. "Yes sir."

"And I know you have training this afternoon, but you are not to get a bloody nose or black eye or any bruise which cannot be covered up." He pointed a finger at her. "That is an order! You think battles are hazardous; they are nothing compared to my wrath."

"I understand, Uncle Unnulf," she replied. "I shall be presentable."

With a curt nod, he spun on his heel and marched out, leaving the door open behind him. A brown and white spotted goat wandered in chewing on a weed.

"Oh, Elyn!" Liv bubbled with excitement. "Jarl Njord has invited you to visit. This is such good news. Everyone says he is seeking a new bride. To think he has included you as a prospect!"

"He could wish to discuss military matters," she offered, hoping such was the case.

"Nonsense!" Liv beamed at her, then she swallowed her enthusiasm. "I'm certain he will interview many young women before making a choice, but what a blessing it would be if he picks you. There is no shame if he decides on someone else," she added. "It is an honor to be considered."

Two thoughts competed for Elyn's attention: first, that marrying the jarl would get her out from under the thumb of her stern uncle, and second, if Njord picked another woman, Unnulf would take his disappointment out on her. He would surely blame her for ruining his chances of advancement. She suddenly felt like the walls of the one-room house were closing in on her. He had beaten her in the past for such inconsequential mistakes as overcooking a meal and for spilling his ale. Even if she did everything perfectly, if Njord chose another wife, she would incur Unnulf's fury. On the other hand, she did not look forward to becoming the property of a man twice her age... well, any husband, really. Thinking of giving herself to a man reminded her too much of the raiders from Raumsdal and the pain and trauma they caused her. Her friend Ingvar didn't count. His touch neither aroused nor disgusted her. It was just something they did from time to time if they had been drinking and the mood struck.

"Aunt Liv, may I be excused to go to my training now?" She had to get some fresh air. "At the feast, Jarl Njord complemented my performance on the battlefield. It might be what he wishes to speak about tomorrow, and I don't want to disappoint him."

"Certainly, dear," Liv allowed with a smile. "But mind what Unnulf said and tell your friends they must not strike you in the face."

"I will," she vowed and leaped up from her stool, eager to change into her gambeson and trousers and take her weapons to the practice yard.

When Elyn arrived at the training grounds, which lay within the jarl's compound, many of her comrades were already there. A palisade surrounded the entire area, which had been erected on a terrace overlooking Kaldrlogr, the village built along an inlet from the fjord. On a lot between Njord's great hall and the outbuildings constructed to the longhouse's north side, spread the practice field with weapons racks, targets, and several strawman dummies attached to posts. Here warriors could hone their skills, engage in sparring, and various contests of strength and endurance. The men also spent much time rowing, climbing, and tree felling to build their muscles.

Along the tall post fence stood other buildings, such as a yard house, smoke house, granary, chicken hutch, and horse stable. Rising above it, stretched a lofty lookout tower with a guard on duty at all times. Njord's compound and village lay in the shadow of towering white-capped peaks and served as a central hub for the farms, fisheries, herds, and forests he oversaw. Elyn was aware the other soldiers lived in Njord's grand longhouse, including her cousin Geir who had moved in with the others a year ago, but so far no one had invited her to join them. Was that what the jarl wished to speak with her about?

Upon seeing her approach, Geir announced in a jovial tone, "Father says we are not allowed to burst Elyn's nose or cut her face or mar her beauty in any way!" The other fighting men laughed.

"Then what can we do to her?" asked Frode, a seasoned fighter with many scars to his credit. "Can we break her leg? Slice off a few toes?" The crew roared in laughter.

Elyn raised her brow and brought fists to her hips. "First you would have to strike me, tricky enough for an agile man in his prime. How would one as old and fat as you accomplish the deed?"

Her insult incited more laughter, but Frode brushed it off, able to laugh at himself.

"Let us practice archery and spear and ax throwing today," Ingvar suggested. Bright sunshine glistened off his fair hair.

"Indeed!" Geir concurred. "Then we can hold a minor contest to see who is most accurate."

"I'll take the wagers," Horik offered, and he extended his cap to collect.

While other fighters practiced with shields and swords or tossed large stones, Elyn notched her arrow and sighted the target ten paces away. Ingvar, a mason by trade, excelled at ax throwing, but she proved highly precise with a bow. The odds shifted in various warriors' favor, as Horik noted who was best at each event. To sharpen their skills even more, Frode suggested they also compete while moving or aiming at swinging targets. Before they were done, each participant won at least once, and the bets they placed had a way of returning to their own hands. The afternoon concluded with a race up the nearest mountain and back down again. Elyn's surefootedness guaranteed she would be one of the first to complete the run.

Sweaty and winded, the quartet drew water from the well to satisfy their thirsts, then plopped down in a circle on the grass. "So, Elyn, tell us what it was like to be locked in combat with Sigrid the Valiant," prodded Geir. He pulled the end of the cord which had bound his curly brown tresses back and shook them out, spraying her with tiny droplets.

"Ya," Ingvar encouraged. "We lost five soldiers in the battle, and two of them were to her blade, yet you bore up well."

The question caught her off guard, and Elyn was not sure what to say. She shrugged. "We didn't have much of a chance to fight because of the storm. She is strong, decisive, with reflexes as quick as lightning." She recalled how Sigrid had snatched her from the path of the spear and marveled yet again. "I consider myself to be any man's equal, but I believe if she had desired to kill me, I would not be here with you today."

"I think she stayed her blade because she favors women," Frode stated.

"What do you mean?" Elyn tilted her head in confusion. She wrapped her arms around her pulled up knees and clasped a wrist with her other hand to hold them there.

"Folks say Sigrid prefers to take female lovers rather than men," Frode replied in a secretive tone. "It is why she has past twenty-six years without gaining a husband."

"I heard all the men of Svithjod are afraid of her," Geir interjected.

"She has the power to cast spells on others," Horik added in a whisper.

"Some people say Olaf was not the true father of the twins," Ingvar recalled. "It is believed Freyr, Balder, or possibly Oden visited their mother while Olaf was away and she conceived Jarls Sigurd and Sigrid, which would explain many things."

Elyn listened to the men spin wilder and wilder tales about the mighty blonde warrior and her brother, but her mind wandered at the declaration she preferred women as lovers. *Can someone actually do that?* She wondered. She was aware they *could,* as from time to time two young women romped off together. She had heard of a man called Vigir who had two wives and the three of them slept and shared pleasures collectively to everyone's satisfaction. Yet Sigrid had no man, no husband, and they say she takes female companions.

The idea set Elyn's imagination ablaze considering the implications and possibilities. *If she can do it, why can't I? Is that what I sensed about her, why my soul seems drawn to her like flies to honey? Does the same attraction dwell in me as resides in her? Is there any action I can take save to dream? After all, she is a powerful woman, joint jarl with her brother. She commands armies, owns ships and land, and does as she pleases, while I am an orphan subject to the rule of my uncle. Besides, the stories could be wrong about Sigrid. But I felt something the day of the battle, and it was real. I could sense she perceived it too, but...*

"What do you think, Elyn?" she heard Geir ask.

She shook her head and looked up, her mouth open like a fish's. "I'm sorry; my mind was elsewhere. What did you say?"

"I asked if you were to face Sigrid again, do you think you could defeat her?"

Elyn did not wish to defeat her. She would prefer to surrender to her, but such was not an option. "I suppose it would depend on who the gods favored that day," she replied. "I would surely not hold back. Now I have a question for you," she countered. "If a shieldmaiden such as myself were to be killed in combat on the field of honor, would she be welcomed in Valhalla along with the men? Would she, by her courage, earn a seat at Odin's table?"

They stared at her slack-jawed and then turned their gazes on each other. "Well..." Geir began but could not complete an answer.

"We know many people who do not die in battle gather at Helgafjell, the holy mountain," Frode said at last.

33

"And Freya takes her portion of warriors to the green pastures of Fólkvangr," added Ingvar. "Most stories do not specify between male and female but assume the champions to be men."

"Mayhap fallen shieldmaidens become Valkyries," Geir piped up. "Of course, Rán takes charge of all who die at sea."

Horik's tone was as bright as his smile. "At least if she dies heroically, we know she will not end up in Hel, as the domain is a place of punishment for those who swear false oaths, commit murderers without cause, or who act as cowards. Some believe anyone who dies of old age upon their sickbed is bound for Hel, but I like to think if they have lived honest lives and shown hospitality and generosity, they will end up at Helgafjell with the farmers and other peaceful folk."

"You needn't worry, though, Elyn," Ingvar added, meeting her gaze. "I believe you are favored by Thor, and he struck his hammer to save you from Sigrid's sword. You have a destiny before you."

So does Sigrid, I am certain, she thought. Then she recalled her uncle's slip when he mentioned the Völva. She had said something to him about her, but Unnulf refused to say what. "Perhaps," Elyn voiced.

CHAPTER 6

*T*he next evening, Elyn and her uncle were seated to either side of Njord at a more private setting in his great hall. A stairstep son and daughter, clearly still in their childhood, sat across from them with an older woman, probably a relative, but none else joined them at the table. The jarl wore a rich blue tunic with a fur collar and a band of twisted gold on one wrist. The smoothness of his chin testified he had recently shaved it and his brown mustache and cheek beard were as well-groomed as his hair.

Elyn only owned three dresses, two for daily wear and this cream underdress topped with a forest-green pinafore. The longhouse attendant who showed them in had hung her gray woolen wrap and Unnulf's fur mantle on pegs near the entry, but she fastened her silver raven cloak pin over the apron strap button at her left shoulder to be certain it would not get lost. Liv had gone with her to the village bathhouse earlier in the day so she would look and smell her best for the occasion. They were fortunate to have an underground hot spring, and the bathhouse had been constructed over it, consisting of a sauna sweat lodge portion and shallow bathing pools for men and women separated by a curtain. Most villagers bathed at least once a week so they had derived a schedule to avoid rushes and crowds, all wanting the steam or warm water at once, but Unnulf had traded time slots with a friend so Elyn could have the afternoon to cleanse herself.

Oiled, perfumed, and dressed in form-fitting clothing which accented her feminine qualities, Elyn felt beautiful, and yet was as nervous as a cat in a kennel. She would have preferred to dine with Njord alone than to have her uncle lurking there to scrutinize her every word and gesture, but she understood the propriety of a chaperone, especially for a first personal visit.

"The reindeer is fresh," the jarl commented as his manservant laid steaming dishes on the table. Another thrall, this one a young woman, filled their cups, keeping her gaze down and her mouth properly closed. "I shot it when I took my son Bjorn on a hunt this morning. I find it is the most tender and flavorful of all the creatures the gods created for us to consume, especially when cooked slowly all day as this was prepared."

Taking a bite, Elyn's features lit. "Indeed, my lord, it is like placing a rainbow in my mouth!" It was rare for Elyn to eat rich foods. They grew peas, cabbage, beans, onions, carrots, and leeks in their garden, which along with fruits, berries, fish, eggs, and cheese comprised her typical summer diet. They dried peas and berries for the winter months to accompany smoked fish, salted pork, small game, and the occasional chicken. Grain, both as porridge and bread, were also important main-stays to her family year-round. Since being included as a shieldmaiden in the jarl's army, she had been granted the right to hunt, and she and Geir brought home a red deer from time to time, but it had not been as succulent and tender as this.

"Most excellent, Jarl Njord," Unnulf praised and licked his fingers after having touched the meat. "By the looks of him, Bjorn will make a marvelous hunter. I can see he takes after his father."

The lad sat up straighter and beamed at Unnulf with pride. "Father taught me how to remove its organs and hide," he boasted. "I helped. I am getting good with my bow, but this reindeer was too far away for my arrow to strike it."

"Do not let that discourage you," Elyn advised with a smile. "You will send arrows sailing far very soon."

"And may I introduce my daughter, Yrsa." Njord motioned to the petite blonde girl with saucer blue eyes. She beamed and giggled shyly.

"Pleased to meet you, Yrsa," Elyn responded. "You must be the prettiest little girl I have ever seen." It was not an exaggeration. Although most children of four or five years were adorable in Elyn's estimation, Yrsa seemed to shine like a rare gem.

"So, Elyn, what made you decide to become a shieldmaiden?" the jarl asked as he ate. He gave her more than passing attention, which she took as a good sign. "If I recall, my wife Hilda encouraged you, didn't she?"

"Yes, my lord. Hilda was quite kind to me after my family was killed. She saw how I wished to retaliate against the Raumsdal raiders who attacked us, but I wasn't big enough to be of much use at the time. Lady Hilda said if I trained and devoted myself to discipline, one day I could be a mighty shieldmaiden like Sigrid the Valiant. I was sad when she died, sad for all of us."

Njord nodded in understanding. "Hilda was an insightful woman, well-suited to be a jarl's wife, and I have missed her. But." He lifted a shoulder and glanced at his children. "Life goes on. Hilda's mother, Aslaug, has been of great aid to me. She has been caring for Bjorn and Yrsa and teaching them all the things they should know, but it is not her place to be at my side. Two years is long enough for me to be alone, and I find myself seeking."

"Which is only natural," Unnulf agreed. "You are an important man, and you deserve the companionship of a worthy woman. I hear King Tortryggr has a granddaughter." A sly smile sneaked onto Elyn's lips at her uncle's clever misdirection.

The jarl shook his head with a wave of his hand. "She is too young. Besides, he will want her to wed a chieftain's son when the time comes. No, Unnulf, I am making occasions to get to know the women of marrying age here among my own people. Surely I will not be forced to seek a stranger."

"I think my lord is wise to pick a flower from his own garden," her uncle praised and took a sip from his cup.

"So, Elyn, I saw you cross swords with the legendary Sigrid," Njord commented, giving her a considering gaze. "What did you think of her?"

"She has earned her reputation," she replied as she considered the tall Nordic hero. "But my lord, there are things I do not understand."

She peered into his rich brown eyes, which seemed to hold ambition, sincerity, and a lusty longing in equal measure. "What things are those?"

Elyn had been thinking a lot about the brief exchange of words she had with Sigrid and about the odd circumstances prompting the battle. "Jarl Sigrid claimed Svithjod did not raid our farms. She seemed to know nothing about it and could not understand why our army crossed their border."

Njord sat back and stared at her, a look of concern filling his face.

"Mayhap she lied, or more likely the culprits were not under her orders. The raiders carried yellow and black shields and flew the raven flag. Many witnesses attested to it, and we found some broken rönds left behind."

"The attack was from Svithjod, Elyn," her uncle confirmed. "But they could have been under the direction of another jarl or King Grimolf. And yes, she may have tried to deceive you so you would lower your guard. You cannot trust the word of weasels."

Weighing their arguments, Elyn could see the merit in them, but her suspicions ran deeper. "That is not all, my lord. I know I am but a common shieldmaiden, only serving in my second summer with the warriors, but why would our peaceful neighbors to the south raid our farms?"

Her Uncle Unnulf squinted and scowled at her disapprovingly, but Njord offered her a patient smile. "I see you enjoy engaging your brain as well as weapons of iron. I will explain. Life in Norvegr is precarious. We grow stronger than southern societies because it is necessary for our survival. Our mountains are high, and our waters run deep, but when winter descends, plunging all into the assault of its long dark, icy winds howling and snow to bury us all, we draw on our strength to overcome. Each year, our farms seem to produce a little less and yet the mouths to feed increase. Our highlands are a bulwark, but one cannot plant vast amounts of crops on them. There is simply not enough farmland to meet the demand. I recall two winters ago when Hilda became sick with the fever, she was not the only soul lost. Many of our citizens perished. This is even a bigger problem with Raumsdal to the north. We do not have the flat fields of the Danes and Swedes or of those farther east and south; we depend on trade and raiding foreign lands for the necessities required for subsistence. I do not believe they attacked us because they hate us or that they are evil. Like everyone, the warriors of Svithjod must fight to survive."

Elyn already knew all this, but it was necessary to remind Njord before posing her next point. "I understand everything you say, it's just…" Elyn focused on the jarl as she felt the searing disapproval radiating from Unnulf's body and sensed his furious stare on her skin. "It is early summer, my lord. The crops are just being planted, and the grain is far from harvest. The flocks and herds are bearing their young and none of the kids or lambs are weaned. It is the wrong season for a resource raid.

When the warriors of Raumsdal attacked our farm and killed my family, it was during the harvest. They made off with sacks of wheat, barrels of apples, and much livestock, but now?" She lifted her palms and her brows at him in honest disbelief. "Something is not right. Are all the leaders of Svithjod slow-witted? Have they no sense? What could they accomplish to their own benefit by such an action?"

"They are dishonorable brutes!" Unnulf bellowed. "They do not require a reason. Perhaps they wanted to steal seed grain or just cause us trouble. Why do you question your jarl's decision? You are the one with no sense!"

"I am not questioning Jarl Njord's decision," Elyn began, but Njord raised a hand.

"Be patient, Unnulf," he said. "I like that your ward has a mind and the will to use it. We must always ask questions; how else can we ever arrive at the answers? Elyn, you have given me much to think about, inquiries I may need to make of the gods. Do you have a theory?"

Elyn lowered her head. "I cannot say," she answered in a hush. "I just think there is more at play than what has been revealed so far in this affair."

Njord brought his hand to rest atop Elyn's. "You have impressed me with your boldness," he admitted with an amused light dancing in his brown eyes. "I see what makes you such an asset in the shield wall."

"I want to be an asset in the shield wall, Father!" declared Bjorn, who had cleaned his plate. "Can I spar with Elyn? Can she teach me to be bold?"

Njord laughed and shook his head. "You are too small to practice with the grown-ups, Bjorn. But continue to play swords and shields with your cousins and one day soon you will be big enough." The little boy with his father's looks about him pouted, crossing his arms over his chest to signal his disapproval.

"Yes, sir," he muttered. His grandmother wrapped an arm around the lad and kissed the top of his head.

"Your father is right," Aslaug told him. They were the only words the woman spoke all evening. Elyn wondered if her uncle thought she should have remained silent, too, but wasn't the point to interact with Njord so he could get to know her? Why did Unnulf have such an attitude toward her? Elyn did her best to ignore him and enjoyed her fine meal and stimulating conversation despite her uncle's foul mood.

. . .

ELYN AND UNNULF walked in silence through the palisade gates and down the path to Kaldrlogr past fields bearing fresh shoots of grain and gardens surrounded by wattle fences under a moonlit sky. She did not realize how angry he was with her until they dipped below a terrace out of the gate guards' sight. With no warning, the back of his hand slammed across her face, knocking her off balance only because she was not expecting it. Her green eyes flashed with insult and a tinge of fear, but she also registered Unnulf's surprise. *He thought he would have knocked me to the ground,* she comprehended. It had been a while since the last time he had struck her and must not have realized how sturdy she had become.

"You are an insulant fool! What did you think you were doing in there? You humiliated me with your questions and unrequested remarks. Who cares about what a woman has to say on such matters?"

Elyn stood fast before her uncle as he shook with rage. She straightened and raised her chin. She was not as tall as him nor as heavy, but he had not been training, and his belly bulged with extra fat. It was not a matter of whether she could take him physically; of which the shieldmaiden had no doubt. But he was the head of her household, and it was her duty to show him respect. A woman who shamed her father, husband, brother, or whomever had charge over her was looked down upon by the entire community, but there were limits. Their law and customs allowed for a woman to defend herself or to employ retribution for a grievous offense. A mild discipline such as being backhanded was not a grievous offense. Unnulf had spent the past six years hugging a line he never crossed.

She bridled her temper to respond civilly. "Jarl Njord appeared to care what I had to say."

Unnulf shook his head and rubbed the back of his neck with his hand. "You conversed with him as if he was your commanding officer, not a prospective husband."

"He *is* my commanding officer, and I am his shieldmaiden." Elyn was unmoved by his complaints.

"You are willfully disobeying me, trying to sabotage my plans for an improved life for us," he accused, pointing a finger at her. "A man has other men with whom to discuss such matters. He wants a woman to bear his children and satisfy him in bed. Do you know nothing?"

"You forget—I knew Hilda better than you did," Elyn countered. "She was not a weak-willed woman. Mayhap I behaved exactly to the jarl's expectations."

He fumed and cursed, working his lips to produce words instead of growls.

"Uncle Unnulf," she addressed with more confidence than she felt; but Elyn had grown weary of being his footstool. "I will be forever grateful to you for saving me from the Raumsdalers and bringing me to stay with your family, but all you have ever done was treat me as nothing, tell me I was nothing, and you do the same to Liv. She is a dutiful and faithful wife who deserves better. But here's what I have learned on the field of honor: I am not nothing. I matter. My spear and shield matter. The man on my left and on my right count upon my valor and skill. We depend on each other for everything and breathe together as one. They do not berate me, but build me up, challenging me to be swifter, stronger, better. My fellow warriors show me the respect you never did."

Elyn held her breath, uncertain how Unnulf would respond. This was the first occasion she had stood up to him, or ever uttered a word in her own defense, but it was time. She was eighteen, a grown woman, and a formidable warrior. She could not let him lord it over her forever. Then again, she could be about to spend the night in a barn.

Unnulf sighed and lowered his hackles, slumping his shoulders as if in disappointment. With his gaze at her feet, he shook his head. "I have only been preparing you to face the harsh realities of life, child. I have no doubt the soldiers treat you as an equal, as one day you may be all that stands between them and an ax in the back. But did you ever think what they must say about you when you are not around to hear it? The jokes they surely tell? You are an anomaly, and while your friend Ingvar may be true enough, the others?" He shrugged, then fixed her with a serious regard. "But the day is coming when you will be too old to play with swords, and then what? Our kingdom needs sons and daughters more than a body to plug a single spot in a shield wall. Let your thoughts dwell on that for a while."

He turned away, his anger waning, and plodded in the direction of the village. Elyn fell into line behind him, saying nothing further. Was being hard on her what she had needed? Did the other warriors truly respect her as she believed, or was it as Uncle Unnulf said? And had she spoiled his chance of uniting households with the jarl? It would be a step up for them, but Njord would certainly forbid his wife from battle, especially once she became pregnant. *Who am I if I am not a shieldmaiden?* she wondered. *And do I wish simply to trade one patriarch for another?* She knew the answer, but she may end up with no say in the matter. Her spear, her sword, her shield—these she could control. As to everything else in her experience… In this one arena, Elyn could take command. The rest of her existence seemed always to be determined by forces outside herself, as if life was something which happened *to* her, jerking her this way and the other, pounding her into a hole where she did not fit, and never allowing her a choice.

CHAPTER 7

Village of Gnóttdalr, Svithjod, the next day.

Sigrid and Sigurd conducted court in their great hall that morning, as was their custom once each week. There were disputes to settle, permissions to grant, and occasional fines or punishments to be issued. But if a matter was grave, carrying the potential for a death penalty or even worse, banishment, the accuser and accused would stand before King Grimolf the Wolf and the gathering of the Thing, where all freemen could cast a vote.

The twins sat on a slightly raised platform at one end of the hall on matching armchairs carved by the finest carpenter in Svithjod at the behest of their father, Jarl Olaf, with the two rangy wolfhounds lounging at their feet. The tables and chairs used for feasting had been moved to the edges to clear the areas left and right of the enormous central hearth in which spectators gathered. For some, weekly court provided entertainment, and it was a place to hear the latest news and gossip. The doors remained open for light and air, but lamps fueled by whale oil perched on their stands to further brighten the windowless structure.

To please her mother, Sigrid wore a white underdress and deep blue pinafore with a braided cord belt and azure ribbons wound in her hair. She wanted to don her warrior attire, as Sigurd did, but decided this was not an issue to argue over. When Olaf was stabbed in the back—yes, some cowardly assassin literally stabbed him in his back three times—and the

43

twins were instantly promoted via their father's will and instruction, Gudred held the keys which were the jarl's wife's to carry. She continued jurisdiction over the treasury, pantry, and valuables of the household and kept the keys on a chain around her waist, often slipped into a pouch or pocket out of sight. Since Sigurd had no wife and Sigrid did not wish to play the woman's role, they had asked their mother to retain her position of authority in the longhouse. Sigrid thought it would help her through the difficult time of losing her husband if she maintained her routine.

A fellow Sigrid knew as Arne Ragnarsson, a lean fisher of Gnóttdalr, stepped forward with a deep scowl on his face, tarnished by a scar across his cheek and nose. "Jarls Sigurd and Sigrid, I have a grievance to claim," he declared. He scanned the crowd with piercing dark eyes until pointing a condemning finger at a stranger standing in the back near the door. "That man stole from me."

"Stealing is a serious offense," Sigurd replied, as he shifted his gaze to the accused. "Step forward and tell us your name."

The man wore clothing reduced to rags and by all indications, hadn't bathed in months. "I did not, my lord," he pled, holding out open palms covered in calluses. "I am Skarde and moved here as the snows were melting. I stay in Cnut the tanner's barn."

"Arne, what was stolen? Did you witness Skarde take your property?" Sigrid charged.

"Over the years, I have gained some silver," Arne explained. "I had some Arabic coins from trading, several ingots, and some hacksilver as well. I keep them hidden in a box in a hole dug under the sleeping bench in my hut down by the docks because one day I will need to buy a new boat. They have always been safe until this newcomer arrived in town. I didn't see him steal them, but the whole box disappeared a few days ago when I was out on a fishing trip, after he showed up."

"Who else knew about your cache of silver?" Sigurd asked.

"Well…" Arne pondered the question.

"He certainly did not tell me," Skarde volunteered. "I am new in town, so how would I know the fisherman even possessed valuables, much less where he hid them?"

"But Cnut's barn is near my hut," Arne pointed out. "You could have seen. You could have searched for it when I was not at home."

"Odo." Sigrid addressed her younger brother, and his attention swung to her with expectancy. "Take a guard with you and search the tanner's barn. If you find a box of silver or anything else out of place, bring it back with you."

With a nod, the young man spun and waved to two warriors of the hall to accompany him.

Sigrid returned her awareness to the claim before them. "You think because he is new in town and no one has bothered your treasure before now, he must therefore be guilty?"

"Exactly!" Arne affirmed.

Sigurd rose from his seat and strolled about as he addressed the hall. "Ours is a law based on honesty above all else. For our society to function, for us to be seen as worthy by the gods, it is essential each man and woman take responsibility for his or her own actions. If you have committed an offense, own up to it. Say you killed a man. You may defend yourself before your peers at the Thing, as is honorable to do. Perhaps you had a good reason to kill him. If you do this in front of witnesses or immediately go to your jarl and admit the deed, then it is likely all will be well. What we do in the open, where others can see and judge for themselves, is surely not a crime." Then his countenance darkened. "But to kill a man in secret and keep silent is to commit murder, and surely such a villain will be punished to the full extent when he is found out."

Every eye fixed on Sigurd when he halted, making a dramatic pause. "Say one man's goat gets his neighbor's goat pregnant. To whom does the kid belong? We can handle these kinds of disputes by the light of day to everyone's satisfaction, but thieving, done in secret where no one sees, is an especially heinous crime. The bandit supposes he will get away with it, but he is even worse than an oath-breaker. Does he not realize the gods know what he has done, how deceitful his heart is? Will they not punish him in due time?"

Sigurd passed his gaze to Sigrid, and she picked up the narrative. "However, if the thief was to come forward and admit his weakness, we will credit it to him as strength. If he returns the stolen items and works to make amends, one day he may regain his good name and the gods might not turn their backs on him. Maybe he will not be taken by Hel to an afterlife of pain and suffering. Any man or woman can redeem themselves by their honesty."

By then Sigurd had come back to the platform and deliberately took his seat. "Odo will return soon," he stated, his scrutiny fixed on Skarde. "If you are hiding anything in your benefactor's barn, this is the time to say so."

The haggard Skarde, with his disheveled hair and beard, shook his head. "He will find only hay and manure."

Sigrid narrowed her focus on him. "You never told us where you were from or what brought you to our village. Would you give an honest answer?"

The impoverished man bowed his head with a slight nod. "Ill luck has beset me," he began. "Everything has gone wrong. I grew up in Sochabrot. I tried fishing, but my employer's boat sunk at sea; I washed up on shore, but he drowned. The villagers somehow thought it was my fault and urged me to leave Sochabrot, so I moved north to Jarl Siegfried Strongarm's lands. I got a job as a freeman farm laborer, and all was well for about two years. I was even thinking of gaining a wife when the farmer's cow bore a calf with six legs. He called for the Völva and she examined the calf and threw her runes. She declared it was a bad omen and asked who had been tending the cow before she gave birth."

Knowing where this story led, Sigrid nodded. "You."

"Yes, I was the last to tend the cow and was present when the deformed calf was expelled from its mother's womb," Skarde continued. "Everyone branded me as bad luck and I was told to leave. That is when I came here. Unfortunately, rotten luck followed me and now I have been accused of a crime I did not commit. What could I have done to anger the gods so?"

"It is often difficult to understand why one is blessed by the gods with all good things," Sigurd consoled, "and why another is cursed by misfortunes. We must all strive to do the best we can with what we are given."

Both twins lifted expectant gazes when Odo and the two warriors stepped in through the open doorway. "We found nothing, as he said."

"He could have hidden it elsewhere," Arne suggested.

"Neighbor, if I had stolen your silver, I would be long gone from this village on my way to somewhere else," Skarde replied to his accuser. "I would buy new clothes, a bath, and a hot meal. But here I stand before you, tricked by Loki again."

"He has a point," Sigurd whispered to Sigrid.

"There is only one action left before us." Sigrid rose, poised with her shoulders back and chin high. In a commanding tone, she directed her younger brother once more. "Odo, take your men and search every building in Gnóttdalr, each hut, barn, and yard house. We will find Arne's silver and cut off the hand of the thief who took it."

Odo nodded and spun on his heel with his attendants, but stopped when a voice shouted, "Wait!"

All attention turned to a boney older fellow with a gray beard who only had one arm.

"Eric, is it you?" Sigurd's mouth dropped, and his eyes rounded in astonishment. He leapt up from his seat and rushed to meet the man, who fell on his knees before him.

"Yes, Jarl Sigurd," he cried with a mournful wail. "Forgive me! I will return everything. Allow me to meet Arne on the field of honor in the tradition of the holmgang, so I may die with a weapon in my hand and have a chance to sit at Odin's table."

"Eric, what happened to you?" Sigrid asked with concern. "I recall you were a mighty warrior in my father's army, but you have dwindled away. How can this be?"

"I lost my arm in battle, but not my life," he explained. "I was of no use on the battlefield anymore and knew no other occupation. My kind and loving wife wove extra cloth to trade for food and I tried my hand at many odd jobs, but the past winter was rough on us. Arne, I was only thinking of my children."

"It was a few years ago, right? I remember the battle and was aware you suffered an injury, but haven't seen you in a long time," Sigurd responded. "We did not know you had fallen on such hard times."

"I recall, you worked for me for a short while last season," Arne realized. "I would never have thought a respected man like you would do such a thing."

"I am not proud of it, but I am no longer proud at all," Eric bemoaned. "Please, Jarl Sigurd, do not take my other hand. Then I will stand no prospect of entering Valhalla. I served your father well for many years. I vow to give back Arne's silver. Let him kill me with a sword in my hand."

Sigrid and her brother exchanged a glance and nodded to each other. Then Sigurd spoke. "You shall return Arne's treasure, every ounce, and then I will employ you in our stables to feed and water the horses, to brush them and tend to them, so you may earn food for your family. But I will not permit you to throw away your life when you are still needed."

"We stand on the brink of war with Firdafylke," Sigrid declared. "If you wish to die with a sword in your hand, let it be standing against our enemies, not in a dispute with a neighbor. We will call on you once again. Therefore, you must eat and regain your strength before they return with a larger army. Arne, will this satisfy you?"

The fisherman nodded. "I only wish my property to be returned," he said. Granting Skarde a glance, he allowed, "I am sorry for falsely accusing you. It seemed the only explanation."

Skarde offered his hand, and the two shook.

"Thank you, my lord, my lady." Eric's face lit with renewed hope. "I am certain I can cut down a few of our foes before one strikes my shieldless side. It is my honor to serve."

"Who shall be heard next?" Sigurd called out. In an aside to Sigrid, he whispered, "How do you always know what I am thinking? Eric deserves the right to die in battle."

"My lord and lady!" A youthful man bounded forward with a joyous glow on his face, clasping hands with a blushing young woman.

"Bragi, you are looking well." Sigrid greeted the young farmer with a smile. Her brother Odo had often interacted with him as a child, and she knew him to be a good-humored fellow who played the flute when not working his father's farm.

"Thank you, Jarl Sigrid," he answered with a broad grin.

"I see you have persuaded the fair Runa to enjoy company with you," Sigurd inserted with a twinkle in his eyes.

"More than just keep company with me," the sandy-haired Bragi boasted. He turned a shining regard on the youthful brunette who gripped his hand. "We wish your permission and your blessing to be wed."

Bragi was a freeman, but his family were tenants on the land the twins controlled, therefore it was appropriate to seek the jarls' consent to get married.

"Congratulations!" Sigrid beamed at the happy couple, wondering if she would ever glow with such radiance out of love for another. Sometimes marriages were similar to contracts, planned and arranged to benefit the families involved. Other times they arose out of convenience because of a pregnancy or to provide security. But Sigrid had witnessed affection blossom like theirs as well and envied it. Then she boxed it away into the category of things she would never experience so her heart would not long and yearn for something which could not come to pass. She had Sveina and her brothers and they would have to be enough.

"Certainly, Bragi Karlsson, on one condition," Sigurd stipulated. "Your wedding will take place here in our great hall and our brother Odo shall stand with you."

"You are too kind!" Bragi almost danced, so overpowering was his enthusiasm. "Thank you, Jarls Sigurd and Sigrid, my lords and my friends."

"And when do you wish this merry occasion to be celebrated?" Sigrid asked with a smile.

Runa answered, "As soon as possible!" Her joyful gaze swung from Sigrid to Bragi, and she giggled with glee.

"Tonight then," Sigurd announced. "We will celebrate with our new couple."

With a bow, the engaged pair scurried off to prepare. Sigurd motioned to his manservant Asmund who rushed to his side. "Go now and tell Gudred. I want a fine feast and musicians for tonight. We are not short of food or funds. Weddings are a happy occasion, and I wish to bestow a gift on a loyal and worthy tenant."

"Yes, my lord," he replied and scampered out of the great hall.

Next up was Gunne Flokisson, another farmer. "My neighbor Bard the Beardless does not keep his goats tied up properly," he stated in irritation. "Twice in a week one or more of them has gotten into my garden and eaten the young shoots to the ground. I demand the offending goats be slaughtered and their blood offered to the gods as a sacrifice for a good growing season."

"Does your garden have a fence around it?" Sigrid asked.

"Yes, but the animals knocked it down and trampled in. If I had not been alerted by their bells tinkling, they could have destroyed everything." Gunne had a right to be angry as his tone revealed.

"Please do not kill my goats," Bard begged. "I need them for milk and cheese. They are part of my livelihood. You cannot take a man's means of providing for his family. I keep them in a pen when they are not up on the mountainside to graze, but they excel at escaping."

"You were alerted by the goats' bells, you say?" Sigurd leaned forward with consideration as Gunne nodded. "That combined with the goat pen means Bard is trying to protect his neighbors' property. But I know goats, and they have no respect for boundaries, nor do they acknowledge such things exist. It is not malicious for them to seek out tender shoots to nibble on, but the fact you keep a fence around your plot indicates you, too, Gunne, have actively engaged in seeking to protect your garden."

"Neither of you is in the wrong," Sigrid pointed out. "However, Bard's goats did harm Gunne's vegetables. We will come out to your farms tomorrow to inspect the damage and arrive upon a suitable sum of reparations for Bard to pay."

"However," Sigurd continued, "as Bard has pointed out, he relies on his goats to feed his family. Therefore, there shall be no slaughter. Just a moon ago we held a fertility rite where sacrifices were made to the gods for a good harvest. We should not insult them by repeating the act as if they were too blind and deaf to notice the first time."

"Yes, my lord, my lady." Gunne lowered his head in humility. "I will accept a fair price for my lost produce, but Bard must find a way to keep those pests out of my greens."

"I agree," Sigrid confirmed. With a glance around and spying no more complaints, accusations, or blissful couples, she rose and Sigurd with her. "Join us this evening as we celebrate with Bragi and Runa. Court is dismissed."

THE WEDDING FEAST was a grand success, and though she had been melancholy to think of how happy the couple was when she had no such love, Sigrid refused to let on to anyone present, even Sigurd who could read her like a toss of the runes. Tomorrow they would go inspect Gunne's garden and Bard's goat pen. Maybe she could stop by Gunnlief's to see how the new ard was working out for him. She would survey the hayfields, hay being one of the most important crops as they would need huge volumes of it to feed the barned and stabled cattle and horses during the deep snows of winter.

Most farms employed several freemen and at least a couple of thralls to keep up with the work of summer and harvest. Barley, rye, and oats were grown on gentle slopes and terraces while most families had a vegetable garden beside their hut or longhouse. Sigrid liked to monitor the progress of the fields so she could predict how much they would have to store for the winter and if any more was required from the trading expeditions. Sigurd focused his attention more on the timber, shipbuilding, and trade aspects of management. Together, they made a successful team. Then there was the constant training of their soldiers to be ready for anything.

She bestowed blessings on the newlyweds, placing kisses to both of their cheeks and then retired for the night. Tomorrow would be a busy day.

As she was undressing for bed, Sigrid perceived a gentle knock. "Lady Sigrid?"

The sound brought a wistful smile to her lips, and she opened a crack to spy Sveina. Sigrid lifted a brow. "Yes?"

"Do you need me anymore tonight?"

"Do you have other plans?" Sigrid extended a bare leg into Sveina's line of sight and rubbed a hand up and down the edge of the door.

"Everyone is going out to Bragi's farm with the couple to sing and beat drums and cheer for them." Sveina gave her a hopeful look which tugged at Sigrid's heart. She truly cared for her servant, but it wasn't what Bragi and Runa shared. It was what it was, and Sigrid was thankful she had that much.

"You should go and enjoy yourself with the wedding party," she consented. "I will still be here in the morning."

"Thank you!" Sveina beamed and pushed her face through the door to give Sigrid a quick kiss.

As she danced away, the image of the red-haired shieldmaiden flashed across Sigrid's mind accompanied by her brother's teasing words: "What are you planning to do? Invite her to dance at the next feast in our great hall?"

If only I could, she thought and climbed into bed alone, leaving her faithful dogs to lay guard at the threshold.

CHAPTER 8

The earliest morning light touched the sky, before the sun had risen past mountains into view, while mist rose off the fjord, and everyone still rested in their sleeping places. Sigrid was experiencing an odd dream with ravens and a serpent and a growling bear when a frantic cry jerked her into wakefulness.

"Raiders are attacking our farms!" Registering the words, she bolted out of bed, disturbing the two huge wolfhounds who slumbered at her feet. She jumped into her trousers and pulled on her boots. "Come quick!"

She recognized the voice of a shepherd named Finn. He must have seen the attack from his pastures on the mountainside overlooking the village and its sprawling farms. Sigrid wrapped on her gambeson, fastening it with her sword belt, and bolted out of her bedchamber into a bustling room of warriors, grabbing up their weapons and rönds to follow Finn. "Come Jotun, Warg," she commanded the dogs.

Sigurd met her with a grave expression where the family space joined to the great hall. "Not again!" He gritted his teeth.

"Thank the gods for Finn's sharp eyes and fast feet," Sigrid allowed. "Let us save what we can."

The twins took spears and shields from the weapons rack by the longhouse entrance and trotted out. "Which way, Finn?" Sigurd asked of the alarmed young man.

"Follow me!" Sigurd, Sigrid, and a band of warriors raced out behind the sheep herder.

"And this time we kill them all!" Sigrid yelled in righteous indignation. Realizing her words, she hoped the red-haired shieldmaiden would not be among the raiders, but if so, it would be her own fault. How dare they attack sleeping families at the break of dawn!

Skirts of cloud loomed about the mountains as the defense forces raced uphill in the chill of early morn, the leggy Cu dashing ahead of their masters. Sigrid spotted the rising plume of black smoke and feared the worst. She pumped her legs, gaining impetus up the path and keeping pace with her brother as they led the soldiers.

"There!" Sigurd shouted and pointed his spear tip at men in battle attire lighting a barn on fire.

Sigrid heard screams ahead and dug in harder to span the distance. Chickens squawked, goats bleated, and pigs squealed. A pony bolted free, galloping past the Svithjod fighters toward the safety of the village below. With the raiders occupied with their pillaging, there was no point in forming a shield wall. The experienced team understood their job was to seek and destroy all who posed a threat to their community, and that is what they did.

Taking only a second to aim, Sigurd hurled his spear, striking an enemy in the torso and knocking him backward and to the ground. Sigrid charged another, who tried to flee, and struck him in the back with her lance. Rangvoldr was joined by Gunnlief who dashed from his farmhouse to engage their attackers in hand-to-hand combat, battering with shields and hacking with axes until the foes lay motionless in pools of blood.

"Don't let any escape!" Sigurd yelled, echoing the command his sister had given as they set forth. Their warriors fanned out with the dogs in the lead, jogging through the fields and their structures, covering every farm-stead on the piedmont.

Sigrid kicked in the door of a burning hut to discover a woman and three children huddled in the one corner not ablaze, coughing from smoke inhalation. Leaving her spear outside, she ducked through the fire and rushed to them, her shield protecting her from the flames.

"This way, now," she commanded, and ushered the family out into the fresh air. A man with the red and black rönd of Firdafylke rounded a corner, and she jumped away from the woman and her children to face him. "Cowardly bandit!" she fumed in scorn. She drew her blade in challenge.

Raising his shield and ax, he smirked as he marched to her, but Sigrid had no time for his antics. She feigned left to draw him off, then stepped right, slammed her rönd into his ax arm and spun in a circle on her right foot, positioning her sword to slice him across the back. He dropped with a cry, and she left him bleeding in search of other invaders.

"Over here!" sounded a woman's scream. Sigrid dashed around a burning granary to spy a farmer trying to ward off his attacker with a scythe. The older man was accustomed to using the tool on grain, not an enemy warrior. The invader's ax smashed the scythe's wooden shaft asunder when he raised it in defense.

"Hey, you cockless coward!" Sigrid snarled, drawing the raider's attention. "You heard me, you mare in season. If you had any balls, you would fight warriors, not slaughter old men!"

"A woman!" the attacker exclaimed. He slung back hair as lengthy and blond as hers when he spun from the defenseless farmer to face her. "You'll see how long my cock is soon enough when you submit to me."

Fool doesn't know who I am. "Come ahead then, and we shall see who gets raped this morning."

With a malicious laugh, the meaty warrior charged with an ax in each hand. Sigrid claimed her ground with a full front stance, leading with her rönd and left knee, her sword arm ready to strike. But when he was in his last stride before making contact, she dropped to her knees, raised her rönd, and his momentum carried him over. As his weight pressed upon her shield, Sigrid pushed up with maximum force, thrusting him onto his back in the dirt, where, in a flash, she skewered him with her sword. He died with an expression of dread surprise on his bearded face.

SIGRID, Sigurd, and their fighting men searched every farm along the terrace. Rangvoldr made certain to finish off any of their wounded enemies while Gunnlief assisted Sigrid looking after the injured and survivors. The farmers and their families hauled buckets from a nearby snowmelt stream to put out the fires and save what they could.

The waste and destruction angered and disgusted Sigrid. The flames of one house faltered with a hiss as neighbors Bard and Gunne drenched them with buckets of water. Black smoke continued to trail upward and mingle with other soot clouds and the mist above, while she tended Finn's wounds. With only his staff, the young man had helped subdue the invaders and sustained a gash to his shoulder.

"You'll be alright, Finn," Sigrid assured him as she wrapped a strip of cloth around the injury. "You will have a story to tell your children about this scar." Jotun, the heavier of her dogs, licked Finn's hand and considered him with compassionate brown eyes.

"I have no children yet, my lady," he replied. "But I hope to someday."

The blessing of a gentle rain began to fall and soon all the fires were out. It was then Sigrid realized one of the burnt-out farmhouses belonged to Bragi and Runa. She leaped up from Finn's side and raced down the path through the veil of drizzle, past distressed tenants, confused farm animals, and her soldiers piling corpses to the smoldering hut and ripped its damaged door off.

"Bragi, Runa!" she cried. The odor of burnt flesh mixed with damp smoke and the coppery scent of blood filled her nostrils. "Oh, no," she moaned. The two brindle dogs trotted up behind her and halted with mournful expressions at the threshold.

Hoping against hope, Sigrid threw aside fragments of thatched roofing and dug through debris to find two bodies. Investigation would be required to determine if they had been killed before the fire started or if they perished in their sleep, but the couple lay together on their sleeping bench. Sigrid's heart ached as she recalled how happy they were at their wedding feast last night. It seemed unreal to her that they had just celebrated their marriage, their whole lives ahead of them, and then this…

Fury tore through her like a wild bear, and she let out a scream of agony. Sigurd burst through the opening and dropped at her side, his comforting arm draping around her. "By Odin, we will punish Firdafylke for this outrage," he seethed.

"We know the time of one's death is decided by the Norn at birth," she breathed. "But the manner of it? It appears he was not offered a chance to fight back. Either they slew him in his sleep or set the house on fire over them and they never woke up." Sigrid raised haunted eyes to her brother. "This is not fair, just like our father's murder was not fair. Every man, every woman should have the right to defend themselves, not to be taken as by a thief in the night."

Sigurd's arm tightened around her shoulders, and she leaned into him, resting her head against his. "They will be happy together on the holy mountain of Helgafjell," he offered in solace. "If Bragi had gone to Valhalla, he would have left Runa behind. This way they can be united until the end of the ages. Do not despair, Sigrid; we will inform King

Grimolf of this attack and then march to Firdafylke in full strength. The guilty shall be punished, even as we have not allowed a single raider to live."

"How many attackers were there?" she asked. "How many of ours are dead?"

"We counted a dozen invaders and found both red and black flags and shields among them," Sigurd replied, then eased her to her feet. "We lost one soldier and six other farmers besides Bragi and his bride, two of them children."

"The monsters," Sigrid seethed, but she allowed her brother and faithful hounds to escort her away from the grim ruins and the death they contained.

Town of Sochabrot in Svithjod, two days later.

Sigrid wore her armor and a blue cape fastened by a silver raven cloak pin to the meeting at Grimolf's great hall. Sigurd sat to her left and Siegfried to her right. Across from them were the other three jarls, Arkyn, Brynjar, and Trygve, with the king directing the assembly from the head of the table. Grimolf was joined by a hairy bald fellow in fine attire, who Sigrid supposed was an advisor. A servant passed out goblets of mead to everyone's satisfaction.

She considered the other jarls, all of whom she had met before, but not since their promotion. Arkyn was a barrel-chested man in his forties, not as tall as her, but possessing an abundance of strength. He looked around the hall with a bored aspect while he sipped his mead, dripping some on his brown, braided beard. Brynjar stood even taller than Sigurd and was renowned as a fierce warrior, but today he wore a noble's tunic and his sandy-blond tresses hung leisurely about muscled shoulders. He appeared to study her with gold-fleck eyes. Trygve sat beside Grimolf, speaking with him in a hushed tone. An older man, like the king, his hair and beard had faded to gray, and he seldom engaged in combat anymore, allowing his eldest son to take that role.

With a nod to Trygve, Grimolf straightened and turned his attention to the circle of jarls. The ruler was in his fifties and had distinguished himself as a seaman and commander of champions. He had defeated three upstarts who thought they could overcome him in a duel, but because of his age and position, he had not appeared in battle for several years. Until the Firdafylke neighbors to the north fell under attack from Raumsdal, their kingdoms had been at peace for over a decade. The fylkes of Norvegr had engaged in infighting to a moderate degree for centuries, typically after harsh winters or in disputes between rulers, leaving much of the experience gained by warriors to be accomplished when they traveled abroad seeking fortunes from foreign territories. But even then, these Northmen were more interested in trade and discovery than usurping the lands of others, and their parties were too small to have done so anyway.

"Thank you all for coming on short notice," the king acknowledged. "It would seem King Tortryggr of Firdafylke is no longer our friend, or at least Jarl Njord, who is sworn to his service is not. Twice raiders from the north bearing the flag and shields of Firdafylke have attacked Jarls Sigurd and Sigrid's land—unprovoked—and their forces have clashed once on the border. Jarl Sigurd," Grimolf motioned, giving him the floor.

"A few weeks ago, they swarmed in destroying crops and slaughtering livestock," he reported. Many of our tenants were injured, two thralls killed, and several women raped before we drove them away, killing six while the rest of the spineless bastards fled."

"We gathered our forces to retaliate in an honorable fashion, unlike the way we were treated, by meeting Jarl Njord's warriors on the field of honor," Sigrid continued. "The battle ended in a tie as a mighty storm with thunder and lightning arose."

"The soldiers all believed it was Thor," Sigurd explained. "They assumed he was displeased, and we decided to call a draw and disperse."

"Then two mornings ago, they attacked at dawn while most men were still asleep." Sigrid tried to maintain a calm and even tone, but she felt the fire blaze through her veins when the image of finding her friends' burnt bodies flashed in her mind. "We suffered far more losses, but none of the raiders escaped this time."

"Did you keep any alive to question?" The inquiry came from the short, stocky, bald man who sat at the king's other side. It struck Sigrid he was exceptionally hairy as the exposed parts of his arms were covered in black furlike thickness and his beard seemed to grow all the way down to mesh into his chest hair. All the tribes and kingdoms of Norvegr spoke the same language, but accents and dialects differed, and it was clear from his speech this man was from a mountain clan.

Sigurd must have been wondering about him as well, for he asked, "Who are you?"

"This is Hroald, an emissary from Gudbrandsdalir in the Fille Fiell mountains," Grimolf introduced. "He came to me from King Hemingr of the village Bjornhellir to negotiate trade agreements and facilitate affairs between our two kingdoms, but I have found him quite useful in a variety of capacities. Hroald has many skills and ideas, and from time to time I listen to his counsel."

Sigrid gave a nod but remained wary of a man from a foreign land whom she did not know. "To answer your question, Hroald, no. We were too busy executing judgement on invaders who would murder women and children in their sleep to ask them any questions."

"Quite understandable," he replied, but she thought the smug satisfaction which blazed on his face seemed inappropriate under the circumstances. "It would have been nice to discover why they had mounted such an unprovoked attack is all."

Despite the fact she had taken an instant disliking to the man, she agreed that would have been a wiser course of action. With a sigh, she turned her gaze to a spot on the table before her.

"We have not been invaded," Jarl Arkyn let out in disinterest. "My lands lay on our southern border, and it is unlikely anyone from Firdafylke will bother us. I don't see why I had to be here."

"We are one kingdom, not five." Grimolf rebuked him with a dissatisfied frown. "What affects one of my jarls affects them all."

"Indeed, my lord, five jarldoms," Brynja commented. He shifted a cold stare to Sigrid. "And yet six jarls sit on the council. I still don't understand why *she* is here."

Sigrid felt Sigurd stiffen at her side and laid a hand on his forearm.

The king raised his voice in impatience. "Because their father, Jarl Olaf, decreed his firstborn twins would rule as one. I have already approved of this arrangement."

"Now let us all be reasonable," the elder Trygve advised in a soothing tone.

"I will stand with Jarls Sigrid and Sigurd," declared Siegfried. "Who is to say which of us will be attacked next?"

"Your fylke is beside theirs and near the border," Arkyn stated. "It makes sense for you to join their fight."

"You fail to comprehend, Jarl Arkyn," repeated the king. "We are all under the threat of war. What I do not understand, though, is why."

"The reason is clear, my lord," Hroald declared. "They are a greedy and dishonorable lot. I have heard King Tortryggr's mind has failed him as well as his sword arm. My trading contacts have whispered about strife between his jarls as they vie for his throne. They are like wolverines fighting over a reindeer carcass, vicious and without mercy."

"Dishonorable is right," Siegfried concurred. "Only a few years ago we supported them when their kingdom was invaded, and this is how they repay us?"

"What do you propose?" Grimolf sat back and waited for recommendations.

"My lord, we must meet force with force," Sigrid demanded.

"I would lead a joint army of all who would rally to our defense and ride to Firdafylke to do battle with our enemies," Sigurd proclaimed. "Send your restless warriors to test their mettle and gain honor in Odin's eyes. We will teach them not to invade our lands killing and destroying without cause."

"I suppose such a course is reasonable," Brynja admitted and downed the remainder of his mead.

"I have warriors who would jump at the chance," Trygve said, "but I cannot put my life at risk in a fight which is not mine."

"One thing troubles me," Grimolf commented. Sigrid turned her attention the king she knew to be a wise man whom her father trusted, and she listened when he spoke. "What if they are merely laying a trap? I mean, to raid farms at planting season is fruitless. If they wanted our food-stores, they should wait for harvest. I am concerned there is more here than meets the eye. I will sanction a full-scale retaliation under Jarls Sigurd and Siegfried's command, and you Jarl Sigrid," he included as an afterthought. "But I warn you to be cautious as a fox."

"We shall indeed, my lord," Sigurd agreed with a nod. "Is anyone else with us?"

"Why not?" Brynja raised an entertained gaze to Sigrid. "I'll lead my warriors at your side. It may be interesting to see Sigrid the Valiant in action."

"Not me." Arkyn waved a hand. "In case it is a trap to lure our army north, someone needs to stay to defend the kingdom."

Grimolf nodded. "A wise idea, Arkyn. Jarls, I will divide my soldiers and send half with you. Now, while you make plans, I have other matters to attend to."

All rose and bade their thanks and farewells to the king as he departed the great hall with Hroald following on his heels. Sigrid heard the odd man with his strange accent saying, "You handled the situation brilliantly, my lord. You are so wise." She wanted to gag at his flattery, but she had a battle to plan.

CHAPTER 9

Firdafylke, a week later.

*E*lyn's uncle was away conducting business, and she used his absence to her advantage, stealing off in search of Astrid, the Völva. Elyn had seen her from a distance on a few occasions but had never dared draw too close to the seer who worked Seiðr, a powerful magic typically reserved for the gods. Her imaginings wouldn't stop racing since her uncle's slip of the tongue. *The seer shared a prophecy with him about me,* she pondered, *but he won't tell me what it is. Perhaps she will.*

"Are you certain we are going the right way?" Ingvar protested. Naturally, she had not been sneaky enough to get past her cousin and best friend. Both insisted on traveling with her.

"I asked Aslaug, Jarl Njord's mother-in-law, and she has no reason to lead me astray," Elyn maintained as they winded their way up a narrow path through a dense, old-growth forest on the mountainside. "She said Astrid was visiting a special spring in a secluded wood along with her attendants to make peace with the Landvættir and elves who inhabit the area and the dwarfs inside the mountain."

Geir glanced about nervously, his grip tight on his spear as he used it as a hiking pole in the rough terrain. "I'm surprised a woman her age could perform this trek," he allowed.

"She has special Seiðr which invigorates her like a youth," Elyn explained. "At least that's what people say."

"People say a lot of things," Ingvar commented. "I would just as soon steer clear of spirits. How do we know there aren't Jötnar on this mountain, ready to throw boulders on the heads of intruders?"

"I've been up here before," Elyn stated with confidence. Then she faltered. "Well, part of the way. When the trail forks, we are to go left."

They scrambled over rocks and boulders along an embankment, leaving the spruce and pines behind with only tenacious scrub bushes clinging to cracks between stones. "I don't think we are going to find any forests up here," Geir pointed out.

Elyn stopped to catch her breath and peered ahead. "See that crevice?" Her faithful guardians raised hands to shade the bright sun from their eyes and squinted. "We pass through there and down the other side. That is where we will locate the forest and the spring," she stated, hoping the seer would be there too.

An hour later, the three were amazed by the lush beauty surrounding them, hidden away from civilization in a high bowl between peaks. Broadleaf aspens and birches joined with evergreen conifers while a carpet of moss and short grass spread before their feet. Flowers and buds bloomed in an array of colors disturbed only by a gentle breeze rather than the bracing winds of the coast. Ahead, Elyn detected the sound of a drum and a melodic voice, and her party advanced in silence so they would disturb nothing important.

Elyn, Geir, and Ingvar stopped at the edge of a little clearing where a spring narrow enough to leap over ran. To the other side, a young woman tapped on a handheld circle-drum and sang in a voice so beautiful Elyn wondered if they remained in Miðgarðr or if, at the cleft, they had passed into one of the other worlds. The air felt warm and energizing, the foliage lush and green, and each of the women appeared more lovely than the last. Four young women dressed in bold colored gowns were positioned at four posts surrounding an older one robed in white, seated in the center on a chair carved out of a living tree. Beside each woman stood a pole bearing a small brazier, which burned with an odd yet pleasing aroma not typical of an ordinary fire. The helpers danced in rhythm to the music, seemingly unaware of the warriors' presence.

Elyn marveled at the half trunk and budding branches which grew from the rear of the Völva's seat while she rested on the stump-half, sculpted and smoothed into an exquisite throne. Long silky strands fell straight over her breasts in front and down her back as white as fresh snow, shrouded with a thin pale linen cloth. A gold cord circled her petite waist, and a laurel of ivy and flowers pinned the veil to her head while on her bare feet she wore silver toe rings. Her face did not show the wear and lines of time that should accompany white hair, and she sat with erect posture rarely seen in elders, making it impossible to determine the seer's age. She was the very embodiment of a goddess.

When the singing ended, Astrid arose and lifted her arms to address the unseen inhabitants of the mountains and their magnificent woodland. "To all the vættir," she addressed in a vibrant voice. "To the mountain spirits, the water spirits, and the forest spirits; to the Landvættir to whom this region belongs, we thank you, we honor you, and we appreciate you. Year after year, you watch over and bless us with bountiful crops from the rich soil. Friendly elves and dwarves who hide away, you share your mountain with us, and we are grateful."

The four acolytes spun in circles, tossing flower pedals into the air as the seer declared her praises. "In this peaceful and beautiful setting, we remember Yggdrasil, the magnificent tree of life, that connects all the nine realms with each other. Your roots run deep, all the way to the bottom of Niflheim, where the well of life is found. You defy the great dragon Nidhoggr and do not fall to his bite. Your branches stretch high, even unto Ásgarðr, where your leaves provide mead for the gods. You bridge worlds and connect the living to the ancestors. Great Yggdrasil, to whom Odin turned to find wisdom, and hung upon your branches in agony for nine days, we recognize you and ask you for knowledge of the past, the present, and the future. You alone shall withstand Ragnarok, when the old worlds are washed away. From your sure root and true branches will spring forth the new worlds and the new gods. Until that day, we honor the earth, water, wind, and flame; we honor the gods and our ancestors. Spirits, I call on you now to show me the things I should see so the people may prosper."

Elyn listened in awe as she stood at a distance with Geir and Ingvar watching as a young woman brought a cup to the shamaness. She drank the contents and picked up her rod. The iron wand bore bands of cat fur wrapped above and below the leather grip bound about its hilt end, further adorned with feathers and colored glass beads. Elyn guessed it was the length of a sword, but more narrow, round, and smooth. Then

Astrid began to dance, disturbing a cat Elyn had not noticed before. The feline trotted out of its mistress' way and laid down in a patch of clover to lick itself.

The songstress tapped her drum and performed a different melody while the dancers' moves became more contorted with waving arms and chants of their own. Elyn was uncertain how long this ritual would continue or if she would have an opportunity to ask her question, but as the days marched toward the summer solstice, the time of the midnight sun, they would have no problem negotiating their way home. She found the ceremony fascinating but frightening at the same time.

Abruptly, the chanting, singing, and drumbeats stopped, and the women all stood still. Elyn could hear her own heartbeat in the stillness as even nature waited in silence for Astrid to speak again.

The old seer held out her wand, pointed directly at Elyn. "Shieldmaiden," she spoke in an ethereal tone, quite different from the one she used in her praises. "Come forward."

She looked at her companions, and they shook their heads with feet firmly planted where they stood. Elyn glanced down, frowning at her worn gray trousers and mud-brown gambeson marred by slices and tears where bits of stuffing stuck out. At least there were no holes in her boots. Taking in a deep breath, she lifted her gaze and marched up to the circle where the Völva took her seat on the living throne. When she was within an arm's reach, Elyn kneeled and bowed her head, uncertain what protocol she should abide by.

"Do not be afraid, my child," Astrid instructed. "What do you seek?"

"My Uncle Unnulf did not tell me he had received a word from you regarding me," she began in a hesitant voice. "But he let slip the other day you had made a prediction involving me, Elyn, the shieldmaiden. He will not say more. I have come... I pray, my lady, you will speak to me so I may know what my future holds."

"Futures are tricky things, Elyn the Shieldmaiden," Astrid began. "They are like clouds. We can see them, but they are always changing their forms. Some things are destined, which we cannot alter; yet fortunes remain ours to step into or shy away from. Each choice we make draws us closer to or pushes us farther from that which the gods have laid out."

Elyn waited with bated breath, unsure if she should say more or stay silent. Astrid closed her lids and waved her wand, swaying left and right, causing Elyn to fear she may fall off her seat.

"Unnulf came to ask about his fortune, if he would rise in power, wealth, and influence," she began. "But the vision I received was of his niece, a feisty girl with flame-red hair. I told him one day you will be joined with a jarl of exceeding importance. I could not see the leader's face, nor was I given a name, but Unnulf seemed satisfied with the prediction. Then I said to him, her name shall long be remembered in the land for her mighty deeds, and she will be called Elyn the Peacemaker, even though she is a warrior. I felt he was no longer pleased, and he asked again about his fate."

Astrid ceased swaying and opened eyes as clear and radiant as the moon, fixing them on Elyn. "I had to tell him I could not see his future. It was all murky clouds and swirls of smoke. He dropped his head in disappointment."

Then I am destined to marry Jarl Njord. The thought which should have filled her with joyous excitement fell over Elyn like a cold, wet blanket and she lowered her head. "Jarl Njord has noticed me," she said in a wavering voice. "He is seeking a wife, but... whatever the gods will."

"I sense trepidation, my dear, but do not let your heart be troubled." The seer reached out her wand and laid it on Elyn's shoulder. At the touch, she lifted a hopeful expression. "Nothing is as it seems. Do not say and do what you think others wish of you, shieldmaiden, rather follow the urgings that whisper to you from within. What we see and hear with our physical senses may be false, but to your own self be true and you shall fulfill your destiny."

"Thank you, my lady," she replied with a respectful bow of her head. Before she rose, Elyn gave Astrid another inquisitive look. "And what of the attacks from Svithjod? Are we to go to war?"

An incandescent glow shimmered in the Völva's gaze. "Nothing is as it seems. Seek, and you will find. I can tell you no more."

Astrid lowered her wand, letting out a heavy sigh, and suddenly she appeared weary and drained, as if she truly was a woman of advanced years. Elyn became concerned and pushed to her feet. "Are you alright? Is there something I can do for you?"

"We will take care of the holy mother," the entrancing songstress assured her as she shifted to the seer's side. The others also gathered around their mistress.

Elyn nodded, and Geir ventured to speak for the first time. "This place is so beautiful, so otherworldly," he praised in awe. "Why does no one live here?"

Now surrounded by all four young women, Astrid raised an amused expression. "And how long would it remain pristine if humans settled here?" Geir lowered his head, and Astrid laughed. "This is a magical spot, preserved by the shy creatures of the mountain and blessed by the gods. There is powerful energy here and the vættir allow us to visit once or twice a year, but not to stay. The continual presence of humans would pollute the Seiðr we Völva depend upon to commune with the other worlds. But let me show you another wonder."

The elderly woman rose from her branched, leafy throne with a sense of renewed vigor encircled by her four attendants. "Come with me."

Elyn, Geir, and Ingvar followed her a short distance from the stream and trees to the edge of a towering cliff. Astrid extended an arm, and they took in the view. The clear brook they had jumped plummeted over the ridge in a rushing waterfall to rocks far, far below where it splashed into a river threaded between the jagged teeth of more pointed, snow-capped peaks. Sunlight struck the tumbling water in such a way it produced a rainbow arching out from the falls down the steep ravine over the river below. The greens of the lower elevation, the blues of the sky, the whites of the clouds, and the grays of the cliffs were so vivid the vision seemed surreal to Elyn. She sucked in a breath and grasped Ingvar's shoulder to steady herself.

"Magnificent!" Elyn proclaimed, filled with wonder. She had spent her life surrounded by nature's majesty and had tried not to take it for granted, but somehow this picture surpassed all which came before.

"Thank you, Lady Astrid," Ingvar breathed in a hush. "You possess true magic, as does this place."

"We promise to tell no others and not return here without your permission," Geir vowed. "As you say, it belongs to the vættir."

Elyn marveled at all that had transpired and pondered Astrid's proclamations in her heart. She wondered about the women who traveled with her, assisting in the rituals. She had heard they dedicated their lives in service to the gods, not to marry or raise families. One day, if they made the sacrifices necessary and excelled in learning a seer's mysteries, they too would become Völvas. Elyn did not fully understand the spiritual world, nor did she desire to be a seer, but these women proved marriage was not required, even if it was expected. *But she says I will be with a powerful jarl, and Njord is a dominant noble who may indeed be king one day.* Trying to wrap her head around the prophecy, she recalled the added words, *Nothing is as it seems. Why do the ways of the other worlds have to be so mysterious? Why can't the gods simply give a straightforward answer?*

Elyn trekked down the mountain with her cousin and comrade in as much confusion as she had come with. But at least she had gotten an inkling of what it was like to touch the hem of Ásgarðr.

CHAPTER 10

*E*lyn and her compatriots walked into a buzz of activity upon returning to Njord's citadel overlooking their coastal village, and though it was late, the sun still cast plenty of light. As a foreboding overtook Elyn, she sped up to keep pace with Geir and Ingvar.

"What's going on?" Geir asked.

Frode turned and cupped a hand to his mouth, answering in a hush. "Svithjod's army is camped on our border. Our scouts say they are led by four jarls and have amassed over a hundred warriors."

Elyn's eyes widened. "Why?" The word dropped from her lips like the last leaf in autumn. She felt as if an invisible fist had grasped her heart and was squeezing the life out of her. After all, what had they done to warrant such an attack? *Is Sigrid with them?* she wondered. *She must be, if they are led by four jarls. She and her brother would be two of them.*

The prospect of a direct confrontation with the legendary shieldmaiden sent the shiver of Hel through her body. It was not so much fear of the woman, though she had every reason to be afraid. Elyn knew her life rested in the hands of the gods, and the day of her death had already been written. No, she did not shrink from battle, but she was terrified of the idea her hand may render Sigrid a fatal blow. She didn't want to kill her admirable foe, but talk to her, learn from her, understand what it was like to be her. Elyn had looked to the woman featured in tales sung by the bards around Njord's longhouse and in the mead halls as a role model and held nothing but esteem for her.

"What are they saying in there?" Ingvar asked.

Frode shot a disapproving glare over his shoulder. "I can't hear if you keep asking questions."

Ingvar dropped his head and closed into Elyn until their shoulders pressed together. He whispered in her ear. "Surely we will battle tomorrow. Four jarls? King Grimolf must be behind it. He is greedy and hungers for our land like the wolf he is named after." She could feel the tension mount in his body as his jaw tightened.

"Let us hear what Jarl Njord has to say," she replied. "Do we know who he is talking to in there?"

Horik, who had been standing nearby, leaned over to answer in a hush. "Jarls Torban and Stefnir War Tooth, and Krum from Gudbrandsdalir, one of King Tortryggr's advisors."

Elyn knew the king was old and seldom raced across the country to the bidding of one of his jarls, but he found the situation serious enough to send a personal representative. She didn't know this advisor Krum, though she was aware Gudbrandsdalir was the rugged region to the east inhabited by miners, hunters, and rough mountain men. Her uncle had spoken of them as if they were barely human, yet twice a year they engaged in trade with them. She had heard of Jarl Stefnir's reputation as a warrior and Jarl Torban's experiences at sea, and while having never met them, viewed them as capable. But would they stand with them against the army of Svithjod?

Murmuring ceased when Njord, accompanied by the other leaders, stepped to the open longhouse doorway. They took positions on the covered porch, and Njord raised his arms to recognize the others. "Friends, defenders of Firdafylke, we bring you news."

The crowd's attention focused on Njord. "Our scouts have reported a considerable force has amassed on our southern border, led by Jarls Siegfried, Sigurd, Sigrid, and Brynja, flying the yellow and black raven banner of Svithjod. For these to have joined forces and lead so large an army, we can only conclude King Grimolf sent them. Krum, tell them what you discovered."

It was at once apparent why Krum had chosen trade and politics over a warrior's path. He rather resembled a crane, with narrow shoulders, a long neck sporting a prominent throat protrusion, and a beak-like nose, all perched on a wider bottom half and twig legs. Gray stripes in his beard hinted at an age near her uncle's. He bore the thick accent of the mountaineers when he spoke.

"My trading partners speak of what they overheard in King Grimolf's hall. They say he is obsessed with power and seeks to expand his kingdom. He also listens to a witch and takes her counsel in contradiction to what his own jarls advise." Then he lowered his voice. "My friend and countryman, who has frequent dealings with King Grimolf, has told me in confidence he has promised his jarls they will divide your lands, farms, villages, and ships between them once you are defeated."

Mumbles and angry scowls followed Krum's report, and Njord had to raise his hands to quiet the assembly. "Jarl Stefnir and his army will stand with us, and Jarl Torban is sending his warriors under the direction of his son, Svenvaldr. We shall form up at dawn and ride out against our enemies to protect our homes and families. Defenders of Firdafylke, my servants shall pass out special tea for you to drink to cleanse your bodies. Go to the sweat lodges and saunas for further cleansing and make your peace with the gods. Get excited, for tomorrow is a good day to die, and an even better day to slay our enemies!" A cheer rang out from the men, but the women gathered their children close with worried looks upon their faces. Knowing she was not the only shieldmaiden in Firdafylke, Elyn would be joined by Helga, who rode with Jarl Stefnir, and Tyrdis of Jarl Torban's band.

She had started to follow Ingvar and Geir to prepare, when she heard the jarl's voice call her name, and pivoted to him with a questioning look.

"Elyn, a brief word," Njord stated as he strode up to her.

"Yes, my lord?"

He halted and gazed at her with such an uncharacteristically indecisive expression that she found it endearing. "Be careful tomorrow," he uttered.

"I am always careful, my lord," she replied. "Concern yourself with tactics to win the day, not my well-being. There are no surprises for the gods. Everything will unfold just as it should."

"You are right, of course," he concurred. "Perhaps you were correct about the raids as well. They were not here stealing crops and livestock, but a precursor to an invasion, merely a way to test our strength and resolve. You have proven yourself to be among my most elite warriors and I trust your valor and the protection of the gods tomorrow. Just know I hold you in esteem and do not wish you to fall."

"Thank you. I will do my best."

Njord nodded and returned to where his fellow jarls stood at the entry to the great hall. *Perhaps he does care about me,* she thought. *But how much?*

ELYN SAT atop a bay mare from Njord's stables holding her spear with her shield slung over her back, her sword and ax both tucked into holders on her belt. Geir and Ingvar rode on either side of her near the front of the army's formation with some thirty or more others on horseback while the rest of the warriors marched at their rear. Firdafylke occupied both sides of a wide fjord, with Njord's lands and Kaldrlogr lying on its south side. Jarl Stefnir and Svenvaldr rode beside Njord, but their soldiers strode behind as they both had to cross the fjord on boats and did not bring horses.

Ahead of their column paced the leaders' steeds. Elyn had been surprised Unnulf chose to join the fighting men, but having inserted himself into Njord's escort, it was doubtful he would be called upon to place himself in any true danger. He had explained to her the wisdom in Njord's style of command. By staying apart, preferably on a rock or hill for a superior view, he could spot traps, weaknesses, and the evolving direction of the conflict and issue orders accordingly, whereas if he was on the ground amid it all battling for his life, he would not hold the same vantage point. She could understand the strategy, but it grated against the long-held honorable tradition of leading from the front and rallying the fighters by example.

They had started out at first light, which at this time of the year was very early. She supposed she had gotten four hours of sleep, but anticipation of the battle kept her sharp and alert. The army trekked over the rounded piedmont and across a plateau, past a high lake, then down the other side sticking between the towering rocky peaks.

While this route was the easiest path to the border with Svithjod, it still presented some rugged terrain. After the ease of a tall-grass meadow, they crossed a narrow stream and proceeded through a forest of mixed deciduous and conifer trees which opened into a rocky clearing cut by a snowmelt creek tumbling downhill through crags and over pebbles. At this elevation she could glimpse the purple silhouettes of ridges in the distance, the snowcapped peaks above, and the green valleys below. Before them rose a gradual incline strewn with stones interspersed with wild oats and shriveling shrub, the air biting with a chill she had not experienced at lower elevations. Positioned near the top of the rise stood the ranks of their enemies like a granite monolith.

"They've taken the high ground," Ingvar noted with a flash of trepidation crossing his scantly bearded face.

"Of course they have," Geir replied in irritation. "They got here first, so they claimed the advantage."

"True," Elyn offered in consideration. "But it is only an advantage when pushing against us with their shield wall. In fact, it is easier to fall downhill than up. All we must do is break through their line and get behind them."

Geir snorted. "Look at them all! How are we to break their line?"

"Jarl Njord will think of something," Ingvar replied in a hopeful tone.

The leaders halted, signaling the warriors to do the same. Elyn could feel the mixed energies among her comrades—nervous apprehension and enthusiastic fervor—and overheard murmurings from the troops. Frode dismounted his horse, and the others took his cue and followed suit to join the foot soldiers.

The jarls advanced at a walk to meet the commanders of Svithjod and remained on their horses exchanging words Elyn could not hear. A frosty gust made her wish she had worn a cloak, but it would only get in the way. Lazy clouds drifted across the blue sky, oblivious to the violence about to transpire.

There is Sigrid, she thought as she witnessed the discussion. A knot formed in her empty gut. The army had moved out without food whose digestion might slow them down, but it arose from nerves, not hunger. Struggling for resolve, Elyn determined she would simply steer clear of the blonde shieldmaiden during the battle.

Soon the commanders returned, and Njord rallied the troops. "Today we defend our land from the dishonorable invaders from Svithjod," he yelled in a forceful tone, his earthy-brown hair blowing in another gust from beneath his silver helmet. "Tyr, god of justice and honor, shall guide us and infuse us with valor even as he kept his word, unafraid when he faced the dread wolf Fenrir. We stand in the mighty power of Thor, god of thunder, storm, and war, who with his indestructible Mjolnir hammer shall smash our enemies. Freya, goddess of love and war, reminds us the reason our cause is pure, to protect our loved ones from the onslaught of the treacherous invaders who have ravaged our farms. And Odin, the

Allfather, god of wisdom and chief of the gods who rules from his hall in Valhalla when not wandering the earth, we call upon you to work your Seiðr this day. Strike our foes blind, deaf, and with such terror they must flee before us. Today, warriors of Firdafylke, victory is ours to be won! See how ravens and crows circle above, ready to feast on the bodies of our adversaries' flesh?"

He lifted his sword arm and Elyn glanced up at the growing group of black birds. She could sense the men's courage mount with every impowering word the jarl uttered, and her own confidence soared.

"Formation!" Njord shouted and the warriors fell into three rows, shields and spears to the fore.

"On me!" yelled the mighty Jarl Stefnir. "Tonight, we feast in Valhalla at Odin's table. Charge!"

Keeping their ranks tight, the army trotted behind Stefnir's lead, absorbing him into the shield wall before colliding with the black and yellow shields of Svithjod. The crash jarred Elyn's whole body as she occupied a spot on the front row of their offense. She dug her feet into holds in the rocks and jabbed with her spear through a tiny gap between wooden rönds pressed together. The enemy had momentum and pushing downhill, pressed against them with tremendous force. It didn't matter if her line stepped backward, as long as they maintained their formation without faltering.

Elyn's breath came hard behind her shield. She winced as an iron spearhead sliced her leg, but it was only a graze, not a piercing. Holding firm, she detected the give of flesh rather than wood when her own lance cut a wound in whomever stood before her. They grunted and groaned, and then it happened. With the enemy above them, several wiry warriors leaped over all three rows to land at her army's rear. She couldn't worry about that, but she was aware they now fought on two fronts.

A cry reached her ears as a man three spots down from her fell and then another. Svithjod was carving a hole in their line. *This is pointless! There are as many of us as there are of them, but as long as they push from uphill, they hold the advantage.*

Just then, Njord's horn sounded a command. The warriors broke ranks, the ends rushing out to the right and left, the second row pulling back, while the third row cut down those enemies who had jumped to the rear with their axes. *Much better!* Elyn spun to face the foe who fell into the hole Ingvar made when he shifted right. With Geir at her back, she thrust with her spear, whose trajectory she changed at the last second, striking the man she faced between his shield and outraised weapon.

As enemies poured through the gaps, she didn't bother to retrieve the lance, but drew her sword. She hacked and slashed with the din of battle encompassing her. The next time she glanced at Ingvar, his face was splattered with blood, more spilling from a gash on his sword arm. *He'll be alright,* she told herself, and focused on the invader who bore down on her.

Just as Elyn sent another man to the ground, a second horn sounded. "My squad to the right," Frode called as he pointed uphill and to the west. "Protect our flank!"

The ten members of the division brushed past enemies and hopped over bloody bodies to take a position farther up the rocky slide where a group of Svithjoders were trying to circle around. Instantly, Elyn recognized the yellow rönd with the twin ravens and the woman who bore it. An electric shock raced through her body and every thought she had entertained about Sigrid rushed into her awareness. In an instant, the rest of the fighting field faded into obscurity and her feet did not know which way to move. Deciding it must be fate, Elyn charged with all her strength. Her shield plowed into Sigrid's, whose sword swipe barely missed her right shoulder, but the fierce shieldmaiden did not yield.

Both women took a step back to raise their weapons and the metal sparked as they clashed. "Do not expect favors this time," Sigrid growled. Furious tenacity shone on her face, hardening Elyn's heart toward the woman she had admired.

"I don't need your favors!" she retorted with a strike of her sword, which her opponent blocked with ease.

They danced surefooted over the rough terrain, trading blows and parries until the shieldmaidens fought apart from the others. Elyn could not afford to glance at her friends; neither did Sigrid's gaze wander but remained steadfast on her. *Are we so evenly matched?* Elyn wondered, *or does she hold back after all?*

With no warning, the ground trembled, and rocks spilled from the top of the ridge, tumbling and crashing in their direction, while at the same time the earth shook loose beneath their feet. Elyn's stomach caught in her throat as she fell through a chasm, down, down, down. Not wishing to look down, she cast her awareness upward, raising her shield to block rocks which rained from above. In seconds, she hit the bottom with a thud and gasped for the breath which had been rent from her lungs.

Elyn waited a moment before trying to move, in case the plummeting were to start again. She was aware of the sound of water falling and glanced around to spy a waterfall plunging into a pool only a few yards from where she landed. A few more pebbles slid through the fissure and dust clouded the air. Everything hurt—her back, legs, shoulders, even her ass. Huffing and coughing, she was finally able to draw a complete breath. They must have dropped into a ravine that had been covered over by a thin layer of stone knocked loose by the rockslide. "Damn Jötnar," she cursed. "Throwing boulders on us!"

The word "us" jarred Elyn's memory, and she rolled, lifting her head to survey the space. Sigrid had fallen in with her, only she lay half buried under the rubble. Her sword rested a few inches beyond the hand which had held it and the shieldmaiden's helmet had tumbled off somewhere. A gash which tore the skin above her left brow trickled blood and her eyes remained shut.

With plenty of light streaming in from above, Elyn searched for her sword but didn't see it. *Did I drop it before or while I fell?*

She pushed up to her hands and knees, testing for steadiness, scanning her body for injuries. While she was certainly covered in scratches and bruises, she didn't think anything was broken. Taking it easy, Elyn hauled herself to her feet, slid off her battered rönd, shook out her arms and legs, and rolled her neck, determining she was in sound but sore condition. With no sword, she drew her ax from her belt and maneuvered a few steps to stand over Sigrid. *She lives*, Elyn considered as she observed her chest rise and fall. *But what do I do?*

CHAPTER 11

$\mathcal{E}$lyn's heart pounded in her chest as she weighed her options. Right here, right now, she could kill Jarl Sigrid the Valiant and gain great fame and renown. With no witnesses, she could concoct any story she liked about how the epic battle in the cave occurred... except without witnesses, people may say Sigrid died in the fall and all Elyn did was chop at her corpse making it appear she had been victorious. A further problem with the option was that the gods saw everything. To kill an unarmed, unconscious opponent was a dishonorable display of cowardice akin to murder.

What would Sigrid do? Elyn lifted her ax but hesitated. *One so well respected would not slay an incapacitated foe, would she?*

But what troubled Elyn the most was the true impetus behind her reluctance—she didn't want to kill Sigrid. She wanted her to live. Lowering her weapon, she gazed at the fair legendary hero. Though caked in dust sticking to blood and sweat, her legs pinned under heavy jagged rocks, she was the most astounding human being Elyn had ever seen. Maybe it was not her beautiful face or toned body, but the songs and stories which hailed her victories over man and beast and saluted her valor and generosity that most fueled Elyn's imagination. Perhaps it was how Sigrid had saved her from a spear hurled on the battlefield when it had been against her own best interest. But maybe it was the strange energy that pulsed through Elyn's sensations whenever they were near each other that compelled her to choose mercy. Then again, it could merely be her own sense of unworthiness.

I am nobody, she thought. *I can't kill a jarl, a female warrior jarl... a lovely, defenseless woman of distinction. She needs my help.*

Elyn shoved the ax back into her belt and lifted heavy stones off the fallen shieldmaiden, tossing them aside. As she worked, Sigrid awoke. Sky-blue eyes blinked and the trapped woman coughed away dust, soon becoming aware she was not alone.

With a startled expression, Sigrid grabbed her sword and swung it at Elyn, who had to jump to avoid its reach. "Do not think of crushing me with a slab of limestone!" she blasted with rage igniting in her glare. Sigrid's voice was robust enough to overpower the burble of the waterfall. "I could carve you like a roasted pig even without the use of my legs."

An admiring smile tugged at the corner of Elyn's lips, and something sprang to life deep within her core. "I am certain you could, Jarl Sigrid, but if you will notice, I am not attacking you, but digging you out of the rubble."

"What happened?" Sigrid raised her left hand to the gash on her forehead.

"The ground gave way, and we fell into this pit chased by large rocks. I think a Jötnar is to blame," Elyn replied in a placid tone that seemed to disarm Sigrid.

As her focus cleared, she aimed it on Elyn's face. "I find myself at a disadvantage," Sigrid admitted. "You know who I am, but I am not familiar with you. What is your name?"

Elyn heaved the last of the big rocks pinning Sigrid's legs to the side and sat on it. "I am Elyn, a shieldmaiden of Firdafylke. I live in a village called Kaldrlogr. It would appear for the moment we are trapped in this crevice. Thus far, no one has appeared at the fissure above to lend aid, and I suspect the battle continues."

SIGRID NODDED. *Elyn! So that is your name.* Satisfaction nestled within Sigrid until she recalled why they were there. Feelings of languid infatuation evaporated, and vengeful wrath rushed in to seize their place. She pushed up on her sword, gathering her legs under her body, and struggled to her feet. She could tell her injuries were more than superficial, and she could not bear weight on her right leg, but she was determined.

Mirroring her movement with caution, Elyn rose from her rock and shifted a hand to the ax on her belt.

Pinning the flame-haired shieldmaiden with a frigid glare, Sigrid snarled. "Why did your raiders attack our farms? It is fortunate you were not among their number as we left none alive."

She cocked her sword arm for a swing, and in an instant, Elyn whipped out her ax to block the whirling blade. The motion of the stroke rendered Sigrid off balance, and she could have easily toppled over, but her opponent pushed against her steel with her weapon until she was upright and steady on her one good leg. Elyn's action surprised Sigrid, though she was glad for it.

"We did no such thing!" her foe declared with heated conviction. She hoisted her ax, poised at the ready.

Sigrid realized she was in no condition to fight, so she had better rein in her temper. She glanced down at Elyn's sturdy legs, shapely hips, rounded breasts, up to luscious full lips, and finally into stunning green eyes and held them.

"Several of my friends were killed," Sigrid asserted, and she felt a quiver go through her body. "A dozen men under the banner of Firdafylke carrying shields with your colors," she testified, motioning to Elyn's rönd lying a few feet away, "attacked the outlying farms of my village, Gnóttdalr. They burned homes, slew livestock, murdered women and children, then tried to flee like cowardly rodents."

Elyn's brows knit together in concern. "When was this?"

"Less than two weeks ago," Sigrid confirmed. With her shoulder stiff and in pain, she lowered her sword but kept a firm grip on its hilt. "Maybe a week and a day after the first time we fought." Sigrid tried to calculate, but her head throbbed. *Has it been three weeks I have spent dreaming of you?*

"That is impossible!" Elyn's declaration snapped Sigrid's thoughts back into focus. "It wasn't us. All of Jarl Njord's warriors are accounted for at the time and none have gone missing," the younger woman insisted.

Sigrid's frown deepened. "I know about Jarl Njord and his intentions for the throne of Firdafylke. With King Tortryggr's mind and strength failing, he supposes to increase his fame by defeating us, but it shan't work."

"What are you talking about?" Elyn fumed and tossed her empty hand into the air. "There is nothing wrong with King Tortryggr's health, mental or otherwise. And while it is true Jarl Njord has ambitions, he is not a traitor. What about your King Grimolf? Greedy to the core! We know about his plans to take over our kingdom, how he has promised all you jarls will double your holdings."

"Nothing but sheep dung!" Sigrid retorted. "That is the biggest load of shite I've ever heard."

Elyn's brows narrowed, and her scowl deepened. "What about the Svithjod raiders who attacked our farms? We had defenseless people killed by your warriors, too. Did they make sport of it? Was it a game to them?"

"We did no such thing!" Sigrid's voice reverberated about the cavern, which only increased the throbbing in her head. "We supported you several years ago when Raumsdal assaulted your land. I personally led a team of wagons to reinforce your army with supplies, and my brother brought volunteers to join your defenses."

"I know," Elyn countered, "which is why we feel so betrayed you have invaded now. Maybe the raiders did not come from your band, but they flew the raven flag and carried the yellow and black shields of Svithjod. Why do you lie?"

She raised her ax in a defiant motion and Sigrid reacted instantaneously, slamming her sword to bear against it. "I do not lie!"

The two shieldmaidens pressed closely together, hot with anger and confusion. Sigrid was not expecting the arousal she experienced at the proximity to her enemy, but her desire could not be denied. It was baffling and unacceptable. Only a handle of wood and a blade of steel stood between them. Sigrid kept her balance on her one good leg, but if Elyn pulled away, she would surely fall. She felt the heat of her breath, inhaled her intoxicating scent, and her body ached for a woman she should not want. *Is this a trick? Have I been bewitched?* A part of her wished to examine Elyn's every feature in intricate detail, while reason ordered her emotions to stand down.

Elyn slowly backed away, almost as if she was being careful to not cause Sigrid to fall. "No, you do not lie." The words rang with sincere belief and Sigrid eased her muscles as she mirrored her foe to relax. They lowered their weapons at the same time. "But neither do I."

A thought took form in Sigrid's foggy brain giving her pause. "We marched here in retaliation for the attacks on our farms, which clearly appeared to come from Firdafylke. If neither of us lies, then what is going on?"

A sigh escaped Elyn's full lips, and she slid her ax back into her belt. "That is exactly what I plan to find out. Jarl Sigrid, may I suggest a truce? You are not in prime condition, but I might still need your aid to escape this cavern. Besides, if we kill each other down here, who will ever know? And who will discover the truth of the raids against both of our lands?"

Elyn made some valid points, but could this shieldmaiden be trusted? Sigrid wanted to trust her. She wanted to touch her, to connect to a kindred spirit, to get lost in her kisses… wait, what? *Where is this coming from? I have Sveina for that.* "How do I know you won't betray me or lead me astray? Your mind could be filled with plots."

"I am not clever enough for plots," Elyn replied. "How do I know you will not gut me with your dagger when I lower my guard?"

Sigrid met her gaze. "If I wanted to kill you, I would do so fairly, not with a ruse."

"When we fell into this pit, I remained conscious while you were struck on the head and buried in rocks," Elyn pointed out. "I could have slain you then."

"Why didn't you?" Sigrid needed to know.

Demonstrating trust and courage, Elyn sat once again on the large stone, leaving herself vulnerable should Sigrid strike. She shrugged. "It was not your day to die, shieldmaiden."

Genuine affection shone through the smile that lit Sigrid's face when Elyn repeated the same words she had spoken three weeks prior. "Very well, then." Bracing herself with her sword, she lowered onto a nearby boulder, which lay just out of reach of the amazing woman who had haunted her dreams, because she didn't trust herself to be too close.

With adrenaline waning, Sigrid glanced around at their surroundings for the first time. Streams of light poured in with the trickling stream of a falls which formed the crystal pool in the center of the rock-walled chamber. White slabs marked in grooves and striations soared upward with a carpet of green moss along a portion of the rise. She couldn't hear anything from the outside for the burbling water and the depth of the cavity.

"You don't suppose this is a troll cave, do you?" Elyn's question swung Sigrid's mind from the natural beauty surrounding them back to the dilemma at hand.

"I can kill a troll if it comes to it," she stated with assurance. The fact was, Sigrid had never seen a troll, though she had heard stories of them.

They were big and strong alright, but sluggish and stupid. She had every confidence she could defeat one if necessary. "Getting out of here concerns me more than a troll showing up."

"Yes, well…" Elyn turned her gaze upward. "That is a sheer rock wall. If we had a rope, 'twould be no problem, but…"

Elyn hopped up as if she had just spotted a gold ingot and she trotted over to the edge of the pool.

"What is it?" Sigrid asked in curiosity.

Elyn lifted Sigrid's lost helmet with a triumphant grin. "I will scoop water from the pool in this for us to drink. I didn't bring my horn into battle."

In a moment she kneeled before Sigrid and extended the headpiece to her filled with clear, cold water and Sigrid drank with gratitude. "Thank you, Elyn. Now, you drink, too."

She did, and then reaching under her gambeson, tore off a strip of cloth which she dipped in the water and tended to the cut on Sigrid's forehead.

"You don't have to do that," Sigrid stated. "You have cuts and abrasions, too, which require attention."

"I'll get to me, but you were hurt worse. If you will allow it, I'd like to examine your leg to see if it is broken. There're no wood planks down here, but if need be, I can construct a splint from your sword and my ax."

Sigrid marveled at Elyn's touch and her willingness to attend to the injuries of an enemy. *Could it be? Could she bear an odd attraction to me as well?*

"You may, and I thank you," Sigrid allowed. "You are not my servant or my vassal, so—"

"I know." Elyn cut her off as she dabbed blood from Sigrid's face. "I wonder what is happening above, whose side is winning?"

Immediately, Sigrid's heart flooded with concern for Sigurd. She closed her eyes and breathed deeply. He was alive. She would discern if it was otherwise. She winced when Elyn touched her hurt leg. "I don't know," she answered as she watched the shieldmaiden unwind the leg bindings that wound up from her boots. "But if it is my side, no harm shall come to you."

Elyn smiled. Fingers which only minutes ago were wrapped around an ax handle now tenderly worked healing magic on her. The tingle of excitement Elyn's touch aroused seem fresh and unexplainable, but not unwelcome. "And if it is my army, no harm will come to you."

Sigrid tilted her head in question. "Do you hold such authority?"

"No," a timid voice admitted. "But Jarl Njord favors me. Besides, he would much rather trade you for ransom than to harm one of your fame."

"He favors you, does he?" Sigrid raised a brow along with the question. *Why does this knowledge stir discontentment in my emotions? He would be a fool not to favor her.*

"My uncle is trying to secure a marriage contract between me and him."

Sigrid looked down at a huge ripening purple bruise with a bleeding gash which split the contusion down the middle, but she did not see a bone sticking out of it. Elyn had managed to bare her leg with no added pain or discomfort. She was suddenly cognizant of the other woman's warm gaze washing over her leg and something involuntary tightened inside her. "Do you wish to marry Jarl Njord?" she asked.

"I doubt I will have any say in the matter," Elyn replied in resignation. "This requires herbs and salves and bandages."

"I have all those back at my longhouse," Sigrid assured her, then considered they would do her no good here and now. "So, you do not want to marry the jarl?"

"I know you must think it foolish of me." Elyn unbuckled her belt and pulled off her tattered gambeson. Sigrid frowned at the state of her battle garment thinking she should have better. But once it had been tossed aside, she gained an enticing image of voluptuous breasts beneath the thin cloth of her gray tunic.

"No," Sigrid stated. "I think you should be able to decide for yourself and do what you wish with your life. Marriage is not something to enter for the wrong reasons."

She watched Elyn rip long strips of cloth from the hem of her garment and tie them around the gaping wound in her lower leg. Once again, the young woman's touch affected her more intensely than such innocent and incidental contact should.

"You are a jarl," she answered as she worked. "You have authority and influence and fame. Naturally, you can do exactly as you please, but I am nobody. I haven't such power."

Sigrid leaned forward, reached out and took hold of Elyn's hands, causing her to meet her gaze. "You are a mighty shieldmaiden, a fierce warrior. I guarantee you have power. All you need is the conviction to wield it."

Sigrid could not explain the connection she felt at the simple touch, but she realized there was something special about Elyn. They had only just met, so how much did she really know about her? *She is a bold warrior possessing skill and instincts, kind and generous enough to care for an enemy's wounds, and beaten down by person or people unknown to the point she cannot grasp her own self-worth. She is smart to look beyond the surface of things, and she trusts me. So there—I have learned quite a bit about Elyn in a short time.*

Elyn glanced away and shook her head. "I am my uncle's ward. I must do as he says, and if Jarl Njord chooses me, how am I to refuse?"

Sighing, Sigrid resumed her prior pose with a shrug, reluctantly allowing her fingers to slide away. "You are courageous enough in battle. Too bad you don't carry that quality with you into every aspect of your life."

CHAPTER 12

*S*he thinks I am a powerful woman? Elyn was taken aback by such a complimentary statement. The gash in Sigrid's leg looked wicked-nasty, but it wasn't the reason she could put no weight on it. Elyn struggled to remain professional as her fingers caressed the smooth skin of her patient's toned knee and calf.

"I am humbled by your praise, Jarl Sigrid," she managed. "I need to remove your shoe to check your ankle for injury."

"Elyn?" The question in Sigrid's voice caught Elyn's attention, and she glanced up into the honesty of her visage. "You and I are well matched in combat, and your mind is as sharp as my blade. Besides, we are trapped in a troll cave with no visible means of escape, so please... call me Sigrid."

Elyn nodded and lowered her gaze, pleased with Sigrid's request, yet still considering herself as inferior. Then she glanced up with sudden concern. "Do you really think it is a troll cave?"

Sigrid laughed and shook her head. "Here, I will remove the boot." She leaned forward with a wince and unlaced her footwear. She had difficulty wiggling it off, but once she did, Elyn saw why. Sigrid's ankle was swollen twice its normal size with purple mottling. Elyn gently laid a hand over it and her eyes shot to Sigrid's again.

"It is inflamed and puffed up," she reported. "When you hit the hard cave floor, you must have twisted it. I need to manipulate it to discover if bones are broken and it will be painful." Elyn didn't want to cause Sigrid any more pain, but it was necessary.

An amiable smile crossed Sigrid's lips. "You have a gentle touch. Go ahead."

Elyn grasped Sigrid's heel in one hand, her toe in the other, and slowly tested the motion of the ankle. Sigrid's muscles tensed. She sucked in a breath and clamped her jaw shut, a muffled "hmph" escaping. Elyn's fingers pressed around the swelling as she tried to determine the placement of the many small bones.

"How did you learn healing skills?" Sigrid asked.

With a shrug, Elyn answered, "By watching Halfdan in Kaldrlogr. He has knowledge of medicinal arts, wound treatment, how to mix the correct herbs to cure fever and disease. When I was little, I was allowed to observe him treat injured warriors. Then when I became a shield-maiden, there was not always time to carry a wounded man to the village and I would set a broken bone or apply bandages to bleeding cuts. Once I had to assist in an amputation, as the man's arm was too badly mangled, and it was draining blood quickly. The cauterization saved his life."

"What does he do now?" Sigrid rolled her foot around, demonstrating she could move it on her own, though with difficulty.

"He has taken a position with the herders watching over livestock in the high pastures in summer and thatching during the winter. There," Elyn pronounced and set Sigrid's bare foot on the floor of the cavern. "A few of the small bones may have shifted out of place, but once we get a brace on it, there is every reason to believe it will heal correctly. For now, I want to move you over to the edge of the pool to soak it in the cold water to calm the fire that burns within and relieve some of the pain. Your leg's bleeding has slowed, but it still oozes. We will need to change the wrappings before long."

Sigrid pinned her with an amused expression. "If you continue to tear off pieces of your tunic for bandages, you shall soon have no shirt left."

Snorting out a laugh, Elyn replied, "I will use a sleeve next. Come, let me help you to the side of the pool."

"I can manage. I feel steadier and I think the tender warmth of your hands has had a positive effect on me." Sigrid pushed herself up from the rock and hopped on her sturdy leg, only touching her right toes to the ground for balance.

Elyn puzzled over Sigrid's manner and her words. *Is she toying with me? They say she prefers women, but surely she doesn't consider me... desirable.*

Sigrid sighed in relief as she eased her foot and swollen ankle into the chilled water. "Now, how will we get out of here?"

"Let me inspect our surroundings." Elyn proceeded along each limestone and marble wall, brushing a hand across them, checking for toe and finger holds she may use to ascend the cliff face. The nearly round hole was much deeper than wide, characterized by the relentless noise of the waterfall. The fissure above allowed plenty of light, but it taunted her as there seemed no way to climb up.

As she stood directly in a sunbeam, Elyn cupped her hands to her mouth, threw back her head, and yelled as loud as she could. "We're down here! Is anyone up there?" She waited for the echo to die away and tried again. No one came.

Not admitting defeat, Elyn continued around to the side of the cave which hung in shadows. Here she discovered an alcove retracting twice as far as her arms could reach before the rock ceiling closed in to just above her head. It was gloomy and colder out of the sunlight. *This may be a good place for passing water,* she thought.

Then she halted with a jerk, staring ahead at a tunnel that appeared to have been chiseled into the wall. It was narrow and low, a dangerously restricted space with jagged stones lining its bottom ready to trip her if she stepped wrong.

"Do trolls chop out passages through the rocks?" she called back over her shoulder.

"How large?" sounded Sigrid's voice.

"Must be dwarves then," Elyn determined as she returned to the spot where Sigrid sat soaking her foot. "It is barely big enough for me, certainly not for trolls. You were right, Sigrid. It is not a troll cave—it's a dwarf cave. There is no sign of them now, but maybe hundreds of years ago they hammered their way in here and carried away all the precious stones just leaving these common ones."

"Tell me about the tunnel." Sigrid gazed at Elyn, setting her heart racing. Here she was, alone in a fantastic chasm with a sensuous woman she had admired for as long as she could recall. Sigrid's presence was overpowering, and yet she remained vulnerable. She commanded authority while displaying equity. The fabled warrior had lashed out at her in fury and also taken her hand in compassion. The flesh and blood woman who bled the same as regular folk was so much more impressive in person than the hero of legend. All Elyn could think of was touching her leg again when it was time to change the dressing.

"It is dark," Elyn reported. "It must go a long way, or… nowhere."

"Then we should explore it," Sigrid suggested. "It is our best chance of getting out of here. I saw you assessing the walls for climbing, and while there is a slim possibility you could do so, the likelihood is much greater you would fall. One of us being lame is bad enough without you suffering a crippling injury as well."

Elyn nodded. "But we can't light a torch. There is no wood down here. Even if we found a striking stone, there is no kindling, no oil, nothing to burn."

"Then we will have to navigate by touch and sound," Sigrid pronounced. "You are not afraid of the dark, are you?"

"No." Elyn took a seat beside Sigrid, thinking, *It is the creatures in the dark we cannot see that unsettle me.* She glanced up, noticing the light had shifted. "We should rest for a while before trying the tunnel. Even if we have nothing to eat, we've plenty of water."

"Agreed," Sigrid said. "You had a good idea about the pool. My ankle is feeling better."

"Not good enough to walk on," Elyn warned. "I wish we had a spear or something to use as a crutch. But the passage is tight. You can press against the sides for support. The bad thing is the floor is littered with chunks of rock to trip on. We will have to move slowly."

Sigrid nodded and gazed ahead at the falling stream of clear water. "So, who has been raiding our farms and villages pretending to be us?"

"An excellent question." Elyn set her brain to task as she thought out loud. "I suspected something was amiss since the first attack. Why would raiders come at planting time when there are no crops to make off with? It also seemed suspicious, even foolish, for them to carry colors. I mean, if you were going to raid your neighbors, wouldn't you wish to hide your identity, not flaunt it?"

Sigrid's mouth fell agape, and her eyes rounded as she turned them to Elyn. "You are right! I may have thought of it, save I have been distracted and distressed of late."

"We heard of your father Olaf's death," Elyn noted with empathy. "I am sorry for your loss but rejoice in Valhalla's gain."

In an instant, Sigrid's entire demeanor shifted into a dark and dangerous place. Her chin became as granite and her gaze as deadly as a serpent. "He was murdered, stabbed in the back in his own house." She spewed the words as venom. "He did not even have the chance to take up a weapon to defend himself. A glorious death was stolen from him, and I will repay the guilty party in kind once I determine who it is." She made a snorting sound like a bull, drew up her good left knee, grabbed hold, and leaned her forehead there, staring at the ground.

Elyn could feel more anguish emanating from her now than at any previous instance. She wished to wrap her arms around her and bring her comfort. An anger rose in her born of Sigrid's pain and she, too, desired to slay the murderous coward.

"We were not told that part," she said at last. "If I can assist in finding this villain, I vow to do so. Do you think the murder was connected to what is happening now?"

"I don't know," Sigrid muttered. "The raids began shortly after he was killed, so there may be a connection… or there may not be."

"If there is a third party trying to goad our kingdoms into war, who stands to gain the most?" Elyn asked, reasoning a jarl would understand more about politics than she would.

Sigrid lifted her head and cocked it at Elyn. "Another good question. Who would benefit? One of our jarls? One of yours? A conspiracy? A nearby kingdom?"

"One thing is certain," Elyn concluded. "If our two kingdoms continue to fight each other, we will both deplete our ranks of warriors. Then, whoever keeps their full-strength could pick us off separately and conquer both Svithjod and Firdafylke."

"Quite true," Sigrid agreed. "And I am beginning to believe that is exactly what is going on."

SIGRID GLANCED around for a smooth spot upon which to lie. As if she had read her mind, Elyn scrambled to her feet and pulled out her ax to scrape rubble into the pile and clear a patch. Sigrid marveled. *How amused the gods must be!*

"How did you read my mind?" she asked aloud.

"Oh, I didn't," Elyn answered as she worked. "I had noticed there was nowhere to lie when I inspected the cave, then when I saw you glancing about and the exhausted look on your face, it was not hard to figure out."

A smile tugged at Sigrid's lips. "And you claim you are not clever."

"Oh, I am not," Elyn confirmed. "My uncle is always complaining about how my mind is as sharp as a ball of wool and that I am as dull as a wooden knife. He says it is my stubbornness alone which makes me a decent fighter."

So, it is her uncle who has convinced Elyn she is worthless. "I'm afraid I must disagree with your uncle. Didn't you realize something was amiss even before we ended up in this pit together? You have presented every good idea as we spoke while I have been too set on avenging my father's murder to notice a thing. Suppose your uncle told you this pool is all dried up and void of water; would you believe him?"

Elyn chuckled. "I can see it is not."

"And I can see you have a keen mind," Sigrid declared. "Why can't you?"

Avoiding an answer, Elyn shrugged. "Here," she motioned. "Come lie down and rest. I will explore the dark tunnel to see if it leads somewhere."

"No." Sigrid tilted her head at Elyn as she concocted a different plan. "You lie down and rest with me, and when we have regained our strength, we will enter the tunnel together. I may have a twisted ankle and gaping rent in my leg, but both of my arms are strong. Two together will be better if we run into anything unsavory in the pitch blackness. Besides, if the passageway splits and divides several times, you could become lost and never find your way out or back to me. It is best we stay together."

It amused her to watch wariness and speculation play across Elyn's features at her suggestion of how horribly a trip into the tunnel could unfold.

"I suppose you are right," Elyn admitted.

Sigrid dipped her hands into the pool, washing off dirt and blood, then splashed her face. After another drink from her helmet, she scrambled over to the cleared slab of rock. She unbuckled her spaulders and breastplate and laid them aside. Intuition informed her it was safe to remove her weapon belt as well. Afterall, Elyn had no reason to nurse her back to health just to murder her in her sleep. The stone floor was hard indeed, but at least it was somewhere to lie down.

She watched Elyn wash her hands and face in the pool and almost suggested she disrobe and take a bath, but the water was frigid, and Sigrid wasn't certain she could stand to see Elyn naked without embarrassing herself with her reactions. She supposed had this not happened, she may be at home with Sveina giving her a hot bath and providing release from her tension by now. Somehow, the thought did not excite her the way it usually did.

Elyn looked at Sigrid's leg and selected a smooth stone which she placed beside her injured ankle. Picking up her worn gambeson, she folded it, set in on the stone, and lifted Sigrid's foot to rest on it. "If you can, try to keep your foot elevated. It will relieve swelling and help prevent more blood from oozing out," she instructed. "If you wish to lie on your side…"

Sigrid nodded at her and smiled, touched by the degree of care Elyn took in aiding her. "I'll be alright like this. I need it to heal as soon as possible to lead my army against our true enemy. You could have used your garment as a pillow for yourself."

Elyn shrugged and laid down an arm's length away from her, staring up at the fissure above. Indirect light filtered in, but the sun had begun its long descent into the western sky. Sigrid wondered what she was thinking. She had so many questions she wished to ask, but one seemed more pressing than the rest.

"So, you are not desirous to marry Jarl Njord," Sigrid began. "Is it him you do not favor, or men in general? Do you prefer men or women?"

It appeared to Sigrid as if all the color faded from Elyn's cheeks, causing her to laugh to herself, but she refrained from exhibiting any sign of humor which may embarrass her cave partner.

A hesitant, but by all indications honest, response came forth in a timorous voice. "I don't know."

Sigrid waited for her to say more. Elyn at last broke the silence. "I have never been with a woman. Men, well Ingvar, my friend, it's fine with him. I was… I had a bad experience at a young age," she settled upon. "But it's alright with Ingvar. We aren't in love or anything, but at least I may know how to please Jarl Njord."

"What about someone pleasing you?" Sigrid suggested. She didn't want to press. Many women had bad experiences with men, but Elyn need never worry about that again. Sigrid was certain she could ward off any unwanted advances at present.

"Pleasing me?" Elyn turned a curious aspect to Sigrid.

"You are supposed to enjoy being touched and made love to," Sigrid conveyed. "It is not only for the man, or your partner, whomever they may be. It is for you, too."

Sigrid could tell by her disappointed expression Elyn had not enjoyed genuine pleasure at the hands of another, and the knowledge saddened her heart.

"I must not know how," Elyn admitted in defeat. "Maybe I am too tense or..."

Sigrid's tone brightened as she wished to cheer her onetime enemy, now potential friend. "No, it is not your fault. You'll experience the most enthralling passion one day. You just haven't found the right person to give it to you yet." With a satisfied smile, she closed her eyes and drifted to sleep.

CHAPTER 13

Despite being exhausted, Elyn had difficulty sleeping. Sigrid's words continued to repeat in her mind as she attempted to resolve them with what she had been told for the past many years. *"You are courageous enough in battle. Too bad you don't carry that quality with you into every aspect of your life."* *"And I can see you have a keen mind. Why can't you?"*

And then there she was, lying so close in all her magnetic confidence, her enchanting beauty, asking if Elyn preferred men or women, teasing about the length of her tunic, suggesting she should experience pleasures. *Could she really look at me in that way? If so, it is only because we are trapped together and there is no one else.* Had she seen a spark in Sigrid's eyes, or was it merely amusement?

In a short time, Elyn's whole life had turned upside down for a second time. Her king and nobles had been tricked into a war with Svithjod, whose leaders had fallen for the same deception. A jarl twice her age was considering her as his next wife. And now Sigrid the Valiant had accepted her as... as what? A fellow shieldmaiden, a partner to seek the truth and stop a war, a friend... a potential lover? All the above?

But I can't forget what the Völva prophesied: I will be joined with a jarl of exceeding importance, remembered for my mighty deeds, and called Elyn the Peacemaker. Then she said nothing was as it seems, and we can change our fortunes by our choices. It is too much for my feeble mind to comprehend!

She closed her eyes and pictured peaceful clouds drifting, drifting...

but she couldn't focus on the clouds. *Do I prefer men or women? I never considered I had a choice.* She thought of how it felt to be with Ingvar, what she remembered anyway, then of how she felt as her fingers stroked Sigrid's leg. Just lying in the same cave with her was more stimulating to her senses than Ingvar's kisses. She knew a few women who tarried around the mead hall touched each other that way, and there were Ingrid and Adelle, two widows who moved in together and ran their farm without the aid of a man, except their own sons. Women had the right to own property, to choose to marry or divorce, and they could rise to prominent positions of authority if they possessed the means to do so. There truly were more options available to her than she had previously considered.

Uncle Unnulf wanted to keep me like a servant until he could arrange a marriage for me which would be of advantage to him, she thought sourly. *That is why he is always berating me for being worthless, so I will not believe I can accomplish anything. Then I will continue to do as he demands.*

Elyn let out a yawn. She glanced over at Sigrid, who made quiet sleeping sounds as she lay in peace. *How wonderful it must be to be Sigrid Olafsdottir, to grow up with every advantage, to have parents and brothers who loved and encouraged her, to possess no fear. My life is like the unknown of the dark tunnel filled with jagged rocks. It is not death I fear, but all the experiences between now and then that unsettle me. Astrid said to be true to myself. How can I when all I possess is doubt? How can I do the right thing when I do not trust my worth?*

Closing her eyes, Elyn finally allowed slumber to engulf her in its sweet embrace.

When Sigrid awoke, it was from a deep chill. The cavern was bathed in the silvery light of the moon, and the waterfall still gurgled. She understood the water had to be going somewhere or the space would have filled up by now and assumed there was a crack or hole in the pool's bottom draining it away into some underground lake or perhaps to the outside.

She glanced over to where Elyn lay, tossed by an uneasy sleep. She was so beautiful! Sigrid could not deny she was attracted to her, but she had been attracted to women before, who did not share her affections. *She says she doesn't know if she prefers men or women,* she mused. *When we get out of here, discover who is causing us trouble and deal with them, then maybe she will be willing to find out... if she doesn't marry Jarl Njord.*

Sigrid could not blame her if she did. Wasn't it every girl's dream to marry a prince or a jarl? Well, everyone's but hers. Her dream was to be the prince or jarl, and while she would have preferred to wait another ten years, having her father to teach and guide her, here she was, living her dream. Only something seemed to be missing. Sigrid and her brother were indeed excellent administrators and courageous warriors and had garnered the esteem of their subjects and their peers, yet... she desired more. She could never be satisfied with the marriage her mother wished for her, but neither did she want to spend her whole life void of intimate companionship.

Sveina, she consoled herself. *It may not be true love, but we are good in bed together and she is loyal and trustworthy. I know what I'll do! I'll make her a freewoman. Then she can decide if she wishes to remain with me or not. That's what I'll do!*

A sudden fear and unease gripped her stomach. *But what if she doesn't really want me? What if she truly never did?*

First, we must get out of this cave. Sigrid pushed herself up to a sitting position and took a drink of the water. She eased her foot off the cushioned stone and winced. Even in the pale light, she could see her dressing was soaked through with blood and the wound throbbed like some tiny elf was beating it with a hammer.

Should I wake her?

As Sigrid sat staring at Elyn trying to decide, the flame-haired shield-maiden jerked up with a start, eyes wide open as if ripped into wakefulness by a bad dream. "Are you alright?" Sigrid asked with concern.

Elyn blinked and found her gaze. "Yes," she replied in a shaky voice. "But I fear a mare may have been sitting on my chest. Perhaps a dwarf died in this cave and his soul remained. I do not wish to die below ground where Freya and the Valkyries can't find me. Are you rested?"

Sigrid shared Elyn's sentiments about being trapped in a hole in the ground for eternity, although sharing imprisonment with the caring warrior may not be so bad. "I am ready to find our way out of here if you are. Let us gather our belongings."

While Elyn wandered about checking under stones, Sigrid reattached her armor, sword belt, slid on her helmet, and picked up her battered shield.

"I can't find my sword," Elyn grumbled. She shot a glance upward to the night sky above the crack in the earth. "Maybe it's up there?"

"Don't worry about it," Sigrid consoled. "It was cheap iron. I'll give you a better one if you get me out of this pit alive."

Catching her attention with a speculative look, Elyn replied, "You don't have to—"

"I don't have to do anything but be born and die," Sigrid stated flatly. "Everything else I do is my choice."

Elyn nodded and skipped over the rubble to her side. "Alright then, but before we head out, I need to change your bandages."

Sigrid relaxed her throbbing limb while Elyn tended to the angry, oozing gash, even more aware of her reaction to the woman's touch than before. She took care as she washed the skin and rewound the bandages. Somehow, she fit them snugly without stirring more pain in the process. *How does she do that? Why do I feel nervous and at ease with her at the same time?*

With a clean dressing on her leg and an arm around Elyn's shoulders for support, Sigrid crossed the cavern to the dark hole in the wall, which presented only enough space for one person at a time to pass through.

"I'll go first," Sigrid instructed.

"I should walk ahead of you to kick rocks out of the way, so you do not trip," Elyn insisted, prompting Sigrid to smile.

"I am impressed by your desire to look after me, Elyn," she admitted with fondness growing in her heart for the younger shieldmaiden. "But it makes more sense for me to take point. I can see the entire floor is covered in stones and you could not possibly kick them all aside. But I will be moving slower and if I'm first, I can't fall behind. Besides, what if we happen upon a creature in the darkness? I will send my fylgja ahead to lead the way. My guardian spirit is a gray and white wolf. I saw her once when Sigurd and I were trapped in a blizzard. It showed us to an outcropping which offered protection from the wind and snow. I believe it saved our lives."

With a look of awe and reverence, Elyn bowed her head. "Please, Sigrid, you and your fylgja lead the way."

Moving her hands over the rough chiseled out faces of the tunnel, Sigrid took her time with careful steps as she hopped along, lifting her injured leg and ankle. She planned on what to do if they came across a fork, how to decide on a direction, but the situation did not arise. There existed only the long, dark worming shaft she hoped would lead them out and not to a dead end.

The two women exchanged some pleasant conversation but remained quiet much of the time as they walked for what seemed to be hours in total blackness. There were moments when icy tentacles of fear tried to wrap themselves around Sigrid, but she banished them with the power of her will. She had to admit having Elyn with her provided both comfort and inspiration; she had someone else she needed to be brave for.

At last, her foot brushed a rat, which squeaked and scurried away. "I think we are nearing an exit," she informed Elyn. "A rat means there must be an opening ahead."

"I beseech the gods for the mouth to be large enough for us to pass through." Elyn's voice sounded steady, which pleased Sigrid. She knew what terror would beset her mother or sister at passing through the bowels of the earth, and Sveina would be a quivering wreck by now, but Elyn remained steadfast and in control.

"You are doing well, Elyn," Sigrid praised. "Your courage has not failed you even in this dark situation."

"How could courage fail me when I journey with Sigrid the Valiant?" she replied in an uplifting tone.

"I think I perceive light ahead!" Sigrid did not rush, for her leg ached and she did not wish to fall so near to success.

They continued, fueled by hope, as the passageway broadened and opened out into the side of a rocky hill. The moon shone overhead, accompanied by the glow of dawn. Summer nights in Norvegr were as short as winter days, which meant they would have plenty of light to return to their homes.

Sigrid's heart soared as she breathed the open air and peered at the scene in jubilation. Could she have made it if she had been the only one to fall into the pit? Surely, because this was not her day to die. But what she learned from Elyn was valuable enough to have warranted gaining her injury to obtain. At least she did not lose an eye as Odin had in his quest for knowledge.

On an impulse, she grabbed the front of Elyn's gambeson and pulled her into a triumphant kiss. Her action surprised Sigrid almost as much as it did Elyn and required an explanation. "We live to fight another day," she declared, as if the kiss had been a typical means of celebration, but deep within her, something stirred. Should she allow it to rise, or stomp it down? Elyn had tended her wound and assisted her out of the cave, but how far could she trust this woman she just met? Sigrid had no intention of letting go of her heart so easily. Love has nothing to do with this, and she couldn't afford to be misled, even if it was by her own desires.

ELYN WAS CAUGHT COMPLETELY off guard by Sigrid's searing kiss, with no idea how to respond. It awakened feelings inside her she never imagined had existed there and left her head spinning as if she had been whirled about by a cyclone. Doing her best to not appear stunned or terrified, Elyn cast her gaze to the landscape and said nothing.

"That didn't mean anything." Sigrid barked the words in indignation. "I am just happy to be alive so we can find out what is going on and warn our people. Don't go thinking my passions have run away with me."

"I—I didn't think anything." The weakness in her tone embarrassed Elyn, and at the same time, she felt a desperate disappointment. *Surely you did not expect Sigrid would develop feelings for you, especially overnight! You are a fool! She says a few kind words to you and... leave it, Elyn!*

Trying to regroup herself, she said, "We should look for the others. I'm certain the battle is over by now. Come, lean on me until we find a branch for you to use as a crutch. And do not think I am foolish enough to believe you would want me. Right now, we need each other, 'tis all. Come, do as I say."

Elyn tucked her shoulder under Sigrid's arm and wrapped a hand around her waist. Both women's shields were slung over their backs, making the arrangement awkward but manageable.

"I did not mean to snap at you," Sigrid responded as she settled part of her weight onto Elyn's shoulder. "I am grateful for your help."

"I know." Elyn welcomed the feel of Sigrid's body pressed to her side as they eased their way down a slope strewn with white rocks. "I see two smoke plumes rising, one on either side of the ridge. They must have lit funeral pyres for the dead warriors. Let's move to the south where yours would be. Sigrid, I'm sure Sigurd is at your longhouse, worried sick about you at this very moment."

Sigrid gave her a squeeze. "I'm sure he is, too. Thank you."

They ran into some vegetation as they neared the smoldering pile, and Elyn selected a strong forked branch for Sigrid to use as a crutch. Sigrid took it and hobbled ahead to inspect the remnants of the fire.

Elyn's gaze fell upon the smoking heap of wood and bodies, mostly burned away, and thought of Geir and Ingvar, hoping they were both safe. She supposed when the fighting ended, both sides retreated a short distance to honor their dead as they were too far from home to carry many bodies back. She wondered who had won and what it meant for the status quo. Presently, Sigrid returned to where she waited.

"Did you see..." Elyn began, but the words fell short.

"There were many bodies, but I am certain Sigurd is not among them. Even if he fell, they would take him home for a stately burial. It was impossible to recognize anyone," she added grimly. "You will find the same on your side of the ridge, I'm sure."

"I should accompany you to Gnóttdalr," Elyn suggested. "It is not safe for you to travel so far alone with your injury."

"No," Sigrid declined. "You need to return to your people, but let us make a pact. I will search for clues under every stone, speak with all I trust, and discover as much information as I can. I will try to convince the other jarls and King Grimolf that Firdafylke is not our true enemy if you will do the same. We shall meet back here two weeks from today to share what we have learned."

"Are you certain?" Elyn searched her eyes, concern weighing heavy in her heart. Besides the feelings which stirred within her for this remarkable woman, she needed Sigrid's support to stop their two kingdoms from being usurped by scheming outsiders. "Will you not allow me to aid you in your journey? It is many hours over rough terrain and your leg—"

"Is not at its best," Sigrid concluded. She reached a hand to Elyn's shoulder and smiled at her. "I have traveled farther under worse conditions. Now, do we have an agreement?"

Elyn considered her proposition carefully. "It is doubtful I will be allowed to speak to King Tortryggr, but I will do everything in my power to uncover who is behind this scheme," Elyn vowed. "I will prove you can trust me, Jarl Sigrid. On my oath, I shall meet you outside the cave tunnel two weeks hence."

CHAPTER 14

Gnóttdalr, Svithjod, late that evening

Exhausted and in pain, Sigrid's vigor was refreshed when she caught sight of the familiar fields and farms surrounding her home. Sveina, who worked in the garden beside the longhouse, glanced up and excitement lit her fair face. She dropped her hoe, ran to Sigrid, threw her arms around her neck, and kissed her cheeks.

"My lady, we were so worried," she gushed. "Everyone feared you were dead, but Jarl Sigurd insisted you would return and here you are!"

Sigrid enveloped Sveina in her arms, savoring the familiar warmth and form of her body. "I am happy to be home."

"Thank Freya for answering our prayers!" Tears of joy streamed down Sveina's cheeks.

"Don't cry, dear Sveina," Sigrid cooed. "I am here now, and all is well."

Pulling back, Sveina inspected her mistress. "You are injured." The delight in her expression faded into concern.

"We will see to it," Sigrid assured her. "Now I need to find Sigurd and let Mother know I am alive."

Sigrid leaned on Sveina for support while gripping the crutch Elyn had fashioned for her in her other hand. Together they entered her longhouse's great hall.

"Sigrid!" Sigurd was the first to notice her and rushed across the room to embrace her. "Thank you Sveina," he offered and took the servant's place as Sigrid's aid. "I knew you were not dead."

Glancing around, Sigrid watched Gudred burst into tears while Girrid and Odo beamed and cheered, along with Rangvoldr, Gunnlief, and the other warriors who occupied the hall. Each hurried to greet her with hugs, to touch her, to be certain she was not a ghost.

Two shaggy Cu dogs trotted to her side with bright eyes and happy grins. "Jotun, Warg, I am glad to see you." Sigrid petted each dog as they basked at her touch.

"Those two have not stopped looking for you," Girrid confessed.

"Asmund, go get the Grædari," Sigurd commanded his servant. "She requires the healer's service. Sigrid, we have been so worried," he said as he led her to sit at the table. "Thora, bring her something to eat." The thrall scurried away obediently while family and friends gathered around and took their seats once more. As the hour was late, Sigrid presumed the others had eaten already, but she was famished.

Sveina stood behind Sigrid's seat at the table and removed her helmet, rönd, and armor, setting them carefully aside while all present extended words of welcome and joy at her return. She combed her fingers lightly through Sigrid's hair, smoothing it before stepping to the side.

"I will heat water for your bath," Sveina offered and excused herself from the hall. Sigrid smiled and gave her a grateful nod, imagining how good it would feel.

"We didn't know what happened to you," Gunnlief began in astounded animation. "Someone said the ground swallowed you and others claimed you had been swept away by the avalanche."

"The ground did swallow me up, but it spit me back out again. I will tell you about it," Sigrid assured him, "but first, what of the battle? How bad were our losses?"

"Svithjod lost twenty fighters, another thirty injured," Sigurd reported in a grave tone. A quick calculation informed Sigrid that accounted for half their army. "But the greatest loss, seeing you are safe, is Siegfried. He lives but suffered a serious wound and requires much care and rest if he is to recover. Five of our men from Gnóttdalr were sent off to Valhalla, and seven, counting you, are injured. Eric did as he promised." Sigurd took on a misty expression. "The old one-armed man took out three warriors before he fell, happy and contented with an ax in his hand."

Sigrid smiled and placed a hand over his. "And Firdafylke?"

"About the same," Rangvoldr answered. He gazed at her in utter amazement, his raven hair falling to the front and back of his broad shoulders. "What happened yesterday... was incredible."

"I did not see how it started," the ginger haired Gunnlief began. "Some say it was dwarves within the mountain, others the Jötnar, and a few people claim it was Thor himself. Our ally Jarl Brynjar and Jarl Stefnir War Tooth of Firdafylke were engaged in a fierce duel in the center of our forces. Many continued the combat, but some of us formed a circle around the two leaders to prevent interference by either side. Sigrid, they were evenly matched and traded ferocious blows, but in one fated motion, both of their swords drove home into the other. It was at that instant the rocks came tumbling down in a mighty river of stone, sweeping away both jarls. We took it as a sign, especially since nobody could find you. Sigurd and Njord both agreed to withdraw to burn the dead and tend to the wounded. We searched for you for hours, but..."

"It was so bizarre," Rangvoldr puzzled. "The avalanche, just as the opposing jarls killed each other, and then you just disappeared! I thought you were lost for good," he lamented. "But Sigurd knew better. He was convinced you would return to us. I..." He lowered his regard and rested his head in his hands. "Forgive my doubt."

"Rangvoldr, there is nothing to forgive," Sigrid assured him as Thora placed a cup of mead and plate piled with food before her. She wasted no time digging in.

"What happened to you?" her mother asked with an expression of dismay streaked with curiosity.

"A shieldmaiden of Firdafylke and I both fell into a crack in the earth that opened up when the rockslide crashed downhill. We were trapped in a cave, and I believe we were put there by the gods." Sigrid cast a glance around the table. The only people here were her family, close friends, and devoted servants. But were they? Could she trust them all?

When she paused to consider, Odo peered at her with interest. "Did you kill her?"

"No."

Sigurd's smile lit his sky-blue eyes as they held hers and silently the twins exchanged thoughts and feelings the others could only guess at. He nodded to her in understanding. "Why do you think the gods put the two of you together?" he asked aloud, then added in an aside whisper, "besides the obvious."

Throwing a smirk to her brother, Sigrid lifted her gaze to the gathering once more. "We are being played, pitted against each other so a third party can benefit."

Rangvoldr laughed. "You hit your head," he said. "I see the gash, and where is the healer? Shouldn't he be here by now?"

"Yes, I hit my head, but that is not why I tell you this." Sigrid's tone and expression were unyielding. Then she conveyed the complete story about the raiders who attacked their farms and the suspicions both she and Elyn harbored. "So you see, we have been tricked into fighting each other without cause."

Gunnlief leaned back and scratched his braided beard. "And you are certain you can trust her?"

"I am," Sigrid stated, and upon reflection, deemed she meant it. She did trust Elyn. Some sixth sense convinced her intuitively everything about the shieldmaiden was true and right. "She had every opportunity to kill me while I was unconscious, but she is a woman of honor and did not strike a blow. Instead, she tended my injury and showed me the highest respect. But there is someone in Svithjod we cannot trust, for this third party, whomever they are, cannot be acting alone. Somebody has given them information or may have even formed an alliance with them. There is a spy among us, and he might have killed Jarl Olaf for discovering the plot. If anyone could have done so, it would have been our father."

"What should we do next?" Odo inquired, eager to be included in the plan.

"The Grædari will mend Sigrid's leg tonight," Sigurd stated while Sigrid ate. "In a couple of days, when my sister's strength has returned, we will go to visit Jarl Siegfried and take gifts and offerings to the gods for his speedy recovery and inform him of the conspiracy. Then Sigrid and I shall travel on to see King Grimolf. He needs to be aware. I will propose he and King Tortryggr should meet to discuss the situation and a truce be called between our kingdoms. If we are going to lead our warriors into battle, it should be against our true enemy, not because we are so foolish as to let ourselves be manipulated."

Sigrid placed a hand over his and smiled at him. His energy seemed to flow into her, making her strong again… or maybe it was the meat, greens, and bread filling her stomach. Either way, she felt invigorated.

"Then I shall go with you," Odo determined, but Sigurd shook his head.

"You should stay here," Sigrid voiced, "to remain in charge while we are away. You will need to keep everyone calm and assist Mother and Girrid visiting our wounded. If any disputes or problems arise, we feel confident you can handle them."

Odo nodded, pleased with the faith the twins placed in him.

"My lord, the healer has arrived," Asmund announced.

SVEINA HAD PREPARED a hot bath for Sigrid who invited the Grædari, a middle-aged man knowledgeable in treating wounds and the use of herbs, into her bedchamber along with her mother. When Sveina started to leave, Sigrid entreated, "No, stay, please. The healer can show you what to do to care for my leg so he need not return day after day."

She nodded and closed the door. Sigrid slipped out of her clothes into the bath to wash, and Sveina assisted her out of the tub and enfolded a sheet around her. Sigrid lay on her bed for the healer to examine her sliced leg and sprained ankle. He treated the gaping wound with herbs and salve, wrapped it in tight bandages, and gave her a pouch of medicinal tea to steep in hot water and drink twice a day. Selecting some strips of stiff leather and a band of soft suede, he adjusted her ankle and tied it fast to hold the bones and sinews in place.

"Do not try to put weight on this leg for several days," he instructed, "or it will take longer to heal. Keep the wound clean and allow it to air a couple of times a day between changing bandages. Here is the salve to use." He handed Sveina a clay jar of ointment that smelled of leeks and garlic, wine and gall. "If it starts to turn angry red or ooze with puss, call for me. I prepared this batch after the last raid to have some on hand the next time I had wounds to treat as it takes over a week for the mixture to ferment. The recipe was passed to me from my ancestors, and it is quite effective at preventing or curing infections," he explained. "The second concern is for the muscle and skin to grow back together. If the swelling has gone down and the oozing stopped, I will stitch it with a needle and thread tomorrow, but the best thing for tonight is to stay in bed." He fixed her with a stern look.

"I will remain right here," Sigrid promised.

After seeing the healer out, Gudred sat beside Sigrid and brushed a hand over her forehead. "You may have a scar here that will show," she speculated with sorrow.

"I can arrange my hair so it covers it if need be," Sigrid responded without concern. "It is not like my cheek was sliced."

"When are you going to stop doing this?" she agonized.

"You mean lead my army from the fore, with a spear and shield and sword?" Sigrid fixed a determined gaze on her mother. "When I am too old to fight, and not a day sooner."

Gudred lowered her chin and placed a kiss on Sigrid's cut brow. "The glow of your father's pride shines brightly in the night sky. Forgive me for desiring you to remain in safety. I am also proud of you and your brothers, but I just lost my husband. I do not wish to bury children as well."

"I know mother," Sigrid replied. "And I have returned. Now, you should get some sleep too."

With a nod of acknowledgement, Gudred left Sigrid alone with Sveina.

CHAPTER 15

Sveina strolled to the side of Sigrid's bed and slid off her dress and undergarments, sending anticipation shooting through the warrior-jarl until that slender, ash-blonde tease produced a cup and handed it to her. "Your medicinal tea," she said with a laughing smile playing on her lips. "I put it in water while you were talking with your mother. Now drink this or no pleasures for you, my lady."

"I'll drink it," she grumbled, but her gaze sparkled at Sveina. She took the mug and downed the herbal mix. It didn't taste awful, which was a relief. By the time she finished, a warm, naked body was nestled against hers, making Sigrid feel relaxed and content.

"You mustn't move around and jostle your leg," Sveina instructed, as her fingertips danced along Sigrid's skin.

Sigrid pushed out of her sheet to free up more flesh for Sveina's talented fingers to caress. "That isn't fair," she protested. "I enjoy straddling you and sending waves of sensual pleasure careening through your body."

"Not tonight," her servant insisted, and brushed a kiss to Sigrid's mouth. "Tonight I shall seduce you with tenderness, arouse your senses with my lips and tongue, send you over the edge into bliss so you may sleep well and put this trying experience behind you."

Sigrid purred and closed her eyes. "I love your touch, Sveina," she sighed. However, a worrisome thought tickled the edges of her awareness, casting the entire experience in doubt—the kiss she shared with

Elyn at the cave. She could not reproduce the feeling it gave her and reflections of the red-haired shieldmaiden lingered, clouding her focus on here and now.

PRESENTLY, Sigrid opened her eyes. Sveina lay nestled beside her, staring at the ceiling with a far-away look on her face. Sigrid recalled what she had wished to do and contemplated how to begin. Rolling onto her side to face her bedmate, she raised a question she had never asked directly. "When we are together, does our lovemaking bring you pleasure?"

Sveina seemed startled by the inquiry and turned a hesitant gaze on Sigrid. "It brings me great pleasure to provide pleasure to you," came her response.

"That isn't what I asked."

"I love you, Sigrid," Sveina confessed. "You are the best mistress any thrall could hope for. You are kind and considerate and always think of me. I am not required to do more than my share of the work, and you protect me from those who may abuse one in my position."

"But does being with me this way bring you pleasing gratification?" Sigrid pressed, even as she felt the weight of an anvil press against her chest in dread.

"My lady, serving you in whatever capacity brings me an abundance of satisfaction. When I go to the market for you and Lady Gudred, I talk with other slaves and you cannot imagine... or maybe you can," she retreated. "Aud says her mistress beats her with a leather strap whenever she spills something or makes a mistake. Felda says she must have sex with all the men in her household—one of them is huge and only wants to take her in the ass. He makes her cry, and then laughs about it. And Erica works on a dairy and while she claims she is not mistreated, she is always exhausted because she has to work all day long with no opportunity for enjoyment of any kind. You, Sigrid, are a wonder, and I love you with all my heart. I am totally devoted to your service."

Sigrid sighed and turned a defeated gaze to the ceiling. One candle still burned illuminating the room in a soft light. "But I thought... years ago when I first kissed you, you acted as if you enjoyed it. You never flinched at my touch and invest so much energy in pleasing me."

Sveina pushed up on her elbow, turning to Sigrid with a frantic look of fear. "It is my purpose in life to please you, Sigrid."

"Then tell me the truth." She fixed her eyes on Sveina's. "There are so few people I can trust, and I count you to be among them. Tell me, Sveina, because I need to know. Prove my confidence is not misplaced. Do not fear reprisal, just be honest: is there someone, a man, who you dream of, one you would rather be with than me?"

Bursting into tears, she cried, "Please, Jarl Sigrid, do not send me away! Please let me stay and serve you. I will do better. I will..."

"Stop this!" Sigrid gathered Sveina into her arms while she wept on her shoulder. "No one is sending you away."

The truth was like a bitter herb for Sigrid to taste. *All this time, I thought she felt as I did. I believed she was as fulfilled by our passion as I was. I thought... that I was not the only one. Oh, what have I done? What can I do?* Sigrid recognized the sting of her own tears, and she tried to focus her attention on consoling Sveina.

"I do not dislike it," Sveina finally said. "In fact, I have come to consider myself fortunate to have gained such favor from a living legend. Do not cry, Sigrid. I never want to make you cry. It hurts like an arrow to the chest to see such anguish on your face!"

"It is not your fault, Sveina," Sigrid admitted. "I saw and believed what I wanted to. Rather than base my actions and belief on your efforts to please me, I should have asked this long ago. I assumed because you never protested... because you anticipated my desires... forgive me, my dear one. I was wrong."

Sigrid may have had doubts which she pushed aside along the way but being hit with this revelation was an awakening blow. In the moment, she felt as if she had fallen into the pit, only this time no one else was with her, and rather than light streaming from above, there was only darkness. She believed Sveina when she professed her love; it was just a different kind of love. *I can't believe I didn't know, that all this time... but she behaved as if she was in ecstasy. Was she simply imitating my responses?*

"No, my lady, you were not wrong," Sveina corrected her. "Your father gave me to you, and I am yours to do with as you like. The fact you wanted me was flattering, that I, a mere thrall, caught your eye, was unimaginable. Please do not send me away." She hugged Sigrid tighter.

Sigrid touched her lips to Sveina's forehead, where she snuggled near her chin. Then she reached around her to remove a gold braided wrist band her parents had given her on her sixteenth birthday. She wore it almost all the time. A wristband was a symbol of status coveted by men and women alike, making them extremely popular, especially so if it was fashioned of gold. She took the bracelet and slipped it over Sveina's wrist.

Sitting up with a shocked expression, Sveina exclaimed, "What are you doing? Only free citizens are allowed to wear one of these."

"You are now and forevermore will be a free citizen of Svithjod, my dear Sveina," Sigrid affirmed. "You were correct to say you were my property for me to do with as I wish. Tonight, it pleases me to grant you your freedom. You are a freewoman now, to come or go as you like. I would be most honored if you choose to remain in my service and of this household, but you may also find other employment or marry if you so prefer."

"Sigrid!"

This time, Sigrid perceived Sveina's tears were from joyful jubilation as she showered her with kisses and bounced on the bed like a child. The glow beaming from her face was brighter than a hundred suns and it warmed Sigrid's heart to know she put it there.

"Of course I wish to remain in your service," she declared. "But to be a freewoman... I don't even know what that means!"

A bittersweet smile tugged at Sigrid's mouth. "Then you will have to take time to find out. Now, tell me about the young man you fancy."

"How did you..." she began. Sveina's whole body shivered with delight. "Finn," she grinned at last.

"The shepherd?"

"Yes." Sveina bit her bottom lip, her brows raised, and eyes widened in a questioning expression. When Sigrid nodded, she continued. "He comes to town once a week to bring cheese to trade at the market and I see him there. We have had many enjoyable conversations. My heart takes wings when I think of his smile."

"Now you will be able to pursue a relationship with him if you like," Sigrid said. "I am glad you wish to remain in my service, but do not worry. I shall not ask you to my bed again and I am not angry with you."

"Are you certain?" Trepidation returned to Sveina's fair face and Sigrid could feel the increase in her heartrate. "I never want to disappoint you, and I fear I have. Oh, Sigrid, please believe me. I do love you... but I'm not the same as you. I didn't want to disappoint you, so I pretended to be. Please do not be angry with me. I would never hurt you or betray you."

Her words rang true with Sigrid, who could sense the conflict of emotions streaming from the woman who sat in bed beside her, probably for the last time.

"I know," Sigrid allowed with a heavy heart. "And you can prove your devotion."

"Yes, I would like to very much," Sveina replied eagerly.

"There is a traitor among our people—at least one, maybe more. One of them murdered my father. I want you to watch and listen. Pay attention to anybody acting suspicious, saying or doing something unusual, men who talk in whispers or break off their conversation when you walk near," Sigrid explained. "You may have an occasion to visit the mead hall with Finn or when you are shopping in the marketplace. Watch and listen, but do not engage or let anyone know what you are about. Then report back to me whatever you witness. And Sveina, be very careful," she charged, meeting the freedwoman's gaze. "You are dear to me, and I will be exceedingly displeased if anything was to happen to you. Is that clear?"

"Yes, my lady," she replied with a serious nod. "I shall be happy to help you find the murdering bastard so you can slice him from crotch to gullet."

Her words brought a smile to Sigrid's face. "Put your nightgown on and then come back to sleep. Tomorrow will be an exciting day for you."

She watched Sveina bound about her bedchamber, putting clothing on this time. She had calmed considerably when she returned. "I will miss sleeping with you in the enormous soft bed," she admitted.

"Does your Finn have a cottage up by the pastures?"

She nodded. "He said it is more than a tent but less than a proper house. I can't wait to share my news with him. Oh, Sigrid, I thank you from the bottom of my heart with all that I am. But I do not want to leave you alone, with no one to hold you at night."

"You must look to your own life now." Sigrid turned and reached a hand to caress her soft cheek. "Do not concern yourself with me in that regard anymore. I will find someone else. But if you are ever cold or lonely in the great hall, you are always welcome to share my bed as a friend."

Sveina turned her face into Sigrid's hand and kissed her palm. "I owe you everything, and I thank you. People do not often notice me so I will be able to overhear much. I will help you find our enemies. Now you must sleep, too."

Sigrid knew she was right. She perceived when Sveina drifted into slumber, but sleep did not come easy for the jarl. Her leg throbbed, her heart ached, and her mind ran through suspicions as to who could be behind the deadly scheme. Nevertheless, between exhaustion from her arduous march home and the effects of the herbal tea, she at last fell into the arms of a dream... a dream who wore a shieldmaiden's gambeson draped with flame-red hair. Sigrid's final thought was, *I promised you a sword... must get Elyn a sword.*

CHAPTER 16

Kaldrlogr, Firdafylke, the same day

ℰlyn's mind tried to process the barrage of conflicting ideas which pushed, prodded, and jabbed at her consciousness like an enemy's spear tips as she trudged back down the rocky slope, over the stream, through the forest and high meadows retracing the path toward home. She had stopped beside the smoldering funeral pyre and paid her respects to the brave warriors who had fallen. But she did not aim wrath and revenge over the lost lives at Svithjod, rather at whoever had tricked them both. "I will make the leaders listen to me," she vowed to herself and to Sigrid.

She kissed me! The impulse on Sigrid's part amazed Elyn, and hours later still filled her with wonder, which grew like a tiny seed planted in rich soil. *She said it meant nothing, but... I felt it did. It certainly meant something to me. She is being cautious, or mayhap she has a lover at home whom she does not wish to betray. But that kiss indicated a great deal of things beyond feeling fortunate to escape the cave.*

She pondered what to disclose and to whom she could reveal it while tamping down dark swirls of worry for her friends, as she did not know who survived the battle and who did not. She had found her sword, broken under huge, split rocks at the top of the crevasse through which she and Sigrid had fallen. Swords were difficult to come by and not all warriors owned one. She would have to make do with her ax and a new spear. *Sigrid said she would give me one, but I will not see her for two weeks. Besides,* she consoled herself, *a worthy shieldmaiden is lethal with any weapon, even with none at all.*

Clearing a ridge, Elyn breathed easier as she recognized the valley spreading before her. Her vision took in the blue-green waters of the fjord and the timber palisade with its lookout spire which designated Njord's compound. Picking up her pace, she made straight for the back gate.

A guard in the tower must have spotted her, for several of her companions met her as she arrived. "Elyn!" Ingvar cried and grabbed her in a bear hug. He showered her with kisses before allowing his fellow warriors their chance to welcome her home. "You are alive! You must tell us what happened."

"And you must tell me what happened with you," she replied as her gaze searched the group of soldiers. "Where is Geir?" The shadowy claws of fear assaulted her imagination when she did not see him.

"He suffered a severe wound," Ingvar answered in remorse. "He lies in the great hall where he is being tended."

"Svithjod lost two dozen dead, with twice as many injured," Frode recounted. He fell in at her other side as she and Ingvar made for the longhouse. "Horik feasts in Odin's Hall tonight, as do Ulfinn and Gustav. We thought you had joined them but are pleased to see the gods were not ready for you yet."

"Were you buried by the avalanche?" Ingvar asked as they passed through the door into the large open space of Njord's great hall.

"In a manner of speaking," Elyn began. "The ground collapsed under our feet, and—"

"There you are, you worthless woman!" Her uncle's fury echoed through the chamber as he pounded across the floor to shake his finger at her. "This is your fault!" Stepping aside, he motioned to the bench where Geir lay under a fur blanket. A maidservant sat upon a stool, blotting his head with a wet rag, while a musician in the corner played soothingly on a lyre.

Elyn's mouth dropped even as she sensed a cord of guilt tighten around her throat. She loved her cousin, and it tore at her heart to see him in such a state, but she could not fathom how his wound was her fault. "How can you blame me?" she asked in stunned disbelief. "What did I do?"

"You should have been at his back, fighting in tandem." Unnulf lowered his voice, but the biting rage remained. "Instead, you left him to spar with that other shieldmaiden. I will never forgive you for abandoning Geir!"

This was always the time Elyn would accept blame, bow her head in shame, and receive punishment for something not her fault, but no more. She was no longer a child dependent on him for everything. She was a formidable fighter, and while still feeling a family obligation to her uncle, no more would she serve as his whipping girl.

Elyn raised her chin and looked him in the eyes. In a tone both firm and respectful, she stated, "I did not abandon Geir. He is a grown man, a warrior in Jarl Njord's shield wall. And I am a grown woman. We were ordered to cover the right flank, and that is what we did. Was I expected to coddle my older cousin, stand watch over him alone, or to engage the enemy as he did? Do not disrespect your son by implying he needed a guardian and is incapable of fighting his own battles. The shieldmaiden was Sigrid the Valiant, and the gods dropped us into a pit together during the fray so truths might be revealed."

"Truths?" He let out a dry, humorless laugh. "You cannot believe the words of such a witch. I am surprised she did not cut out your entrails and strangle you with them. Or perhaps you are the one who lies, and you merely hid behind a boulder until the battle was over."

Holding her ground, Elyn refused to back down or be dragged into a pointless argument. She stepped around him and strode to where Geir lay. Noticing her approach, the servant woman arose and offered her the stool beside her cousin.

Her soul overflowing with concern, Elyn gently stroked Geir's face as she peered down at him. "Hey, you weren't supposed to let them get a blade on you," she said in friendly jest, hoping he could hear her. When he moved his fingers, she took his hand and gave it a squeeze. "I'm right here, Geir. I'm going to take care of you now."

She pulled back the fur to inspect his wounds, still overhearing her uncle's grumblings. Ingvar joined her. "Halfdan has already been here and applied medicine and bandages." Elyn could tell from the placement of the cloths and the bloodstains he had a gut wound. These varied in severity, depending upon whether the bowels had been perforated or not.

"We will offer prayers and sacrifices to Eir on his behalf," she said.

"The Valkyrie goddess did not take him from the field of battle, so I conclude it was not his day to die."

"As it was not yours." Recognizing the voice, Elyn rose and spun to face Njord.

"My lord," she addressed him with a slight bow of homage. "The gods spared me to continue in your service. I have an unbelievable tale for you if my lord is inclined to hear my account."

Njord held out a hand to her, but Elyn glanced down at herself. "My lord, I have just walked many miles after enduring a night in a dwarf cave and should make myself presentable before I take your hand."

"My dear Elyn. Do not think you must impress me by displaying a beauty I already know you possess. Come and share my table," he invited. "You must be hungry, and I wish to hear your account, as I am certain you are curious about what happened with us after you landed in a cave."

Ingvar and Unnulf followed as Njord escorted Elyn to sit beside him at the table with his children and Aslaug where servants passed out food and drink. Elyn was certain Unnulf was biting his tongue to remain civil, for above his desire to berate her rose his quest to please the jarl. With a refreshing meal before her and feeling welcomed by Ingvar and Njord, Elyn relaxed.

"Tell us what happened," the jarl implored. "Frode said you were there one minute, battling against Jarl Sigrid, and the next you had both disappeared. Everyone was distracted by the landslide and the duel between Jarl Stefnir War Tooth and that burly Svithjod jarl. They killed each other or perhaps were finished when the stones rolled from the mountain onto them. Jarl Sigurd and I called a truce because of the strange occurrence. The warriors were murmuring about giants and Thor's displeasure and…"

"Yes," Elyn agreed. "I believe Thor has intervened twice now, and for a good reason, but I will get to that. The ground shook when the mountainside slid upon us, and a crevasse opened under our feet. Sigrid and I were swallowed into a deep cave, where we fought some more, then talked and discovered both our kingdoms were being manipulated into warring against each other. We worked together and found a dwarf tunnel just large enough to squeeze through leading to the outside, but by the time we arrived, everyone had gone home."

"Sigrid would lie to you, child," Unnulf ventured in a cautionary tone. "She would say anything to gain your confidence, only to betray us all."

"I was the first to suspect things were amiss, and it was I who convinced her, not the other way around."

"The suspicions you told me about before?" Njord inquired. He followed her story with interest.

"Yes, my lord, and more. She swore raiders bearing our shields and flag attacked her farms while I vowed we did no such thing. She also gave her oath they did not attack us," Elyn explained.

"But the marauders carried the yellow and black of Svithjod," Unnulf asserted.

"Exactly!" Elyn passed her gaze between her uncle and her jarl. "Why would they do such a thing? I suggested if we were to raid our neighbors, we would surely not want to announce who we were to invite a retaliation, and she agreed. We concluded a third party, perhaps another kingdom or a conspiracy of ambitious men from one or both sides wish to drain our armies of their numbers so the usurpers could sweep in and pick us off, thereby conquering both Firdafylke and Svithjod with little effort or loss of their warriors. If we did not raid their farms and they did not raid ours, we must conclude someone else did using deception to start a feud."

"If." Unnulf raised concerns. "It is also possible Jarl Sigrid lied about her farms being raided in order to appear to be the victim, to invent an excuse for their attacks on us."

"Jarl Sigrid is a person of honor," Elyn stated in robust defense of her fellow shieldmaiden. "She does not lie, and neither do I. Jarl Njord, I beseech you to take these concerns to your fellow jarls and to King Tortryggr. He should be informed, even if it is only a theory at this point. He needs every bit of available information to make the correct decisions."

Unnulf shook his head as if embarrassed by her, but Njord gave his chin a thoughtful stroke. "Frode, Ingvar, Lady Aslaug, what are your thoughts regarding Elyn's report?"

As a senior warrior and underling commander, Frode spoke first. "I have heard many stories about Sigrid Olafsdottir, and some seem too fantastical to be true. But I have never heard it said she lies or engages in deception of any kind."

"She is a pawn in King Grimolf's scheme," Unnulf inserted. "She may have no choice in the matter."

Njord sat back in contemplation. "What would I do if my king ordered me to concoct a story to mislead others? I suppose I would have to weigh what is to be gained against the value of my honor. Many rulers have obtained their thrones by less than honorable means. Such is often the price of glory."

Elyn pinned him with a curious expression. "My lord, how can one hope to gain glory without honor? I realize I am a simple woman, naïve in games of political nuance. I am merely one who defends my family, village, and country with skill and valor. They call a battleground a field of honor where the gods choose who they will take to their halls of glory and who they will leave behind to fight another day. These are the values we live by. Jarl Sigrid is a shieldmaiden, like me. Honor is everything to her."

Njord responded with a warm smile and placed his hand over hers on the table. "My dear Elyn, Sigrid is not like you at all; she is like me. A jarl is more than a warrior who survived the most battles. Our minds must calculate, like we are playing a game of Hnefatafl, deciding which pieces we can afford to lose and which we cannot as we march toward the prize of ultimate domination. She must employ strategy, and unfortunately, that can include subterfuge. Ingvar, Aslaug, thoughts?"

"I trust Elyn's instincts," Ingvar stated with conviction. "If she says we are being manipulated, I wish to seek who is behind it."

"I know nothing of these matters, my lord," faltered Aslaug's timid reply. "But I have lived more years than you all. I recall my grandparents telling me how in the past Svithjod and Firdafylke were one kingdom, strong and prosperous as they commanded a long portion of seacoast. A division arose between the king and a high-ranking jarl, and everyone in the kingdom took sides in the feud. No one remembers what the argument was about or who started it, but my grandfather always believed an enemy had sewn seeds of discontent between them. You see, the high-ranking jarl was the king's half-brother. Anyway, the kingdom split and now we stand at the brink of war with our other half. Is it not worth the effort to investigate Elyn's claims for the sake of peace?"

"Lady Aslaug, you are wise indeed," Njord praised and inclined his head to her. "I will take this all under advisement. Now, let us be glad Elyn has been restored to us." He raised his cup. "Skol!"

"Skol!" they all repeated and drank to Elyn's safe return.

CHAPTER 17

Bjornhellir, village in the Kingdom of Gudbrandsdalir

ing Hemingr the Unwashed sat atop a raised platform on a heavy pine armchair adorned with antlers and skulls matching the dominant decor of his great hall high in the Fille Fiell Mountains east of the coastal kingdoms. His thick mane of umber brown hair spread over the fur mantle draped around his shoulders. At forty-four years old, only the slightest hint of gray frosted the beard flowing to the middle of his barrel chest. Muscular and tough, he could chop through a tree trunk in minutes and a row of men in half the time. With vicious determination, he epitomized the mountaineers whose ancestors had ventured into the wilderness to mine ore and precious metals from the earth, to hunt muskox, wild boar, red deer, and reindeer, to take on the fearsome wolverine, lynx, and mighty brown bear. Theirs was a challenging existence where few crops could grow, and winter conditions descended harsher than near the seashore. Hard times made for stalwart men and sturdy women. The resources gleaned from the mountains were valuable for trade, but the lack of a waterway to the sea hindered their ability to engage in profitable commerce.

Alongside the king, Brunhildr assumed her position as queen and partner in leadership. The big-boned, blonde-haired mother of five children was swathed in silver chains, bracelets, and rings and her deep blue woolen dress bore a luxurious arctic fox fur about her impressive shoulders.

The hall bustled with servants performing their duties, women weaving at their looms or preparing food, and warriors swapping stories, drinking from horns, or playing games, but all stopped to stare when an odd-looking pair walked through the doors. One man was short, stocky, and as hairy as a bear. His older companion resembled a knotted twig, with a long neck and nose, bony chest, and knobby middle. They both grinned from ear to ear.

King Hemingr considered them with cold russet eyes peering over a hooked nose. "I expect to hear news of success."

"Indeed," Krum proclaimed with a bow before the ruling couple.

"We also brought fresh dairy, produce, and many bags of grain acquired in trade, my lord," Hroald reported with his own display of homage. "Everything is working out as you predicted."

A smile stretched across Hemingr's wide face as delight danced in his countenance. "Come," he said, rising from his throne. "Let us enjoy refreshment while you tell me all the details."

The two emissaries joined Hemingr and Brunhildr at a huge pine table while a serving girl brought them yarrow beer, bread, berries, and roasted meat smothered in a savory sauce.

"My lord is too generous," Krum declared as he inhaled the delicious aromas.

"That all depends on the report you bring," Hemingr replied. "Krum, tell me of Firdafylke. Have you gained the ear of King Tortryggr the Navigator?"

"I have, my lord," he boasted. "I gave him the gems from our mountain as a gift, negotiated a fair-trade settlement which slightly favored his kingdom, and remained to advise him for several months. It took only a few rumors and a well-timed story to convince him what a greedy, power-crazed king Grimolf the Wolf has become. As evidence, the first farming raid arrived on schedule, further convincing him Svithjod had turned against them."

"Have you been able to sway the loyalty of any of his jarls?" Brunhildr inquired.

"Doing so is proving more difficult, my lord," he admitted with a frustrated expression. "But I have enlisted the support of a few underlings upon whom the jarls depend. There is one who has gained the ear of Jarl

Njord, who has cast his lot with us. He vowed his loyalty in exchange for a jarldom in the new kingdom. I gave him a ring as security in your name." Krum shrugged his skinny shoulder. "I figured you would honor the pledge or have him killed, but either way he is your eyes, ears, and voice in Jarl Njord's court."

Hemingr nodded to Krum. "Well played. We must first have pawns before we can decide whether to sacrifice them for the greater good. Hroald?"

"King Grimolf was most impressed by the gifts you sent and has proven easy to persuade, my lord." Hroald's round cheeks appeared rosy above his braided black beard. "King Tortryggr is older than he, so it is simple to pretend his health is failing. It only took a few hirelings to arrive from trips north to Firdafylke spreading rumors of plots by his jarls as they vie for power to seize the throne from Tortryggr's son once he dies. I, of course, lamented the sad state of Firdafylke's king and how he cannot remember who he is from day to day. But the raids came as powerful evidence. Twice now, the two kingdoms have fought along the border, first as a skirmish, and the day I left to travel here as a full-scale battle."

"Excellent!" The king struck the tabletop with his fist and the gleam in his eyes brightened.

"But we do not know the outcome," Brunhildr pointed out.

"Who won does not matter, as long as they kill each other," Hemingr explained. "However, my wife has a valid concern. You two must hurry back down the mountain with more trading goods to discover how much their armies have been weakened. I will send an escort of several guards each so you can return word as soon as you arrive."

"Yes, my lord," Hroald replied. "And like my friend Krum, it has been difficult to enlist a jarl to our cause. Those in Svithjod are even of greater comradery than the leaders in Firdafylke, but I was able to shake things up a bit, which will give us an edge, and, like my counterpart, I have secured a few important underlings with promises of power."

"You are learning to play the game, Hroald," Brunhildr praised with a regal smile.

"This is a most excellent meal, my lord," Krum proclaimed between mouthfuls. "It is true you reward those in your service quite handsomely."

"And what reward do the two of you expect upon our success? Surely not positions of authority?" Hemingr queried.

119

The men laughed and shook their heads. "You mentioned a tidy sum of wealth with which we could live comfortably," Hroald answered.

"And you alluded to using your influence to secure us attractive wives," Krum added with a hopeful gaze. "What would we want with power and authority?"

"It is our pleasure to serve a strong and crafty king such as yourself," Hroald confirmed between bites.

King Hemingr smiled. "Tell me about Kings Grimolf and Tortryggr."

Krum lifted a finger as he swallowed a morsel. "King Tortryggr was once a great seafaring adventurer where he gained fame and wealth enough to secure his ascension to the throne of Firdafylke. Now he is an old man—not feeble minded nor weak of limb, as my capable counterpart has made him appear to the people of Svithjod, but he has become soft. It has been more than ten years since he stepped onto a battlefield. He sits about his hall doting on his grandchildren, singing and dancing to the tunes of his musicians, while his only living son, Erling, trains his warriors and carries on much of the administration. The king still holds court once a week and attends every sacred rite and observance."

"I wonder how Tortryggr would react should something happen to his son and heir?" Brunhildr considered aloud.

"If someone murdered Erling, he would stop at nothing to gain revenge," Krum warned. Then an amused expression crossed his long face. "But if his darling only son was to die in a tragic accident or of a mysterious illness, robbing him of a warrior's death, it may be the blow to undo the king."

"Something to consider," Hemingr smiled at the devious minds he surrounded himself with.

"King Grimolf is not as old, but not as youthful and robust as you, King Hemingr," Hroald testified. "I have seen him spar with his captains and engage in games of skill and strength, but neither has he fought a battle in many years. He enjoys the company of a beautiful wife and has numerous sons and daughters. His eldest son is now a young man eager to prove himself, but because he has other children, losing him would not be so life-shattering. Grimolf's weakness lies in his inherent goodness. He is a man of honor and sees those around him as honorable too, which is why the stories I feed him of Firdafylke's ambitious jarls circling like vultures waiting for their king to die makes him so angry."

"You have both done well, my emissaries," Hemingr praised. "It is time for stage two of our plan. When you return tomorrow, I will send a personal token of mine to each king. You are to assure them Gudbrandsdalir stands ready to support their cause against their insolent, raiding neighbor. Krum, if you and your cohorts manage to arrange an accident or slow poisoning of Tortryggr's heir mimicking an illness, it would be most fortunate. Hroald, do what you can to undermine the alliance among Grimolf's jarls. You are most expert at sewing discord."

"Yes, my lord," both men vowed.

"Sune," called the king. A brawny man with a square jaw and trim beard approached the table with an expectant look. "Select some helpers and unpack the trade wagons, then repack them with ore, furs, and smoked meat for the emissaries to take back tomorrow. Pick six trusted men to accompany them, three for Roald and three for Krum. If all goes according to plan, we will march on the remnants of both armies at the height of summer."

The underling bowed and turned on his heel to fulfill the king's directive.

"The two of you are welcome to sleep in my hall tonight," Hemingr offered. "I am ready to retire now. Brunhildr, will you be accompanying me?"

King Hemingr rose, extended a hand to his wife, and escorted her from the great hall to their private chambers where a woman watched over their children at play.

"It is time to get ready for bed," Brunhildr said, and she dismissed the servant.

"We want a story!" the youngest boy exclaimed. Two other boys and two girls, all with bright faces and bouncing curls, gathered around their parents. Hemingr and his wife sat on their enormous bed and the children piled in, the youngest little tot crawling into her mother's spacious lap.

"I will tell you a story about Loki," he said with a wink.

"Loki was your grandfather, wasn't he?" the oldest girl asked.

"Yes, he was," Hemingr grinned, "but he is also one of the gods who lives in Ásgarðr. Loki is a trickster who can take many forms and has fathered many children, some who are good and others who are not so good. Odin, Thor, and Frigg count on his cleverness to get Ásgarðr out of trouble, but sometimes Loki causes mischief of his own."

"Tell the story of how Loki tricked the dwarves into crafting Thor's hammer, Mjöllnir," suggested his oldest son. Hemingr smiled at Ulfvar and ruffled his hand through his chestnut hair.

"Once long ago, Loki became bored, and do you know what that means?"

The children giggled.

"Mischief!" Ulfvar shouted. Hemingr's swift fingers tickled the boy before he could move out of reach.

"Mischief," the king repeated. Brunhildr laughed and hugged her little girl, beaming with joy at her husband.

"Loki thought he would entertain himself by playing a prank on Thor, so while the god of thunder and his wife Sif were sleeping, he sneaked into their bedroom and cut off all of Sif's beautiful golden locks. When Thor found out, he was so angry." Hemingr made a silly, enraged face at the children, threw back his head, and howled, sending them into rolling laughter.

"Thor was about to beat Loki in retaliation, but Loki was quick to use his brain. 'I wish to make amends,' Loki said. 'I will go to the dwarves and have them spin her hair of actual gold to repay what I cut off,' he vowed. So Thor decided he would wait and see what Loki would bring to replace Sif's fabled tresses he had ruined. Loki traveled deep into the mountain and found the sons of Ivaldi, who were known for their fine craftsmanship, and convinced them to spin the golden hair. They did, but in their eagerness to please the gods, the brothers made more magic items—a deadly spear which could slay any foe and a fast ship that could be folded small enough to fit in one's pocket."

The children hung on the storyteller king's every word, bringing delight to his heart. "But Loki saw an opportunity to gain more favor with Thor and the other gods while he was in Svartalfheim. He found two dwarves who claimed to be the finest forgers in all the nine realms. Their names were Brokkr and Sindri. He played on their pride and bet they could not produce three items as spectacular as the ones Ivaldi's sons had made. Of course, these dwarves accepted the wager, for they wished to prove they were the best.

"Loki wanted to observe their craft, so he shifted into the guise of a fly, buzzing around the forge, teasing the dwarves as they worked. First, they fashioned a living boar out of gold, and then a magic golden ring that produces eight rings more every nine days. Last, they began production on an invincible hammer. Loki was feeling frisky, so as a fly, he bit

Brokkr in the eye and he could not see what he was doing. Sindri blamed the fly for almost ruining the hammer."

"But it wasn't ruined," one of the king's daughters asserted.

Hemingr winked at her. "To make it up to Brokkr, Loki invited him to return with him to Ásgarðr to present the gifts to the gods. He gave the giant-slaying spear Gungnir and the magical ring Draupnir to Odin, and the golden boar and shrinking ship to Freyr. Then he presented Thor with the golden headdress for Sif and the mighty hammer, Mjöllnir. The gods agreed the best of all the items crafted by the dwarves was Thor's hammer, so Brokkr won the bet, but Loki won the favor of the other gods... at least this time."

"I like this story," the youngest boy said. "Tell us another, please!"

Hemingr stood, scooped the child into his arms, and carried him to his bed. "Not tonight. It is time for sleep so you can grow up to be big and strong like Thor, or crafty like Loki. Either way, you must sleep."

Brunhidlr placed the smallest girl, who was almost asleep, into the children's bed and the others climbed in. "Close your eyes and go to sleep now, children, and do not bother your mother and I, even if you hear we are still awake," Hemingr charged.

"Yes, Father," Ulfvar promised.

Hemingr and Brunhildr crossed the room back to their sturdy, broad bed. Hemingr tugged his tunic over his head, revealing his muscled chest strewn with sprouts of dark hair. As he pulled off his boots, he said in a hush, "I am encouraged by our envoys' reports. It was one thing to keep to the mountains generations ago when our numbers were but a few miners, but now our population has grown while our food supplies have not. It is not fair that other kingdoms monopolize the coasts and the fertile land for growing crops, while we do not even enjoy river access to the sea. We are completely landlocked up here, cut off from easy trade routes. We build no ships as our ancestors did and neighbors do because we have nowhere to use them. Another generation, and our carpenters will lose their expertise for lack of practice." With a sigh, Hemingr slid under the covers and lay beside his wife.

"I understand, my love, why you must employ deception to be victorious in our cause," Brunhildr responded. She had slipped out of her gown and wore only a short white linen underdress with a plunging neckline. A ruby hung at the hollow of her throat, and it caught Hemingr's eye. He fingered it and the skin lying beneath.

"Our army is not large enough to defeat either kingdom in their strength and without a passage to the sea, we are lost."

"We could have sought an alliance with one of their kings," Brunhildr mentioned as her hand roamed over his scarred chest and powerful shoulder.

"I tried six years ago," he reminded her. "When Raumsdal invaded Firdafylke. I sent a message to Tortryggr offering our support against the invaders in exchange for rights to one harbor where we could moor our ships, but he turned me down. He said Grimolf and Svithjod had already granted aid asking for nothing in return." His face darkened, and he rolled from his wife to lie on his back, his gaze staring upward. "I have considered for a long while how to gain the port we need, and nothing sounded as sweet as to turn those two against each other. We shall have victory, my love, and I hope they both live through the fighting so I can banish them from what once were their lands."

Brunhildr rolled and straddled him, her golden braids falling across her ample breasts. "We will show them to insult you, a king, their equal. No, they are not your equals. Sagas will be told of Hermingr the Unwashed and how he amassed the largest kingdom in Norvegr to pass on to his sons. You will be remembered as the cunning grandson of Loki who tricked his enemies into defeating each other for him."

"And they will sing about Queen Brunhildr, who was as fierce a fighter as she was a lover." With an amorous grin, she lowered her mouth over his.

CHAPTER 18

Svithjod, four days after Sigrid's return

"You can't be considering traveling so soon!" Gudred protested while Sveina assisted Sigrid in dressing for her journey.

"I am not considering it, Mother—I have already decided. It is only one day's ride to Siegfried's hall, and I will not sit about these rooms another day while he lies at the point of death," Sigrid announced. She laced her right boot as tight as she could without undue pain and stared up at Gudred in dismay. "I do not understand you. First, you try to convince me to marry the man and now you protest my going to visit him when he is in need."

"It is raining, and you are far from recovered yourself," her mother fretted. Staying out of the argument, Sveina shifted behind Sigrid to braid her hair.

The past few days had been slightly awkward for Sigrid as she settled on how she and Sveina would relate to each other when so much between them had reversed. As it turned out, little had changed at all, except for bidding farewell to sexual encounters. They had been friends before, and remained so, only now Sveina seemed to be even more attentive out of gratitude for her freedom. Sigrid enjoyed seeing the glow on her face when she told stories about Finn. The feel of Sveina's fingers gliding through her hair was as pleasurable as ever, perhaps more so. *I did the right thing,* she consoled herself, *only I should have done it sooner.*

"A little rain does not bother me, and time is of the essence. Who knows what plot is in motion? Siegfried is our friend. I must go to him," Sigrid insisted. "Besides, I will ride, not walk the distance, so having an injured leg is of no concern."

Sigrid pushed herself up and took her crutch in hand. Whenever she touched the straight branch with the broad fork on top, she remembered Elyn and wondered how she was doing, if she would truly meet her at the appointed time, and if the other shieldmaiden thought of her. Gudred had affixed a small pillow in the hollow of the staff's divide which made it much more comfortable to lean on. She glanced down at her attire, consisting of brown trousers and a moss-green knotwork-edged tunic, and fastened her studded leather sword belt around her slender waist. Sveina picked up a summer-weight oiled hooded traveling cloak and stood ready to follow when Sigrid moved.

With a hopeful aspect, Gudred made her last ploy. "You could let Sigurd take Odo and you remain in charge here."

With a humorous smile, Sigrid brushed a kiss to her mother's cheek. "Odo needs experience. We will return in a few days' time." With a glance and a nod to Sveina, she leaned on her crutch and struck forth.

Sigurd waited with Rangvoldr and Gunnlief near the open longhouse door while a soft rain fell outside. Girrid handed him loaded saddlebags. "I packed some rations and a change of clothes for your journey."

Falling in beside him, Sigrid inquired, "So you two insist on coming along?"

"My lady, we would never allow harm to befall you or your ornery brother along the road," Rangvoldr replied with a cheerful grin. "Besides, who else will entertain you with stories and songs?"

Sveina handed Sigrid a leather pouch with a shoulder strap. "Here are clean bandages, your healing salve, and the tea you are to drink. Do not even think of neglecting the care of your wound," she charged in a commanding tone.

The men laughed. "Look what you created by granting her freedom," Gunnlief teased. "We can see how she will order her husband about."

"It isn't Sveina's fault," Sigurd excused with a jest. "She learned how to be demanding from my sister." This time, even Gudred joined in the laughter. Sigurd added with a wink, "Do not worry. I will insist she care for her leg, or I'll do it myself."

With an embarrassed smile, Sveina wrapped the cloak around Sigrid's shoulders and fastened it with a silver raven pin. "Thank you, Sveina," Sigrid offered with affection. "Look after Girrid, Odo, and Mother while we are away."

"I will," she promised, and the party of four headed out into the morning rain.

As THEY RODE along the way to Hafrafell, Gunnlief took point, scouting the trail several lengths ahead for potential danger while Rangvoldr guarded the rear, leaving Sigrid and Sigurd side by side in the middle, leading an ox by a rope around his neck. After a while, Sigurd asked in a low voice, "How are you coping?"

"My leg is healing," she replied. "The treatment has kept infections away."

"That is not what I am referring to." He pinned her with an intuitive gaze as their horses clipped along at an energized walk. "Things are different between you and Sveina. I'm glad you granted her freedom; she deserves it. But there is something else."

Sigrid had not wanted to speak of it. She felt embarrassed and guilty, as if she had only used her loyal servant all these years, but she didn't honestly realize... or had she simply not wished to know? She shook her head, unable to look at her brother.

"Sveina loves me," she finally said, "but she doesn't love me in that way. She has only been my companion out of gratitude for being well-treated. Now her heart leaps for a young man she has been seeing." She sighed, and added, "How do I feel? Like I violated her or took advantage or deluded myself. I feel... as if I am so different, I will always be alone. I care for Siegfried the way Sveina cares for me, which is like a dear, respected friend, but I can't marry him or any man."

Sigrid sensed Sigurd's warm smile and turned a curious expression on him.

"It is for the best," he asserted. "It is better to close one door before opening another. You are now free to pursue Elyn's affections."

Her jaw dropped open while her blue eyes rounded, astonished by Sigurd's bold suggestion. "I... I don't know if she is even interested. I hardly know her at all." Sigrid scrambled to find words.

"And yet from the moment you saw her, you cannot stop thinking of her," Sigurd recalled. "You are not the only woman who loves other women, Sigrid, so do not single yourself out in that way. Clearly, something draws you to her."

"And what about you and Birgitta?" Sigrid was eager to turn this path of conversation back on her twin. "You will be seeing her when we arrive and have ample opportunity to keep company with her. What will you do?"

Sigurd straightened in his saddle and lifted his attention to the trees and mountains surrounding them. He took in a deep breath of the fresh air. "I have been thinking a lot since Father was killed. It is time for me to step up, embrace responsibility, take a wife and start a family. It would be of great advantage to Siegfried for me to marry his sister and become part of his family to look after his interests while he is recovering. There could be power seekers who would vie for her hand just to gain a jarldom since his son is not of age to assume his place."

With a snorting laugh, Sigrid replied, "You'd better not tell her that!" Sigurd presented her with a puzzled expression. "A woman does not want to be 'a responsibility' that her man must 'step up' to shoulder. She wants to be the apple of your eye, the object of your passion, to know that she matters to you. Do you understand nothing?"

"So, what should I say? You see how much I admire her."

In a tone of sage wisdom, Sigrid explained. "You may compliment her beauty, but also her mind. Women have them too, you know. Find something she is skilled at to praise, like, I don't know, her weaving or cooking or whatever women do, so that she knows you appreciate more than her body and her womb. Listen to what she has to say and take it as seriously as anything Rangvoldr or Odo would convey—then you will gain her ardent devotion."

"Is that why you are devoted to me?" Sigurd asked. "Because I treat you as an equal?"

"My dear Sigurd, it is more than that." With a tone infused with unfailing love, she affirmed, "You are the other half of me, body and soul, as if we began as one seed and were split apart in our mother's womb. What you think, I think; what you feel, I feel. That is how I knew you were not killed in the battle. Though my eyes could not testify to it, my heart surely could."

"And that is how I knew you lived, dear sister," he concurred. "You have given me wise counsel. I feel an undeniable attraction to Birgitta, but we are also well suited for each other. If she is agreeable and feels the same, I shall ask her to marry me. I know it is not as easy for you, but I must confide something to you that may be of solace."

Sigrid brought her gaze back to Sigurd's. There was very little that went on inside his head she was unaware of.

"I can feel the attraction to Elyn as well. There was a spark about her, fighting on that battlefield, her flame hair swirling with her motion, the look of fearless determination in her eyes. It was more than her presence, which is compelling enough... she felt familiar, like I already knew her, though I had never seen her before that day. Do not be distressed," he instructed. "I do not desire to lie with her—I will reserve that for Birgitta from now on if she says yes—but there is something there. You feel it too, don't you?"

Taking a moment to gather her thoughts, Sigrid answered, "Yes. It is as if Freya tossed an invisible rope around my soul that pulls me toward Elyn. What I do not know is whether she feels the tug as well, and if so, what do we do about it?"

He shrugged. "You could enlist her in your service if she is willing to leave her home."

Sigrid contemplated the suggestion. *Her uncle demeans and abuses her. I don't think she would mind leaving his house, but...* She shook her head. "It will not work for me to hold authority over her like I did Sveina. Then how can I ever know for sure she wishes to be with me for the right reasons? There must be another way. But first, we approach Hafrafell. Let us focus our attention on Siegfried... and his sister," she added in a teasing tone.

BIRGITTA GREETED SIGRID, Sigurd, and their two companions at the entry to the hall they had gathered at only weeks ago to plan their attack. Sigrid suddenly felt angry with herself for not realizing the deception sooner. *Siegfried would not be in this condition, had I paid more attention and deduced what was happening.*

"We are so glad you are here, Jarls Sigurd and Sigrid," she said with relief filling her honey eyes. "Especially you, Sigrid, as we weren't certain you lived. Please, come in. I have prepared a room for you and your men are welcome to stay in our great hall."

"Thank you for your kind hospitality, Birgitta," Sigrid bade and hugged the young woman. "We would have come sooner except for my injury."

Sigurd followed Sigrid's example and greeted Birgitta with an embrace. "I am prepared to do whatever I can for you, Siegfried, and his children. We brought an ox to sacrifice to Eir to blow her healing breath down to him."

"Thank you, Sigurd," she cooed in appreciation. "My spirits have been raised just by your presence."

Sigrid took a moment to glance around the somber hall and noticed a few unfamiliar faces. "Who are those people?" she asked, pointing to a woman with a white apron over her apple-red underdress and a man in a gray robe who sat at the end of a long table.

"She is Estrid the Revivor, our village Grædari, who has been treating my brother's wounds," Birgitta explained, "and the man with her is Trygg the Sightless. He is a Gothi with the ability to see into the other realms. Both are highly esteemed in Svithjod. I will tell him about the ox you brought, and he shall perform the Blót. I can prepare a broth from the blood and bones of the sacrificed animal to help Siegfried regain his strength."

"You are a devoted sister and an asset to your people," Sigurd said to her. "Any man would be fortunate indeed to win your affections." The words no sooner fell from his mouth than Sigurd began to look around, shuffle his feet, as timid as a lamb. Sigrid decided to rescue him.

"Where is your mother?" she asked.

"She is with Siegfried. Come; I'll take you both to see him."

Birgitta led the twins into Siegfried's private chamber where his step-mother Frida sat at the side of the jarl's bed, mopping his face with a wet cloth. A young man around Odo's age, a tall lad void of facial hair, and two younger girls occupied the room with them. The younger boy blew softly on a wooden flute while the oldest girl drew a bow across the horsehair strings of a Tagelharpa. They stopped playing and gave their attention to the visitors.

"Mother, Jarls Sigurd and Sigrid are here to lift Siegfried's spirits," Birgitta said.

"Of course," Frida responded as rose from her seat. Still attractive for an older woman, her hair of variegated hues of brown and gray was wound into one long braid which she wore over her shoulder tied with a yellow ribbon. "Here," she offered it to Sigrid, when her gaze fell on her crutch. "Children, let us go out now for a while." She touched a hand to Sigrid's arm, a weary expression playing over her face. "He might wake and talk for a few minutes, but he has a fever and may only sleep. I am trying to keep him cool."

Sigrid nodded, and the family stepped out, leaving the twins with Siegfried. Sigrid sat, picked up the wet cloth from the bowl, and continued to soothe his face while Sigurd stood vigil.

"Siegfried, can you hear me? It is I, your ally Sigurd, and I brought my stubborn sister along. We are here, my friend."

The wounded jarl stirred, and his lids fluttered open. His lips parted, but he was too weak to speak. "Greetings, Siegfried Strongarm, and do not forget your name. I survived when many had given up hope." Sigrid spoke to him in an encouraging tone as she smiled at him. "So will you."

"Yes, he will." Sigrid glanced over her shoulder at the unfamiliar voice to spy Estrid, who had slipped in unnoticed. With her stood the blind religious leader.

"Let us gather in the great hall for the sacrifice," Trygg instructed. "We sacrificed a goat and a lamb the day they brought him home and he has fought to remain with us. I believe we shall see even more encouraging signs today because Olaf's children have arrived bearing gifts and their good wishes."

"Everyone recognizes how luck follows the two of you wherever you go," Estrid added. "All are encouraged because you have come."

Sigrid smiled and nodded, then turned her attention back to the patient. "Siegfried," she said, comforting his hot skin with the rag once more. "This fever will break overnight and tomorrow you will be more yourself. Believe it my friend, because I do not lie. You must get better, for we have important matters to discuss with you. Your sister shall prepare a broth for you from the blood and bones of the sacrificed ox to make you strong again. Rest now, and we'll talk tomorrow." She placed a kiss on his forehead and pushed up from the chair.

Sigurd took the seat briefly to place his hand on the older jarl's shoulder. "I saw you in the fray, my friend. You were skillful, mighty, and brave. You fought like a legendary hero of old. Your father and grandfather look down from Valhalla and say, 'One day you will join us to feast and fight and stand with Odin on the great and terrible day of Ragnarök, but not today. It is not your time,' they say, and I agree. Rest now, Siegfried. We are here with you."

The twins followed the healer and the Gothi into the great hall for the blood-letting ceremony.

CHAPTER 19

"*M*y heart leaps to see you feeling better today." Sigrid beamed at an awake, alert Siegfried, who sat up propped on pillows in his bed.

"Eir has heard our prayers," Sigurd added. He pulled a stool beside the chair Sigrid occupied while Frida and Birgitta sat on Siegfried's other side. A servant departed carrying a chamber pot, leaving the five alone in his room.

"I believe Sigrid is responsible for my fever breaking," he confessed. "Your life-energy fills every space with a radiant presence. You know I spoke with Olaf about you in the past. Does your answer remain the same?"

"It does, dear friend." She smiled and took his hand. He gave it a squeeze and nodded. Sigrid poked Sigurd in the ribs with her elbow. When he turned to her with a nervous expression, she flashed him an exasperated look and shook her head, rolling her eyes.

"What?" Siegfried's face perked in curiosity. Across the way, Birgitta beamed, a shy blush rising in her cheeks, and her mother hugged her with a joyful countenance.

Sigurd cleared his throat and sat up straighter. "I have asked your sister to be my wife, and she has agreed," he stated boldly. "As the head of her household, we ask for your blessing."

A bright smile crossed Siegfried's pale face. "I give it with all my heart." He glanced over to Birgitta's joyful visage and nodded. "You have chosen well. Now I must recover fully, so I may stand with you for the ceremony. Let us hold it here so I may open the hall to all for a grand feast. Then I suppose you will take her with you to Gnóttdalr," he added, shifting his gaze back to Sigurd.

"Yes, I shall, but you are welcome to visit anytime."

Sigrid was proud of Sigurd for summoning the courage to ask Birgitta and to speak with confidence to Siegfried. She thought of how she had been bold enough to kiss Elyn at the cave's mouth but immediately retracted the sentiment with a denial. It had meant something to her, but she had feared rejection and covered up her vulnerability with bravado. *How will she react when we meet again?* The reflection reminded her of the other reason they had come.

"Siegfried, there is an important development we need to discuss with you regarding the recent trouble and the events leading up to the battle in which you received your wounds," she addressed in a solemn tone. She glanced at the women who sat on his other side. "You may wish your family to hear, but not those who serve in your hall, for there are hidden enemies among us."

She could see by his expression she had gained his full attention.

Sigurd laid a hand on Siegfried's shoulder and bent in close to his ear. "Hear my sister's report as if it came from Odin's ravens," he charged. "I believe what she says is true." He straightened, then stood, rounded the bed, and moved behind Birgitta, resting strong, tender hands on her shoulders.

The recovering jarl shifted his regard to Sigrid. "Tell me."

When she had finished relaying the entire story, suspicions, and evidentiary logic, Siegfried leaned back into a pillow against the wall and sighed. "There are several possibilities to consider," he mused aloud.

Frida had become tense with fear and Sigurd held Birgitta tighter, her head against his abdomen and his arms around her shoulders, as he stood steadfast behind her.

"Jarl Arkyn refused to participate in our joint assault on Firdafylke, so I must wonder why," Siegfried posed. "He claimed it was because his fylke lies farthest south and is in no danger from their raids, but could he be waiting for us to spend our warriors in vain, so only he retains a full army and then uses it against King Grimolf?"

"It is an angle to consider," Sigurd admitted. "But I would prefer to believe a foreign power is behind the plot than that we have a traitor in our midst."

"It would have to be a kingdom nearby," Siegfried considered. "We know Raumsdal tried to take over Firdafylke a few years ago. They could have conceived this scheme to weaken their forces enough that this time they could succeed."

"Hördaland lies to our south," Sigrid observed thoughtfully. "They are a strong and populous land. King Vikar has won many victories and placed his sons in charge of lesser kingdoms in the interior."

"And there is Gudbrandsdalir, home of the mountain men to the east," Sigurd asserted. "Since Vikar or his sons rule everything directly south and southeast of us, that leaves Gudbrandsdalir and Raumsdal as our only other close neighbors."

"So," Siegfried concluded. "It is one of them or we have enemies within our own kingdom."

"Or an alliance of like-minded opportunists from both Svithjod and Firdafylke," Sigrid added. "Either way, we must be vigilant, and we should bring these suspicions to King Grimolf."

"I agree," Siegfried affirmed. "But I am in no shape to accompany you to Sochabrot."

"We know." Sigrid took his hand once more, giving it an encouraging squeeze. "And I fear we cannot wait. Oh, Siegfried, I am overjoyed at your breakthrough, but you require many weeks of rest and recovery before you are strong enough to fight again, which I know you will be in time."

Birgitta tilted her head up to Sigurd. "I could come with you to speak to the king."

Sigurd bent and kissed the top of her head. "Your brother needs you still, and we don't know what danger we may face."

"Besides," her mother inserted on a cheerful note. "We have a wedding to plan." She took Birgitta's hand and smiled at her.

"It is settled," Siegfried decreed.

Sigrid fixed her attention on Frida. "Do not allow any but your most trusted servants to tend Siegfried. Better yet, do not admit any but the two of you and his children to enter this room until we return. If you did not prepare his food and wine personally, have a thrall taste it before bringing it to him. I don't trust anybody, and neither should you. Someone murdered Olaf, so what is to stop them from coming after Siegfried, especially while he is vulnerable?"

Fear swept into their visages at Sigrid's suggestions, but both mother and daughter nodded. "We will take special care," Frida vowed.

"You aren't leaving yet, are you?" Siegfried's usually stalwart expression took on the aspect of a lost puppy.

Sigurd laughed. "Not until tomorrow. You owe me a game of Hnefatafl since you beat me the last time we played. I will set up the board while you rest and come back with it afterwhile."

Siegfried relaxed and nodded in satisfaction. "Be sweet to my little sister," he instructed, as his weary eyes closed.

All but Frida quietly vacated the room while she remained to watch over his rest.

AFTER DINNER, when Sigurd had wandered off with Birgitta clinging to his arm in jubilant adoration, Sigrid lingered in the great hall with Rangvoldr and Gunnlief. Several servants, a dozen fighting men, and the musicians also filled the common space. A skald approached and bowed to Sigrid.

"Jarl Sigrid the Valiant," he addressed in nervous glee as if he had been whisked up to Ásgarðr and was speaking with one of the gods.

She laughed with a twinkle in her blue eyes. "That's me. What is your name?" She sipped more ale from her horn and leaned on Rangvoldr as she considered him in amusement.

"I am Thorgeir, teller of tales, singer of songs," he announced. "Several of my fellow skalds repeat the story of how you wrestled a tremendous brown bear and killed him with only a dagger, but I wish to tell it better than any of the rest. Could you please relate the tale as it really happened?"

Sigrid felt very relaxed as she had drunk several horns of the barley ale. "The beast attacked our party and I killed it," she said. "What more is there to tell?"

"No, no, silly Sigrid!" Rangvoldr corrected. "Let me relate the story, for I was there to witness it."

The storyteller took the bench across from them eagerly, waiting to lap up the narrative as if it was a bowl of cream. Bright-eyed, he responded, "Please, mighty warrior—share what occurred."

"See there?" Rangvoldr grinned at Sigrid, and she shifted away from his shoulder to sit upright. "He called me 'mighty warrior.' You should take my advances more seriously."

Sigrid laughed, shook her head, and gestured for him to proceed.

"We were returning from a hunting trip into the mountains when we were hit by an early snowstorm and had to stop and wait it out," Rangvoldr relayed in his best storytelling voice. "There were only four of us—Sigrid, Sigurd, Leiknir, and me, and we took refuge under an outcropping. Amazingly, Sigrid claimed to have followed a wolf to find the shelter, but none of the rest of us ever saw it. Anyway, we fell asleep waiting for the storm to subside and awoke to discover ourselves surrounded by a wall of snow, so we started digging our way out. Soon the pale light of an overcast sky offered hope, and we pushed out of the snowbank only to spy a tremendous grizzled brown bear snuffling through the new snow. Immediately, we retreated under the outcrop to collect our weapons, but the beast charged.

"Sigrid earned her nickname that day as she blocked the bear's path and roared a challenge to him. It replied by stretching up on its hind legs, far taller than she stood, and thundered back. Without hesitation, Sigrid drew her boot-knife and buried it into the giant creature's belly. It howled and slashed at her with its massive claws, but she hugged its body and jabbed her blade repeatedly into its side until it fell on top of her in the snow. By then, we had returned with spears and swords and pulled her from beneath the beast's weight. To this day, I have never witnessed such a display of fearlessness."

Thorgeir absorbed every word with wonder and clapped his hands at the end, turning an admiring gaze on Sigrid. "It that what happened, truly?"

She shrugged with a consenting nod. "I have claw scars on my back to prove it," she confessed, "and that bear skin is my favorite winter cover."

"She saved our lives," Rangvoldr affirmed. "Sigurd declared from that day forward she would be known as Sigrid the Valiant, though to watch her in battle alone is enough to convince anyone the name applies."

"Sigurd, Rangvoldr, and Gunnlief are every bit as courageous as I," she told the skald. "As is our friend, Jarl Siegfried Strongarm. I wish to hear a song about him."

. . .

A FEW DRINKS and an hour later, Gunnlief and Thorgeir left to visit some others who lounged about Siegfried's great hall. Sigrid, being tired from the journey and relaxed from her ale, bid Rangvoldr a good night.

"Don't leave," he begged, taking hold of her wrist as she stood. "Or better yet, invite me to come with you. There is no one else you know here, and Brenn would be angry if you slept with Gunnlief. There is no need for you to be alone and unattended."

"It is kind of you to offer, Rangvoldr," she replied with a humorous smile. "But you realize that is never going to happen. You are like a brother to me, and you know I prefer women."

She gave her arm a shake, but he held firm. "That is because you have not yet allowed me to show you the pleasures I can evoke from a woman," he insisted with a seductive look in his dusky eyes. "And I am not your brother."

"You have had too much ale," she laughed. "Go find a willing wench. I am sure a man of your prowess shall have no problem convincing one."

"I am not drunk!" Rangvoldr threw her wrist out of his grip with an angry pout. "One day you will change your mind," he predicted.

When goats take to the skies on goose wings, she thought, but said, "Get some sleep. Tomorrow, we go to see the king."

Sigrid gathered her crutch under her arm and ambled to the guest quarters Siegfried's household had prepared. It had two small beds—Sigurd's noticeably empty as he was off courting Birgitta. The space was adjacent to Siegfried's private chamber, separated by silk drapes, not a wooden wall. *This is good,* she considered. *It will be easy for me to know if he has a restful sleep.* She changed into a knee-length linen sleeping tunic and replaced the dressing on her leg so Sveina would not be cross with her, pleased to see the healing process was going well. Then she nestled down and fell fast asleep.

SOMETHING WOKE Sigrid in the middle of the night, though as she drew her awareness into focus, she wasn't clear what. She blinked as her vision adjusted to the pale light. Sigurd slept soundly across from her, but an eerie sensation pecked at her intuitive senses and the hairs on the back of her neck prickled. Hearing a creek in the floorboards coming from Siegfried's room, fear for him shot into her chest. *Mayhap he has fallen and is trying to get up,* she thought.

Springing out of bed, a voice in Sigrid's imagination suggested she move quietly, and she acted on it, creeping past her brother's bed to the silk divider hanging between their rooms. The pressure on her ankle shot pain through her leg, but Sigrid's anxiety blocked it out. She slid a hand into the folds and pulled them back far enough to peek through. A man stood beside the jarl's bed holding a pillow, which struck her as very out of place. Frida or Birgitta maybe, but some man in the middle of the night with a cushion for him? No, that was wrong.

The instant he bent to push the pillow over Siegfried's face, she bolted through, grabbed the interloper by the arm, spun him around, and slammed her fist into his jaw. The startled man dropped the pad and swung back.

The fistfight which ensued woke Sigurd, Frida, Birgitta, and Siegfried's children, who were piled on pallets on his floor. When things settled down, Sigrid would realize she and Sigurd had been given the children's beds for their stay.

One of the women lit a lamp, one screamed, and the sturdy arms of her brother caught the would-be assassin in a bear hug from behind. Sigrid hooked another punch to the man's cheek, snapping his head around, before she registered Sigurd's voice shouting, "That's enough! I've got him."

By then, the entire house had been rousted as two of Siegfried's guards appeared in his doorway with swords drawn. Siegfried pushed up in bed and stared incredulously at the wiggling, bruised traitor Sigurd gripped in his powerful arms.

"Hallbrandr!" he exclaimed in dismay. "Why? What have I done to prompt you to steal into my bedchamber to murder me in my sleep like a coward?"

The villain's scowl deepened behind the light-brown scruff covering his chin as he squirmed some more, but his jaw remained clamped shut. Sigurd tightened his hold and Hallbrandr's flexing ceased, a flicker of fear lighting in his pensive eyes.

"Answer me!" Siegfried demanded.

"How dare you!" Frida, who had been making her way forward, slapped the prisoner across his face with the ire of a mother protecting her young.

Sigrid flicked her gaze to Siegfried. "He has been paid off by the conspirators," she stated with more certainty than speculation, "like they employed someone to murder Olaf."

Realization flashed in Siegfried's expression, and he snapped his regard to Hallbrandr. "Tell me who paid you and you will be spared from torture," he promised. "I will even keep you until the Thing meets on the new moon where you may plead your case before the people."

She guessed he might jump at his jarl's generous offer, but after a moment, Hallbrandr shook his head and lowered his chin. "I acted alone," he said. "My family has been overlooked. My cousin is a great warrior, yet you have not promoted him. I thought since you were already dying, if I hurried things along, he could compete for your title. Stigandr would be an excellent jarl but know the truth—I acted on my own accord. My cousin is unaware I am here and would disown me if he knew. He is a man of honor, while I... am an opportunist."

"Take him away," Siegfried commanded with a motion to his warriors. "Lock him in the guardhouse while I determine how we shall get the truth from him."

Sigurd released his hold as Siegfried relaxed against the wall at the head of his bed. "Sigrid, I owe you my life," he gushed in gratitude. "How did you know?"

"The gods must have awoken me," she replied in humility, "because it is not your time to die. Do you believe his story?"

Siegfried shook a weary, sorrowful head. "I believe yours. Perhaps he will talk. If not..." He let the words hang, for everyone present understood the course of action which lay before him, the difference, Sigrid was certain, being her friend would take no pleasure in it.

Once everybody had settled back to sleep for the remainder of the night, Sigrid remained awake on her bed digesting what had just occurred. Her world had changed the day her father was murdered, only now she realized hers was not the only world under attack. All Svithjod, possibly all Norvegr had become unsafe, and it was only getting worse. It was critical she and Sigurd discover who had undermined the kingdom and stop them.

Elyn, be careful. She closed her eyes and breathed the thought out into the air of Miðgarðr. *Trust none but your own soul. Firdafylke needs you; Svithjod needs you... I need you, so be safe.*

CHAPTER 20

Two days after Elyn's return

*E*lyn sat beside Geir, spooning broth into his mouth. "That's good, swallow it down," she coaxed. She stopped feeding him long enough to lay a new cold cloth on his forehead as he shivered under a pile of blankets. "You must get well so you can return to teasing me and attempting to keep me in my place."

Njord had placed all his longhouse's resources at her disposal to aid in her cousin's recovery. Two other injured warriors shared this corner of the hall, each tended by a loved one. The healer had been in to check on his progress and declared the wound free of sepsis, but he was still in extreme pain and running a fever.

She was torn between refusing to leave his side and eager to take her vital concerns to King Tortryggr.

"Are you planning to turn in your spear and shield for a bag of healer's herbs?" he managed weakly in a stab at humor. She spooned in more broth.

"I believe I am needed in both capacities at the moment."

Hearing footsteps behind her, Elyn peered over her shoulder and straightened with expectancy as she saw Njord approach. "How is our patient?" he inquired.

"Halfdan said his infection is not spreading and the wound should

141

heal," she answered with optimism. "My lord, have you given more thought to warning the king?"

Njord took a deep breath and released it slowly. "I am making inquiries. The Thing meets in two weeks' time, and it would be the best venue to present our suspicions."

Elyn's heart sank like an anchor dropped with no rope attached. That would be too late. She must meet with Sigrid before then and could not show up, having made no effort. "But my lord, we should speak to King Tortryggr privately. Everyone will attend the Thing, including any enemy agents who work to undermine our kingdom. What if another raid occurs before then? We cannot afford to wait," she insisted.

A sparkling smile lit his face. "Please, Elyn," he bade in a charming tone. "Call me Njord." With a hand resting on her shoulder, he bent and brushed his lips to her cheek. "I have posted scouts and assigned warriors to patrol our farmlands. If raiders attack, we will be ready to expel them before they can cause harm. You have a sharp mind, but you understand nothing of politics. We cannot simply show up on the king's doorstep and demand to be heard. Do not worry, my dear. Take care of Geir, for he needs your attention now."

She felt as though she was drowning in disappointment and every piece of floating wood she grabbed dissolved in her hands. She couldn't just let this go. *There must be something more I can do. Maybe if I go to see the king. Ingvar will help. But Njord is correct in saying Geir needs me, too.*

"Yes, Njord." The words fell from her mouth without conviction even as her brain spun alternative plans.

"Will you join me for dinner tonight?" he asked.

"I will," Elyn answered, thinking she could strike out early in the morning.

Njord beamed at her and then at Geir. "You will be on your feet in no time, Geir," he cheered. "Elyn has a way about her, and I am certain you will thrive under her care." The jarl gave her shoulder a pat. "I look forward to your company this evening," he cooed before breezing away.

Geir grimaced. "You are planning something," he muttered. "Going to leave me and do something foolish."

"Shhh." Elyn placed a finger to his lips. "If anyone asks, tell them Ingvar and I went fishing because I needed some fresh air. You can manage one day without me."

He smirked and rolled his eyes. "I am in no shape to argue with you."

Elyn poured another bit of broth into his mouth. "Rest now," she instructed. "I have to find Ingvar."

EARLY THE NEXT MORNING, while everyone else still slept, Elyn and Ingvar borrowed two horses from Njord's stable and struck out for Gimelfjord, the town where the king made his residence. Fog shifted across the dirt road which led over hill and dale through a forest, and it was not long until a soft rain began to fall.

"Tell me again why we are disobeying Jarl Njord," Ingvar elicited as their horses plodded along. He pulled the hood of his traveling cloak over his blond hair against the raindrops.

"Because time is of the essence." Elyn carried two axes in her belt and a dagger in her boot, but she wished she had a sword. *Sigrid is going to give me a sword,* she reminded herself. *But that is not why I am doing this.* "Jarl Njord believes us, but he doesn't understand. There could be a spy in the king's court," she suggested. "One of the other jarls could be behind the conspiracy. We can't just announce to the whole kingdom we suspect a plot. I will persuade King Tortryggr to send an envoy to King Grimolf, asking for a face-to-face meeting. We must convince the kings to connect, like when Sigrid and I were thrust together in the cave. As long as they each believe lies about the other, we cannot have peace. Besides, my cousin and your best friend lies gravely wounded while the one responsible laughs at our stupidity."

He sighed. "I understand your concerns, but I don't think they will allow two mere warriors anywhere near the king."

Elyn considered Ingvar, the haphazard way he slouched in the saddle, his gaze staring blankly ahead. "Something else bothers you," she observed. "We are both worried about Geir, but I believe he'll make a full recovery, even without my constant care."

Her companion shook his head. "I agree, but... it is clear Jarl Njord is smitten with you," he begrudged. "He will ask you to marry him, and where will that leave me?"

"You must be mistaken," she replied, hoping such to be the case because she remained uncertain what she would say or do if he should ask. "I have done nothing to encourage him."

"That's exactly why," Ingvar explained. "Jarl Njord admires a strong woman, not one who throws herself at him."

"I suppose you are right. Let us not put the stern before the bow," she chirped with as much cheer as she could muster. "No proposals have been made yet—from either of you," she added, pinning him with a sarcastic expression and a snicker. "Of course, Uncle Unnulf rejected your unspoken proposal when I brought it up to him. What is more to the point is the question of do I wish to marry at all?"

Ingvar turned a puzzled aspect to her. "What do you mean?"

She shrugged, trying to keep the topic light, but Elyn desperately craved input from someone who's opinion mattered to her. "There are far more women to go around than men, so it is reasonable not all would take a husband. Take Jarl Sigrid, for example. She would not go wanting for lack of marriage requests, yet she remains unwed."

"I understand you admire Jarl Sigrid," he admitted. "You aspire to become a legendary shieldmaiden as she is, but would you refuse a husband to emulate her?" Elyn said nothing for fear of appearing foolish, but it did not take long for her good friend to press her further.

"What exactly happened between the two of you in the cave?" Ingvar demanded.

"I told you," she replied, but she could not make herself sound convincing when her emotions and imagination ran amuck.

"You told everyone the parts you wished to convey," he corrected. "Now it is only me. Were the two of you intimate?"

"Not in the way you suggest." Elyn was quick to reply. "But I felt an intense attraction, as did she. There is something between us, Ingvar. I am just uncertain yet what it is. Please do not tell anyone. It is a fool's dream to think of becoming attached to one such as Jarl Sigrid the Valiant." She turned her attention back to the road and let out a long sigh. "Mayhap I am a fool."

"If there is one thing you are not, dear Elyn, it is a fool," Ingvar pronounced. "In truth, I can bear witness you are not a typical female. Oh, there are other shieldmaidens, and they are just as energetic in bed as most women, if not more so. But you only consent when drink has lowered your resolve to abstain. I've had to stay close to you to make certain other men did not take advantage, and I have until now supposed it is because of the rough treatment you endured at the hands of the raiders when you were younger, but there may be more to it."

"I thank you, Ingvar, for watching out for me and for your tender touch." Elyn meant it. Most unmarried youths and adults alike were free with their affections, but she had always been reserved. "I thought that was the reason too… until I was forced into proximity with Sigrid. Oh, I have admired many an attractive woman, but never suspected I would say or do anything about it. Now…"

Ingvar shrugged. "You feel how you feel," he said. "It is a relief to discover it is not me you lack passion for, but men in general. I consider myself privileged to know you in that way. So, if you end up together with Jarl Sigrid, how would it work?"

Elyn snorted a laugh at him. "One matter at a time, please. Let us pick up our pace lest we dally the day away."

With a smile, Ingvar nodded, and they kicked their horses to a canter.

THE SUN HAD COME OUT, turning the moisture to hot humidity by the time they reached King Tortryggr's grand longhouse in Gimelfjord. Elyn and Ingvar were permitted through the gates, where they secured their horses and walked toward the king's great hall. Elyn marveled at the huge carving of Odin dominating the common space of Tortryggr's compound. Warriors trained in the yard, their swords and shields clinking with effort. A merchant's wagon passed them on its way to exit the main gate. Chickens and goats wandered about freely. Unlike Njord's fortress, this one lay in the center of the town, with craftsmen's shops, houses, mills, markets, and farms all creating a buffer between attackers and the king. A short path led from a gate in the palisade to a pier where several ships were moored ready for action at a moment's notice.

"I am Elyn of Kaldrlogr, and this is Ingvar," she announced to men standing guard with spears outside the longhouse door. Their attire declared them to be warriors. "We have an important matter to bring before the king."

The sentinel to her right was as big as a bear and just as burly. He narrowed his brows at her, forming a deep frown of disapproval. The one on her left was not so massive, but taller and broader than either she or Ingvar, with tawny hair and a ruddy complexion. "The king is not accepting visitors today," he allowed in disinterest.

"You don't understand," she replied in an insistent tone. "I have news of the most vital urgency which the king must hear."

The hulk to her right retorted in a deep, gruff voice, "*You* do not understand, shieldmaiden. King Tortryggr is otherwise occupied today."

The two stood as staunch and unyielding as mountains, frustrating Elyn to no end. She feared this may happen, but she had to try. Ingvar exchanged a glance with her and shrugged. But she was not ready to give up so easily.

"Then I wish to make an appointment for tomorrow," she declared, raising her chin with the bearing of a woman of substance. "This matter cannot wait for the Thing to meet. I must inform him at the king's earliest convenience."

"We don't take appointments," the first guard stated. "We just keep people out."

Finally, Ingvar spoke up on her behalf. "Who do we speak with then?"

The door opened and an odd man swathed in fine silks stepped out. Elyn recognized him from the meeting of jarls Njord had held a couple weeks ago. He pinned her with a curious gaze over his hawkish nose. "May I be of assistance?" he asked in the thick foreign accent of Gudbrandsdalir.

Elyn hesitated. She recalled King Tortryggr had sent him to Kaldrlogr as his representative, so he must trust the man, but she did not know him from a random tree in the forest. She sensed an unease just standing near him she could not explain. But he was offering to help.

"Krum, is it?" she asked. "You visited Jarl Njord in Kaldrlogr not long ago."

"Yes." The middle-aged ambassador flashed her an appeasing smile and motioned away from the longhouse entry. "I recall seeing you—quite unforgettable, a shieldmaiden so striking in her beauty. Not many of those have I run across. But alas, I did not catch your name."

He walked with them to a grouping of benches under the branches of a large tree, where they took seats out of the sun. "Elyn," she answered. "And this is my friend, Ingvar."

"Did Jarl Njord send you?"

"Not exactly," she hedged. "But he is informed of the situation."

Krum cocked his head in concerned curiosity. "Situation? There's a situation?"

"Yes, about the recent raids and confrontation with Svithjod." She wasn't about to divulge sensitive information to this stranger, but everyone was aware there had been raids and a battle.

"Ah, I see." An assured smile replaced anxiety in his features. "My dear, there is nothing more to worry about. I have just returned from Bjornhellir where I spoke with King Hemingr about this very problem. In fact, I was leaving my meeting with King Tortryggr when I ran into you just now. King Hemingr is most eager to build a robust ally in Firdafylke and has vowed to throw the full support of his army behind your cause. Should the greedy treacherous usurpers from the south cross the border again, he has made an oath to lead our mountain warriors to join you and your fellows in defense of this great kingdom."

Distrust squirmed in Elyn's gut like a writhing serpent. She met his placid beam with a deep frown. "Why would King Hemingr commit his soldiers to our cause? What profit has he to gain?"

Krum nodded, practiced smile in place. "Because Firdafylke has become an important trading partner to my homeland, while Svithjod's merchants tried to cheat us. Did you know King Grimolf demanded twice the value of his grain and fish for our ore and furs? King Hemingr was so insulted, it took all his advisors to hold back his wrath. Mountaineers are a proud lot and do not tolerate being cheated. On the other hand, your fair and honest King Tortryggr sealed a trade deal which benefits both our kingdoms. That is why King Hemingr is so agreeable to lend his aid. I appreciate the reason for your visit, but let me set your mind at ease. They next time you are called upon to face the barbarians of Svithjod, it will be at the side of a strong ally. There shall be no more stalemates, only total victory."

He rested a bony hand on her shoulder before engaging in more flattery. "I see Jarl Njord has at his disposal a shieldmaiden who is both fearless and cunning, one who seeks to understand the motivation behind the battle rather than remain content to merely slay her foes. I deem the two of you will make a formidable team."

"Ambassador," she addressed strategically. "Has Jarl Njord spoken to you of his intentions? If so, you know more than I do about his plans."

Raising innocent palms, he fudged. "I know he seeks a new wife. I only meant he would be wise to consider you. After all, you possess every attractive asset."

The way his inspection sized her up as if she was a commodity he may wish to buy or sell ignited an intense dislike for the man and she worried her personal distain for him might influence her search for the truth.

Elyn pushed to her feet and took Ingvar's arm as he stood beside her. "Thank you for explaining things to me, Emissary Krum. I feel much more at ease. Ingvar, at least our travel today was not wasted. We must be getting back," she said, excusing them. "My cousin fights for his life. I bid you a good day."

Once they returned to their horses, far from Krum's earshot, Ingvar asked, "Are we leaving now? I was sure you had some other scheme in mind to get to King Tortryggr."

She shook her head and glanced around the compound once more. "If we snuck in without permission, he would have us removed without listening to a word. Besides, I gained quite a lot of information from Krum."

Ingvar swung into his saddle, a relieved look on his face. "I feel much better knowing Gudbrandsdalir will join our side in this dispute. We will surely win with such an advantage."

From her seat atop her mount, Elyn fixed him with an impenetrable expression. "Don't you understand? King Hemingr designed everything. He is our true enemy."

CHAPTER 21

Twilight engulfed Njord's fortress overlooking Kaldrlogr when Elyn and Ingvar rode through the gates. Unnulf stood like a gnarled oak, his arms crossed over his chest, exuding his displeasure. *This will not be pleasant,* Elyn surmised.

"Where have you been?" he demanded, though in a quieter scold than she expected. "You should have been here nursing Geir back to health instead of gallivanting around with that boy."

"Ingvar is not a boy," she protested as she swung down from her horse. She handed her reins to her trusted companion, and he rode on, sparing her uncle a polite nod in greeting.

"Well, that was the last outing you will spend alone in his company."

Elyn approached Unnulf warily. "Why? Are you so displeased you are sending me away?"

A gleam shone in his eyes which belied the glower on his face. Unnulf opened his arms to her and relaxed his tense shoulders. "No, child." She stiffened under his embrace, worried it was a trap, and at any moment, she would feel the pain of his retribution. "I have wonderful tidings to share with you."

Despair dampened her core when she absorbed his words. There were few things Unnulf would consider wonderful tidings, fewer yet that would sound delightful to her ears.

"Jarl Njord and I have negotiated a marriage contract. You shall be the wife of a jarl, the most important woman in Kaldrlogr," he pronounced with pleasure oozing from his spirit. "You will wield tremendous influence and can implement all the plans you used to dream of by the fire on long winter nights. I am so proud to be your kinsman!"

Elyn's entire body, mind, and soul went numb at the proclamation. There had been a time it would have thrilled her heart to hear such words of praise which had never passed his lips, but not this, not now. She tried to stop her limbs from trembling, as she was sure he would perceive it as he hugged her. After an enthusiastic pat on the back, he loosened his hold, and pushed her to arm's length smiling at her ashen face and wide, glassy green eyes.

"I know! Isn't it amazing?" he declared. "But you shouldn't be so shocked. After all, there were indications."

He agreed to a marriage without consulting me? He pledged a contract with the jarl when I wasn't even present? His actions should have come as no surprise. It was the story of her life since her parents were killed. But this was beyond any of his prior assumptions. And Jarl Njord? Did he not wish to hear the words, "Yes, I will marry you," from her own lips?

"When?" She could barely form the word, but it was the most imperative. Mayhap she was stuck in a marriage she had not desired, but the timing was crucial for the security of the entire kingdom. She *must* meet Sigrid, as agreed.

"Nine days from now, on Freya's day next." He gleamed with pleasure as he explained the date. "Nine is an important number, as you know. There are nine worlds held up by the sacred tree, Yggdrasil. Odin hung from that tree for nine nights before he could glean the secret knowledge from the waters below. And most symbolically, the god Freyr waited nine days before marrying Gerd. It is wonderful luck to plan the wedding on a Freya's day, and," Unnulf added triumphantly, "you will be the jarl's wife when we all attend the Thing in Gimelfjord. Everyone will congratulate you and present you with gifts."

And you'll be standing right there, no doubt, to bask in every bit of glory you can wiggle out of it, uncle of the bride.

Then it struck Elyn as a blow from the incomparable Mjolnir—next Freya's day was exactly two weeks since the pact she had sworn with Sigrid, the day she was honor bound to meet her on the mountainside.

"Why do you stand there dumb like one who cannot speak?" Unnulf's frown returned. "You should dance for joy at this blessing! You are but a common, poor woman whose only skill is to wield a weapon well enough to keep herself alive, and here you have been handed the grandest of honors. Speak!"

"I, I," she stammered as the gravity of the trap's vise closed in on her tighter and tighter. "I am overwhelmed, Uncle Unnulf. Give me a moment to process."

He grabbed her wrist with a jerk, causing her to flash a terrified gaze to him. "You will not ruin this for me, for your aunt and cousins," he growled in a low rumble. "There is no backing out, no running off with that fool, Ingvar; do you hear me? It is likely you will outlive Njord by many years. Once you are a widow, you may do as you please. Now, come home with me so I can lock you in the house overnight."

"No!" Elyn yanked her wrist free of his grasp and she registered the surprise in his expression at both her strength and audacity. "I must stay in the hall with Geir. I was gone all day, and it is my duty to him. You may ask one of Njord's guards to monitor me if you wish, but I am staying with my cousin. Do not forget your place, uncle," she warned in a hiss. "Once I become the jarl's wife, the tables will be turned, so you should think about how you treat me from now on."

Pleased with the alarm she triggered in his beady eyes, Elyn brushed past him and into the great hall. The action took all her strength, and she rushed to the seat beside where Geir lay under his blankets. Her head swirled with dizziness and her stomach felt as though she would retch. With her elbows on her knees, she lowered her head into her hands, trying to steady herself.

"You are back." Geir did not even open his lids, yet he knew her presence. "Did you talk to the king?"

"They wouldn't let us," she uttered. "How are you feeling?"

"The gods have been fighting over me," he said, followed by a weak cough. "None of them wants me, so they have decided to let me lie here a bit longer."

"Never mind about the gods," she issued in a shaky voice. "I want you, so you must stay."

"What is wrong?" This time his eyes opened, and Geir reached a hand up to catch hold of hers.

"Your father and Jarl Njord planned my marriage to him while I was absent." The words still sounded unfathomable to her ears. "I was not even consulted."

"You are a freewoman," he stated, rubbing his thumb along the back of her wrist. "You have the right to decline."

"But what reason would I give? And Uncle Unnulf would beat me, disown me, or worse. If I run away from this, I could never return." The reality of the statement struck her with the finality of a fatal arrow.

"Why don't you want to marry Jarl Njord?" he asked in honest concern.

"They set it for the day I am to meet Jarl Sigrid by the cave," she whispered. "And I learned important information today she must hear."

Geir's lids fluttered shut, and he sighed. "Talk to him. He may be willing to postpone the ceremony." In a moment, he was sleeping soundly.

Weak and trembling with fear and indecision, Elyn claimed a spot on the bench such that she lay head-to-head with Geir. She didn't bother to remove her boots, supposing her hands would tremble too much to unlace them, but she could not sleep. What she did next would frame her future for the rest of her life.

Elyn took several calming breaths to steady her nerves and began making mental lists. *Njord is not a bad man. He respects me and I would gain authority to do as Uncle Unnulf suggested, take actions to improve life for our citizens. And I would be out from under his thumb. Ha, did you see the look on his face when I said he had better start treating me right?* She paused a moment to take glee in the thought before continuing.

But I swore an oath to Sigrid I would meet her on that day by the cave, and I cannot break my oath. It is vital she know about King Hemingr's plans. And I need to find out if he promised the same to Svithjod. Saving both our kingdoms is of far greater importance than securing an advantageous marriage.

Fluffing a flat pillow, Elyn rolled onto her side. She was still too warm to need a cover and pushed her blanket off. *But what if I forsake my uncle and jarl, run off to meet Sigrid and she does not show? Can I be certain she will keep her word? And even if she has the intention to, something could come up for her which would be a conflict as it has for me.*

That line of thinking unsettled Elyn. She understood far more about her feelings for Sigrid than about how the famed jarl regarded her. *She kissed me,* Elyn argued with herself. *But she said it didn't mean anything. She is a jarl, like Njord, who says and does as she pleases. What makes me think she feels anything toward me? I could be but a playing piece in her strategy game. She needs me for information, nothing else.*

Elyn flopped onto her back once more, her fingers rubbing along the torn edge of her gambeson. If she was on a battleground, she would know what to do, but this was untested soil. The thoughts in her own mind assailed her as so many adversaries on a field of combat, only she did not know the right moves, the weapons and tactics she should use to come to the correct conclusion. *If I go to Sigrid in nine days, I can never come back.*

Amid the whirl of confusion, one idea emerged in triumph. *I will return to the mystic forest where I spoke to the Völva! Surely in that place permeated by Seiðr, I will find clarity.* Having a plan allowed Elyn to drift into sleep.

THE NEXT MORNING, Elyn struck out alone up the mountain trail she and her friends had followed not long ago. The air was brisk and fresh, and her spirits soared in anticipation of receiving some revelation in the sacred place. Her cheerful countenance also derived from Geir's improvement that morn as his fever was gone, and he awoke hungry.

She climbed over the ridge with a spring in her step, down into the high valley, over the stream, to the same grassy spot surrounded by foliage where the seer's unique tree-stool remained. Elyn ventured to reach out her hand and glide it over the living throne, but she dared not sit on it. Instead, she made a small circle around the holy ground, taking deep breaths. She could smell the scents of pine, clover, fresh water, and wildflowers. Lifting her face to the sky, streams of light trickled down through the leaves to warm her skin. She could even feel the prickle of Seiðr dance along her arms, raising goosebumps.

Peace descended over Elyn as she reveled in the serenity surrounding her. *Mayhap I could become a Völva.* The thought was fleeting, as she had no magic powers or connection to the gods. Her uncle was right. The only thing she could do well was fight, a realization which struck her with an added worry. *I can't be a jarl's wife—I don't know how! I've never been responsible for others or valuable property. And his children. They are delightful, but what do I know of children? I would be a terrible jarl's wife. Oh, Njord, whatever were you thinking?*

Elyn settled on a fallen log, its bark spotted with moss and rot, its earthy scent grounding her back into her idyllic haven. *Let me recall the words the Völva Astrid imparted to me.* She said them aloud to be certain she remembered the cryptic message correctly.

"Futures are tricky, Elyn the Shieldmaiden," she began. "Some things are destined, yet we can step into or shy away from our fortunes. Our choices matter." Elyn paused, considering the action she was about to decide could seal her fate for better or worse. She wished she could consult the seer again but hadn't time to try to find her.

"You will join a jarl of exceeding importance. Well," Elyn concluded, "Jarl Njord is important. So does it mean I should forget Sigrid and marry him? But she didn't stop there. Astrid said I will be remembered for my mighty deeds and known as Elyn the Peacemaker. How can a jarl's wife fulfill that part of the prophecy? Will Njord allow me to march with the warriors and fight in the shield wall? Will my actions on the field of honor be what turns the tide for peace?"

She peered around at her tranquil setting, the farthest from war she had ever experienced. Nearby a spotted woodpecker hammered away at a tree pursuing its meal while two yellow and black orioles sang to each other in the treetops, reminding her of Sigrid's rönd. "But she also said nothing is as it seems and I should follow my own voice, not what others want me to do. Be true to your own self and you shall fulfill your destiny, she said. Seek and you will find. Well, Astrid," Elyn called out as her gaze poured over the majesty of nature surrounding her. "I am seeking."

Waiting, she heard nothing. Elyn sighed and rose, walking over to the spot to view the fabulous waterfall. It plunged down the rock wall into a sparkling pool of blue. "It never runs out of water," she marveled. Gazing higher, she beheld mountain peaks still clothed in white mantles even as summer neared its apex. "Snowmelt," she supposed aloud. She decided she should come here in the depths of winter to see if the falls would be frozen over or flowing.

Elyn strolled back to the clearing, listening to the bird whistles, the sound of leaves rustling in the breeze, and the steady fall of the water. There had been a waterfall in the cave she shared with Sigrid, constantly spilling its life-giving liquid into the clear pool, and after a while she had grown so accustomed to the gurgle, she no had longer noticed it.

"Astrid, I wish you were here," she sighed. "Odin, where do I find wisdom? What must I sacrifice? You value honor and look with scorn on oath breakers. I pledged to Sigrid to meet her on that day, but Uncle Unnulf made a vow I would wed Njord. I cannot keep both oaths."

Gazing at the sky, Elyn's soul pleaded for a sign, some direction as to which action to take. "To remain guarantees me security, but there are no promises if I go. It is a total risk into the unknown." She plopped to the earth and sat cross-legged on the tender grass. "Nothing is as it seems. Why can't seers speak plainly?" She let out a frustrated sigh.

A sudden thought popped into Elyn's mind which she had not considered before. *What if Njord is not the jarl Astrid spoke of? What if the jarl I am destined to be joined with is Sigrid?*

CHAPTER 22

Sochabrot, Six days after Sigrid's return

Sigrid and Sigurd left their weapons at the door to Grimolf's great hall as two guards escorted them inside. Their footsteps echoed around the spacious chamber, which stood relatively empty at midmorning. Rangvoldr and Gunnlief had remained in the yard watching over the horses and trading stories with the king's warriors. This time there were no other jarls, no feast or musicians, only a few servants, a handful of guards, and Hroald, the short, hairy fellow from Gudbrandsdalir. Sigrid's first thought was, *what is he doing here?*

A handsome middle-aged woman in fine silk garments approached them. "I am Gyda, King Grimolf's house supervisor," she said with a pleasant smile. "You must be Jarls Sigurd and Sigrid from Gnóttdalr."

"Yes," Sigurd replied. "We are very grateful to King Grimolf for agreeing to speak with us on such short notice."

"He regards you both with esteem," she confessed, with a slight bow of her head. "Won't you join Emissary Hroald at the lord's table?" She extended her arm in invitation, and the twins walked with her. "I will let King Grimolf know you have arrived."

"Thank you, Gyda." Sigrid no longer leaned on her crutch but gripped Sigurd's arm as she limped to the seats Gyda offered them.

"It is so good to see you both again!" Hroald beamed at them from behind his black, braided beard and opened his palms to them. "Do you have concerns to bring to Grimolf?"

Sigrid eyed him warily. *I think you are being a bit too familiar with our king,* she thought in disapproval. "Our concerns will be made to King Grimolf, Hroald, and do not involve you. However, our blacksmiths have enjoyed working with the ore you traded for our grain and cheese."

He inclined his head to her with a satisfied grin.

Sigrid was relieved to see the king enter the hall. Sigurd started to stand, but Grimolf waved him down. "No need to get up," he declared, and took a seat at the end of the table. "This is an informal meeting between friends. May I offer you refreshment?"

"Thank you for your hospitality, King Grimolf," Sigurd praised, "but we do not want you to go to any trouble. Our issue will not take too much of your time, as we realize you have many important matters to attend to."

"As you wish." Grimolf considered them with cool ice-blue eyes. He was clean with combed hair and beard but arrived in a padded tunic and thick leather vest presenting as a warrior rather than a lord. "First, tell me of Jarl Siegfried. Will he live?"

Sigrid noted honest compassion in his expression, which set her at ease. "His strength is returning slowly but surely, my lord. He wanted to come with us, but we insisted he rest."

The king nodded with a smile. "Now, twins of Olaf, what troubles you?"

Sigurd nodded to Sigrid, and she addressed the king with assured authority in her tone, explaining why she believed Firdafylke never raided their farms and someone else was playing them like game pieces. "And that is not all," she added. "While we were visiting Jarl Siegfried, someone tried to kill him as he slept in his bed. The man is being interrogated but thus far has given up no information."

Worry wrinkled Grimolf's brow, and he stroked his beard in contemplation. "You believe these are connected?"

"Along with our father's murder," Sigurd added. "Someone is working to destabilize our kingdom, or Firdafylke's, or both."

"If true, that would be very unsettling indeed." Grimolf turned to Hroald. "What have you heard? You are just back from a trading run."

"As I told you yesterday, King Hemingr has pledged his support to you and Svithjod should there be any further fighting. He is disgusted with the reports he has received from Firdafylke's jarls fighting over who will succeed poor King Tortryggr. My counterpart in Gimelfjord said Tortryggr's son had to negotiate their trading contract because his father did not have enough wits about him to know what was going on. It is a very sad situation."

Sigrid shook her head. "Elyn said King Tortryggr is in excellent health and suffers no mental weakness at all."

Hroald lifted his chin in defense of his report. "And this shieldmaiden has direct access to the king, or is she merely repeating what she had been told?"

Doubt clouded Sigrid's face. Elyn did not enjoy keeping company with her king and had admitted she would probably not be allowed to see him. "She is a companion of Jarl Njord, and he has direct access to King Tortryggr. But even so, what would the situation there have to do with Olaf being murdered, and an attempt having been made on Siegfried's life?"

"I agree with Sigrid," her brother stated. "There is more going on here than we have been led to believe. If someone is trying to whittle down our forces, they surely have their eye on your throne, regardless of Tortryggr."

Inspiration seemed to light in Hroald's eyes, and he lifted a finger, then dropped his hand and his chin. "What is it, Hroald?" Grimolf asked.

The dwarfish man shook his head. "It, it's nothing. I shouldn't say. I could be wrong."

"If you know something which could help sort this out, say so," the king demanded.

"It's just..." he fudged and ran a hand down his face. "I noticed that within less than two moons, three of your jarls have died or been incapacitated: Olaf, then Brynjar, in the battle where Siegfried was wounded, and now someone has tried to kill him. We know it was not Sigurd and Sigrid, but neither Arkyn nor Trygve took part in the fight with Firdafylke—Arkyn did not even send any of his warriors. I don't have any evidence or witnesses, but it just seems odd to me. If we are looking for someone who wishes a shift in power, I would look at those two." Hroald shrugged and leaned his elbows heavily on the table.

"There could still be a foreign foe at work," Sigrid pointed out. "I suppose Arkyn could disguise some of his fighters in the red and black of Firdafylke and raid farms near our northern border, but his fylke lies at the southernmost edge. He would have logistics to manage. My lord, has he given you a reason to doubt his loyalty?"

"It would be easy enough to send raiders by ship and land the boats far enough away no one saw them," Grimolf reasoned. "He has brought no complaint to me, no grievance. You all understand how power is structured. Each jarl is free to administer his or her domain as they see fit within the guidelines of our common law. We share culture and belief in the gods, and all freemen receive a vote. The Thing will meet soon where differences will be settled. The king's only claim on the jarls is the right to call up their military service in time of crisis. I do not dictate to you all as if I was a high lord with all power. Each man is his own master, the master of his household and his slaves. The primary function of the king is to unite all the fylkes and make certain wealth is distributed fairly so none starve or freeze when winter falls. I have only called for taxes on a few occasions to build new ships or to repair major damages from a calamity. Are you suggesting one of my jarls would kill off his peers and hundreds of Svithjod warriors to usurp my position?"

"I have traveled extensively in my trade dealings, King Grimolf," Hroald testified. "To the south and east lie kingdoms in which the ruler amasses great wealth and control to himself with the power of life and death over his people."

"That is not our way," Sigurd stated with an offended frown. "But land produces wealth and with wealth comes the power. You say King Hemingr has promised to send warriors to our aid, but how do we know they will not come to attack us and take our land, our rivers, fjords, and seacoast?"

"Such an idea is ridiculous!" Hroald declared. "We do not have your numbers or your strength. Our army could never defeat yours, but we could turn the tide of battle in your favor against Firdafylke, or Arkyn's army. Sigurd, you are right—land is power. What if Arkyn and Trygve have formed an alliance to take all the land in Svithjod and divide it between them? I am not saying they have, but if you are throwing about suspicions anyway..."

"We can speculate all day and get nowhere," Sigrid declared. "King Grimolf, I would respectfully suggest you send an invitation to King Tortryggr to meet him face-to-face and talk. Tell him we did not raid his farms. Find out for certain if he is in sound health or not. Look him in the eye and you will know what is true and what is false."

Grimolf suddenly appeared old, weighed down by worry and distrust. "What if that is what my enemies wish me to do? I cannot leave the capital and march to the border in case a traitorous jarl captures it while I am away. Besides, why should I reach out to him first? I have confidence in you and Sigurd to lead our army to victory. I do not need to hold out a flag of truce. If King Tortryggr is innocent of crimes against us, let him request a parley."

Sigrid inwardly groaned in frustration. They had made some headway, but not achieved their prime objective. "So, you are saying if King Tortryggr solicits a meeting under a banner of negotiation, you are willing to talk with him?"

The king worked his jaw with furrowed brows for a moment, then nodded. "If the king of Firdafylke requests a meeting and is in robust enough health to ride to the border, I will speak with him."

"My lord, is that wise?" Hroald asked with the sound of deep concern. "What about protecting your capital?"

Grimolf turned a calculating gaze onto the stocky ambassador. "You have stated King Hemingr vowed to support me with the aid of his warriors, correct?"

"Indeed. See, you wear the ring he sent as a token of his oath," he motioned.

With a raised brow, Grimolf replied, "Then what have I to worry about?" Returning his attention to Sigrid, he affirmed, "You have my answer."

Sigurd and Sigrid rose from their seats and bowed in respect to their king. "Thank you, my lord," Sigurd said. "Please rest assured, we are loyal jarls who keep our oaths of fealty."

"As I do mine." Grimolf stood giving them a nod. "When we discover who murdered your father, my own hand will perform his execution."

THE TWINS MET their friends outside the king's longhouse. "How did it go?" Rangvoldr asked.

"A mixed bag," Sigurd replied. Rangvoldr gave him a pat on the back in consolation.

"He listened, and he is now suspicious as well," Sigrid reported. "But he is not convinced. I don't understand why he has a foreigner as an advisor. That Hroald had a statement to counter everything I presented, and he is throwing suspicion on our fellow jarls."

Rangvoldr shrugged. "Maybe he's right. I mean, we don't know who killed Olaf or why."

"Hey, at least he listened," Gunnlief added in cheer. "And he will be on his guard, which makes the trip worthwhile."

"It does," Sigurd concurred. "Now let's see if we can make it to Siegfried's without having to stop and sleep outside on the ground where my sister may have to fight another bear." He winked at her with a grin.

"You just want to rush back to exchange kisses with Birgitta," she smirked.

"Indeed, I do!"

The thought of kisses conjured Elyn's image in Sigrid's mind as she relived the memory of touching her lips to the beautiful shieldmaiden. A tingle shot through her senses which drew color to her cheeks. She experienced a moment of blissful anticipation of what may lie in their future until interrupted by an unsettling question. *Do I accept her ideas and suspicions because they are reasonable and sound, or because I desire to share pleasures with her?*

With a laugh at Sigurd's enthusiasm, the quartet mounted their horses and trotted out the gate toward Hafrafell.

CHAPTER 23

Gnóttdalr, ten days after Sigrid's return from the cave

Sigrid and Sigurd had remained with Siegfried for two days and nights after their meeting with Grimolf before returning to their longhouse. The would-be assassin had concocted one story after another but confessed no believable name who hired or coerced him to act. Before he could succumb to torture, Hallbrandr hung himself in his prison cell. Rangvoldr had sustained his attempts to charm Sigrid whenever Sigurd was away with his fiancée, and she continued to dash his hopes. This game had gone on for years, Sigrid recalled, and she never took it seriously.

All conceded it would be best to delay a marriage ceremony until the situation with Firdafylke had been resolved and Siegfried had fully recovered from his wounds, and Sigrid agreed with the plan. She liked Birgitta. The young woman was bright, kind, and good-humored, but direct enough to keep her brother in line if he was to suggest something foolish. *She is a good match for him,* she thought, and conjured images of how handsome and intelligent their children would be. *He must be sure to have a quiver full since I will not be producing any heirs.* The idea did not trouble Sigrid, as she was assured Sigurd's seed would carry their father's legacy into the next generations with the same qualities she may have reproduced. After all, she and her brother were almost identical... almost.

The four entered their gates devoid of fanfare as people went about their productive summer work. Farmers had waved to them when they passed the laborers cutting hay with long handled scythes in the field. Sigrid had calculated the immense stores of fodder they would require to keep all the livestock fed through the coming winter and was aware without the added efforts of thralls, they could not produce enough. She thought of her sweet Sveina, and while understanding it was impossible to free all the slaves, considered holding a special feast in their honor as a thank you at the end of harvest time.

Once I have visited with mother and assured her all is well, I must ride out to each farm to inspect the grain and see if the farmers require anything, especially those affected by the raids. Poor Bragi and Runa. Her heart sunk at the thought of the young newlyweds, the sorrow stiffening her resolve.

"There you are!" Proclaimed Odo, who was out in the yard sparring with one of the more experienced warriors. He dropped his shield, sheathed his sword, and jogged up to meet them. "It is about time you returned!"

Sigurd slid agilely from his mount to hug his little brother. "What? Tired of responsibility after less than a week?"

"Me?" he laughed. "Nay." Then he added in a whisper. "Mother is driving me crazy."

Sigrid dismounted and tested her right leg, glad it was gaining strength. While not battle ready yet, she felt she could move around without assistance. Two lanky Cu dogs loped over to her, bright-eyed with grins on their drooly faces. They rubbed against her thighs and raised their heads under the palms of her hands.

"I missed you too, Warg and Jotun. Were you good boys while I was away?" Their panting smiles and lolling tongues assured her they had been.

"Sigrid, Sigurd!" Girrid raced out the door to join Odo in the greetings. "What news have you? How is Jarl Siegfried? Did King Grimolf accept your theories?"

"Patience," Sigrid laughed as she hugged her sister. "Siegfried's health is improving, but first, where is Mother? Your brother has exciting news."

Gudred appeared in the doorway with Sveina by her side. An enthusiastic glow overtook the younger woman, and she ran to embrace Sigrid, filling her heart with bittersweet delight. "I am so glad you are back safe and sound, and without your crutch," Sveina gushed.

But her mother propped hands to her hips and stared suspiciously at the twins. "What is this news? Anything worth my while to hear?"

Sigurd took on a proud swagger as he crossed the yard to the longhouse entrance. "Only that Birgitta and I are to be wed, as soon as we clear up the current situation."

She threw her arms around his neck and cried for joy. "Oh, Sigurd, you have made me so happy!" Girrid bounced over and joined them in a three-way hug.

"My leg is gaining strength," Sigrid replied to Sveina. She wrapped an arm about the slender blonde's waist and strolled to the garden with her, away from the others allowing Sigurd his moment to be the center of attention. Sveina beamed at her with admiration.

"That gladdens my heart, and such cheerful tidings for Sigurd!"

Sigrid motioned to a stone bench under a shade tree near the garden which occupied one end of the longhouse yard. "You have been doing an excellent job with these vegetables," she praised as she surveyed the leafy greens and tender shoots. "Not a weed in sight."

They sat together under the boughs of the red maple. The two wire-haired hounds stretched out on the grass at her feet, content to be near their mistress.

"Thank you." Sveina bowed her head and folded her hands in her lap.

"And how is charming Finn treating you?"

She caught Sigrid's gaze with delight. "Very well, thank you. He was so happy to learn of my new status and squeezed in two trips to the market this week especially so he could see me. He bought me drinks at the alehouse, and we danced and listened to the skald's songs. But I have been keeping an eye out for anyone suspicious," she promised. "I haven't forgotten. I'm just not certain what to look for."

"I can tell you one thing for sure," Sigrid said. She reached over and took Sveina's hands in hers, holding her regard in sincerity. "There is a man, an envoy of sorts, from Gudbrandsdalir named Hroald. He is easy to recognize by his odd appearance and foreign accent. Watch for a short, stocky man with hair as black as Rangvoldr's only much more of it, who rather resembles a large dwarf. He has gained King Grimolf's ear and I do not trust him. I believe he is up to no good, though I do not hold specific evidence, nor have I pieced together the whole contorted scheme. I only know he is someone to watch. If you see him in the village, or anywhere on our land, inform me immediately. He may have a spy in our very midst, and I must discover the traitor's identity."

"I promise, Sigrid," Sveina vowed gravely. "And I have been watching out. One night while you were away, Odo invited many friends and warriors to feast on a reindeer he killed, and I stayed in the shadows listening to everyone's conversations. Mostly they told stories and boasted of their exploits, so I didn't learn anything relevant."

"It's all right, Sveina. You did well. You did exactly what I asked, and I am proud of you."

Sveina glanced down with a blush at Sigrid's hands on hers. Suddenly aware of what had for years been habit, Sigrid pulled them back. Sveina did not belong to her anymore; what was worse, she never had. "I worked with Lady Gudred on her weaving and attended your sister as she dressed for Odo's feast. She wanted me to braid her hair the way I do yours. I think she has her eye on some of the young men, but no doubt your mother will have something to say about it."

Sigrid laughed. "No doubt, indeed!" As she studied her former thrall, Sigrid began to settle her emotions. This was a good thing. Sigurd was right—she should close one door before opening another, and she very much wanted to open a door between herself and Elyn... if she didn't end up as Njord's wife, that is.

"What's wrong?" Sveina's gentle fingers brushed her arm. Sigrid hadn't noticed her expression fall at the thought of Elyn and Njord, but her faithful servant had.

With a shake of her head, Sigrid replied, "Nothing. I'm going to be meeting someone in a few days to exchange information we have learned to try and determine who is behind all the trouble and put a stop to it once and for all. Then Sigurd and Birgitta will have a fabulous marriage feast and you and Finn can figure out what you want to do."

"And you?" Sveina's voice steeped with affectionate compassion. "This person you are meeting, is it the other shieldmaiden I have heard Sigurd tease you about?"

Sigrid nodded. She didn't know what to say about Elyn. *Does she think of me each day as I do her? Do I fill her dreams as she does mine? Or is she like every other woman who thrills my heart and will turn out to marry some man?* She stared out at the garden, not seeing the little white blooms on the early peas or the honeybees hovering around them.

"You have good instincts about people," Sveina commented. "I am certain she will meet you as agreed and will have collected valuable information to share. Together, you will devise a plan. Sigrid, no warrior, no beast, no circumstance, no force of nature has ever beaten you, and the current crisis is no exception. I have faith in you. If this shieldmaiden has even half as much sense as I possess, she will too."

"Thank you, Sveina," she said, blinking back a tear threatening her unwavering composure. "You have been my loyal companion through it all. It is hard to say if I would have become legendary without you."

"Of course you would have!" Sveina let out a laugh. "You are Sigrid the Valiant! I didn't do anything. I never taught you, helped you train, or accompanied you on adventures. All I did was stay around the longhouse performing domestic chores."

"You're wrong, Sveina." Sigrid battled with the sentiment desiring to flood her soul. "You believed in me. You always were the first to run and greet me, to make me feel as if I had returned triumphant even if I was empty handed. You tended to my wounds, kept my spirits high during long dark winters, and... by Thor's hammer, you gave yourself to me night after night when... when you didn't even..."

"Shhh," Sveina cooed, and hugged Sigrid close. "I told you why. Sometimes I would wish I was like you. I would say, 'why can't I feel what she does? Why am I attracted to men instead?' I wanted to please you. Now, do not cry. I am not worth it."

"You are," she stated, and swiped at an escaped tear. "That is why I had to free you from your servitude. You deserve to pursue your own path, your happiness, after all the happiness you have given me. Now, neither of us shall cry. And as for Elyn, the shieldmaiden... we shall see what the three fates have in store for us."

THE NEXT DAY while Sigrid rode about the countryside visiting farms and inspecting crops, she passed the sacred burial grounds of her ancestors and was compelled to stop. She tied off her horse to a branch and walked into the field distinguished by a dozen or more grassy mounds outlined with large stones in the shapes of ships. One hill along the outer edge remained brown with fresh dirt and only a scattering of grasses and some clumps of clover. A harrier circled overhead, its outstretched wings gliding on the updrafts as its keen eyes searched for a mouse or other prey.

Sigrid's leg had improved, and she only had a slight limp as she strode to the site where her father had been buried. The whole village along with Siegfried's family and a few others from across Svithjod had come to pay Olaf homage. Fifty men had labored an entire day to dig a great hole where Olaf was laid to rest inside his personal ship, with the mast taken down. He had been dressed in his best armor, an expensive chainmail shirt with shoulder plates, and his silver patterned broe helmet. Accompanying him to the afterlife were his finest sword, raven shield, axes, and spears, his swiftest steed, and a draft horse with a cart filled with his special belongings. An older thrall who had served Olaf for many years volunteered to travel with him over Bifröst, the rainbow bridge into Ásgarðr, or to whichever of the worlds had been reserved for her father.

Sitting on a broad, flat-topped monolith, Sigrid speculated where Olaf's spirit resided and if she would see him again. He had not died in battle, yet it was a violent death. No weapon was found in his hand, though no sooner than Sigurd discovered his body lying on his chamber floor, he had thrust his own sword into their father's fingers. *Do you feast in Valhalla with Odin's bravest warriors?* she wondered in mournful doubt. *Mayhap Freya chose you to dwell with her in Folkvangr. Our people also believe in the holy mountain, Helgafjell, which is for good folks whose professions never allowed them to distinguish themselves in combat. I know you are not in Niflheim, the cold, dark, misty world beneath the roots of the tree of life ruled over by Hel.*

"Father." Sigrid spoke aloud so mayhap he could hear her. "A part of you, your Hamingja, is still with me. I can sense your protective spirit, perceive your words of counsel in my mind, and feel your presence with each breath I take. That part of you is ever present in each of your children and will be passed down through generations, aspiring your line to greatness. I realize that."

She lifted her gaze to the azure sky above, searching the clouds for a sign. "But your body is gone from my sight. No longer can your strong arms embrace me. But where is your Hugr, the essence of who you were in this world? I know you live on somewhere in one of the other worlds. I wish you could hear my voice. I wish I could look into your wise eyes once more."

This time, she did not try to stop the flow of tears, as there was none but a scampering squirrel around to witness them. "You taught me to fight, to be brave and true. You showed me how to administer our lands so we would remain prosperous. Under your guidance, I learned strategy and discernment, but now… Sigurd and I were not ready to step into your shoes. The kingdom is in peril, and somehow, we have to find the right solution and implement it. That's not even mentioning my personal dilemma. I barely know Elyn, and yet I must trust her if we are to sort out this plot and uncover the cowardly assassin who murdered you, who took you away from me."

Sigrid brushed at her tears and passed her foggy gaze around the still and quiet of the graveyard. She spotted where her grandfather lay and the runes on stones marking other jarls who came before them. There was a separate place where commoners were laid to rest, those who could not afford to be buried with longboats and treasures. Studying the shapes of the stones, Sigrid could picture her ancestors' ships sailing at sea, cutting through massive waves, saltwater splashing on their faces. An eternity of never-ending adventures, feasting with the gods, fighting, dying, and rising again each morning held powerful sway over the imagination. There were many things they knew about the afterlife, but vast amounts of details mortals were not privy to.

Cocking her head, Sigrid said, "I believe once we have crossed over, we can visit our loved ones, even if they go to a different land. Like a seer can pierce the veil between worlds, our Hugr can travel from place to place. How would Valhalla be a reward if it separated a warrior for eternity from those he or she loves? Father, I intend to be with you again one day. I feel your love for me deep in my core, but someday I shall see your face once more. I will spar with you on the seashore, and you will see how strong I have become. We can dine with my grandparents and visit their fathers and mothers. It will be a glorious day—but not yet. There is much for me to do. I wish you could meet Elyn. I would like for her to have known you. Is she The One, Father? Can you view my destiny from your vantage point? Whatever lies ahead, fill me with the courage I require to follow it through. It is my truest desire to make you proud."

CHAPTER 24

Kaldrlogr, twelve days after Elyn's return from the cave

"*R*aise your cups to Elyn, the beautiful shieldmaiden who has captured my imagination," Njord called before all present in the hall.

"Skol!" they cheered. Njord's family and friends gathered around him while his warriors and their women occupied other tables in the comfort of his longhouse. Elyn was terrified.

She drank with the others while he beamed at her and his innocent children smiled and talked about how happy they were to have a new mother. "I like she is a skilled fighter, proven in battle, and can help me become a great hero," Bjorn chanted.

"I like she is pretty and will brush my hair each night and tell us stories," Yrsa said with a shy grin.

"I am glad to have a daughter again." Aslaug smiled at Elyn from across the table where she sat between the children. "Do not worry. I will teach you everything you need to know about being a jarl's wife."

Elyn was ninety percent sure she was going to run away tomorrow to meet Sigrid, but she had been afraid to say anything to Njord for fear of what her uncle would do. She simply could not break her oath to Sigrid, even if the famed shieldmaiden did not share the same spark in her heart. Many lives were at stake, and she had given her word. Odin saw and heard all. He would know, and besides, it was her uncle who made the pledge with Njord, not her.

But neither did she want to let her family and friends down by simply running away. How embarrassing it would be for Njord to stand with all the merrymakers gathered and his bride just not show up. Dread dug deep in her soul, pulling up the roots of her emotions as she pondered what to say or do. It would take her a full day to walk to the agreed upon spot, so she would need to leave tomorrow to be waiting for Sigrid on Freya's day. She would have to pack her belongings without her uncle seeing her. What would she tell Aunt Liv? She had already spoken with Geir and Ingvar and sworn them to secrecy.

"My dear, you have hardly touched your food," Njord said with concern. Elyn's stomach was far too tied up in knots to allow her to eat anything.

"Don't pressure her, Njord," Aslaug soothed. "She is probably nervous about the ceremony."

Elyn granted her a weak nod, then glanced around the hall. Her aunt and uncle sat at the other end of the table with Frigga. This was the best time to make a move.

"My lord," she said, looking up at Njord. "Lady Aslaug is correct about my nerves. I feel I must excuse myself, but I will return soon."

"Whatever you need, dear." His smile was genuine. He may not be in love with her, but he did like her, and she respected him. *I don't want to hurt him. How will I ever accomplish this?*

Elyn struck out for the yard house and watched to see if she spotted anyone about. Convinced the coast was clear, she made a mad dash for her uncle's cottage. Once in the door, she dug a large traveling sack out of a wooden trunk and filled it with her most important items. She folded her best woolen blanket and stuffed it to the bottom. Thinking she would need to cook, she took the old iron pot her aunt seldom used, a big ladle, a wooden bowl, a small spoon, and her drinking horn and packed them. Next, she considered her clothes. She was wearing her finest dress, so she put in her two pairs of trousers, two tunics, her gambeson and boots, and her hooded cloak. Uncertain how long she would be living on her own off the land, she collected a miniature wooden box with some sewing tools and thread for mending or making new garments.

A quick glance around reminded her of ribbons for her hair and a brush, so in they went. Her pouch of herbs and bandages in case she sustained an injury was good to have, and ah—her sharpening stone. All her weapons, belt, and shield were at the longhouse in her storage cubby, so this was probably all. Wait! Spotting the silver raven cloak pin which had been her mother's, Elyn grabbed it up and slid it into her bag, then pulled the string tight. She hoisted the pack onto her shoulder and crept out of the house. The summer sun still lit the village. *If anyone asks, I can tell them I am gathering things to move into Jarl Njord's longhouse,* she decided.

Once back at Njord's compound, she hid her sack in a haystack in the stable and returned to the great hall with her heart racing in her chest.

"Feeling better?" Njord asked as she took her seat. Elyn nodded.

"You have been uncharacteristically quiet," he noted with concern. "All is well, Elyn. Geir is up walking now and will soon be at full strength. I promised I would raise your concerns about Svithjod and the inconsistencies regarding the raids at the Thing next week. Please tell me what troubles you."

He laid his hand over hers and she entwined her fingers with his. "May we speak privately after everyone has gone home?" Her eyes must have been misty with apprehension, for he gave her hand a squeeze.

"Certainly, my dear. Now, will you try to eat something?"

Elyn knew she would need the strength and had already enlisted Ingvar to sneak some small loaves and salted herring out for her to take with her. To console Njord, she nibbled a block of cheese.

THE PROBLEM WITH WINTER, besides blizzards, was it was always dark; the problem with summer was it was never dark. With dinner, dancing, and storytelling over, Njord's children tucked into bed, and Elyn's family gone home, he took her hand for a stroll outside, away from the smell of smoke and whale oil, into the cool of the evening, but because it was still light out, Elyn felt they lacked privacy.

"Will you show me the new stallion you have added to your stables?" she asked.

"I would be happy to."

To Elyn's relief, no one else was in the barn. The drowsy horses perked up when they entered, probably hopeful of getting a treat. They strolled past several stalls. "Here he is." Njord stopped before a spirited solid black stud, who whinnied and shook his head at them. He pawed the ground impatiently, clearly perturbed by being locked in a stall.

"He is grand," Elyn praised, and he was, all muscled and full of spirit, with intuitive onyx eyes and a sassy swish of his tail. He reminded her of Sigrid.

"When I breed him to our mares, we will have the finest stable in all Firdafylke." Njord smiled at the horse and stroked his neck. The animal nodded his head up and down before retreating to the back of his box.

Elyn began to shake. She had never been so afraid of anything in her entire eighteen summers.

"Are you cold?" he asked in concern. Njord whipped off his silk mantle and draped it around her shoulders.

"No, my lord, but thank you."

"There, there," he soothed, caressing her cheek with an ungloved hand. The jarl leaned in and kissed her, tenderly at first. She responded as she always did—in the way she deemed she was expected to. Njord deepened the kiss, parting her lips with his tongue, and she could sense his rising desire. Nothing. No fire, no thrill like she had experienced at Sigrid's touch. She knew in an instant she had made the right choice.

Elyn pulled back, raising her fingers to stroke Njord's face, and peered at him with a despairing look. "I was just going to run away," she confessed. "But it would have been dishonorable, and I am not a coward."

Confusion flashed across his features. "What do you mean, run away?"

Elyn leaned against the stallion's stall wall and crossed her arms over her chest, hugging herself in assurance. "I esteem you most highly, Jarl Njord. You are a fair and decent man, a good father, and a brilliant tactician, but I cannot marry you."

"What do you mean?" His voice rang with alarm, and he passed a searing gaze over her. "We have been engaged for over a week. Announcements have gone out. My children are excited to add you to our family."

"I know," she agonized, balling her hands into fists, which she pounded against her thighs. "And that's why I couldn't just leave without telling you. I couldn't allow you to be humiliated. Now you have time to send out a retraction."

"Why were you going to run away?"

"Njord." She addressed him familiarly with regret permeating her tone. "My uncle made arrangements with you without consulting me first. He proclaimed to me all was done and sealed when I returned from my outing with Ingvar."

The jarl swallowed his pain, took her elbow, and pinned her gaze. "You love him, don't you, that young warrior?"

In exasperation, Elyn shook her head. "No, I mean I do love him, but not as a husband. He is my best friend, but not the reason."

"Then is the thought of being my wife so repulsive to you would leave me the day before our wedding?"

"No, no!" Elyn strained for the right words to say, but they kept eluding her. Her shoulders tensed and she began to pace in a short pattern while he stood dumbfounded. "I don't know how to explain it. I made an oath to meet Jarl Sigrid on Freya's day, a day and a half from now, so we could compare our findings and devise a plan to spare both our kingdoms from further violence. I gave my word, Njord. I must be there."

"But what do you have to report to her that is so valuable?" he protested. "I'm certain she has gained far more information than you."

"I know King Hemingr of Gudbrandsdalir is behind the raids," she blurted out. "His man Krum, who has flattered King Tortryggr with gifts and gained his ear, is an enemy working to undermine us and ensure we keep fighting with Svithjod until neither of us can field a viable army. King Hemingr sent word to King Tortryggr promising the support of his warriors in our fight against our neighbors, but he plans to use them to wipe us out."

The jarl stared at her with an unbelieving aspect. "How can you know these things?"

"Because Ingvar and I did not go fishing," she confessed. "We went to Gimelfjord."

"And you spoke with the king?"

"No," she groaned. "But Krum fed us enough lies which when combined with what Sigrid and I already had ascertained, I could easily deduce their plan. Njord, I have to go meet with Sigrid. If you lock me up, I will escape. You will have to kill me to keep me here. I mean no disrespect, my lord. In truth, it is my desire to save your fylke from being stolen from you and protect you and your family in the process. So you see why I was going to run away, to ensure no one stopped me from fulfilling my oath, only... you have been so kind to me, ever since my parents were killed. Your wife Hilda was my mentor and I owe her so much. I simply couldn't leave you to be humiliated. I never wished to hurt you."

Njord's temper calmed as he seemed to grasp the gravity of the situation. He exhaled a long sigh and nodded. "Then let us postpone the ceremony. You were right to be offended. Unnulf and I should never have made arrangements without your input. To be fair, I never asked you if you wished to be my wife. I was prideful and assumed you would, but I intend to remedy my mistake."

Straightening, Njord took Elyn's hands in his. He raised one to his lips then lowered it. With humility and unease reading in his expression, he asked, "Elyn, will you marry me? I see so much of my Hilda in you, but I realize you are your own person, not her come back to me. You are intelligent and lovely to behold, fierce and bold in combat, but amiable and peace-loving off the battlefield. I believe we could enjoy many adventures together before I grow too old. I can provide you with comfort and security for all your days, even after I pass to the next life. What is your answer?"

Elyn smiled, stood on her toes, and kissed both his cheeks. "That was the grandest proposal any woman could dream of." Steadier than moments ago, her hands no longer shook, and her stomach had calmed. "But I do not believe I am destined to be your wife. How do I explain it?" Her eyes searched his, and she saw there the sting of disappointment. "You like me, and you respect me, but you are not in love with me, not like you were with Hilda. I like and respect you, but my heart soars on the wings of another. It is not Ingvar, nor any of your warriors, so do not be jealous. Once I suggested Jarl Sigrid was like me. What I have discovered is I am like her, if you understand what I mean. You would never be completely satisfied with me as a wife, Njord, nor I with any man. Please do not hate me."

Njord took a step back, eying her in surprise. Giving his head a little shake, he blinked before his expression shifted from dismay to understanding. Relaxing, he answered, "I could never hate you. Everything you said is true. But if King Hemingr's plot is real…"

"I cannot return home for a long time," she admitted. "My uncle will despise me for sure and people will ridicule and loathe me for breaking our engagement. It would be good for you to act offended and outraged, even if you are not. You will draw the sympathy of every unmarried woman and have your pick of them. Sigrid and I are going to try to get our kings to talk to each other. It is the only way they can be certain of the lies each has been told. Your part will come in encouraging King

Tortryggr to meet with King Grimolf and maybe even escort him to ensure his safe travel. There are traitors among us, I am certain. Be watchful. You are an important leader of our people, and we all depend on you."

"I think for the next few weeks, we will all depend on you, though no one will know it," he said and rubbed her arm. "People will curse your name without realizing you are their hope for salvation. I understand why you wish me to remain silent. If I speak of your true actions, our enemies will know we are on to them and switch tactics. They may even speed up their plans or send an assassin after our king. It is wise for us to hide this knowledge until the precise moment." Njord placed a kiss on her forehead. "Thank you for not running away. Thank you for your sacrifice to protect us. Is there something I can give you? Anything you need?"

Elyn glanced around at the animals surrounding them. "It would be very helpful to me if I had a horse."

He stepped back and extended an arm. "Take your pick."

With a relieved smile of gratitude, Elyn skipped to the stall of a bay gelding she had ridden frequently. "How about him?"

"He is yours." Njord moved near and placed a hand on her shoulder, brushing a lock of hair gingerly to the side. "Be careful. You are an asset I cannot afford to lose."

"I give you an oath on my mother's silver raven pin: I swear to act with the greatest care for my life so you will not be angry with me for arriving at Odin's table before you." Elyn winked, Njord laughed, and her tension drifted away.

CHAPTER 25

On the border of Firdafylke and Svithjod

*E*lyn's blanket lay spread under a birch clump at the northern end of the trail Sigrid would take to reach their rendezvous point, while her bay gelding grazed tied to a log nearby. She had arrived the night before and found the rocky terrain near the cave mouth unsuitable for a campsite. So she ventured farther south until coming upon an inviting spot at the edge of a forest with a stream for fresh water, grass for her horse, and shelter for her under the tree branches. Soft ferns, rotting leaves, and loose soil made for comfortable bedding. She had used her pack as a pillow and her cloak as a cover while keeping her collection of weapons close at hand. Now Elyn sat eating unleavened rye bread, hard cheese, and some berries she had collected along the journey.

She was certain Sigrid would use this route as it was the most direct. Elyn could not see the tunnel opening from here, but it was not too far uphill from her camp, so even if Sigrid went a different way, it should be easy enough to find her. *If she comes.*

While confident Jarl Sigrid the Valiant would do all in her power to keep her word, Elyn didn't know what had been happening in Svithjod or what challenges may delay Sigrid from arriving. It was also difficult to tell time this near to the summer solstice. *It is early,* Elyn determined. *If I was at home, I would probably still be asleep, but I am too anxious to sleep. I mustn't let my imagination or my emotions run wild. Sigrid is not coming to meet a lover, but a fellow warrior. We have a mission of the utmost import to complete.*

Nevertheless, the young woman could not stop the tingle of anticipation at seeing Sigrid again. With nothing else to do, she took her sharpening stone out of her bag and dropped it into the pot of water sitting near the smoldering fire from last night. Once it was thoroughly wet, she set it on the blanket in front of her and scraped her ax blade over the rectangular slate at an angle, stroking one side, then flipping the blade to the other in an even action. A sharp ax head was essential, and she had cut firewood with this one. The routine repetitive motion was relaxing and aided in calming her nerves.

It was not long before a flock of birds launched out of the trees down the path, squawking as if in warning. Jerking her gaze up, Elyn spotted the tall blonde warrior riding along with two tremendous hounds trotting at her sides. A thrill leaped into her heart and a smile formed on her lips of its own accord. Elyn pushed to her feet, leaving the ax behind, and walked forward to meet Sigrid.

"Good, you are here!" Sigrid called to her with cheer. That was a positive sign.

"Indeed, I am," Elyn replied. "I promised I would meet you, didn't I?"

Elyn was delighted to witness Sigrid slide nimbly out of her saddle and walk the last few steps with no limp at all. The two gray brindle Cu approached to sniff Elyn and make certain she posed no threat. Seeing they had no intention of attacking, she patted each pot-sized head.

"Jotun and Warg. They insisted on coming. They like you," Sigrid commented with a sparkle in her blue eyes.

Impressed by the gentle giants, Elyn said, "I like them too. Hi there, boys. You are good protecting your mistress." They stood beside her for a moment, chests heaving and tails wagging as they panted huge breaths. "Jarl Njord has a few of these he takes hunting, but they aren't personal companions, as these seem to be."

"Oh, they think they are people," Sigrid said with a laugh. "Go on, now," she instructed and gave them a hand signal. The dogs trotted a few steps away and lay down, one on each side of the trail near where Elyn's camp was set. "So you spent the night, I see."

"Yes. It was easier for me to make the trip yesterday than this morning. I am pleased to see how well your leg has healed." Elyn tried not to glow, but she wasn't sure she was succeeding. Surely she was making a fool of herself, but in the moment, gazing at the lanky living legend who smiled at her conversing like a friend, she really didn't care. *Better for Sigrid to think me a foolish admirer than for her to believe I don't care for her.*

"Between my family, the healer, and Sveina all constantly tending to it, I suppose the wound had no choice but to surrender."

Elyn wondered at how at ease Sigrid seemed compared to the butterflies she felt beating their wings against her insides. *Wait—who is Sveina? Does Sigrid already have a lover? Of course she does, you idiot! How would one as fabulous as Sigrid be without a lover? You are such a fool!*

"I have some gifts for you," Sigrid stated, and reached to a bundle tied behind her saddle. "I might as well give them to you before we get down to business."

Elyn took hold of the horse's reins to keep it still while Sigrid retrieved a brown woolen blanket with something rolled inside. It wasn't until Sigrid raised a nervous, expectant gaze to Elyn's that she felt the exchange of emotion again as she had in the cave. Mayhap this Sveina was an old woman who serves in their longhouse, or an aunt or cousin, and not the object of Sigrid's passions.

She set the bundle on the ground, took a shiny sword from it, and held it out to Elyn. "I hadn't time to have our blacksmith make you a new weapon, but this was my first sword, the one I originally trained with and carried on my sea voyages with Jarl Olaf and Sigurd."

Sigrid placed the blade in Elyn's hands, and she marveled at how light and balanced it was. "Sigrid, this is… beyond my expectations." The flat of the blade was smooth, with a fuller groove down the center of its length. The grip was bound with black leather between a pommel resembling a silver hat and a curved crossguard, while its length tapered near the tip. "It is so light!" she exclaimed is disbelief.

"It's made from Damascus steel, not heavy iron like your old relic. My father bought it from a Frankish trader and gave it to me for my fourteenth birthday. See." Sigrid's fingers brushed Elyn's as they slid along the sleek blade up to the hilt to point to some etchings. "He had a silversmith engrave twin ravens on the crossguard and another just like it for Sigurd."

"This is an important heirloom, given to you by your father," Elyn protested. She could not fathom the notion of Sigrid parting with such an item of sentimental value. "I couldn't possibly—"

"Please." Sigrid wrapped her hands over Elyn's around the sword. "My father left me many things to remember him by. It would honor me if you were to carry this weapon into battle."

In that moment, Elyn wished nothing more than to throw her arms around Sigrid and kiss her until the sun went down... which may be in a couple of more weeks. Never had anyone given her an item of such value. Even iron swords were scarce, but Damascus steel...

"I don't know what to say," were the only words she could put together. "Thank you so much! I will treasure it always."

"Try it out," Sigrid suggested with an exuberant grin, her eyes dancing with delight.

Elyn took a step backwards, gripped the leather-strapped hilt, and whirled the weapon with the greatest of ease. "It is so graceful. I can be so precise with this. It is truly amazing—you are truly amazing!" The last part wasn't supposed to leave her mouth, but Elyn was thinking it, so it wiggled out with the other words of praise. Now she was embarrassed, but it was too late to backtrack, so she just pretended she hadn't voiced such a declaration. "Let me set this on my blanket where it will be safe." It was as if her feet did not touch the ground when she glided to her bed and back, savoring the tingle of sensations informing her how magical life could be.

By the time she returned, Sigrid was holding a garment, which she laid over Elyn's arms. Her first impression was how heavy it was, so she grasped the shoulders and held it out to inspect. She thought it was a new gambeson, but it turned out to be so much more. The stunning, deep blue padded fabric had been embossed with overlapping coin-sized metal bits resembling the scales of a fish or snake. It had a head hole at the top, a V-neck which fastened with a toggle, and short sleeves ending above the elbows.

"It's like a cross between a gambeson and scale armor," Sigrid explained. "It was specifically made lighter than traditional chainmail or lamellar armor and cut for a woman's figure, but it is too big for me. I thought it would be just right on you, with your stronger curves, though it may fall below your knees as you don't have my height."

Elyn felt she would drown in astonishment at the beauty and functionality of the armor, and in addition to the fabulous sword, she was truly at a loss to express her feelings in words. She pressed it close to her body, testing the width around her breasts. "I think it will fit perfectly," she managed. Each of the hundreds of sewn on metal scales shone in the filtered sunlight. "It is so beautiful," she gushed in appreciation.

"These go with it." Sigrid bent down to collect a few more pieces from the wrap at her feet. "These leather bracers and greaves were dyed to match the blue. The set was a gift from the king of Vestmar after Sigurd and I saved his daughter when her ship broke up in a horrific storm on the Baltic as she traveled to Estonia. I never grew into it. Oh, and another piece."

She grabbed up a coil of chainmail and placed it on top of everything Elyn cradled in her arms. "It's a coif. I had no extra helmet and not enough time to commission one to be made, but this will provide some protection, especially for your neck."

"Sigrid, I... I wasn't expecting all of this." Her mouth hung open like a gaping maw.

"Well, not to criticize, but your gambeson is really worn out, and, well," Sigrid stammered as it was her turn to struggle with words. "It's important to me to keep you well protected."

Elyn's gaze passed from the costly, fine-crafted armor to the hopeful look residing in Sigrid's aspect. And there was the impulse again, screaming at her to kiss the woman! But... Elyn thought she had been terrified to face Njord and call off the marriage until that moment. She could feel sweat break out on her palms, her chest heaving with each breath, and her heart thundering like a blow from Thor's hammer.

"I don't know how I'll ever thank you," she admitted. "But I shall endeavor to try. Let me put these in a safe place and then we can talk."

While she laid the armor on the edge of her blanket alongside the fabulous sword, Sigrid unsaddled her horse and walked him out to the grassy spot where hers grazed. Elyn was sitting on her pallet with a horn she filled with fresh water when Sigrid returned and plopped down beside her.

"You must be thirsty," she said, and offered her the drink.

Sigrid smiled and downed the whole thing in one long, languid swig. Elyn couldn't keep her focus off her, studying the fit of her trousers, the cut of her tunic, her bare arms protruding from her sleeves, sleek neck, chiseled jaw, kissable lips, stunning eyes, and golden hair hanging loose about her shoulders save for two little braids framing her smooth face. Elyn had never felt this way before, so she wasn't certain what it meant. She only knew she never wanted it to end.

"I have no gift for you," she admitted with a tinge of sadness.

Sigrid smiled and handed her the empty horn. "Yes, you do."

Elyn could have dived into those passion filled eyes and never left them. *Could she truly be feeling what I am?*

"Information," Sigrid concluded. Elyn felt her spirits plummet, but then Sigrid asked her first question. "Are you to marry Jarl Njord?"

Eagle's wings lifted her up again, and Elyn answered with a simple, "No," which elicited a smile from Sigrid.

"Good. He is too old for you, and I believe you have an exceptional destiny ahead. I'd hate to see it spoiled by a husband."

Elyn tried to read Sigrid's intentions, but she had little experience in matters of passion, and merely inclined her head. She considered sharing what the seer had told her but did not want to appear forward or presumptuous. Perhaps later.

"He does believe my testimony, however, and is ready to assist in whatever plan we devise."

Sigrid's body responded with alertness. "That is good to hear. I discovered many suspicious happenings to share with you. My friend, Jarl Siegfried, suffered a severe wound in the battle and we went to visit him on the way to see King Grimolf. While we were there, one of his tenants tried to murder him in his sleep but hung himself in his cell before Siegfried's interrogators could wrangle a name from him."

Elyn's eyes widened in shock at the notion someone would attempt a thing so foolish. "I am glad your friend was not killed," she avowed. "Will he recover?"

"His strength is returning, howbeit in no rush," Sigrid affirmed.

"What did your king have to say?" Elyn asked. "Did he trust your testimony?"

"That is where things became interesting." Sigrid's tone took on an air of animation as energy radiated from her perfectly fit body. "There is this envoy from Gudbrandsdalir named Hroald who has latched himself to King Grimolf's coattails—"

"Who fills his ears with lies and reeks of corruption." Elyn declared, completing her sentence.

Sigrid's expression morphed into astonished recognition. "Yes! How did you know?"

"Because King Tortryggr has one of those mountain men sent by King Hemingr filling his ears with flattery and deception and his pockets with gifts," she explained. "Did this Hroald say King Hemingr has pledged his warriors to fight on your side against us?"

"He did." Sigrid's eyes flashed and her tone turned heated. "He also tried to convince King Grimolf one or two of our other jarls were behind the plot as they wished to take his crown and divide all the fylkes between the two of them. Did you talk to King Tortryggr?"

"No." Elyn lowered her gaze in disappointment. "They wouldn't let Ingvar and I in to see him, but we talked to Krum, the trader from Gudbrandsdalir, who I'm convinced was sent by Hemingr to persuade King Tortryggr to waste his warriors fighting with you so he can seize both our kingdoms and claim the whole stretch of seacoast. He assured me Svithjod would not get away with your plan to conquer Firdafylke because Hemingr would send his army to our aid. He claimed King Grimolf tried to cheat them in a trade agreement and lots of other obviously false accusations."

"We must find a way to bring our two kings together to communicate with each other," Sigrid declared. "I tried to convince King Grimolf to propose a parley, but he is a proud man. He said he was willing to meet with King Tortryggr only if he requests the meeting. But I know there are other spies and agents, other players in this conspiracy besides the envoys. There has to be, and I am more convinced than ever one of them murdered my father."

"You are right. The two of them couldn't do everything by themselves." Elyn racked her brain, trying to think. "I have two close friends who I know are innocent: my cousin Geir, who was also gravely injured but is recovering, and Ingvar, a fellow warrior my age. We are always together, and neither of them are traitors. I strongly believe Jarl Njord is honorable, although someone near to him, a servant, an advisor, or a friend, could be a spy for our enemies."

"It is actually a sound strategy," Sigrid admitted with a contemplative aspect. "Turn all of us against each other so we fight until we spend the lives of our warriors, promise his alliance to both sides, manipulate us into one final battle. Then when he rides down from the mountains with his army, he attacks and defeats whatever soldiers remain on the battlefield. He can then execute or banish our kings, do what he wishes with any jarls who survive, and triple the size of his kingdom." Sigrid fixed her gaze on Elyn with inspiration. "When you return home, here's what I want you to do."

Elyn's heart sank along with her countenance. "I can't go home."

CHAPTER 26

$\mathcal{E}$lyn's reply surprised Sigrid, and she slowed her racing mind. With deep concern welling in her chest, she asked. "Why can't you go home, Elyn?" She watched Elyn try to shrug it off, mask any disappointment she may be experiencing.

"It's this whole big misunderstanding," she said, casting her gaze down to hide her distress from Sigrid.

Perceiving the seriousness of the matter, Sigrid, who already sat with only a sliver of air between herself and the woman who had captured her imagination, inched closer. With gentle fingertips, she guided Elyn's chin upward so she could read what lay in those stunning, jewel-green eyes. "Is this about Njord or your uncle?"

Elyn sniffed. "Both. You see, when Ingvar and I snuck off to try to talk to King Tortryggr, my uncle and Jarl Njord made all these plans for our marriage ceremony without even asking or consulting me. When we got back, I was told what was going to happen and Ingvar said I had the right to say no, but Uncle Unnulf insisted I couldn't back out and what a wonderful opportunity it was, what a blessing for the whole family, and the Völva had divined I would be joined with an important jarl and people were telling me you didn't need me, that you may not even come, and... They set the date for today, Sigrid. I had a choice to either marry Njord, or honor my oath to you, so I chose to keep my vow. Besides, there is more at stake here than one person's future. You needed my half of the puzzle to fit with yours, and we still must devise a plan of action. I hate to be limiting your choices, but if I went back, first my uncle would kill me —maybe literally—and everyone would be so disgusted with me, no one would heed my words anyway."

While Elyn nervously chattered nonstop explaining what had happened, Sigrid sought to process not only her words, but the intent behind her actions, what she must be feeling, the incredible sacrifice she had made just to get here and meet with her. She tried to imagine if anyone else she knew would have done the same under those circumstances.

"You gave up the chance to become a jarl's wife simply to come and talk with me?" Sigrid found the reality unfathomable. "With no guarantee of reward, or that I would even keep my word, after only one night in a cave, you abandoned a future secure with ease and position to meet with a woman you barely know?"

Sigrid's heart was as stirred as her passions had been for this young woman with flame hair, verdant eyes, and a body which tightened her loins just to gaze upon. She was far more than a pretty face or a strong arm.

"But I do know you, Sigrid. Everyone has heard the skalds sing and recite poems about your heroic deeds," Elyn explained. "I know you always honor your vows, and what good is a reward or marriage to a jarl if our kingdoms are destroyed by the mountaineers? I don't love Njord, so why would I want to marry him? My uncle is a demanding taskmaster who has never been kind to me; why should I care about his wishes? So you see, I sacrificed little, and would give up considerably more to be here with you, to gain your trust and friendship, and to foil the plot of a devious enemy."

"Be careful, my sweet," Sigrid warned, with a misty expression filling her face. "I am not a god or a hero from the sagas. I have never slain a giant or traveled to Álfheim to mingle with elves. I am not perfect, no matter how hard I strive to be, so do not think more highly of me than you ought."

Elyn smiled at her with genuine affection. "I know you are human and am very glad for it. Otherwise, I could never dare dream of touching you."

As a magnet draws steel, Sigrid's hand moved to caress Elyn's fair face. She brushed her thumb across her lips and cupped her chin in her palm, allowing her fingertips to trace circles on her skin. "No one has ever done anything like this for me," she confessed. "Sigurd would rearrange the stars if I asked, as I would for him, but that's different. No one else..." Her words trailed off as her heart raced and her brain fogged. All she wanted to do was kiss the girl.

As she leaned in, Elyn moved to meet her. The kiss shot a myriad of sensations racing through Sigrid's body, mind, and spirit, like an unusually strong drink or fallout from a lightning bolt. Elyn was not pulling away, not even hesitating, which encouraged Sigrid more, arousing her desire, stimulating her senses with a captivating allure unlike any woman she had known. She nibbled at her lips, flicking them with her tongue, savoring their taste, yet hungering for more. Sigrid increased the pressure, opening her mouth with a delirious craving. Elyn's fingers curled in her hair, lengthening the intimate encounter which threatened to consume Sigrid in its seduction.

Forcing her lips from Elyn's, she issued a husky request, cautious against falling yet again into her own trap. "Please tell me if this is truly what you want or not, Elyn. Say no, as you did to Njord, for I can't abide the thought of taking what you do not freely give." *Not again; never again.*

Elyn cupped Sigrid's face in her hands and answered with a penetrating gaze. "I have never wanted anything more."

The wolfhounds who had been lounging about, perked up and raced off after some rabbit or squirrel, or who cares, leaving Sigrid and Elyn alone at a lovely forest's edge high on a hillside far from civilization.

Ardor shone on Sigrid's face while a thrill of pleasure cascaded through her. *She wants me! She wants me the same way I want her.* There had been a few women, those who are insatiable, who go about searching for new sexual experiences, who had been enthusiastic about a night with the famed warrior, but none who meant anything. Elyn, on the other hand, meant a great deal to Sigrid, and she intended to show her just how much.

She claimed Elyn's mouth with unabashed fervor as her hands explored her body. Sigrid took her time, guiding Elyn, enjoying introducing her to new pleasures, delighting in her rapturous sounds and expressions. It further thrilled her to discover what a quick study her partner was, or perhaps she just possessed natural talent. Clothing was discarded and territory staked, as they wrestled each other in tantalizing bouts of ecstasy, each determined to outlast the other. Sigrid ascertained she had reached an undiscovered plane of existence before they collapsed in each other's arms, drenched in sweat, with their energies spent.

Sigrid lay with her eyes closed and a silly smile of pleasure lighting her face, her head spinning, her entire body tingling, both completely satisfied and eager for more. "I should have found you sooner," she breathed, feeling as though she rested on a cloud.

"I may not have been ready sooner," Elyn confessed. "But I am so glad you found me now."

Secure in one another's embrace, Sigrid and Elyn drifted into sleep.

ELYN FELT as if she soared among the stars. Even the gods of Ásgarðr and Fólkvangr could not possibly experience such bliss! She floated in and out of awareness, exhausted from their lovemaking, marveling at all the pleasures she had never imagined she could feel. If her life was to end today, she could leave Miðgarðr content and fulfilled, but she suspected the gods would at least allow her to complete her important task of securing peace before taking her.

Sigrid's head was a delightful weight on her shoulder, as was the warmth of her body leaning on hers. One muscled arm lay across her bare belly while a long, toned leg stretched between her thighs. Was this real? Elyn pinched herself to make certain. She took a deep breath and smiled at the marvelous wonder of the day.

With a light touch, she traced the lines and swirls of Sigrid's warrior tattoos which adorned her shoulder and upper arm. Elyn recognized the symbols carried meaning, though she was not sure what these relayed. *Perhaps I will wear markings like these someday.* She had never felt so satisfied and happy, as if this was truly where she belonged. Blanketed by a lazy haze, she drifted back into dreams.

Her eyes were still closed when an inkling of something out of place tickled her senses. Intuition tugged her from slumber, warning her to wake up. Then Elyn heard a twig snap and popped into alertness. A man with his ax raised crept toward them from only a few feet away. "Sigrid, move!" She shouted. Throwing back her cloak that half covered them, she pushed her lover off and aside, rolling her across the pallet. The man's ax blade dug into the dirt, angering Elyn with the hole it sliced in her best blanket.

In an instant, a completely naked Sigrid sprang into action, attacking the would-be assassin with a vengeance. She threw kicks and punches which disarmed him in no time. Watching Sigrid spurred a variety of feelings in Elyn, ranging from admiration to unquenchable lust. Toned and buff, with precise strikes landed with incredible force, Sigrid was simply amazing! However, Elyn's brows furrowed with discontent as she noticed the many scars which etched Sigrid's body. *She must learn to take more care and not dash headlong into every danger.*

When their attacker turned tail and ran, Elyn picked up her ax. The fact she was naked also, did not hinder her actions one bit. Jumping to her feet, she cocked her arm and hurled the sharpened weapon with all her might. It buried itself in the villain's back, and he fell forward to the ground.

Trying to avoid stepping on anything hard or sharp, Elyn ran after Sigrid to the place the man lay moaning. Sigrid yanked the ax from his ribs and flipped him over. "Who sent you to kill us?" she demanded.

His eyes were stricken with fear and when he coughed, blood spilt from his mouth. Elyn knew that meant her blade had punctured a lung. There was a chance he would live, but only if he received treatment right away. "I brought my medicinal supplies," she mentioned. "I could treat his wound."

"Not until he answers me." Sigrid grabbed the front of his shirt, pulling his torso up as she squatted over him.

The man's gaze swept her form before he gasped for air, which sent him coughing again. "Can't breathe," he managed pitifully. With an angry grimace, Sigrid lowered him back to the ground where he rolled onto his side, struggling to suck in a breath.

"There is a chance I can save you," Elyn offered. "But you must answer Jarl Sigrid. Who hired you to do this?"

Doubled over in pain as he lay on his side, the man coughed up more blood. "Water."

Sigrid nodded to her, and Elyn raced for her horn and filled it from the little stream. But the time she returned, he was no longer alive to drink it. "Did he give you a name?"

"No." Sigrid pushed to her feet and Elyn retrieved her ax. She took a sip of the water then handed it to Sigrid. She felt the jarl's enchanting gaze sweep over her nude body as they walked back to her campsite.

With a disappointed sigh, Sigrid pulled her tunic over herself, so Elyn did the same. "How did you know?" Sigrid peered at her in amazement. "You saved my life."

Elyn shrugged. "I had a feeling, and it woke me."

Sigrid hugged her tight. While they stood locked in their embrace, the two big dogs loped up with cocked ears and expressions of concern. One stopped at Sigrid's side while the other trotted over to investigate the dead man.

"You two are a little late!" Sigrid exclaimed with a laugh. Drawing back, she secured a hand behind Elyn's neck and pulled her into a kiss. "Thank the gods for your intuition. He would have killed us both."

"I don't think so," Elyn countered with an air of consternation. "I expect his plan was more devious. He was going to kill you and blame me. It would have been perfect if it had worked. An eyewitness runs to Gnóttdalr testifying he saw a shieldmaiden of Firdafylke murder Sigrid as she slept. Jarl Sigurd would gather his army and attack my homeland with unbridled fury to avenge you, and lay waste to Kaldrlogr without a doubt. It would have accomplished everything Hemingr has designed."

"Except you awoke and stopped him." Sigrid shook her head with a look of awe. "By the gods, what instincts and intelligence you possess! It would be scary, if you were still my enemy."

Overcome with a soft warmth, Elyn beamed at Sigrid, whose fingers combed through her long red strands. "Sigrid, sweetling; our kingdoms may have been at war, but *you* were never my enemy."

Sigrid pulled her close again, wrapping both arms around her. She trailed kisses from her throat up her neck to her ear, sending shivers through Elyn who held on, cherishing each heartbeat. Sigrid whispered, "And I never will be."

CHAPTER 27

With reluctance, Sigrid loosened her hold on Elyn, though she would enjoy nothing more than diving in for more incredible sensual pleasures. Unfortunately, a corpse lay nearby, and a strategy required devising. She brushed her lips to Elyn's in confirmation of her affection, then asked, "What shall we do about him?" She threw a glance over her shoulder.

"If we plan to spend any more time here, we need to do something with him, I suppose. Do you recognize him?"

Sigrid frowned. "He looks familiar. I'm certain I have seen him around Gnóttdalr, but I don't know his name. He isn't a farmer." She focused on remembering what she had witnessed him doing. "He may have been a crewmember on a ship which frequents our harbor. I'm more concerned with who hired him. Only a handful of people knew I was coming here today, and..." She paused, a dread twisting in her gut. "If it was one of them..."

"Anyone could have seen you leave town headed up into the mountains alone," Elyn countered. "He could have merely followed you, waiting for an opportunity to catch you off guard, as he certainly couldn't have hoped to defeat you in fair combat."

The knot in her belly loosened a tad, but the unease remained. "If I carry his body back home, the scoundrel who sent him will know he has failed and may suspect I gained information from him," she mused aloud. "That could throw him off balance, causing him to make a mistake, or he might simply flee."

"Alternately, if we bury him, whoever sent him will wonder what became of him when you return unharmed. He may even ask you if you had any trouble," Elyn suggested.

Sigrid's expression brightened. "Yes! Even if he doesn't present so bold a question, uncertainty is always less desirable than knowing for sure we dispatched the assassin. I'm hungry."

Elyn laughed and shook her head. "I have a few bites left of the food I brought with me."

With a beaming countenance, Sigrid posed a suggestion. "If you can stir your fire to life and pile some rocks over our unwelcomed guest, I will bring back some fresh game."

"I could do that," Elyn replied, returning her smile. Sigrid laid a peck on her lips for good measure and collected her bow and quiver from her saddle lying nearby.

Sigrid pulled on her trousers and laced her boots. "It is always wise to make important decisions on a full stomach," she said, while Elyn finished dressing as well. "I have some ideas, but yours are probably better."

"Doubtful!" Elyn chuckled and rolled her eyes.

"Jotun, Warg," she commanded as she pushed to her feet, and the two jumped to attention, ready for instructions.

"Which one is which?" Elyn asked. "They look so much alike."

"The heavier fellow with the white diamond on his chest is Jotun," she explained, petting his head. "And this energetic guy is Warg." She stroked the leaner hound as they both grinned eagerly at her. "Come on boys—let's go hunting!"

"You two watch out for Sigrid!" Elyn shouted after them.

Sigrid had always enjoyed hunting, but today she scampered through the forest lighter on her feet than she had been in years. It didn't even bother her an assassin had tried to kill her. Although it wasn't an everyday occurrence, it was more routine than the excitement she felt over an amorous relationship with Elyn. Here was a woman who understood her way of life as a warrior, who shared her peculiar orientation, and whose body complemented hers so well.

What had begun as a physical attraction had grown into so much more. Elyn was smart and strong, yet tender and naïve. She was neither needy nor bossy, too shy nor an incessant chatterbox. Her parents may have been common farmers, but Elyn had the makings of a person of high rank. Njord had seen it, or he would never have asked her to be his wife. And her scent aroused Sigrid in a way Sveina's had not. *She really seems to like me, beyond just the sex, which was incredible!*

Drawing her focus back to food, Sigrid slowed her pace to a stealthy creep, placing her feet deliberately amid the underbrush. She motioned for the hounds to halt, and they waited, alert and expectant. Sigrid scanned the area littered with small shrubs, hollows under large roots, and porous soil where rabbits liked to dig warrens and build nests. Their grayish brown coloring was effective camouflage, but she was blessed with sharp eyesight. Spotting an ear flicker among old leaves and tall grasses, Sigrid carefully notched her bow and let the arrow fly. It struck its mark and half a dozen other rabbits shot out in all directions.

"Go!" The two Cu were off, engaging in one of their favorite pastimes —rabbit chasing. While they were bred for size and strength to tackle foxes, wolves, and even challenge wolverines, these wirehaired hounds had long legs and enjoyed stretching them out in a good old-fashioned chase.

Sigrid retrieved her kill and whistled for them before they strayed too far out of sight. She was halfway back to camp when Warg and Jotun trotted up, each carrying a bunny in his jaws. "Good boys," she praised. "You each get your own, and Elyn and I can split this one. I'm sure I saw some wild strawberries around here."

By the time Sigrid and the dogs returned, the fire was crackling, and Elyn was placing the last of the stones over the dead man's body. "Success!" Sigrid called, holding up their lunch by its ears. "I gathered a pouch of strawberries, too."

"Because you are an awesome huntress," Elyn praised with a smile and greeted her with a casual kiss. "One fire and one burial."

An hour later, the two women sat on the blanket eating their meal. The dogs didn't wait on them to devour theirs.

"What we must do is find a way to get King Grimolf and King Tortryggr to meet together and talk," Sigrid began.

"I agree," seconded Elyn. "The problem is, I can't get near my king and yours refuses to call for the meeting."

"True." Sigrid had been pondering a few options and decided it was time to share the most promising one. "But King Tortryggr would receive me, would he not?"

Elyn's eyes rounded. "Yes, but would it be safe for you to travel in Firdafylke? Everyone believes you sent the raiders, that you are our sworn enemy. It is too dangerous."

"Ha!" Sigrid laughed. "As if sleeping in a jarl's own chamber is not dangerous enough sport in Svithjod these days, or going for a ride in the highlands," she added, motioning at the pile of stones fifty yards away. "You are so precious to be concerned for my safety. No. If I ride in alone, in a nonthreatening manner under a flag of truce, nobody would dare assault me. Helsike, if they believe half the stories skalds tell, they would be afraid to raise a hand to me!" she asserted with humor.

"So, you think you'll just travel by yourself all the way to Gimelfjord? Do you know how to get there?" Elyn did not seem quite as concerned, but still skeptical.

"I have been there on two occasions in the past, though my entire plan would gain legitimacy if someone of import was to accompany me." She considered Elyn with a raised eyebrow.

"I hold no station," Elyn declared, sitting back with a surprised expression. "No one outside my village even knows I exist."

"While I am prepared to admit you are very important to me," Sigrid replied, reining in an amused grin. "I was thinking more along the lines of your Jarl Njord. You said he believes you and is willing to help."

Elyn nodded, relief and a little blush shone in her face, and she averted her eyes with a shy smile. "We can easily persuade him to take you to speak with the king."

"Oh no, not we." Sigrid caught Elyn's gaze with a glow in her own. "You will be traveling with Sigurd to bring a message to King Grimolf."

The color drained from her shocked visage and Elyn squeaked out, "Me?"

"This plan includes some harmless deception, but under the circumstances, it is certainly worth the risks."

Elyn took a bite of her meat and waited with an uncertain expression, but Sigrid smiled at her in assurance. "I will go as King Grimolf's emissary with a personal directive from the king requesting they meet for a parley on the border near the seacoast, where we had our first encounter. That way, they will enjoy the luxury of being able to travel by ship and the terrain is more hospitable than up here. We will set a date, probably a week to the day, so our enemies will have no time to mount another raid but will have a chance to send word up into the mountains to Hemingr so he can arrive with his warriors. While I am doing that, you go with Sigurd to speak as King Tortryggr's representative. Our people will not know who you are and assume you are a high-status woman. Sigurd can testify to the same and lend your message credence."

"But neither king has asked for such a meeting." Elyn blinked innocent green eyes at her, enticing Sigrid even more. She felt her heart leap in her chest and wondered at a strange thought. *Is this how it feels to be in love? Surely, I am not... am I?*

"Hence the benign pretense," Sigrid rationalized. "We will act for them with the initiative they should have undertaken for themselves. Hopefully, by the time they discern they have been duped, they will not be too angry about it. I shall accept full responsibility for the ruse and submit myself to any retribution they may be inclined to dole out."

"But..." Elyn's features filled with fear. "King Grimolf might be outraged and strip you of your jarldom."

"Ha! Let him." Sigrid's confidence soared, fueled by Elyn's fervent distress, the kind only one who truly cared could express so candidly. *Might her heart be just as touched as mine? Is it possible she loves me?* Laughter bubbled up from her soul as Elyn's jaw dropped in disbelief.

"Do not waste a care, Elyn my dear," Sigrid explained. "I am not my title, and who I am no man can take from me. I built a fortune and a legend once, so I have no doubt I can do it again. And while it is true my father and twin were a part of it, I am still Sigrid the Valiant, with or without a longhouse, farms, and ships. All I require is my sword and the air in my lungs." *And maybe you,* she mused to herself.

Elyn nodded, an appreciating aspect overtaking the former doubt. "Indeed, Sigrid, you speak the truth. Forgive my unworthy assumption. You are above the need for titles and worldly wealth. It is just I care so much what happens to you, that sometimes—"

Sigrid leaned forward and captured her lips, not allowing her to finish her excuse. After the pleasure of a prolonged, languid kiss, she replied, "You are forgiven." She straightened and eased a strawberry into her mouth with a flirtatious smile. "Are you onboard with the plan? Any additions, corrections, observations?"

"I have had practice at pretenses," Elyn admitted and batted her eyes at Sigrid. "Although not while in the presence of a king. It is a sound plan, but I think it is also important these two agents, Krum and Hroald, should be there as well, so we can expose their treachery. If they return to Gudbrandsdalir, we may never get the chance to enact punishment upon them for their crimes. They are probably behind all the assassinations and attempts."

"You are right," Sigrid concurred. "What did you bring with you to wear? We need you to look the part of a noble woman, not a foxy, alluring shieldmaiden."

Elyn blushed and giggled. "How will we accomplish all this when you keep saying things that make me want to kiss you?"

Sigrid caught Elyn's cheeks and planted a big smack on her lips. "Clothes!" she laughed.

"I have a suitable gown," she answered. "Surprised?"

"I love being surprised by you," Sigrid cooed. "Let me see it."

Elyn dug into her bag and pulled out a neatly folded cream underdress with a forest green apron dress slashed on the sides which fit over it with shoulder straps. Both pieces were woven of linen threads, and it was clean with no holes or tears. Sigrid held up the underdress, noting the decorative stitching around the hem.

"This looks full enough for you to ride in, though from its condition I'd say you never have."

"No. I always wear trousers when riding. Well, I mostly always wear trousers," she added. "But when I turned eighteen and had no husband, my aunt insisted on making me a nice dress for feasts and occasions. I helped with the weaving, but she sewed and embroidered it for me."

"If we add some jewelry to this and let mother arrange your truly beautiful hair in the latest fashion, it will do." Sigrid refolded the garment and handed it to Elyn. "And just so you know, you are very attractive in a pair of trousers, as I am certain you will be in this dress." Seeing Elyn's delighted response, Sigrid could not resist one more kiss.

"So," Elyn posed with a hand on her hip and a query in her voice. "Are we going to ride to your longhouse or make love again?"

A flutter winged its way through Sigrid's core, and she sensed the heat in her cheeks as she gleamed back at Elyn. "I have the most incredible, enormous bed at home in my private chamber."

With an enthusiastic hug, Elyn proposed, "Then let's get packing!"

CHAPTER 28

*E*lyn put on the fabulous steel-studded blue armor set Sigrid had given her, minus the coif, so she would look presentable riding up to Sigrid's homestead. They enjoyed pleasant getting-to-know-you conversation, playful banter, and games of I spy for hours as they rode. It was so magical, Elyn would not have wished it to stop, except for Sigrid's mention of the enormous private bed waiting at the end of the road.

The sky bore a kind of twilight look with the sun hidden behind a ridge of mountains when the women and dogs arrived in Sigrid's courtyard. Few people were out as most had retired for the evening, but Elyn spotted a slender young blonde woman unpinning sheets from a drying line and folding them into a basket. Jotun and Warg raced ahead to elicit pats from her.

When the woman turned toward them, her face lit, and she hurried to greet them. "Asmund!" she called out. "Jarl Sigrid is back. Come see to the horses."

Sigrid dismounted and Elyn followed her lead, suddenly feeling nervous about meeting her family. "Sveina, why are you still up?" Sigrid and Sveina embraced in a very fond greeting.

"I couldn't sleep until I knew you had returned safe." The woman turned an amused and curious aspect to Elyn. "And your friend?" she asked in a teasing tone of delight. "Is she the one you and Sigurd have been talking about?" She inspected Elyn with an intense gaze.

"This is Elyn of Kaldrlogr, Firdafylke," Sigrid introduced. "Elyn, this is

Sveina, my…" The pause had Elyn speculating all kinds of things. *So this is Sveina, quite young and attractive. Please say cousin.*

"My dear friend," she concluded. As Asmund arrived to lead their horses away, Sigrid chided, "You didn't need to stay up waiting for me."

Sveina turned her amused smile to Sigrid. "I can see that now," she answered with a grin. "If Lady Gudred's room is lit, I will let her know you are back safe. I am very happy to meet you, Elyn."

She watched Sigrid's eyes as they followed the woman who walked ahead of them into the longhouse. There was definitely something between them, or there had been. But Sveina did not seem jealous or incensed by Elyn's presence. Indeed, she appeared quite pleased. It was baffling. Elyn only knew she was the one invited to Sigrid's bed, not the waif, for which she was relieved.

They crept past men and women who slept on benches along the walls of the great hall. Sveina whispered, "Shall I bring you something to eat and drink?"

"That would be lovely, thank you."

Sveina nodded and turned in the direction of a pantry.

"Through here," Sigrid motioned, and opened a door leading to a sectioned off wing of the longhouse with four divisions. She gestured to the far left, pulled back a drape, and showed Elyn into her bedroom where she stopped to turn up the wick to an oil lamp resting on a small table by the ingress.

Elyn looked about at the paneled walls, two with colorful tapestries woven with pictures, one with hooks bearing Sigrid's clothing, and one with shelves containing a variety of items. She spied a second larger table with a stool, wash basin, comb and brush, and a wooden box which may hold hair ribbons or jewelry. A large trunk rested at the foot of the spectacular bed with carvings in the head and footboards, mounded with pillows and a light-weight striped wool blanket. Lying on the trunk was a folded bear skin. *Too warm for a fur in summer,* she thought. In the middle of the wood planked floor sat a hearth ring of stones where Sigrid's winter fire would burn. In one corner stood a five-foot wide oval barrel tub with a drying sheet spread over the edge.

Sigrid unbuckled her belt and hung it on a hook near the doorway. Elyn unfastened her belt buckle and reverently handled the sword Sigrid had given her safe in its scabbard with a glance around.

"Here," Sigrid offered in a whisper. Elyn handed it to her, and Sigrid laid it on top of the bear skin.

Sveina appeared at the threshold with a basket of leftovers and a quart-sized tankard, handing them to Sigrid with a bemused smile. "Have a good night," she chirped, and let the curtain fall closed.

Sigrid turned a hungry gaze on Elyn. "Let's sit on the bed and eat this so we will have strength to see us through the night."

Elyn joined Sigrid, where they shared the simple supper of bread and honey, raw vegetables with goat cheese dip, and two skewers of roasted reindeer cubes. It wasn't hot, but it was delicious, as was the sweet mead they both drank from. Enchanted with her surroundings, and especially her hostess, Elyn deemed this the most intimate meal she had ever partaken.

"So, that's Sveina." Elyn was dying to know. "I'm guessing she is not a relative?"

Sigrid considered her question with indecision before settling on what to say. "Sveina is very important to me. She has been my companion since I was fifteen, a thrall my father provided to serve me. But we became closer than I am to my blood sister. I granted her freedom as a reward for her loyal service."

"You were lovers?" Elyn feared the question pushed too far, but she wanted to know, and how Sigrid responded would tell her much about both women.

Sigrid laid the empty food basket aside, took Elyn's hand, and traced circles in her palm with a finger. "We were... for my part, anyway. She... she just wanted to please me. We still care for each other deeply, but no longer in the same way. That's why it is imperative I know for certain you want me as much as I want you, that this is not a pretense."

Elyn's heart was touched by the lament and insecurity in Sigrid's expressive blue eyes. This was the first time she had seen any vulnerability in the famed shieldmaiden, and it only drew her emotions closer to her. Elyn reached out, catching her face between her palms, leaned in and kissed her with all the aspects of passion she could knit into the gesture. "I am here because there is nowhere I'd rather be, and no person I would rather be with. When I was little, I was bitten by a snake. Ever since then, I have not cared for snakes and have made a point of avoiding them because I do not want to get bitten again, so I understand your hesitation. But Sigrid, I am not a snake, nor am I a thrall whose duty it is to please you. However, it is my goal to please you as much as you please me. And you do please me, very much."

As confidence returned to Sigrid's gaze and a satisfied smile blossomed across her lips, she unfastened the toggle at the neck of Elyn's armor. "Let's get you out of these clothes then, shall we?"

They undressed each other, teasing with strokes and kisses as they went along, until they lay under a thin sheet, flesh to flesh, savoring each tantalizing caress as they explored each other's bodies with fervor. In between climaxes, Elyn ventured a reprimand. "All of these scars tell me you are not careful enough." She placed a kiss to one on the hollow of Sigrid's shoulder. "Your body is magnificent, but too many wounds are telling."

"It's not like I rush in naked to battle giants," Sigrid quipped in her defense. "Sometimes a warrior must take risks in order to achieve greatness."

"If you intend to persist in taking such chances, then I shall simply have to always fight at your side to deflect the spears and blades which might slice another piece of you," Elyn vowed as her fingers skimmed a scar across Sigrid's belly.

"How do you manage to remain in pristine condition?" Sigrid asked as she drew a line down the middle of Elyn's chest between her breasts.

"I have only been active in combat for two years," she answered, "and have not seen considerable serious warfare."

"But you are so good!" Sigrid seemed surprised to hear of her inexperience.

"I have been training much longer," Elyn explained. Then she relayed the story to Sigrid of how her farm was attacked and her parents and brothers killed, and how even at twelve years old, she had fought back. Sigrid remained pensive through the story. When Elyn finished, Sigrid drew her close to her breast, with powerful arms holding her in their safety. She kissed Elyn's forehead and cheeks before working her way to her lips.

"I pity the fool who tries to assault you now. In case you are not aware how amazing you are, let me tell you, because as you know, I do not lie," Sigrid stated in sincerity. Then she shrugged and added lightly, "Unless I'm manipulating kings into doing the right thing."

That drew a laugh from Elyn and lightened the mood. They shared tales of adventure, hopes, dreams, and heartaches, until finally Elyn could not keep her eyes open any longer and she fell asleep on Sigrid's shoulder, wrapped safely in her arms.

ELYN WORE her good dress to breakfast with Sigrid's family the next morning. She was presented as "a woman Sigrid picked up from Hafrafell," so any spies in the hall wouldn't know something was afoot. However, Elyn could tell her strikingly similar brother Sigurd recognized exactly who she was.

Elyn spent the meal conversing amiably with Gudred, Girrid, and Odo, who did his best to charm her. She supposed Odo to be a little older and Girrid a little younger than her. What Elyn noticed most was how no one thought it strange Sigrid had brought a woman home to spend the night, so she had to deduce it was a common occurrence. *Nothing wrong with that,* Elyn told herself. *It is good she is experienced. That's how she was able to guide me so well. I only hope she doesn't become bored with me after a few weeks and wants to move on to someone else.*

Sigrid spent most of the meal whispering with Sigurd or speaking aloud in nonsense words. Elyn presumed being twins, they had concocted their own language in their childhood, a code they were privity to which outsiders couldn't comprehend. *Ingenious!*

When a servant came to clear the table, Sigurd pushed up and slapped Odo on the shoulder. "Little brother, let's you and I give Elyn a tour, shall we? Sigrid has other things to do this morning."

Elyn went with them, and once they were outside and a fair distance from anyone else, Sigurd said, "Odo, I need to let you in on our plan. Here's what we are going to do."

SIGRID REMAINED at the table watching the men in the great hall, noting who looked cheerful, who did not, and who conversed with whom. As she studied people, some of whom she had known from her childhood and others only more recently, Rangvoldr wandered over and took the seat beside her.

"Girrid, we need to work on a new tunic for Sigurd's wedding," Gudred said. "Sigrid, I suppose you won't be assisting us."

"I have my own plans for a gift for Sigurd and Birgitta," she answered with a grin. Her mother just shook her head and left the table with Girrid in tow.

"She is attractive," Rangvoldr commented. "The woman, I mean, not your sister... I mean, of course Girrid is attractive, but she is too young for me." Stumbling, he tried to pick himself back up.

"How was your ride yesterday?" When she didn't answer right away, he continued. "You seem distracted. Did you sleep at all? Hey, maybe the two of you will invite me to the party next time."

The last statement caught her attention. She replied with a sarcastic expression. "Does anything else ever cross your mind?"

He shrugged. "Not really."

Sigrid huffed out a laugh and returned her gaze to the hall. "There is a traitor in our midst, Rangvoldr, and I must uncover who it is. The ride was fine. As you see, I found my red-haired shieldmaiden. By Freya, who could it be?" She started to slam her fist onto the table in frustration but caught herself just before it could land and rattle the cups. She shook her head.

"What are you going to do next?" he asked.

"Can't tell anyone, old friend," she replied. "I'll be gone a few days, so I'll need you and Gunnlief to keep an especially close eye on things here."

"What about Sigurd?"

"He's got an errand to run as well," Sigrid answered in vague terms. This was typical behavior for Rangvoldr. He always wanted in on whatever they were doing. However, a creeping doubt unsettled her soul. He was one of only four people who knew she was going to meet Elyn. Surely a man who had wanted to do nothing but sleep with her for years didn't try to have her killed!

"Why don't you let me come with you?" he asked. "I went with you to see King Grimolf. You need an escort, and there's no better choice than your brother's best friend."

Sigrid shook her head, tense at Rangvoldr's attention. She took a gamble and turned to meet his gaze. "Are you, Rangvoldr? Are you Sigurd's best friend? Do you love us as much as you claim, or did you only attach yourself to Jarl Olaf's children for your own advancement? What would you do to gain power and wealth?"

"Sigrid! What are you suggesting?" Insult flashed in his visage, followed by hurt, and he turned away, lowering his face. "I can't believe after all the battles we have fought side by side, you could suggest such a thing. You know I care for you and Sigurd, and I would if you were but ordinary warriors." Tilting his head, he looked back at her. "Only you would, under no circumstances, ever be ordinary. If you don't want me to come with you, just say so."

Is he sincere? Searching her feelings, her memories, her instincts, Sigrid honestly did not know. "I'm sorry, Rangvoldr. You know how suspicious I have been since Olaf was murdered. It's not that I don't want you to accompany me. It's only this is something I must do on my own, just Elyn and I, understand?"

He tipped back his head and let out a sigh. "Right."

For an instant, she caught the jealousy flash in his dark eyes. Then it was gone. *What if I wasn't the assassin's target after all? What if he was after Elyn?*

CHAPTER 29

Kaldrlogr, Firdafylke, the next day

Sigrid came dressed as a noble lady rather than a shieldmaiden when she rode through Njord's palisade gates with her armor and weapons all packed away and tied to her chestnut stallion's saddle. The warriors in training, blacksmith, fletcher, carpenter, and common laborers all stopped what they were doing to stare at her in disbelief.

She nimbly swung a leg over her horse's head, slid to the ground, and smoothed her skirts. "I am here on behest of King Grimolf with a message for Jarl Njord," she announced in a regal tone with her chin high. Sunbeams glistened off her honey hair as a breeze caught the loose strands which tumbled down her back.

A man in commoners' attire soiled with a workman's dirt rushed over. "I will look after your horse, my lady." He bowed before her, and she handed him the reins.

"Thank you, good fellow."

With the company still staring at her, Sigrid strode across the lawn and through the front entrance to Njord's great hall.

"She should be tied and quartered!" An older man with gray streaks in his ash-brown hair and beard bore an expression of bitter contempt, his hooded eyes shooting fiery darts. "I cannot believe my stupid ward could have done such a thing as this. You should send soldiers to drag her back, my lord. I'll take a lash to her myself."

"That shall not be necessary," Njord assured him in a tone displaying no ill will toward the woman in question. He glanced up, spying Sigrid and a curious expression enveloped him. "Unnulf, please do not upset yourself so. If you will excuse me, I have a guest."

Unnulf's raging eyes rounded in shock at the sight of Jarl Sigrid standing only a few yards away. She recognized his name as the cruel uncle who had belittled and browbeat Elyn, and she regarded him with icy steel in her visage. His face paled in terror. "Yes, I see. I'll just be going now. Do not worry, my lord. I will make this up to you somehow."

Njord waved a dismissive hand and the disgusting man scurried past Sigrid, careful to remain out of her reach.

"Jarl Sigrid Olafsdottir," he greeted cordially. "What a pleasant surprise. Won't you come in?" He inclined his head and offered a welcoming gesture.

"Thank you, my lord," she answered as if they were old friends and joined him where he stood near the center of the grand chamber. "I have an important message from King Grimolf to relay to King Tortryggr. An associate of yours suggested you may be willing to serve as my escort to Gimelfjord."

It seemed to Sigrid he was studying and assessing her as he paused before stating a reply. She had known who Njord was since she was a small child and had seen him on numerous occasions, but this was the first time she had spoken with the man up-close and personal. The impression she received was of a reputation well deserved. He struck her as calculating, formidable, and in control of his emotions.

"I believe it will be best if we speak in private," he concluded. Raising a hand and his voice, he directed, "I wish you all to vacate the hall. I have a sensitive matter to discuss with Jarl Sigrid of Svithjod."

"But my lord," protested one of his professional warriors. "I cannot leave you alone with our enemy. What if she tries to do you harm?"

He set his jaw and narrowed his brows at the guard. "Do you think I cannot handle myself in the company of an unarmed woman, no matter how fierce her reputation? Go!"

After ensuring the hall had been cleared, Njord offered Sigrid a seat at his table, where he joined her. "You will do me the favor of being my honored guest at dinner tonight?" he asked.

Sigrid relaxed with a friendly smile. "I would if you wish it."

"You're quite compelling up close, Jarl Sigrid; a perfect blend of beauty, power, and presence. I can see how you stole Elyn from me, but I am still not happy about it."

"While I cannot express regret for that, I would like to extend an apology for the insults I hurled at you on the battlefield," Sigrid offered. "I was attempting to goad you into coming to the fore, but you were too self-controlled to fall for it. Indeed, Elyn speaks very highly of you."

"As she does of you." Njord laced his fingers together in front of him at his place at the end of the long table, Sigrid seated directed to his right. "We did not raid your farms or kill your friends."

"And we did not invade your farms and slay yours," she repeated in candor. "Elyn has told you all this."

"Yes, but it adds weight to hear it from you. Does King Grimolf send a message?"

Sigrid contemplated whether to be completely upfront with Njord. She decided what he did not know, he could not later be held accountable for. The man was helping her and the last thing she wished was for him to earn the displeasure of his king.

"Yes. He has sent a request for King Tortryggr to meet with him on neutral ground, the location on the border by the seacoast where you and I first fought each other, so the two of them may parley under a banner of truce and hopefully get to the bottom of the deception."

"Elyn maintains it is King Hemingr and his lying emissaries," Njord said, a furrow in his brow.

"That is indeed what we believe and can prove it," Sigrid affirmed. "We want to ensure both Krum and Hroald attend the peace talks so they can be exposed as liars. Hroald told King Grimolf that Hemingr had promised his army to support us in the fight against Firdafylke."

"And Krum vowed to King Tortryggr Hemingr would send his fighting men to our aid." Njord shook his head. "We should have never clashed on opposite sides of a shield wall," he acknowledged in bitter regret.

"And we should have left none of your warriors dead on the fields," Sigrid agreed. "We were deceived, and cannot undo the damage, but hopefully our kings can agree to terms which will prevent such a thing from occurring in the future. We both should have first opened a dialogue to discuss what happened, but with all the evidence pointed at each other being at fault, we both rushed in. It is no excuse, but mine and Sigurd's emotions were still raw over our father's murder. We supposed it may have been you behind it."

"I swear on Odin's Spear, I had nothing to do with Jarl Olaf's death."

Njord's tone and expression brimmed with honesty and Sigrid acknowledged him. "I know that now."

"I suppose Elyn is staying in your longhouse?" he half spoke, half asked.

Sigrid nodded. "She believes she is not welcome here, and after hearing her uncle's rant, I must conclude she is correct."

"We agreed not to divulge her reason for calling off the marriage until all the spies have been rooted out. It showed courage and resolve for you to ride in here alone and unarmed, and I commend you."

With a smile, Sigrid inclined her head. "Thank you for your kind words of praise, Njord, but I must applaud you for your wisdom to accept Elyn's testimony."

"Her argument was sound," he replied with a humble shrug. "You will not use her and toss her aside, will you?" He pinned her with a critical expression, having suddenly pivoted the conversation. "I would be angry to lose her to you when you have no serious aims."

Sigrid lay her hand over his and spoke from her heart. "Jarl Njord, you recognized a seed of greatness in Elyn. I see it too. I have no intentions of using her for my political gain nor for my personal pleasures and do not intend to discard her when my mission is concluded. You should know, it is not you she lacks passion for—it is men in general. She told me she did not wish you to be trapped in an unsatisfying marriage, nor did she want the same for herself. You are a good man, and she values your friendship."

He nodded, satisfied with her response. "I am aware she suffered some unpleasant experiences, and her uncle is an ambitious man who disrespects her as often as possible. He wished to advance himself through the marriage, a fact I am not blind to. It will be interesting to see if he shows his face in my hall tonight. I shall be happy to escort you to deliver your message to King Tortryggr tomorrow. Will you be ready for an early start?"

"The sooner, the better." Sigrid grinned.

NJORD KEPT HIS WORD, and the two set out with an escort of his four most trusted men, one of whom was Ingvar who Elyn talked about. Her cousin

Geir was still recovering from his injury but was well enough to join them for dinner. Unnulf, however, did not show, even though an invitation was sent to his house. His wife had replied he left suddenly on a business trip—likely story! *The worm is afraid of me*, Sigrid concluded.

Her companions remained quiet on the half-day ride and Sigrid enjoyed the scenery. What had begun as a misty morning with moisture permeating the air and whiffs of clouds encircling the mountains ended up bright and inviting. Flocks of geese flew overhead while smaller nesting birds chirped from the branches. Sigrid's thoughts wandered to remembrances of gliding her hands over Elyn's luscious curves and firm muscles, intoxicated by her allure, and wanton craving. Feeling the heat fill her as if she was back in her bed, Sigrid deemed she should steer her imaginings in another direction. *What shall we do when this has been settled?* she pondered. *I wonder if Elyn has ever sailed east to the Götaland? I shall take her on a trading expedition so she may visit the exotic market and meet the Sviar.*

Upon arriving at Tortryggr's great hall, they were admitted and announced. The king, aging but appearing quite robust, sat in his high-backed armchair on the short rise of a platform at one end of the chamber with his son Erling, a mature man nearing Njord's age, at his right side. Sigrid recalled the stories of his seafaring adventures from decades ago and approached him with admiring respect.

"My lord," Njord began with a bow. "Jarl Sigrid Olafsdottir has arrived with an urgent message from King Grimolf of Svithjod." He stepped aside and presented Sigrid.

"Word of your mighty deeds is widespread in Svithjod, my lord," she affirmed. "My king does not wish us to live as enemies, but as friends." She went on to issue the request to parley, including the particulars of time and place.

The king with short gray hair, a neat white beard, and sea-green eyes listened with interest to her communication. He nodded, raised a finger, and leaned over with a hand in front of his mouth to consult Erling in private. Tortryggr's son was not strikingly handsome like Sigurd, but neither was he homely. He wore his autumn-leaf hair back in a braid exposing a high forehead and arched brows over eyes a shade darker than his father's. His physique suggested he was an asset in a shield wall, and the scars visible on his arms and face indicated he had seen action. She was aware Firdafylke sometimes carried out raids in the east and along the coast to the south. Tortryggr had even sailed west to a green island called Eire where they had not faced a warm welcome, but it is most likely Erling received his wounds in the war against Raumsdal, the kingdom to the north.

Sigrid took note that Krum, whom Elyn had described to her, was not present in the hall. *What could he be up to?* she wondered. *If he is anything like Hroald, he would never miss a meeting where pertinent information may escape his notice.*

Tortryggr straightened and returned his focus to Sigrid. "I know who you are, as your reputation also proceeds you. King Grimolf the Wolf and I were once allies, and it would be advantageous if we were so again."

Just then, the birdlike man rushed into the hall draped in an orange silk mantle pinned around his tan tunic. "Wait, my lord!" he shouted. "Do not listen to this woman. Grimolf has devised a trap in which to ensnare you." He scurried up to stand between Sigrid and the king and folded his hands with a slight bow. Then he turned and pointed at her. "You cannot trust her word nor that of a greedy king who wishes nothing more than to usurp your kingdom and add it to his own."

Tortryggr tilted his head and scrunched his chin at Krum. "This 'woman' is Jarl Sigrid the Valiant, Krum. Her word is above reproach throughout all Norvegr."

Krum frowned and passed a frantic gaze over Sigrid. She crossed her arms over her chest, regarding him as though he was an insect. Returning his attention to Tortryggr, he suggested, "Mayhap she believes she is telling the truth. Grimolf has deceived her as well in his eagerness to lay a trap for you."

Erling bent close and Tortryggr lent an ear to listen to his son's counsel. He nodded and fixed his focus on Sigrid. "Suppose my army was to join me as an escort to these peace talks," he proposed. "Just in case this is a ruse to ensnare me. Would your king find those conditions unreasonable?" He raised a brow at her.

Sigrid smiled, for such had been her intention all along. "No, my lord. I doubt King Grimolf would expect you to travel anywhere without such a precaution. Bring as many warriors as you like—a hundred, two hundred," she shrugged. "Ask Njord to bring his as well. In fact, my king would not be offended or intimidated if you brought all your jarls and their forces with you because we do not intend to do battle, rather to converse as equals on neutral ground. I'm certain he will retain an escort also."

"My lord, I must protest," Krum began in a desperate plea.

Sigrid threw Njord a glance and he stepped forward. "King Tortryggr, I propose you bring Ambassador Krum to the talks. That way he may attest to your safety. Besides, didn't he promise King Hemingr's support? Perhaps he can send word to his king letting him know peace is on the horizon and his troops will not be needed."

"I, I," Krum stammered. "I should take such a vital message back to King Hemingr in person, my lord, so I won't be able to join you at the meeting."

"Nonsense!" Njord exclaimed in a jovial voice. "Anyone can deliver a report. You are too important to be a mere errand boy, isn't it so, King Tortryggr?"

The king passed a considering eye across every face in the room, ending with a questioning look at Erling. Sigrid had noticed how Erling had scrutinized Krum ever since he burst into the chamber hollering objections. He gave his father a curt nod.

"I agree," he decreed. "Krum, you shall accompany me. Then you can bear witness and have a substantive story to take up the mountains if the talks break down due to lies and treachery. This is my decision." He raised a hand and waved for a hulk of a warrior who marched to the front and bowed. "Karr, please keep a close escort on our friend Krum until we arrive at the parley. He is concerned about foul play."

"Yes, my lord," he avowed and moved to tower over the twiggy emissary.

"Jarl Sigrid, Jarl Njord," Tortryggr motioned. "I shall see the two of you along with King Grimolf one week from today. We shall travel by sea, and I intend to bring a considerable force as an escort to deter any tricks. Krum, pack light for the journey. Erling, will you oversee the arrangements?"

"Certainly, Father," he replied.

"Thank you for your time and your wise decision to avoid war," Sigrid said as she bowed to the king. "I promise you will not be disappointed."

Sigrid and Njord exited the king's longhouse to meet their escort who had waited with the horses. "That went well!" she declared with a grin. "I pray Elyn has equal success. You played your role brilliantly."

Njord laughed and took his reins. "You could coax a bear away from honey, couldn't you?"

She was about to banter back with a clever reply when someone caught her eye. Sigrid peered around the horses trying to get a better look at a middle-aged man with a visible belly and irritated stride. In a hush, she inquired, "Is that Unnulf?"

Njord snapped his head in the direction she indicated. Dark suspicion veiled his visage. "I do believe so."

"What is he doing here?" she demanded.

"What indeed?" Njord repeated in a tone frigid enough to spear Sigrid with dread.

CHAPTER 30

$\mathcal{N}$jord invited Sigrid to spend the night in his longhouse again as their travels had taken all day and the hour was late when they arrived. "I appreciate your hospitality," she replied.

They enjoyed light conversation over a meal before retiring for the night. Sigrid had been welcomed to share Aslaug's room on both occasions she stayed at Njord's residence. The first night they had remained quiet and just slept, but seeing how the older woman was still awake spinning at her wheel, Sigrid ventured to strike up an exchange.

"I appreciate you sharing your space with me, Lady Aslaug," Sigrid said as she undressed for bed.

"Not at all," she smiled as her fingers guided the woolen fibers. "I am happy to entertain one so renowned as you." A twinkle lit her old eyes.

With her dress hung on a hook and wearing only her chemise, Sigrid plopped onto the side of the bed nearest where Aslaug sat on her stool spinning at the wheel and considered her with an interested gaze. Sigrid had had never desired to spin, weave, embroider, or sew. She only learned to cook out of necessity, and because her father indulged her so, allowing her to join in her brother's education, she never had to. Regardless of a woman's status, much important work of the household fell to her, especially when the men were out on hunting or fishing trips, sailing on trade expeditions or to discover new lands, or away at war. Women tended gardens, fed the animals, milked cows and goats, sheered sheep, cooked, cleaned, did the laundry, and still engaged in textiles making most of the clothing for the family. Some men became adept at leather crafting, fashioning vests, armor, saddles, belts, shoes, and such, but it was up to the women to spin fibers—whether flax or wool—into thread, to weave the thread into cloth, and to cut and sew the fabric into all kinds of garments. Mayhap they did not face the constant threats to one's life from dangerous animals, storms, ruffians, and foes, but just to think about the mountain of women's chores—not to mention caring for the children—made her head hurt.

"I admire what you do, your invaluable contributions to your household," Sigrid said. "My mother engages in these activities, but she is younger than you and has my sister and our servants to assist."

"I have servants, too," Aslaug admitted, "but I assign them other tasks. I want only the finest threads, the tightest woven cloth for my family's clothing, which means I must do this work myself." She smiled with pride in her craft. "My daughter, Hilda, was more like you. She was a fierce shieldmaiden, but only when required to be, not as a profession. She engaged in the business of being a jarl's wife, was a loving mother, and ran the household efficiently. It took the unseen, unknowable enemy of a sickness to bring her down. Njord could have had me evicted from the longhouse after her death, but he asked me to stay on and help raise his children. I was pleased with the prospect of his marriage to Elyn because I thought she would want me to continue in my position, allowing her to pursue martial activities, but..." She shrugged. "We will see who he chooses next."

"I have a proposition for you," Sigrid announced in inspiration. "If Njord's new wife wishes to bring her own mother in to take your place, you are welcome in our longhouse. I have no intention of ever engaging in such domestic necessities, nor shall I push them off on Elyn. My mother can't do for everyone in our household. You would be an appreciated asset."

Sigrid smiled, pleased with her idea, until struck with a sudden thought: *will Elyn be staying with me?* They hadn't discussed it. Sigrid assumed she would want to, that they could build a life together, sharing adventures and protecting her village from dangers. Elyn had said she would not be welcome back here, and she would have to live somewhere. *I should not assume,* Sigrid chided herself. *I will have to ask.*

"What a kind offer, Jarl Sigrid," Aslaug answered. "I will keep it in mind."

Eager to change the subject of living arrangements, Sigrid noted, "My grandparents passed many years ago and I lost the opportunity to hear their tales from the old days. It strikes me I could learn much from you."

"I recently told Njord of how your kingdom and mine were one in generations past before being rent asunder by conflict," she began. "But the part I left out for brevity was the great calamity which precipitated the problems."

Sigrid's attention was peaked. "What great calamity?"

"This story has been passed from my grandmother's grandmother down to me and I shall teach it to my grandchildren soon." Aslaug stopped spinning so she could use her hands to illustrate her tale. "Going back four generations, over a hundred counted years, there fell a great disaster in the sky and on the earth. Some say it was the wrath of the gods, others alleged a war broke out between Ásgarðr and Muspelheim, and many believed Ragnarök had come. One interpretation claimed the serpent Jörmungandr had become restless and uncoiled himself from about the seas."

The story and Aslaug's tone and animation drew Sigrid in like a child. "What happened?"

"Those who lived through it testified how the ground shook so hard some roofs and less sturdy structures collapsed. A few days following the shaking, a haze akin to a thin smoke cloud streaked through the sky. Each moon it grew thicker and thicker until it blocked out the sun and daylight in summer took on the shadowy hue it holds in winter. Temperatures dropped and frost killed the crops at the time they would have celebrated the summer solstice. This prolonged winter continued for several years, and no one could produce crops. With no hay for the cattle, they died. The land was thrust into famine. Some neighbors banded together for security, some people got into their boats and rowed away seeking a better place to live, while others turned violent, raiding and killing for whatever food they could find.

"My ancestors survived off resources from the sea, though the account tells even the fish and seaweed became harder to find during this terrible period. Eventually, the dust in the sky cleared, the sun shone again, summer's warmth returned, and the people rebuilt their lives. My grandparents said perhaps half the inhabitants were lost to hunger, cold, violence, or disease."

"It is a frightening tale indeed," Sigrid responded in a mesmerized hush. "Especially when one considers it may repeat in the future. So, not even the seers could agree as to the cause of the catastrophe?"

Aslaug shook her head. "After a while, people forgot about it and went about their lives. The two brothers were but small children when these things befell Sogn, what the kingdom was then called. The eldest was the king's legitimate son, and while he suffered, not so much as the younger brother, whose mother died of starvation. He was left to fend for himself and carved his mind and body into one of a mighty warrior to survive. Seeing how fine a man he had become, the king, his father, granted him a jarldom to rule over while his elder son inherited his throne. The younger brother never forgot how they abandoned him to face the cruelties of the disaster alone, while his father and older brother dwelled in greater security.

"While no one recalls exactly what the quarrel was about which split Sogn into Svithjod and Firdafylke, it is certain the harsh conditions they endured as children during the calamity played a role."

Sigrid soaked in Aslaug's story and could not wait to share it with her family and to seek any elders who may also have had a version of events passed down to them. "That is a very fascinating and informative tale. Now I shall take even more care in managing our fylke to ensure granaries house not only grain for one winter, but for several. I wish to be prepared to feed my people, so none will starve, should something of this magnitude occur again."

"And this is why your father decreed both you and your twin should be joint jarls." Aslaug's eyes danced at her from the winkles and folds surrounding them with such youth and life, it astounded Sigrid. "I suppose we should get to sleep sometime tonight."

"Indeed." Sigrid rose and walked to the other side of the bed where she had lain before. "Thank you for sharing your wisdom with me, Aslaug. Njord is fortunate to have you as a grandmother for his children."

Aslaug folded down her covers and sat wearing a white linen sleeping gown. "Thank you. I tend to think so," she added with a laugh.

SIGRID WAS DREAMING of a dark summer with snow covering grainfields when suddenly Elyn's look of alarm filled her vision. "Wake up!" she cried. Uncertain what was real and what was a dream, Sigrid's eyes popped wide just in time to roll off the bed away from the arrow which struck an empty spot where her torso had rested.

With a surge to her feet, Sigrid dashed after her attacker who fled and chased him down as he sprinted out the backdoor of the longhouse. She probably passed a dozen men and women sleeping in the great hall, but her focus was fixed on the fleeing assassin. With superior speed and a ton of determination, she overtook the man and tackled him to the dirt. His bow fell from his hands as he tried in vain to wiggle free of her grasp.

She flipped him over and the man sought to throw a punch at her. She aptly dodged the blow and pinned his wrists to the ground as she straddled him. "Who are you and who sent you to kill me?" she blasted, fury pouring off in waves.

He kicked and used his superior weight to turn the tables, reversing their positions as they grappled. But Sigrid was aware of her powerful legs and curled one up so the bend of her knee caught him around the neck. Her burst of energy propelled him off, and she spun on top once more, delivering a pounding blow to his nose which broke the cartilage, causing it to gush blood.

Terror seized his face as the man surely feared the end of his life. He stretched a hand up, groping for her throat in the pale light of the midnight sun, but she lifted her head, avoiding his reach. His fingers clutched the top of her chemise, ripping it open with his efforts.

Taking hold of his wrists, she forced his arms back to the soil. "If you want to live one minute longer, you will tell me who sent you!" He quivered under the intensity of her threat and the fight left him, rendering him prone in defeat.

Familiar footsteps rushed up behind her, stopping at her side. "I know this man," Njord declared. She spared a glance to see him pointing at the would-be assassin. "He is Unnulf's apprentice."

A more dreadful horror widened his eyes further as the man paled. "I am a carpenter, not a killer!" he cried in his defense. "My master ordered me to kill Jarl Sigrid while she slept in your longhouse. I pleaded with him, but he said he would dismiss me and spread horrible rumors about me. I didn't want to be forced to flee the village with my pregnant wife near time to deliver. Jarl Njord, Jarl Sigrid—can my life be spared long enough to see the birth of my child?"

Sigrid pushed to her feet and stepped off the man. "I don't care about him," she spat. "I want to kill that conniving, spineless traitor with my own hand! He doesn't even have the courage to face me himself, sends this hapless soul probably hoping we would kill him before he could talk. Let me get my sword," she demanded as she held the top of her chemise together in some form of modesty. "Which way is his house?"

"Wait." Njord laid a firm hand on her arm to hold her back. "Fury may serve a warrior well in the heat of battle, but it is not the proper emotion with which to make decisions."

Struggling to push down the surge of temper whirling inside, Sigrid sighed and nodded. "You are correct, of course. But you are not the one who had an arrow shot at her head while trying to sleep."

Njord granted her an understanding look, then turned his gaze on the man with the broken nose still spilling a stream of blood. "Did he say why? Halvar, isn't it?"

He nodded. "Yes, Halvar is my name, and no, he did not say why." Njord traced the moustache which framed his bare chin in consideration. "Surely this is not in retaliation for you messing up our wedding plans. When I told him the marriage had been called off, your name never came up."

"No," Sigrid affirmed with conviction. "This is about ensuring there be no peace between our kingdoms. He was present when I arrived to tell you King Grimolf wished to form a truce with King Tortryggr. When we saw him in Gimelfjord, he must have rushed to warn Ambassador Krum. That is why Krum burst in late voicing his protests. Both you and Elyn have spoken of Unnulf's ambition. I'd wager King Hemingr promised him a jarldom for his collaboration in the scheme."

In stunned realization, Njord voiced his immediate thoughts. "I wonder what his plans for Elyn and I were? Execution, banishment, slavery, or did he just not care?"

"So, you aren't going to kill me?" Halvar eked out in hopefulness.

The midnight activities had not woken everyone, but a few people from Njord's longhouse had ventured out to see what was going on, including Ingvar and Njord's son Bjorn.

"I think we should let Jarl Sigrid fight him in front of the whole village tomorrow so she can humiliate and kill him before an audience." Bjorn's bitter words came from lips twisted in an angry scowl. "She is our guest, under our protection. Besides, he could have killed Grandmother by mistake."

216

"I'm not so bad a shot," Halvar allowed. "I would never harm Lady Aslaug!"

"But you would harm Jarl Sigrid," Bjorn countered.

Sigrid's gaze passed from the boy to Halvar, who still lay on the ground, his fate resting on her recommendation. She knelt beside him, grabbed his nose, and popped it back into place, causing him to let out a yowl of pain and cover it with his hands. "I know that hurt," she said, "but it was also necessary so it will not cause you difficulty breathing in the future. Your baby won't like being awakened by you snoring louder than a bear."

As Sigrid stood, Njord asked, "Then what shall we do with him?"

"He owes a debt to your household, Njord. Perhaps he can pay it with free carpentry work or some other form of labor if he has no silver," Sigrid suggested. "But for now, I have an idea." She glanced around and caught the young blond warrior's gaze. "Ingvar, bring me a sword."

Njord gave her a curious look while Bjorn crossed his arms over his chest. "Carpentry work as penance for attempted murder? Shouldn't we at least subject him to a lashing?" the boy asked.

Sigrid smiled and placed one hand on his shoulder. "You are eager and fierce, Bjorn, fine qualities. But so is mercy." Raising her regard to Njord, she suggested, "Why don't we engage in some deception of our own?"

His expression brightened. "I'm listening."

"We lead Unnulf to believe I killed his apprentice, and we know nothing of his involvement. Halvar, I'm afraid your wife will be mourning your loss for a few days, but won't she be pleased when she sees you alive afterward? Njord, you must then ensure he accompanies you to the peace talks, where Halvar will expose his treachery in front of everyone. If he is the coward he appears to be, Unnulf will turn on Krum, who likely gave him instruction on what to do. After allowing my temper to mellow, as you so wisely recommended, I no longer care what becomes of him, so long as he never says or does anything injurious to Elyn again."

"Once all has been revealed, the freemen who gather for the Thing can vote on his punishment, be it death or banishment," Njord concluded. "The assembly would have met this week but has been postponed for King Tortryggr and his escorts to travel to the parley."

Sigrid nodded, and Ingvar returned with a sword. Sigrid whispered to Halvar, "Play dead." Then, taking the hilt in her hand, she shouted, "This will teach you to try to murder the daughter of Olaf in her sleep!" With a

217

vigorous motion, she thrust the sword tip into the ground an inch from the man's throat, which was already covered in blood from his nose. He lay still.

"Ingvar, please dispose of this traitor," Njord ordered. With a nod, Ingvar threw the limp man over his shoulder and carried him away.

Bjorn's inspired gaze passed from Sigrid to his father. In a hush, he marveled, "That was pretty clever!"

CHAPTER 31

Svithjod, the same day

*E*lyn rode along on the bay gelding Njord had lent her between Sigrid's two tall, blond brothers, struck by how much Sigurd's features resembled his sister's. Odo looked enough like the twins to tell he was related, and his youthful exuberance was apparent in the stories he told to entertain her. But after the first several hours of the journey, he ran dry.

"My sister is overjoyed with you," Sigurd commented, surprising Elyn with his candid openness. "She has done nothing but grieve, brood, calculate, and suspect every human in sight since our father was killed, but from the moment she laid eyes on you across the battlefield, at least some of her moods have been uplifted."

Blinking, and uncertain how to respond, she said, "I am glad to be of help to her, in whatever way I can."

"I know you have been intimate," he stated, as if such topics were casual conversation. "It's obvious by the glow she's been wearing, but I have to ask." He shifted his focus to her, contemplating Elyn with the same blue eyes as Sigrid's. "What are your intentions in the relationship? I mean, there is no one tougher than Sigrid, but she has a tender core. She may have had other lovers, but she has never been in love... before. She is my big sister by five minutes and while she does her share of protecting everyone else, it is my duty to protect her."

"What has she told you?" Elyn's heart leaped at his use of the word 'love' and deep down, a thrill tore through her. *Could it be? But how? Why? Uncle Unnulf repeatedly reminded me I'm the most undesirable person on earth. Is Sigurd playing with me, or did he speak the truth? Could it be Sigrid desires a relationship with me, not just a good time?*

His gaze sparkled when he laughed, and he glanced back at the road. Odo didn't seem to be interested and rode ahead to lead the way. "We share a unique bond," he explained. "More often than not, we can read each other's thoughts and feel one another's emotions. She hasn't *told* me anything, and yet I perceive it all."

"What about Sveina?" Elyn hesitated to ask, but it seemed she and Sigrid were especially close and had been for years, even if things didn't work out as Sigrid had wished.

"Sigrid never looked at Sveina the way she looks at you, nor glowed with radiant joy at the sight of her." Sigurd shrugged. "I'm sure she loved her and still does, but not to the same extent. I went through a string of young women before setting my sights on Birgitta. Sigrid recognized she was The One before I did, but I came around. Now we are to be wed." He pivoted in his saddle to face her in astonishment. "You have turned this inquiry on me, Elyn. I am attempting to determine your intentions toward my sister, not convey all her secrets to you!"

A pink blush rose in Elyn's cheeks. "I had heard stories and songs of Olaf's twins since my childhood and long aspired to be like Sigrid the Valiant but knew such would never happen. After my family was killed and I went to live with my uncle, Jarl Njord's wife Hilda took me under her wing and saw I received training as a shieldmaiden. I excelled at it, pushing myself to achieve every milestone reached by the boys and men, and to surpass them when possible, but I was still expected to complete all my domestic chores besides. To be honest, I didn't think I would ever meet Sigrid, and if I did, had convinced myself she would find me laughable. But..."

"Sigrid is more than a legendary warrior," Sigurd reminded her. "She is a real person."

Elyn cocked her head as his words sunk in. "She is. She has opened every door to me, encouraged me to believe in myself, inspired me to be my best. To even speculate she may care for me, is too much to comprehend, too wonderful to be true. You asked what my intentions are, and I'm uncertain I have ever had intentions other than to fight in the shield wall and defend my home from enemies. It hadn't occurred to me I may have choices, but now that I do..."

Elyn paused, hesitant to reveal her feelings. *This is Sigurd. Anything I say to him, I may as well be confiding to Sigrid herself. Could I summon the courage to tell her? It is easier to relay it to him, I think.*

"If she wishes it, I would be more than happy to remain with her in whatever capacity she wants me to fill."

A satisfied smile crossed Sigurd's handsome face, and he nodded to her before turning his attention back to the road. "There is no tradition, no precedent among our people for a woman to take a wife or a man to have a husband, although it still happens without a ceremony or acknowledgement by the community. That is what Sigrid desires, to have a woman as a life partner, not merely to have sex with. Mother can't understand, but I suppose most people don't. They say, 'Sigrid, you may have all the lovers you wish, but you should marry a man and have children. It is what women are supposed to do.' But my sister is not like most women. I'd hate for her to set her hopes on you, only for you to turn away and seek a more acceptable arrangement. I couldn't stand the agony of another broken heart."

"Sigurd." Elyn sensed a rush of emotion, feelings she didn't believe dwelt inside her before that instant. A tingle rushed across her skin, and she felt weak in the knees, as if had she been standing, she may have fallen to the ground. He returned a soft, soulful gaze to her, and she swallowed before making her reply. "I could not endure her heart to break, either. I truly love Sigrid but have been afraid to say so lest I make a fool of myself."

He flashed her a grin. "I hoped that was the case. Now, let's plan how we will convince King Grimolf."

They had been riding all day when the trio arrived in Hafrafell at Siegfried's longhouse where they were welcomed and escorted inside. A lovely young woman with light brown hair and dancing eyes rushed across the hall for Sigurd to scoop into his arms and twirl about. *Birgitta, I presume.* Elyn stood with Odo while Sigurd concluded his greeting with a kiss.

"You are being remiss, my dear." Birgitta peered around Sigurd's impressive frame with a curious expression. "Introduce me to our guest."

"Yes, but of course," he replied happily. "Can't I be excited to see you?" He laughed and slid an arm around her slender waist. "This is Elyn from Jarl Njord's household in Firdafylke. Elyn, meet my fiancée Birgitta. You know Odo."

"So nice to meet you, Birgitta." Elyn felt so awkward. She never knew what to say to people.

Odo rolled his eyes. "I'm off to mingle," he announced and waved to someone he recognized as he strode away.

"How is Siegfried?" Sigurd asked.

"Better," Birgitta replied. "Elyn, did this big oaf tell you about what happened?"

"Yes, or rather Sigrid did. I am glad your brother's health is improving." Elyn felt suddenly as if every eye in the hall was focused on her. Jarl Siegfried's wound was delivered by one of her countrymen, perhaps one of her friends. She had killed warriors from Svithjod in the battle and here all their friends and relatives gathered like a pack of wolves to tear her apart. She inched up to Sigurd and took hold of his other arm.

In her dress with no weapons, she felt vulnerable, and a slight bit guilty. While it was every warrior's dream to die courageously in battle, not a one ever wished it to be 'today.'

But wait—it was not her they had their gaze set upon. It was Sigurd, and not vicious snarls on their lips, but grins. "Congratulations on your upcoming marriage!" one called out.

"You are one lucky bastard," another admitted with a laugh.

The warriors of the hall gathered around to pat Sigurd on the back and shake his hand.

"And who is this beauty on your other arm?" Elyn recognized Jarl Siegfried as he gingerly crossed the floor.

"Siegfried, please do not get up!" Sigurd left Birgitta and Elyn behind to rush to his friend's side. "We were on our way to visit you where you sat."

Siegfried batted a hand in the air. "I can't rebuild my strength lounging about on a bench, now can I? But just between you and me," he said in friendly comradery. "It was much easier to bounce back when I was younger!"

Birgitta introduced them. "This is Elyn, a representative from Firdafylke. Sigurd and Odo are escorting her to deliver a message from King Tortryggr to King Grimolf."

Siegfried's eyes and smile brightened as he bathed her in his gaze. Then Sigurd spoke in a hush which Elyn could still make out. "She's Sigrid's friend."

The host jarl's mouth opened, then closed, and he nodded, the heated expression evaporating from his face. "Ah, that's nice." It was clear he didn't mean it. Elyn could not believe the admiring looks she received from all the men. Was it the dress? It had to be the dress. Mayhap it was the hair style Lady Gudred had given her or the borrowed jewelry. "Welcome to my home, Elyn. You will be safe with us."

"You are so kind, Jarl Siegfried," she gushed in honest appreciation. "I thank you for your hospitality and am sorry for any inconvenience."

Siegfried raised a hand and smiled at her. "There is no such thing as an inconvenience regarding a friend of Sigrid's. We have spoken and I am aware of the situation. Come, let us sit and eat, but remember." The older jarl with tawny-brown hair and a burnished wiry beard lowered his tone. "There may be spies among us."

Elyn was tired from the long ride, but excited to visit Siegfried's home as she had never been to Hafrafell before. It struck her the traditions observed here were no different from in Njord's longhouse. They served the same foods and drinks, enjoyed the same music, and stories, and she could swear she had seen one of these very skald's perform in Kaldrlogr. *How can we be other than friends and neighbors? It makes me sick to think my hand injured or killed people so engaging, so much like mine.* A sudden rage rose inside her toward the lying Krum and Hroald and their conspirators when she saw a young pregnant woman sitting off by herself, draped in a brown shawl with her head lowered in sorrow. *Her husband must have been killed in one of the battles, perhaps by my own hand, and all because we had been deceived! It would be different if these people had raided our lands, stolen our stores, and killed our farmers, but they didn't. Oh, Odin, Allfather, god of wisdom, grant me the words to present to a king! I am but an ordinary shield-maiden, not eloquent of tongue. May you guide my speech so King Grimolf perceives my sincerity, so he will agree to my request.*

Birgitta invited Elyn to spend the night in her room, which was arranged and decorated quite differently than Sigrid's. However, Elyn had fallen fast asleep before Birgitta returned from her walk with Sigurd and never heard her come to bed.

· · ·

SIGURD MADE certain they were off to an early start the next morning as they rode to Sochabrot to meet with the king. Once in the grandest great hall Elyn had ever seen, Sigurd introduced her as an emissary from King Tortryggr the Navigator.

She studied the king, who sat in his seat of judgement on a small, raised platform. He appeared robust, in his early fifties, with plenty of brown still competing with the gray in his hair and beard. An attractive woman at least fifteen years younger with auburn hair and a splendid summer white and golden gown sat regally at his right hand.

"Elyn of Firdafylke, what message do you bring from King Tortryggr? Is he well?" Grimolf asked, inviting her to speak.

People had gathered around, and all the attention made Elyn nervous. At least Sigurd and Odo stood close by, so she did not have to face the assembly alone.

"Yes, he is well, my lord. Any rumors of his ill health are false, and while not so vigorous and youthful as yourself, he is still strong and active in both mind and body."

Grimolf let out an amused laugh and turned to his wife. "Do you hear that, Tori? I am youthful!" He slapped his knee, Tori chuckled, and he returned his attention to Elyn. "I am glad to hear such fortunate news."

When Grimolf said nothing else and looked at her expectantly, Elyn took a deep breath, steeled herself, and spoke with confidence as Sigrid would do. "King Tortryggr wishes you to believe the truth—neither he nor any warrior of Firdafylke raided or attacked your lands, but someone made it seem as if we did to suit their own purposes. He invites you to meet with him in person under a banner of truce so you may reason with one another and form a pact of peace and discern who our true enemy is. This parlay would take place at a spot on the borders of our two lands near the seacoast, easily accessed by ship, one week from today."

"King Grimolf do not listen to this woman," asserted a short, stocky man with an excessive amount of black hair.

That must be Hroald, Elyn figured and narrowed her eyes at him.

Grimolf turned an inquisitive gaze to the man with the mountaineer accent. "Why not? I have already promised Jarl Sigrid if King Tortryggr requested talks, I would agree."

"But my lord, this is clearly a trap," Hroald elaborated. "They will be lying in wait to kill you when you arrive. If King Tortryggr truly wishes peace, demand he come here to your great hall."

The king seemed to consider his words and Elyn knew she must devise something convincing to counter Hemingr's agent. "My lord, this is no trap, but I can understand your concerns. Perhaps you would wish to bring with you an armed escort, even a large one, even an army if you feel your life could be in danger. Already an assassin tried to kill Jarl Sigrid and I to prevent such negotiations from taking place."

"See!" Hroald declared pointing a finger at Elyn. "She wants you to bring an army so they can wipe out your forces and sweep in to conqueror your kingdom."

"No!" Elyn was at her wits end. That infuriating little man was going to ruin everything. Why wasn't Sigurd helping her? Didn't he know how to talk to a king better than she?

Stepping forward, Elyn dropped to her knees before the lord of all Svithjod. "If you believe my testimony is false or that my king, respected throughout all Norvegr for a lifetime of worthy deeds, is a deceitful schemer out to ruin you, then hold me here as a hostage. Let my life be forfeit if my words are not true. You have an enemy, King Grimolf; but it is not Firdafylke."

Hroald opened his mouth to speak again, but Grimolf raised a hand to silence him. "You are a friend of Jarl Sigrid? Ah, yes," he answered himself with a nod. "Jarl Sigrid mentioned you to me when last we spoke. You say an attempt was made on her life?"

"Yes, my lord, it is true," Sigurd affirmed and stepped forward placing his hands on Elyn's shoulders.

Now he decides to say something! she thought and waited with bated breath for the king's decision.

"King Tortryggr requests a parley and you told us if he did so, you would talk to him," Sigurd said as a reminder. "I suggest you not only take an armed escort but bring Ambassador Hroald as well. It would be most advantageous to have his insights on any proposals King Tortryggr may voice. And Hroald, didn't you promise King Hemingr would come to our aid in force if needed?"

"Well, yes," Hroald squirmed and cast his gaze to the floor. "But it would be better for me to return to Gudbrandsdalir to update King Hemingr on the situation."

A curious look overtook Grimolf's expression, and he turned a suspicious eye on Hroald. "First you try to convince me Tortryggr is on death's door and Jarl Njord is attacking us to gain enough prestige to challenge the prince for his father's throne. Then you try to convince me my own jarls are plotting to kill Sigurd, Sigrid, and Siegfried so they can come after me and usurp my rule. Now you say Tortryggr is strong enough to prepare a trap and threaten my kingdom. Which is it, Hroald?"

Elyn beamed in satisfaction as the dwarfish man withered under the king's scrutiny. "I, I just want what is best for you, King Grimolf."

"Good," the king quipped. "Then you shall accompany me to the border. Elyn, I have no need to hold you as a hostage. Sigurd will keep an eye on you, and if he does not, I am confident his sister shall. We will have to postpone the meeting of the Thing until this is settled. Odo, my fine lad, would you mind serving as Hroald's protector? He will need you every hour of the day and night from now until the talks to ensure nothing happens to him."

"Indeed, my lord!" The eager young man stepped forward. "I won't let him out of my sight and vow not a hair on his head shall be harmed."

Thank Odin! Relieved for the ordeal to be over, Elyn allowed Sigurd to assist her to her feet. "Thank you, King Grimolf," she said with a bow. "I look forward to seeing you again in one week's time. You will be very pleased with the results."

CHAPTER 32

Sigrid returned to a near empty longhouse, with only Asmund and Thora milling about the great hall. "Where is everyone?" she asked.

Asmund stopped sweeping and propped himself on his broom. "All the men have gone to a barn raising. There's a lot of rebuilding required after those raids."

"And Lady Gudred and Girrid went to prepare food for the workers," Thora added from the stool where she pumped the handle on the churn making butter.

So much for my welcome home, Sigrid thought. *Sveina knew when I was due to arrive, and she always has a bath ready for me. Maybe she will be along soon.*

"Thank you," Sigrid bade the servants. "I know lending a hand, especially under these circumstances, takes priority. Have Jarl Sigurd, Odo, and Elyn returned?"

"Not yet," Asmund replied.

"Can I get you something?" Thora asked.

"No, thank you. I may come out for a bite later. I'm just going to unpack and rest for a while." Sigrid strode past them into her private room. She couldn't remember when the house had been so quiet. Even Warg and Jotun were not here to greet her.

As she undressed, Sigrid wondered how she would tell Elyn her uncle was a traitor. Would it come as a surprise or not? She scooped water from the basin and splashed it on her face, then blotted it with a towel and sat at her dressing table to brush her hair. *I want to look good when Elyn returns. I shall ask her to stay with me and I hope she agrees. But she'll need to have a position. I'll bet she would make a wonderful fighting instructor, but that's Rangvoldr's post, when he isn't running off with Sigurd.*

Hearing a noise behind her, Sigrid smiled. "Sveina, would you heat water for my bath?"

"Sveina isn't here."

Sigrid spun at the sound of Rangvoldr's voice. It was quite presumptuous of him to enter her quarters uninvited, and she was only wearing her chemise, howbeit a fresh one without a tear down the front. "What is the matter?" she asked in concern, supposing an emergency could excuse his intrusion.

"Your insistence on peace talks is the matter." His muscular body blocked her doorway with arms crossed and a perturbed expression.

A confused frown formed on Sigrid's face. "I know you enjoy fighting, but since when is peace a problem?"

"When it stands in the way of our jarldom," he answered with stony conviction.

"*Our* jarldom?" This was very wrong. A seed of dread sprouted in Sigrid's gut as she hoped she misinterpreted Rangvoldr's meaning.

"Precisely." He crossed the room, rounding the dormant hearth, to stand closer, but still between her and the exit. Sigrid rose from her stool and faced him, her eyes demanding an explanation.

"You do not take my proposals seriously because we are not peers and you see me as beneath your station," he expounded.

"No," Sigrid retorted. Her heart raced at his implications. She had uncovered no evidence he was a traitor. What would drive him to reveal these things? "You are my brother's friend, like kin. I am not attracted to you that way. You know this, so I considered your proposals to be a game."

"This is not a game!" Temper rang in his voice and shot through his gaze. "Do you understand how it feels to grow up with Sigurd and Sigrid, children of Jarl Olaf, to be just as proficient as them, but never good enough? I was there for most of your exploits, fighting at your sides, and yet who recounts the tales of my heroic deeds? Where is my name in the songs and praises?"

"Rangvoldr, I do not compose the ballads nor repeat the accounts,"

Sigrid responded. "I asked no one else to, either. I am sorry you do not feel you get the credit you deserve, but that is not Sigurd and mine's fault."

"It doesn't matter now," he quipped. "A restructuring of power is on the horizon, and I shall have my seat of rulership. The question is, will you be at my side? Think of it, Sigrid," he began in an animated tone intended to convince her. "What if you and I shared control of a larger fylke than you currently hold? More farms, more ships, more warriors? We could mount expeditions to the Volga and beyond. Our names would be remembered in the sagas, Sigrid and Rangvoldr."

Oh, he was a traitor, all right. But how to handle it was the question. She had not brought her sword with her to her room. Her trunk held a few weapons, but it was locked at the foot of her bed. He was a capable fighter and physically stronger than she, and while she might incapacitate him, she needed to learn every detail of the plot he may convey to her.

"And where would we get this expanse of land?" she asked, as if she was considering it.

His dark eyes brightened. "I have made a bargain with someone who can make it happen."

"And what about Sigurd?" She raised her eyebrows with the question. "Do you plan to leave him out?"

"I promise no harm will come to Sigurd," he vowed. "Beyond that, I have no control."

The deal was obviously with King Hemingr, but what did he have to do to earn a jarldom? A dread realization shot through her as a flaming arrow and catapulted her into a furious temper.

"You!" Shaking with rage, she pointed a finger at him. "Did you kill Olaf? Was a sorðinn title more important to you than my father's life? Odin's beard, man, he treated you like another son!"

"No!" He lifted his palms in innocence and shook his head, reeling in shock. "I did no such thing," he vowed. "And if I had known he would, I'd have never let the man in."

"You let his murderer into our house?" she fumed. *No, Sigrid, don't kill him yet. There may be more he can tell you.* It took all her self-control to not gouge out his eyes with her fingernails.

"I didn't know he was going to murder anyone," Rangvoldr stressed. "He said he was here to propose a deal to Jarl Olaf. Since your father so often boasted of having two heirs but only one jarldom to pass on, he thought to persuade Olaf to agree to a pact guaranteeing you and Sigurd would each have a fylke to rule, but your father would have nothing to do with it. Afraid he would go to King Grimolf and ruin everything, he..." Rangvoldr's voice trailed off, and he hung his head. "He stabbed him in the back."

"Who?" she demanded. "Who stabbed Olaf in the back?"

"Now, Sigrid," he began, inching closer to her. "I can't give you a name. You'll run out and slice off his head and while I'll be happy to present it to you on a platter as a wedding gift, right now, we need him to complete the deal."

Right now, I'm ready to slap your head onto a platter! Amid the infuriating shock of betrayal, the repugnant whirlpool of molten anger, and the savage desire for revenge, Sigrid was struck with an even more chilling thought.

"Where is Sveina?" She struggled to keep fear at bay while every muscle in her body tightened.

Rangvoldr closed the last few inches between them and smiled at her, reaching up to stroke a lock of her hair. "You won't need her anymore," he answered in a soothing tone. "You have me now. And you won't need the red-haired girl either. I will take care of you, love you, give you pleasure. Don't you know I've always wanted to do?"

Sigrid became as still as granite, her voice a menacing whisper. "By Thor's death, what have you done?"

Seeing the violent resolve in her aspect, Rangvoldr took a step back and glanced away. "It's your own fault," he retorted. "You should not have sent her to spy on me. I couldn't let her tell you, not before I had the chance to explain."

"You... killed her?" The glacial chill in her tone could have frozen a fjord in an instant. He was a dead man. She may have allowed him to live for the role he played in Olaf's murder, but this was beyond forgiveness. Rangvoldr would never leave her room alive.

"She was only a slave, Sigrid!"

The man thought he could use that as an excuse?

"Still, you chose her over me, time and time again. It was infuriating, emasculating, and besides," he declared, waving a hand in the air, "she shouldn't have been sticking her nose into my affairs, following and watching me."

"Why? Because she saw you talking with Hroald?" Sigrid trembled. A part of her wanted to choke the life out of the conspirator, while another longed to crumple in a heap on the floor and sob.

Rangvoldr froze and blinked at her. "Oh, you know about him?"

"Yes, I know about him, and King Hemingr." Sigrid bit off the words in disgust. *But how am I going to kill him?* She pondered. *Everyone is gone, the servants are no help, I have no weapons, and my room is not a conducive setting for a fight.* She considered the water pitcher, her hairbrush, the washbasin, but those were not viable options. She doubted she could overpower him in a fistfight, even when she was fueled by wrath. Then an idea crept into Sigrid's mind.

"You do?" A blank look passed over Rangvoldr's visage before he reached to touch her shoulders.

"So, Hroald stabbed my father in the back, and you did nothing?"

"You must understand what is about to happen." Rangvoldr insisted anxiously. "The Gudbrandsdalir ambassadors will make sure the peace talks go wrong, so our army and Firdafylke's break into battle. When few remain, King Hemingr's forces will charge down from behind the ridge and wipe out whoever refuses to surrender. Then, we get an enormous jarldom in the new kingdom."

"Enormous, you say?" It curdled Sigrid's stomach to put a curious intonation into the words. She softened her gaze and relaxed her muscles, ready to play the praying mantis. She reached a hand to caress his shoulder, thinking, *let's see how you like a little deception.*

His expression radiated with hope. "Indeed. Twice the size of this one, and King Hemingr promised no harm would come to Sigurd. If he does not object to joining us, he may have his own jarldom."

"You know him well," Sigrid said in a languid tone, batting her eyes at her prey. "Do you think he will agree?"

"Together, we can convince him."

Sigrid eased backward toward her bed, a 'come-hither' expression slyly teasing him to follow. "How may I be certain you will keep your word? Is there a way we can seal the bargain?"

Rangvoldr mirrored her steps, desire ripe in his smile, as he undressed her with his wanton gaze. "I'm sure we'll figure out something. Oh, Sigrid, at last you see me as worthy!"

As worthy as a worm-infested dung pile!

Sigrid lay on the bed and rolled to the other side, making room for him, then bit her lip in a flirtation. "Let's see if you can live up to the boasting you've touted all these years."

Rangvoldr grabbed the hem of his tunic and yanked it over his head, revealing a muscled chest and shoulders adorned with tattoos and scattered scars. Without bothering to remove his boots, he climbed in and covered her body with his. "How I have dreamed of this moment! I knew one day you would truly look at me, and you would invite me to your bed."

With a playful grin, Sigrid flipped him, so she straddled his sides with her thighs. "I like to be on top."

He let out a laugh and reached a hand to fondle her breast. "Whatever pleases you. Gods, what a pair we will make! You'll see, Sigrid."

Sigrid had realized a strength she possessed he could not counter, and squeezed with all her might, compressing his ribs, and restricting his lungs.

"Hey," he laughed, and slid his palms to her thighs. "Not so tight. I can't breathe."

Her demeanor switched on the point of a blade. "Good." The frigid bite of her tone combined with the icy intent in her eyes triggered Rangvoldr's fear response. She recognized it the instant it flashed into his gaze.

"You don't mean it!" His hands groped, pushing, pulling against her powerful legs, but he could not pry them from the vise-grip which held him captive.

She leaned closer and seethed, "You should not have killed Sveina."

When he grabbed for her throat, she threw her head up and arched her back out of his reach. "Don't do this!" he cried.

"Where is she?" Sigrid hissed. "What did you do with her body?" Sveina would have a proper burial and Sigrid would have a tender goodbye with her trusted companion.

Rangvoldr opened his mouth to speak but could not produce a sound. His eyes widened in terror, and he slapped a hand to her arm. Sigrid relaxed the muscles in her legs long enough for him to inhale a shallow breath. "Tell me!"

He gulped and cried, "In the sweathouse."

As she slammed the pressure powerfully between her thighs once more, tears squirted from his eyes. She ripped her arm from his grip and uttered, "That will save you from torture and agony, but not from justice."

His gasp was a sweet sound to her vengeful ears. Sigrid gripped Rangvoldr's wrists as they flailed to make purchase and plummeted her weight down with a mighty jerk, pinning them to the bed on either side of his head. Taking a deep breath herself, she pressed her thighs tighter. "Mayhap I could have forgiven you for falling prisoner to your ambition, for hiding an enemy plot, for betraying your jarl and your king," she rattled off in menacing speculation. "But you knew what Sveina meant to me. You didn't kill her to protect yourself," she snarled in a tirade. "You were jealous because I desired her instead of you. What inconceivable folly clouded your mind into thinking I would ever want you?"

Rangvoldr struggled beneath the might of her rage, endeavoring to raise his arms. He tried to jar her loose by kicking his feet and twisting his hips, but Sigrid's singlemindedness equipped her with a puissance he could not overcome. Each time he attempted to draw breath afforded her an opportunity to strengthen the clamp, which robbed him of air. Though a face so familiar from her youth pleaded with Sigrid, her vehement resolve did not waver.

"You are an oath-breaker, a defector, and a murderer," she pronounced in judgement. "You will descend into the murky depths and never raise your horn in Odin's Hall. I don't care how good a warrior you were—Valhalla is only for the worthy." With shaking muscles, Sigrid kept the pressure firm long after Rangvoldr lay still.

CHAPTER 33

"*I*s anyone home?" Sigurd's cheerful voice echoed through the great hall as he and Elyn entered that evening. Though she knew the hour to be late, light streamed in behind them through the open doorway.

At once, a depressed spirit settled over Elyn like a shroud, and she sensed something terrible had occurred. Thora sat in a corner weeping, and Elyn's heart leaped into her throat with dread.

"Sigrid?" Her lips and voice trembled as they formed the name.

Asmund, seated beside Thora with an arm about her shoulders, pointed to the family's private chambers. Sigurd took Elyn's hand, and they rushed through the ingress. Sigrid sat on the floor outside her room wearing trousers and a tunic with her head buried in her knees. Elyn did not see any blood, but when Sigrid raised her gaze, her eyes were red, moist, and haunted.

Elyn kneeled on one side of her and reached for her hands while Sigurd squatted by her other side and rested a steadying hand on her shoulder. "What happened?" His tone reflected the tender compassion in his expression. Elyn was much relieved to see Sigrid safe, but sensed pain and grief weighing on her like an anvil.

Sigrid turned her sorrowful countenance first to Elyn, then to her twin. "Rangvoldr." She inhaled a shaky breath. "All this time, acting like your best friend, he has been sick with envy. Hroald promised him a jarl-dom, power, wealth, and influence. He wanted us to join him," she relayed, then lowered her head with a humorless laugh. "He didn't precisely spell it out, but Hroald murdered Father, and Rangvoldr let him do it."

When Sigrid lifted her gaze again, the blaze burning there was preferable to the previous helpless despair. "I had requested Sveina to keep an eye out for Hroald because we suspected him. I asked her to watch and listen for any signs of treachery." Fresh tears quenched the fire from her eyes. "It's my fault."

Elyn gripped Sigrid's hand tighter, fearing what may follow. She felt Sigrid's agony tear through her soul and wished more than anything whisk it away. Not knowing what to say, she lifted Sigrid's fingers to her lips and kissed them, wrestling back her own tears. *You must stay strong for Sigrid. She doesn't need you crying, too.*

"Rangvoldr is a traitor?" Disbelief permeated Sigurd's voice. "A spy, who assisted that rat's bastard in killing Father?" Pushing shock from his visage, his muscles stiffened, and his sound hardened. "Where is he? I want to talk to him."

Sigrid whipped her head toward her bedchamber door and back with a solemn expression. "He's dead." Her red-rimmed eyes met Sigurd's. "He killed Sveina."

Elyn felt her heart break for Sigrid. She understood how much Sveina meant to her, what they had shared, how horrendous a blow this was to the woman she loved. "Oh, Sigrid," she uttered in empathy, before drawing a hand to cover her mouth. Elyn refused to fall apart, but she could not halt the tears from forming for Sigrid's loss.

Sigrid pried one hand from Elyn's grip to wipe at the stream flowing down her face while holding tight to her with the other. Elyn wanted to wrap Sigrid in her arms, to kiss away every tear, but she did not dare overstep. Her brother was here, and he would be of greater comfort.

"I brought her body here and laid her on my bed," Sigrid stated in a dull cadence, void of inflection. "He choked her and broke her neck, so there's no blood. I couldn't leave her in the sweathouse."

"By Thor, how did I not know?" Sigurd let out in dismay. "How could I allow myself to be fooled? You are not to blame, Sigrid. No more so than I."

"He deceived and betrayed us," Sigrid affirmed. "All out of ambition and jealousy." Tilting her head to Elyn, she continued, "The assassin in the forest may not have been for me after all. Rangvoldr stated I didn't need

Sveina or you. He's always had this fantasy about us. I should have taken his delusions more seriously. He killed Sveina because I chose her, and he may have tried to do the same when he realized I had chosen you, too. But he was wrong—dead wrong." Meeting her gaze with ardent longing, Sigrid confessed, "I do need you, so very much."

It was the stone which broke the basket, and Elyn wrapped her arms around Sigrid, placing gentle kisses on her cheek. "I'm here for you, Sigrid, and I'm not going anywhere. I'm only sorry you killed the cockless swine, so I don't get to do it for you."

Sigurd pushed to his feet with a look of bitter resolve. "I'm going to find that snake Hroald and execute my vengeance on him for killing Olaf."

"No, wait." Sigrid laid a hand on his calf and gave it a squeeze. "We should allow this to play out. There will be time for executions after Kings Grimolf and Tortryggr see and hear and comprehend the truth. We must do something with Rangvoldr and plan a burial for Sveina."

He let out an angry puff and rubbed the back of his neck. "I suppose I can wait a week. But dead or not, I'm giving that skitr-faced false-friend a piece of my mind!" He stomped through the curtain into Sigrid's room.

Sigrid's arms enfolded around Elyn's neck, and she hugged her close. Elyn shifted to sit on the floor beside her, extending an aura of warmth, love, and comfort over her as the embrace lingered. Minutes passed in silence until Sigrid loosened her arms and leaned back to focus her gaze on Elyn.

"I fear I have more ill tidings," she conveyed. "Unnulf is also a conspirator bought by Hemingr's promises of wealth and power. We caught his apprentice, Halvar in a weak attempt on my life and he testified against your uncle."

Horror overcame Elyn at the thought her wicked uncle may have hurt Sigrid. She set her jaw and hardened her face. "Sadly, it does not surprise me to hear of it. He has always been an ambitious man. But if he had succeeded in harming one hair on your head, I—"

"He didn't." Sigrid assured her with a kiss on her lips. "We have taken no action against him yet but will present Halvar as a witness before the kings." She let out a mournful sigh. "Is there no one we can trust?"

Elyn brought her palms to Sigrid's face and steered it into her honest gaze. "You can trust me." For a moment the two women peered into each other's souls, afraid to move or breathe lest the spell of connection be broken.

"She's telling the truth." Sigurd reappeared in Sigrid's doorway, much calmer than he had been. "She proposed to remain as King Grimolf's hostage against the possibility of the parley being a trap, even offered to forfeit her life if our message was false."

"Elyn!" Sigrid's eyes widened, and she blinked, her lips parting in astonishment. "You mustn't do such things."

"Oh, Sigrid!" Sigurd groaned and shook his head. "You must allow those around you to be strong, too. You aren't the only valiant one, you know."

The hint of a smile peeked across Sigrid's face for the first time as Sigurd's delivery lightened the mood. She entwined her fingers with Elyn's and nodded. "I admire your conviction. I just can't bear to lose anyone else close to me right now."

With a soft glow in her aspect, Elyn replied, "I understand."

"Well, I think I hear everyone returning at last," Sigurd acknowledged. "Where have they been, anyway?"

"At a barn raising," Sigrid answered.

Two gangly gray-brindle Cu dogs loped in to let their mistress know they had returned. As if by some deep intuition, they halted, eased nearer with bowed heads and distressed eyes, and lowered their bulks to the floor near where she and Elyn sat cuddled together. Sigrid smiled and stretched out a hand to pat each head.

"I'll get Gunnlief and Finn to help us with them," he said with a nod in the direction of her room. "Poor Finn. You should allow him to assist with the arrangements."

"She was so excited about building a relationship with him," Sigrid bemoaned, her shoulders slumping once more. "I can't believe she's gone." She rested on Elyn's shoulder and Elyn kissed the top of her head. There were no words she could offer. Sigrid needed to grieve, and Elyn would be there to share her sorrow.

Out of the blue, Sigrid lifted her gaze to Sigurd as he started to walk away. "Where's Odo?"

"He stayed to monitor Hroald and ensure he did not flee the kingdom," Elyn replied in a tranquil tone. "He is a capable young man and will do well."

Seemingly satisfied, Sigrid relaxed into Elyn's embrace.

· · ·

LATER THAT NIGHT, after the house had quieted and bodies been removed, Elyn reclined in bed with an exhausted Sigrid, who leaned on her for intimate support, her head nestled upon Elyn's breast. Sigrid could not tolerate food at dinner, and despite her urgings, Elyn refused to eat without her. It had been a horrendous day for Sigrid—for both women, really. Elyn reflected on all the times her uncle had rebuked her ideas as foolish, had insinuated Sigrid lied, and it all came together. He wormed his way into Njord's circle to influence him in ways to benefit the conspiracy. Then why had he been so set on her marrying Njord when he probably calculated they would both wind up dead? Was it merely to keep up pretenses, or was it his backup plan if Hemingr's ploy was a failure? She simply didn't care.

What she cared about was the woman in her arms. She stroked Sigrid's silky shoulder and upper arm and touched a kiss to her brow, aware her mind trudged through a mire of woes and regrets. "Tell me about your happiest memories with Sveina," Elyn encouraged. "The times the two of you laughed and enjoyed life together."

Sigrid's energy shifted and brightened. Opening a treasure box of memories, she conveyed story after story of youthful mischief, swimming nude in the fjord, playing pranks on Odo and Girrid, and being chased by Lady Gudred wielding a rolling pin, the image prompting them into a roar of laughter. "She may have been my servant, but aside from Sigurd, she was my best friend. She knew what I wanted or needed before I did and never failed to give it to me. I picture her sitting in a meadow of clover on Helgafjell, conversing with skogvættir and fjallvættir, the spirits of the forest and mountain. The Ljósálfar will invite her to dine with them, for she was as fair as the light elves, and they would enjoy her pleasant company. She never complained, never said a harsh word to anyone. I believe wherever she is now, it is the most peaceful of the realms. That is the comfort I hold onto."

"I am certain you are right," Elyn concurred. By then, their positions had reversed, and she lay on Sigrid's shoulder with her hand atop her abdomen.

"I loved her, you know," Sigrid confessed. "But not the way I love you. You are the missing part of me, the soul I could never find. Something struck me deep down in the unknowable core of my being when I first saw you. My mind was unaware if you were a stone-cold bitch or a fun-loving tart, but my heart rang a bell, waking me to your existence. I couldn't allow harm to come to you on the field of battle that day, because I needed the chance to get to know you, to discover for myself why the sight of you stole my breath away. I love you, Elyn, and I believe we were meant for each other—not only to save our kingdoms, but to complement each other's strengths and weaknesses, to share a life of discovery and joy, trials and disappointments together as a team. Two oxen equally yoked can easily handle a load which would be a burden for one alone, or a strong ox paired with a weak one.

"Elyn, would you consider remaining here with me, not to be my servant, but my partner? We find ourselves in need of a captain of our warriors, since the position used to be Rangvoldr's. And I…"

Sigrid and Elyn inclined their heads toward each other at the pause, catching one another's gaze. The hopeful, vulnerable look in Sigrid's sky-blue eyes was endearing and totally irresistible. A coy smile danced over Elyn's lips. "And you?"

"And I would be lost without you."

Elyn pushed up to meet Sigrid's mouth in a vital kiss, her hand trailing its way to trace light fingers across her throat and into her golden hair. "I love you, Sigrid. Not because you are a legend, but because you are real. You believed in me before I accomplished a thing, and because of you, I now believe in me, too. I would be honored to share your life and adventures, your pain and responsibilities, to train and lead your warriors, to cool your temper by day and heat your bed each night. But this I insist upon—I will fight at your side, protecting your back, ensuring no sword or spear can strike you. My shield shall be your shield, and my blade will repel your enemies."

Unspeakable joy washed over the two in an encompassing wave and their lips found each other once more. This was not the occasion to dive headlong into physical passions, but for a deep understanding, a union of souls. Elyn and Sigrid held each other in pure satisfaction throughout the bittersweet night.

CHAPTER 34

*S*igrid and Sigurd each commanded a longboat as four ships embarked from Gnóttdalr the day before the kings' peace talks were scheduled. Even though the journey would take half the time by sea, the twins wanted to set up a meeting spot and scout the area for any awaiting trouble. Both wore their armor and brought their weapons. They had called upon every able-bodied man and part-time shieldmaiden in the village to join their party with the mission of safeguarding Grimolf and as a deterrence to violence. Gunnlief, who had been as shocked as Sigrid by Rangvoldr's betrayal, was accompanied by his wife, Brenn, who left the children with their grandmother. Arne, the fisherman, and Skarde the Unlucky helped man Sigurd's boat while Gunne and Bard, the farmer and goatherd who had argued in their court not long ago, pulled side by side on an oar.

Standing at the bow, Sigrid's gaze fell on the stern of Sigurd's ship, which had taken the lead. She thought about racing him just for the fun of it but spared the men's vigor as they heaved at the fourteen rows of oars. Crafted of oak in clink-type construction, these low-draft ships had speed and flexibility for travel over the open ocean or up rivers as shallow as half Sigurd's height. Thirty yellow and black shields hung on the sides of the vessel while the warriors kept their axes and swords close at hand. A plentiful number of spears were piled in the center of the craft, along with campsite supplies.

They ventured north with the vast expanse of ocean churning to the port side while the rocky coastline and green timbered mountains etched a silhouette to starboard. Taking a deep breath of the salty air filled Sigrid with the thrill of adventure as she recalled past voyages with delight. Though packed with tedious boredom and scattered with life-threatening danger, her experiences at sea had been some of her most memorable.

They had held separate memorial services for Sveina and Rangvoldr. Sigrid was pleased with the crowd who gathered to say farewell to her beloved servant, and they lay her to rest in a burial mound reserved for non-noble free citizens. Friends and relatives relayed words of fondness and placed flowers on the earth to honor her. Word traveled quickly about how she died, and few paid their respects to Rangvoldr. Sigurd could not forgive his betrayal, but as a fierce fighter who had battled by his side many times, he deserved to be hastened on his way on a warrior's funeral pyre to wherever the gods saw fit to send him.

Sigrid turned a look of anticipation over her shoulder to Elyn and grinned. Wind whipped her lover's hair like a wave of fiery silk, causing Sigrid's heart to flutter. The blue and silver armor she had given Elyn fit her full breasts and rounded hips perfectly, presenting her as the very image of a Valkyrie. *How could she have never realized how magnificent she is?*

Memories of sparring with Elyn in the yard filled Sigrid with pride. She taught her a few fresh moves as Elyn accustomed herself to the new blade, but Elyn had shown her a trick or two in exchange. Sigrid had been amazed by her tenacity and strength when they had played a game of shield push where each opponent dug in to shove the other past a line drawn in the dirt. Elyn's agility nearly matched her own, and Sigrid was certain it would with more practice. *Training with her is like matching my skills against Sigurd, only she is not so tall... and my brother doesn't get me hot and bothered in the same way.*

She had enjoyed bathing with Elyn in the warming waters of the fjord and dancing with her in their hall. They had spent hours telling each other stories about their lives and considering the monumental questions of mankind. Her tantalizing touches and seductive looks had kept Sigrid in a constant state of arousal throughout the week, and she found it hard to keep her mind on anything other than getting Elyn alone in her bedroom whenever possible. She had never been so delirious with passion, nor flown so high on the sharing of it. With Elyn, she not only felt alive, but reborn.

And now she joins me on our first quest as a team. The thought brought

Sigrid immense satisfaction and eagerness which hummed through her systems with a bright and shining energy. There would be danger if Hemingr and his army arrived as she expected them to, but she would be at Elyn's side protecting her delectable rear.

The vessel rose and fell as it cut through moderate swells, and Sigrid noticed Elyn's firm hold on the gunwale. "When was the last occasion you traveled in a longboat?"

"This is my first time on a warship," she answered. "I am enjoying the exhilaration, but my stomach is not so thrilled as my spirit."

"Why didn't you say something?" Sigrid chided. "Our next voyage I will give you some ginger root to chew and a tight coiled bracelet to prevent seasickness. Also, after you get used to the motion of the waves, it won't bother you anymore."

"I'm not incapacitated," Elyn assured her. "I'm just feeling a little woozy, is all. Don't worry about me. I am enjoying the salt air in my face and watching you in command."

Sigrid's heart jumped in her chest as she beamed adoringly at Elyn. Remembering the ship full of warriors, she decided turning back to the front was the wisest course of action.

When they arrived at the spot, the crew beached the boats and prepared a camp. Besides their tents and campfires, Sigrid and Sigurd erected a regal canopy furnished with wooden folding chairs and table for the kings and jarls to sit for their conference. A barrel of the twin's finest mead was rolled in for the occasion as well. By the time they had completed the arrangements, Elyn had set up their tent and had a crackling fire going.

After a cheerful meal shared with their crew and friends, Sigrid and Elyn retired to their tent, which did not promise enough privacy for the activity Sigrid wanted to engage in. Once again, she struggled to contain her desires.

"Thank you for doing all this while Sigurd and I arranged the meeting place."

"It was no problem," Elyn assured her. "It gave my stomach time to settle down. What do you think will happen tomorrow?"

Sigrid laid beside Elyn on a blanket in her trousers and gambeson, having removed her shoulder and breastplates. Elyn had set her armor aside and was draped in a gray tunic. Sigrid reached for her hand and wove their fingers together.

"Predicting what occurs in the future is tricky," Sigrid responded in a contemplative manner. "I know what I hope to happen, but even that is general. I couldn't guess what Jarl Njord and King Tortryggr will decide to do about your uncle. I suspect someone, whether Sigurd, King Grimolf, or myself, is going to kill Hroald for murdering Jarl Olaf. He shall not get the chance to plead his case before the Thing. I truly wish for an agreement securing better communication lines to be established between our leaders which will extend far into the future so misunderstandings like this no longer happen."

"Me too." Elyn ran her thumb along Sigrid's hand. "They can do what they wish with Unnulf, but I am sorry for my aunt and cousins. I wonder if Geir will be well enough to attend."

"I'll wager Siegfried will come," Sigrid stated. "There is no reason to believe a dispute will break out between our armies, considering the wealth of evidence against Gudbrandsdalir, but if something goes wrong..." Sigrid would never stand against Elyn, even if it meant she desert the battle completely.

"My place is with you," Elyn vowed. "I am now and shall ever be a shieldmaiden of Svithjod. I would be sad to fight my friends and countrymen, but let us say such a thing isn't going to happen. Just be confident, Sigrid. I am always at your side, no matter what."

Sigrid's fingertips guided Elyn's chin toward her face and she kissed her with languid contentment, savoring the bond between them. "And I will always be at your side, no matter what."

OTHER CONTINGENTS from both kingdoms arrived during the night and early the next morning until all were present. They comprised two vast armies of hundreds of warriors, both trained and volunteer, who remained several hundred yards apart while the canopy, seating, and refreshments Sigrid and Sigurd had established lay in the middle.

Washed, hair combed, and dressed in her royal blue armor, Elyn marched with Odo, Gunnlief, and Siegfried's man Sweyn in Svithjod's honor guard escorting Jarls Sigurd, Sigrid, and Siegfried to the meeting place. Grimolf had two aids with him, one on each side of Hroald. She saw Jarls Arkyn and Trygve for the first time. Sigrid had suggested they were in attendance as evidence they were not assassinating jarls or trying to oust the king.

Nerves stirred in her gut as she and the rest of the guard halted and assumed positions outside the open-sided tent. *Odin grant them wisdom. Forseti, son of Baldr, remove the scales from their eyes so they may see the truth and embrace peace and justice.*

With the security of Sigrid's gift sword at her side, the spear in her hand, and the shield strung over her back, Elyn and her fellow guards assumed postures of relaxed readiness. From her vantage spot, she could witness the entire meeting.

Tortryggr and his party made a point of arriving at the same time. His son Erling marched on the king's right and Njord on his left with Ingvar and Frode a stride behind. Krum seemed as nervous as a cat when two soldiers escorted him under the canopy. Elyn recognized Jarl Torban in the group and another distinguished man whom she had not met before. *He could be Jarl Gudbrand,* she suspected. She did not see Unnulf or Geir, but they may be across the field with the army.

The two kings appeared stiff when they shook hands, but Sigrid's air of amiable confidence set the tone for the parley. "My lords," she addressed them and motioned to the folding chairs and table already set. "It is good to come together to discuss these events. Sigurd and I have prepared a comfortable space for you. A drink to wet your mouths?" While Grimolf and Tortryggr settled, she dipped a cup into the open mead barrel and drank from it to show both leaders it was safe. With a nod from Grimolf, she poured each a goblet and placed them before the kings. Then she stepped back into a semicircle made up of the jarls from Svithjod.

"Tortryggr, it is good to see you well and strong," Grimolf opened in greeting.

"And I am pleased you are in good health as well," Tortryggr responded. The kings nodded to each other. "Skol." Tortryggr raised his cup.

"Skol," Grimolf repeated, and they both drank deeply. "I have been informed you had no part in the raids against my kingdom. Is this true?"

"On my oath," the older man vowed. "We thought you had attacked our farms."

"I swear by Odin's beard, we did no such thing, despite any so-called evidence to the contrary. The twin jarls believe you and I have been played for fools."

"Indeed. Jarl Njord has advised me of the same." Tortryggr took another drink and turned calculating scrutiny on Krum. "This emissary from Gudbrandsdalir flattered me, showered me with gifts, and offered counsel which seemed wise, so I consulted him from time to time. He would have me believe you are a greedy, ambitious ruler who sought to steal my kingdom."

Grimolf cast a scornful glance at Krum, then jerked a thumb at Hroald. "This envoy from Gudbrandsdalir insisted you had lost your wits and lay on death's door while your jarls fought over who would succeed you. You seem to me to possess all your faculties."

"These lies are all preposterous!" Tortryggr exclaimed. "Grimolf, many seasons ago, you and I were friends. What has happened to us over the years?"

Grimolf shook his head. "We stopped visiting each other and ceased communicating. I guess we were both wrapped up in our own families and affairs of state."

"I think our true enemy lies to the east in Gudbrandsdalir," Tortryggr suggested. "Speak, Krum," he commanded in a harsh tone. "What did King Hemingr promise to Firdafylke?"

Shaking and wide-eyed, the twiggy man with the gray-striped beard lowered his head. "I said speak up!" thundered Tortryggr.

Krum swallowed and eked out, "He told me he would support you against any foes who may attack, but I am just a messenger! I have nothing to do with making vows," he plead.

"Interesting," Grimolf mused with a smile to his counterpart. "Hroald, repeat what you assured Hemingr promised to Svithjod."

Hroald's gaze darted to all the taller men surrounding him, then to Krum. Pointing a finger, he accused, "That man is nothing but a liar! King Hemingr promised Svithjod his support, not them."

For an instant, Elyn feared this accusation may garner consideration, until her attention fell on Sigrid. If looks could have killed, Hroald would lay dead in the dirt already. In her characteristic boldness, Sigrid raised her voice in controlled fury. "The liar is you, Hroald!" She took an intimidating step toward the stocky little man, and he blanched.

"My lords, King Grimolf, King Tortryggr, I beg your pardon for my outburst," Sigrid addressed to the leaders. "But additional evidence has come to light regarding this cowardly weasel, and I cannot remain silent. He murdered my father, Jarl Olaf, your friend—stabbed him in the back like the spineless worm he is because he had not the fortitude to face him like a man!"

"Wait, what?" squeaked Hroald.

Sigrid spun to him with fire blazing in her eyes. "Rangvoldr told me exactly what happened. You thought to convince Olaf to agree to your scheme and Rangvoldr, who you manipulated through his ambition and pride, let you in to speak with my father when no one else was present. When Olaf turned you down flat, you feared your treachery would be exposed, so you stabbed him in the back repeatedly until he was dead."

Hroald's eyes widened, and he faded between the guards stationed at his sides. "No, no! It was Rangvoldr! He is the man who killed your father, not me!" Holding out palms in feigned innocence, he uttered, "I am but a merchant and ambassador, not a man of violence. I could never—"

"You could never defeat a skilled and powerful warrior in a fair fight," Sigrid barked.

"Where is Rangvoldr? Where is my accuser?" Fear poured off Hroald in waves, to Elyn's great satisfaction.

"He has paid the price for his crimes, Hroald." Sigrid's tone and her stare had frozen to an icy point. "It is time for you to do the same."

"But, but, this is hearsay!" Hroald passed his hopeless gaze around the assembly. "Rangvoldr lied to protect himself."

"Do you want to learn why I know he told the truth?" Sigrid scanned the circle of guards, jarls, and kings, standing tall and speaking with authority. "Because Rangvoldr was many things: a traitor to his jarl, king, and kingdom, a glory-seeker, a murderer, an obsessed and jealous man. But one thing he was not, was a coward. He fought beside Sigurd and me in the shield wall in numerous battles. He did not flinch before the power of the sea when it roared or the steel of an enemy who challenged him. Rangvoldr might have killed Olaf if he thought it would advance his position, but he would never have stabbed him in the back. He had too much pride for that. I know his words are true because he would have had the courage to look my father in the eye when he drove in his blade."

Quivering in horror, Hroald succumbed and dropped to his knees. "I was under orders from King Hemingr!"

"So was I!" Exclaimed Krum. "But I didn't murder anyone." He turned his plea to Tortryggr. "I didn't murder anyone! I only misled you about Svithjod because I had to, or King Hemingr would do terrible things to me."

"Jarl Sigrid, your outburst is excused." Grimolf gave her a nod and rose from his seat. "Tortryggr, my friend, pardon this slight interruption, but I made a vow to the twins, and I must keep it." He motioned to the two guards on either side of Hroald who hoisted him to his feet and followed Grimolf, dragging the wailing man with them.

"Mercy!" cried Hroald.

The guards removed Hroald from the tent and slammed him to his knees. Grimolf's ire against the spy who had gained his trust, manipulated his actions, and murdered his faithful jarl announced his intentions to all. Since he had come to the parlay unarmed, he held out an empty hand. Elyn moved in an instant, desiring to be the warrior to place a sword in his fist—her sword, the first one Jarl Olaf had given Sigrid. It was symbolic, and she felt the most fitting weapon for the circumstances.

The king gripped the hilt she offered him, and with a powerful stroke, separated the murderer's head from his body. He wiped the blade on Hroald's tunic hem and returned it to Elyn. Afterward, Krum could not spill details of the plot fast enough.

When he had finished confessing all, including enlisting Unnulf and two other key players across the kingdom as spies, Tortryggr looked to Grimolf. "It is very fortunate indeed you requested this meeting, my friend. Let us plan how to proceed."

Surprise lit Grimolf's expression. "I didn't request the meeting—you did." Both kings turned perturbed faces to Sigrid.

A slight knot clenched in Elyn's stomach, though she doubted the rulers would be too harsh on the woman she loved. Sigrid had done what she always does—weighed her best interests against the greater good and forged ahead with gusto toward the right choice.

"Yes, I sent the messages," she confessed. "You can reprimand me later. Let us be happy we now know who our true enemy is and form a strategy of how to defeat him."

"Oh, there will be a later, I assure you," Grimolf growled. "But I understand why you did it." Then the leaders set to work mapping out their plan.

CHAPTER 35

*D*ressed in chainmail forged and linked on his own mountain, with a sliver broe helmet, Hemingr perched atop a sturdy pony awaiting word from scouts on the backside of the ridge overlooking the field of combat. At his side, Brunhildr sat tall in her saddle, a most impressive shieldmaiden whose blonde hair fell in two braids to her broad armor-clad shoulders and plated bosom.

"Soon we shall have our seacoast, Brunhildr," he promised. "I'll build you the grandest ship in all Norvegr."

"I wish those dispatch runners had given a more detailed report," she replied with concern.

The king recalled the day the message bearers had arrived with the date and location the armies of Svithjod and Firdafylke had set to meet. One had reported his envoy mentioned a possibility of peace talks while the other only stated the king was bringing his whole army.

"I have confidence in Krum and Hroald," Hemingr replied. "They will ensure the armies end up fighting each other. We must be patient."

Just then, a wiry young man scampered down the hill with an eager expression. "My lord!" he called as he neared. Skidding to a halt, he announced, "They have struck down the meeting pavilion and the two armies are lining up to face each other! Gunnar is staying to observe. He will report on the battle soon, but I wish to run back and watch too. Do you give me your leave?"

Smiling at the excited youth, Hemingr waved his hand. "You may, but make certain none see you. Our strategy relies on absolute surprise."

"Yes, my lord," he chanted with enthusiasm and raced away.

"See, Brunhildr?" the king beamed at her with pride. "All is going to plan. You and I shall ride to victory once more."

Her tense muscles relaxed at the report, and she returned his grin. "You truly are the grandson of Loki. How else could your clever schemes work so well?"

"And you must be a Valkyrie reborn in Miðgarðr, for how could the greatest of all shieldmaidens stand as an equal at my side? Come, let us prepare." Hemingr dismounted his pony and his wife followed. All the mounted warriors did the same, and they readied their shields and spears, axes and swords.

Hemingr could hear the clash of iron and steel and the shouts from over the ridge as they tarried until the precise moment. His heart swelled in expectation as visions of victory danced in his head. Three kingdoms joined under one king. He would choose only loyal jarls to administer his lands. He would requisition the ships of Svithjod and Firdafylke as his own and press their best shipbuilders into service to craft a vessel worthy of his Brunhildr. His sons and daughters would rule over the most expansive kingdom in Norvegr, and he would die a famous man, sung about throughout the land. His nerves tingled with delight as his blood raced, ready to take possession of all he deserved.

The minutes seemed to pass like a long winter awaiting spring, but at last, his scouts rushed down the hill. "Their warriors fall, my lord!" the young man from before announced.

Gunnar issued his report next. "They contended in their shield walls for a long while, but cracks broke, and they shifted to man-to-man combat. Now over half lay dead or dying on the field."

The king nodded, his soul reveling in the image formed in his mind. "Formation!" he called out. "We don't want them to flee in separate directions. Keep your eyes on me. At first, both sides will think we are there to reinforce them. We want them to hold on to that belief for as long as possible." Hemingr drew his sword and raised it high, his left arm snug in the straps of his black shield. "Forward!"

With Brunhildr at his right hand, they led their warriors to the top of the ridge. A thrill leaped into Hemingr's throat when he saw the soldiers of Svithjod and Firdafylke whacking at one another. He watched a red shield fall, then a yellow and he felt as if his spirit was soaring with the gods. Hundreds of them lay on the ground, some writhing in agony, others motionless. Never in his life had he experienced such glorious satisfaction.

"Charge!" He gave the order and the mighty men of Gudbrandsdalir, the miners and timber-cutters, the hunters and forgers, all with exceptional valor and zeal, raced behind Hemingr and Brunhildr to certain conquest.

Closer and closer they ran, the thrill of battle carrying them like eagles' wings. While both sides continued to fight, their attention had shifted to his band of warriors. Faces beamed at them eagerly from both armies, pushing Hemingr's spirits to a higher plane.

Just as he could taste his triumph, the unthinkable happened. The dead and dying warriors arose from the earth as if completely unharmed. First one, then another, as if he was faced with an army of wraiths no weapon could destroy. His mouth dropped as the terror of an apocalyptic nightmare seized the breath from his lungs. Combatants from both sides spun their shields and weapons on the mountaineers, and a line of fresh soldiers bearing a mix of yellow and red rönds raced from behind the trees to encompass his rear. *How can this be?* he puzzled in disillusionment. *How could they have known? This is MY trap, not theirs!*

Panic surged through King Hemingr's soul as his gaze shot left and right. There was no escape for them. They would have to fight their way through, only they were surrounded and vastly outnumbered.

"Form a circle!" He commanded. "Shield wall! Turtle formation!"

But the coastal warriors had already begun to cut down his fighting men.

"What is the meaning of this?" Brunhildr cried out as she pushed her shoulder to his locking shields. They tried to keep their enemies at bay with jabs from their long-handled spears.

"I don't know!" he shouted back. "They found out. Somehow, they knew we were coming."

Hemingr's exuberant bliss transformed into shocked terror in an instant and he couldn't think, only react. Everything appeared as in a fog to his eyes, blurry images moving too fast for him to process. The confident fighters of Firdafylke and Svithjod poked holes in his shield wall until they were reduced to a circle of soldiers vying for their lives.

Amid the haze, he spotted a singular sight: a striking shieldmaiden, not unlike a younger Brunhildr, with flowing strands of red hair which appeared to glow in the sun attired in amor only a partnership of elves and dwarfs could have crafted, glided toward him as if riding on a cloud. "Valkyrie!" he called out to her. "Have you come to take me to Valhalla? I never felt the wound. How can I be dead? Yet I will gladly go with you."

He lowered his sword and shield, holding out his arms to her, his mind a haze melding dream with reality. The last thing he recalled was the heel of her boot striking him between the eyes.

SIGRID STOOD in a circle of leaders around where King Hemingr lay unconscious on the ground. They had captured Brunhildr with only minor injuries and held forty of the fighters from Gudbrandsdalir captive while decisions as to their fates were reached. An equal number littered the field, their blood soaking the earth. Sigrid was annoyed with Siegfried for taking part in the fighting, as he had reopened his prior wound. He stood with them, pride gleaming on his face, insisting the blood seeping through his gambeson was nothing. Not to mention her own blasted brother, who let himself get cut in two places and now sported a purple bruise under his eye. Did he really believe that was necessary? She shook her head at him in disapproval.

At least Elyn had come through the fighting unscathed. Sigrid glanced over to where she stood a short distance away behind the ring of jarls and kings conversing cheerily with Ingvar and her cousin Geir. Two guards gripped Unnulf by the arms as he scowled awaiting his fate. Krum sat on a stone with his head in his hands under Erling's watchful eye. Everyone's attention shifted to the midst of the group when Hemingr stirred.

He sat up and stared at kings with crossed arms and dire expressions while jarls voiced their suggestions.

"Banish him," Jarl Torbin demanded. "Let him live out his days a fugitive with no home. Because of him, my friend Jarl Stefnir War Tooth died in a useless battle which should never have been."

"I say execute him," Svithjod's Jarl Trygve proposed beneath narrowed brows. "And all his conspirators with him!"

"Nay," Njord countered. "He is a king. Allow me the honor to engage him in single combat so the gods can judge his fate. He may die at my hand like the warrior he is or suffer banishment should he defeat me."

"He cannot be allowed to keep control of his kingdom," Grimolf concluded as he rubbed the hair on his chin."

"What about his children?" Siegfried asked. "Who will rule Gudbrandsdalir?"

"Do not think to harm my children!" Brunhildr erupted in fury as her strong arms struggled against the grips which secured her.

"We could turn it into a jarldom under our joint control, Grimolf," suggested Tortryggr. "The population is not so large as to demand a king anyway."

"Why?" Sigurd addressed Hemingr rather than speak around him as the others did. "Why plan this scheme? What did we ever do to you, and why did my father have to be sacrificed to your greed?"

The mountain king's mournful gaze locked onto Sigurd's, and he opened his mouth to answer. "First, son, I never ordered Hroald to kill your father or any of the jarls. I instructed him to seek men of prominence who were discontent with their existing situation and enlist them as allies. I suggested they engage in ploys to stir hostilities between jarls to destabilize your power structures, but on my oath, I never ordered him to kill Jarl Olaf or any other person."

Sigrid examined the defeated, haunted look in his eyes, the conviction in his voice, and felt the disappointment in his spirit. "Mayhap you did not order his death, but because of your plot, many good men have perished, some of them your own. You sent the raiders disguised as Firdafylke fighters to our farms and disguised as ours to theirs, did you not?"

"Yes."

"Innocent farmers, women, and children died in those raids," she continued. "They were sacrificed to your greed and ambition, were they not?"

He shifted his focus to Sigrid, peering up at her from his seat in the dirt. "May I stand?"

Grimolf granted him a nod and Hemingr pushed to his feet, keeping his palms open and in view of all. "My motives were not greed and ambition, but survival."

Tortryggr exhaled a derisive snort. "How so? We never bothered you, attacked your people or stole your goods and resources."

"No," he answered, turning to Tortryggr. "But you denied us access to the sea." Hemingr shuffled in a small circle so his gaze could fall on each jarl and leader as he explained his case. In a voice more robust, he continued. "Generations ago, daring men ventured high and deep into the wilderness of the Fille Fiell mountains. They were strong and brave and discovered valuable resources of amber and ore, great herds of reindeer and elk, and timber so thick the trees were as hairs on a person's head. Some returned to the seacoast with their treasures, but others elected to stay and carve out a home there. They brought women and grew families and increased in number, prospering from trade. But mountain life is harsh," he stated in a pragmatic tone. "Crops cannot grow, and it is difficult to keep livestock alive through the winters. We are men and women of Norvegr, like you, with common ancestors. I'll bet, King Grimolf, if we trace our lineages, we will discover we are related."

He raised his palms to the kings and shrugged. "But we have no rivers that flow to the sea... no fjords, no massive lakes upon which to launch ships. We have almost forgotten how to build a longboat and are losing a portion of our heritage. Transporting heavy ore over land by wagon is difficult, and we are limited in our trading partners because we command no harbors or ships from which to embark. Remember King Tortryggr, when I offered you my aid against your Raumsdal invaders in exchange for a port—one port—where we may launch and moor ships? But you turned me down." Hemingr's beseeching gaze scanned the circle. "What else are we to do?"

Grimolf and Tortryggr whispered between themselves while the jarls scowled and grumbled. "We command a fjord," Siegfried stated. "You never offered to purchase land along its edge from us."

"When did you invite our kings to discuss this issue?" Njord inquired with a heated glare. "Never. Instead, you sent spies to deceive us and raiders to destroy our early crops. Let me fight him in a duel, King Tortryggr. I will settle this matter."

"If anyone is going to engage in a duel, it should be me," Sigurd declared. "No offense, Jarl Njord, but I am younger, stronger, and more motivated than you, for personal reasons. I will lay the conniving weasel in the ground."

Sigrid was uncertain whose suggestion held the most merit and was glad the decision was not hers to make. As she stood listening and weighing the options, she sensed a frustrated energy from behind and turned to view the anxious expression on Elyn's face. She shifted from one foot to the other, her hands moving from her hips to cross her chest, to dangle at her sides. A strong intuition tugged at Sigrid, and she ventured to throw a twist into the discussion.

"My lords," she spoke, taking a step forward. "I understand this is a debate between leaders and the final decision rests with Kings Grimolf and Tortryggr, but..." She glanced back to Elyn and waved her over. "I believe this worthy shieldmaiden has something substantive to add."

Sigrid smiled at the surprise which lit Elyn's eyes and gestured for her once more. Hesitantly, Elyn ambled over, and Sigrid guided her to the fore with a pat of assurance on her shoulder.

"Elyn is one of mine," Njord affirmed. "Or, rather, she was. It was she who first voiced her concerns and who brought to me her suspicions and evidence of Hemingr's plot. I'd wager if it was not for her quick wit, keen observation, and dogged tenacity, we would find our situations reversed today. Elyn, what do you wish to say?"

"Thank you, my lord," she replied to Njord. "But Jarl Sigrid deserves far more credit than I. It's just that... it is come to my attention..." She paused and bowed her head.

"Elyn, my dear." Tortryggr spoke to her in mild reassurance. "You have distinguished yourself in my eyes. Please, tell us what is on your mind."

Sigrid could feel her anxiety at addressing the assembly. Her uncle had been a conspirator and now awaited his sentence, and she had not quite accepted the idea she was indeed an extraordinary woman worthy of being heard. Sigrid reached forth with waves of confidence pouring from her heart and pressed mental encouragement in her direction. *You can do it, Elyn. Share your solution with the same spirit you display in battle.*

Lifting her head, Elyn continued in a stalwart tone. "Thank you, my lord. It occurs to me we have two choices before us this day. I have worked with healers, and they have taught me you can treat the symptoms of a disease and gain temporary relief, but the same pain and discomfort will return after a while. Or you can treat the root cause of the ailment and cure it for good. You all have been offering ways to treat the symptoms, but no one has addressed a solution for the underlying problem which precipitated today's events. It is true King Hemingr's actions caused pain and suffering to both our kingdoms, which could have been far worse than what we have endured, and we can kill or banish him, strip his kingdom from the rule of his family, sell him as a slave, humiliate him with defeat in single combat, or an array of other punishments for his crimes against us, but it will not solve the problems which caused him to take these actions. We may get rid of him and live in peace and prosperity for years, but Gudbrandsdalir will still have no access to the sea. Will rivers spring up where none exist? Will their steep slopes suddenly flatten out or their winters warm to the temperatures we enjoy on the coast? Our growing season is short and precarious enough; imagine what theirs is like."

Every eye of the gathering was on Elyn, and every ear trained to the persuasive quality of her voice. She had no agenda, made no pretense, and entreated only what flowed from her heart. With no title, no lands to defend, no political goal to achieve, no vengeance to enact, and no point to prove, she demonstrated the meek perspective of a mediator. Sigrid's heart swelled with love and pride for Elyn, grateful, in a strange way, to Hemingr for making it all possible. Perhaps they would have eventually met had their armies not clashed that day on this very field, but it was equally likely they would not have and Elyn would have married Njord as her overbearing uncle dictated. Sigrid questioned her desire to punish the offender, her heart softening as she considered the wisdom in Elyn's words.

"It is true King Hemingr has wronged us," Elyn continued, "but did we ever consider his point of view? What would you or I have done in his situation? Did anyone offer to sell him land to build a port? Did we not turn down his proposal to trade military aid for a harbor? I suppose it would be within our rights to impose judgement on him, to pay him back for the trouble he has caused. It might make us feel better, but it will not return our departed loved ones. We can punish him in our spite and anger and the mountain folk will be afraid to stand against us... for a while. But in time, they will be back, attacking us again, and mayhap with greater success, because their problems and needs would not have changed. Their challenges would not have been addressed."

Turning in a slow circle, Elyn lifted her hands. "So you see, my lords, we can treat the symptoms and feel better for a short while, or we can seek to resolve the root problems which have created the irritating outcomes. Do you believe King Hemingr is an evil man deserving of retribution? If so, execute him. That is your right. But consider the alternative: he may be a decent leader who is trying to secure the best possible future for his people. Who among you does not strive to do the same? I am but a common shieldmaiden with no experience in leadership, unknowledgeable of politics, and unsophisticated in my reasoning, so you may wish to brush my suggestions aside. I am only thinking of our children and future generations. Leaders come and go, but our people remain here in this land. Whatever problems we do not fix, we simply pass on to them. Thank you for allowing me to speak."

With her head lowered, Elyn faded behind Sigrid, but the jarl caught her arm and put her lips to her ear. "You were brilliant, my love! Whatever they decide, you won me over. Thank you. I know it took more courage for you than facing down a brown bear required of me."

Releasing Elyn's arm, Sigrid turned back to the silenced ring of jarls and kings.

"Perhaps it will take longer than a few minutes to make so weighty a decision," Grimolf admitted.

"Indeed," Tortryggr concurred. "The fate of a king, even an enemy, is no matter to be taken lightly. Let us see to the wounded and the dead, then sit down together with Hemingr and Brunhildr to consider these matters with the wisdom of Odin rather than the short temper of Thor."

CHAPTER 36

Four weeks later, Hafrafell, in Jarl Siegfried's hall

Sigrid and Elyn danced to the gay music of court musicians at Sigurd and Birgitta's marriage celebration. Imported wine flowed along with ale and mead for the occasion, and everyone wore their best attire. Flowers of every size and hue adorned the bright hall while smiles lit each countenance. Games had been played that morning with enjoyable prizes for the winners and playful teasing for the losers. Sigrid and Elyn had entered a race where their inside legs were tied together, and they had to run as if on three legs. Their attempt ended when they toppled into a clover patch, laughing too hard to get up. Odo won a contest for who could stuff the most apple tarts into his mouth, at which Gudred had covered her face and purported not to know him.

As they swirled to the sound of drums, lutes, lyres, pipes, and flutes playing cheerful tunes accompanied by clapping hands and tapping feet, Sigrid pretended the festival was for her and Elyn, and all their friends and relatives had turned out to celebrate with them. Even Kings Grimolf and Tortryggr were in attendance.

Thanks to Elyn's courage, King Hemingr kept both his head and his kingdom under conditions recognized by all parties. She had earned her title of Peacemaker. Tortryggr and Grimolf consented to grant an unoccupied portion of land close to their border featuring an inlet large enough to provide a safe harbor to Hemingr, who agreed to pay his lease in amber each spring. There his people could build and maintain their ships under Sigurd and Njord's watchful attention. After his initial trip home, Hemingr returned with wagons of treasure whence he paid reparations to the families of each citizen of Svithjod and Firdafylke who had been killed in the raids or fighting he had caused. While some remained bitter, still thirsting for Hemingr's blood, the kings had taken Elyn's words to heart and determined this was the best solution to forge a lasting peace in the region.

Hot and perspiring from the exertion, Sigrid took Elyn by the hand. "I'm going to sit with a drink. Would you like to join me, or do you wish to dance some more?"

"I could use a cup," she replied with a dazzling smile. Elyn looked so tempting as her breath heaved and droplets of sweat lined her brow, the same way she appeared after sparring when Sigrid could not wait to get her back to her room. The desire to kiss her right there in the hall was a real temptation, but this was Sigurd's special day, and she would do nothing to detract attention from her brother and Birgitta. She could feel the bubbling delight springing forth from his soul and rejoiced with him in hers. Taking a glance over her shoulder, Sigrid spied Sigurd across the room, beaming at the young woman who held his hand, hopping out the steps to their dance. It had been a perfect day.

Frida poured the wine into Sigrid and Elyn's silver cups, and Sigrid found an empty spot on a bench along the wall. She plopped onto it and pulled Elyn down beside her, laughing at her startled expression. It was hard for Sigrid to keep her eyes off her body in that new form-fitting dress and even harder to tear her gaze from her radiant face. She wore a dress too, with a stylish cut and embroidered details to compensate for lacking Elyn's physical attributes. Her lover didn't seem to mind, confessing her attraction to long legs, modest breasts, and lean muscles.

As if materializing from nowhere, two shaggy hounds the size of small ponies appeared before Sigrid beseeching her with soulful expressions. "I see you Jotun and Warg," she acknowledged and scratched them behind the ears. Elyn also extended a hand of affection to the wolfhounds. "I'll bet you don't know what to think about all this merrymaking, huh boys? Now, lie quietly at my feet. Afterwhile, there will be scraps and leftovers for you."

After each woman had drunk deeply from her cup, Sigrid stretched her arm around Elyn's shoulder and pulled her close, taking joy and comfort from feeling her body pressed to hers. "Are you having a good time?" she asked.

Elyn leaned into her more heavily. "You know I am. You should go dance with Sigurd. You needn't feel you must entertain me."

"Says the woman who robs my breath with laughter and fills my heart with songs." Sigrid laid her cheek to Elyn's head. "I'll grace my brother with a dance soon. This party will go on for hours yet. But later, when they retire to Birgitta's bedchamber, I know a private spot to take you before we stretch out in the hall with all the others to sleep."

Sigrid felt the pull of anticipation. In the weeks which had passed, she had grown even more intense in her feelings for Elyn, who seemed to surprise her in the most delightful ways. She invented a game whereby each would cast their dice and the one with the lowest number would have to remove an article of clothing. If they rolled a tie, they each removed an item, but they were not allowed to touch each other until both had nothing left to shed. It was the most tantalizing and provocative game Sigrid had ever played, and she was immeasurably glad it was a secret frolic just for them.

"I look forward to retreating to this private spot of yours. Where is it?" Elyn tilted her head back to shoot a questioning gaze at Sigrid.

"Why don't you try to guess?" Sigrid teased.

"I hope it is not a fish-cleaning hut," Elyn replied. "Because if so, you will be going there alone."

Sigrid laughed and brushed a kiss on Elyn's forehead. "Not a fish-cleaning hut."

Their banter was interrupted when Grimolf stood and raised his hands. The drums, strings, and flutes quieted, and the dancers' feet stilled. "Jarl Siegfried, may I share a few words with your guests?" His auburn-haired wife Tori remained seated beside him and smirked in amusement, perhaps knowing what he would say.

"Indeed, my lord." Siegfried smiled and extended a hand toward the multitude of merrymakers. "My hall is your hall."

Grimolf inclined his head, then raised his goblet to the newlyweds. "Jarl Sigurd Olafsson and the lovely Birgitta, Siegfriedsdottir, today you begin a new chapter in your lives together. Cherish every moment, both the good and the bad, the joyful and solemn, your quarrels and your agreements, because variety is the spice of life. You should love and fight with passion, so you know you are alive. And now, Sigurd, we must look to find a husband for your sister, Girrid, so she may move to his house and make room for the children you and Birgitta will soon add to the family."

The comment produced a few laughs and a blush on Girrid's cheeks. Sigrid cast her eyes about the hall, noting who was with whom. As Grimolf continued his speech, she whispered into Elyn's ear, "Who is the young woman beside Grimolf's son, Tyrulf?" She made an inconspicuous gesture to a slender youthful man with sandy hair and a scant beard sitting with a pretty girl she did not know.

Elyn studied the couple and murmured back. "I'm pretty sure she is Erica, the daughter of Erling and King Tortryggr's granddaughter."

A speculative grin crossed Sigrid's lips. "They seem quite cozy."

By then, Grimolf had concluded his words of encouragement and advice. "Skol!" he cheered, lifting his cup.

"Skol!" repeated the attendants, and all drank to the happy couple.

"We have another announcement," Grimolf declared, and the hall quieted again. "We thank our neighbor, King Tortryggr the Navigator, for joining us in this celebration. He and I have been catching up and reminiscing about old times. Did you know a few generations ago, there were no kingdoms of Svithjod and Firdafylke?" A few people stirred and others responded with curious gazes. Sigrid smiled, a light sparking inside as she recalled the story Aslaug had recounted when she stayed at Njord's longhouse.

"Instead, we were all part of Sogn," he expounded. "Sogn was a strong, prosperous kingdom, one of the largest in Norvegr, but the king and his half-brother had a falling out and it split in two. King Tortryggr and I have decided it is time to repair what was broken. Tortryggr?" Grimolf waved the older king up from his seat and motioned for him to speak.

"My son, Erling, is a capable administrator and a fine warrior. He is of an age to come into his own. It also seems my granddaughter, Erica, has become quite smitten with Grimolf's son, Tyrulf, who spoke with me of marriage no sooner than these two voiced their vows." The elder king pointed to where Sigurd wrapped his arms around the shorter Birgitta, who stood in front leaning into him. "As you can see, I am not getting any younger, but I still have a few adventures left in me. Grimolf and I agreed we do not wish to die as feeble old men in our beds, but as warriors fit for Odin's Hall. To drink mead and feast at Odin's table has always been our dream, but now, safe in our capitals surrounded by hundreds of warriors, no longer competing on the field of battle, how will such a dream come to pass?"

"So, my friend and I have sworn a blood oath to rejoin our kingdoms under the red and yellow banner of Sogn," Grimolf proclaimed. "Inspired by Olaf's twins, Erling has agreed to share the rule of this joint kingdom with Tyrulf, sealed by the marriage of his daughter Erica to my son. Erling is older and more experienced, but Tyrulf is eager, brave, and strong. Their qualities complement each other and as brothers-in-law they shall govern in our stead. Erling has no sons, only daughters, and has consented to pass his right to rule to his first grandson, who will be Tyrulf's son with Erica."

"What if they only have daughters?" someone one called jokingly from the crowd.

"Then they will have to look to Sigrid for instruction on how a woman is to lead!" Grimolf replied with a laugh. A blush rose in Sigrid's cheeks, and she lowered her chin shaking her head. As "punishment" for having sent out false invitations to Tortryggr and himself, he had charged her with the added task of devising and implementing a plan of aid to every widow and orphan in the kingdom so none would endure a harsh winter.

"Do you not recall the many goddesses, including Freya, who epitomized leadership?" Grimolf asked. "Our gods set a precedent for this very thing. Were not the Vanir and Æsir once at war? Freya agreed to marry Odin to create peace between their clans. Even after they went their separate ways, their bond remained strong, and that is why Odin and Freya divide courageous warriors who die in battle between them still today."

"Grimolf and I have spent our lives loaded with the burdens of responsibility, compelled to put the well-being of our kingdoms before our own. Therefore, we have decided to relinquish our thrones and embark on a grand adventure." A brilliant spark of lively mischief lit Tortryggr's eyes.

"We are setting off in King Tortryggr's newest ship, featuring the most innovative construction yet, with a crew of carefully selected warriors, seamen, traders, and our wives to visit all the places we have never been," Grimolf added in excitement.

"And if the sea or a hostile native's spear should strike us down, we will rejoice because of the rewarding afterlife we shall embrace!" Tortryggr beamed and exchanged a triumphant glance with Grimolf.

Surprise was the standard reaction, but with smiles and shrugs, the people began to cheer, clap their hands, and converse with each other in tones of wonder.

"I did not expect that," Sigrid admitted.

"I think it is endearing," Elyn cooed. "Promise me when we grow old, you will carry me off on a grand adventure so we will not die of some weak woman's ailment."

"You have my word," Sigrid vowed, with love for Elyn creating a flutter in her heart.

A FEW HOURS LATER, Elyn lay with Sigrid on a blanket in a little green meadow outside Siegfried's yard walls, gazing up at a gleaming quarter moon and a sky flooded with a river of stars, Jotun and Warg lying guard. With the summer solstice passed, nights were still short, but it got dark enough to see the stars for a few hours.

Satisfied and relaxed, Elyn luxuriated in Sigrid's nearness, breathing in her scent and tingling with the energy radiating from the singular shield-maiden's body. When the Thing met a couple of weeks ago, the case had been brought against her Uncle Unnulf. He had asked her to speak on his behalf, and she refused… at first. She testified how six years past he and Geir had saved her life from the Raumsdal invaders and offered her a place at his hearth but would say nothing more in his defense. She refused to lie for him and if she elaborated on her story, it would only make him look more guilty. The freemen of Firdafylke voted to banish him, but not his family. Liv elected to stay in Kaldrlogr with her children, and Unnulf was put on a boat with a bag of his belongings the next day. Elyn would be pleased if she never saw him again.

The assembly also took action against Krum and two other spies who were uncovered. All three were forced to march naked through the streets of Gimelfjord while residents jeered and hurled insults, manure, and rotten produce at them. Then they were sent back to Gudbrandsdalir, where they became King Hemingr's problem.

"There's Thor's chariot," Sigrid said, pointing to an arrangement of stars. "And over there are Tjatse's eyes. See?" She pointed again. "The real bright ones."

"Do people actually use the stars to navigate their ships?" Elyn asked. "How do they know where to go?"

"We may not be certain *what* they are, but our ancestors have known for hundreds of years and passed down to us the significance of star patterns in the sky. Their slow march around in a circle takes a full year, and they always keep their order and timing. See that one?"

Elyn followed Sigrid's finger in a straight line off the back corner of Thor's chariot. "Yes."

"It's the North Star, always pointing north, as if it is the hub of a wheel and all the others move around it. The arrangement of stars assumes differing positions throughout the year, and the navigators can use their locations in certain seasons to determine east and west and how far south they have traveled."

"You know so many things," Elyn marveled, and brushed a kiss to Sigrid's cheek.

Sigrid laughed. "I was required to learn so many things! Father raised me to fill his place one day. I wonder if his eyes are up there, if he can see us lying here gazing up at him?"

Her heart brimming with adoration, Elyn turned on her side, propping up on an elbow to face Sigrid. She couldn't stop her fingers from their need to touch, stroke, and caress the woman she loved. "If so, Sigrid, I know deep in my soul he is indeed proud of you. You rose to the occasion, uncovered his murderer, and kept his legacy alive. Could what makes the stars bright be the loving pride of our parents, grandparents, and ancestors' radiant faces glowing down so we know they have not forgotten us? I wonder if my mama and papa are up there, too? Are they shining down at me?"

Sigrid rolled toward Elyn and tangled her fingers in her hair. Pulling her close, she met her lips, nibbling, flicking, possessing, until Elyn's brain turned to a foggy blur of bliss. "If they can see you, Elyn, I assert with absolute assurance they are proud of you, more so than you could imagine. You stopped a war, reunited a kingdom, laid the groundwork for a lasting peace, and you haven't even reached your twentieth year yet. You are a power on the battlefield, a wildcat in bed, with amazing intuition and a brilliant mind. Add to that a sense of humor and a body I can't resist, and I thank the gods daily for bringing us together! I love you more than I knew was possible."

Stirred and impassioned, Elyn reclaimed Sigrid's mouth, desiring to delve deeper, to lose herself in the sea of joy splashing against her senses. "I love you, Sigrid," she affirmed in a delirious tone, husky and warm with relaxed intimacy. "I pray you won't tire of me and seek another."

"Never!" Giving Elyn a scrutinizing look, she addressed her with speculation. "Didn't I just finish saying how brilliant and intuitive you are, and then you say something dumb like that?" She shook her head, prompting laughter to bubble forth from Elyn's lips.

"Yeah, well, even a clever girl can have an off day," she admitted in good fun.

Then a mischievous gleam lit in Sigrid's blue eyes just long enough for Elyn to wonder what she was up to, when Sigrid pushed her onto her back, straddled her body, and tickled her without mercy.

"I'll teach you to voice ridiculous things! Tire of you?" she whooped. "There hasn't been a moment when I wasn't thinking about getting my hands and lips and tongue on you! Does one tire of food and drink? Do you think I will grow weary of breathing next? You silly woman!" Her tickles slowed to light caresses and her playful teasing tapered into lush longing. "I desire you more than meat and bread, more than water or air. You are my everything."

Elyn had not known her heart could expand even wider than it had already, but under the comforting weight of Sigrid's body, the tingling sensation of her hands on her, the absolute candor in her eyes, and the conviction of her words sent Elyn over some invisible edge. She let go of her image of inadequacy, released the barrage of slights and insults she had become accustomed to, and dared to believe she was worthy of being happy and loved. Besides, she knew for a fact Sigrid the Valiant did not lie... unless it was to save a kingdom.

EPILOGUE

Gnóttdalr, five years later

rost bit the twilight air as Sigrid rode through the gates to her longhouse yard on an autumn evening. She slung a leg over the horse's head and slid from the saddle, allowing a bend in her knees to absorb her impact with the ground. *I suppose I could dismount normally, but where's the fun in that?* she thought as she handed off the reins to a stable boy. With low-hanging clouds obscuring light from the setting sun and rising moon, she was glad to see several torches had already been lit.

Two gangly, wirehaired pups bounded over, with ears flapping and tongues wagging. One was a gray brindle and the other an oat colored wheaten. Barely weaned, they were already to Sigrid's knees with their long limbs and squirming bodies. "I see you Fenrir and Freki." They leaped at her leg, their tongues licking whatever they landed on. "Down, pups! Yes, I love you, too." The Cu who were fixtures in noble households throughout Norvegr and beyond, were powerful dogs, intimidating in size, unmatched in speed, and fiercely loyal to their owners, but the gentle giants were short-lived. A warrior may ride the same steed his entire career but would go through three or four of the great hounds during a horse's lifetime. Jotun and Warg were gone, and when Njord heard the news, he sent a gift of two pups from his bitch's summer litter. She could swear they grew an inch every night.

Before choosing a direction to move, Sigrid scanned the grounds until her gaze fell upon the vision she had been dreaming about all day. Elyn had stayed out late to work with Gustav, a lanky lad who had sprouted a foot over the summer. Sigrid tarried a few minutes, leaning on the timbers of the main building, soaking in the sight of her marvelous lover patiently instructing the awkward teen on his footwork, encouraging him with every correct placement. Sigrid beamed at her with pride, admiring her luscious curves, beautiful features, and physical strength, but more powerfully, her unyielding, kind nature.

Cognizant of the time, Sigrid pulled herself away and trotted around to the front door, the dogs having run off to play somewhere. The hall was warmed by the long blazing hearth running down its center and saturated with the aromas of delicious food and sweet mead. She hung her fur wrap on a hook and smiled greetings to the servants, warriors, and family members who filled the chamber, then made her way straight to where Birgitta sat with the children. While she nursed the smallest babe, two other youngsters giggled and chased each other in circles with carved wooden animals in their little hands.

"How is the harvest coming along?" Birgitta asked. The young woman had filled out to sport a mother's figure but remained as bright and attractive as ever.

"We got the last of the barley safely into the granary today, but we still have to wait for the last crop of hay to cure before we can stack it in a barn. The approaching rain will set us back a few days, I fear, but you cannot store damp hay. It's a fire hazard and may spontaneously burst into flame," Sigrid explained. "But all is well," she added with a smile. "And tell me about your day?"

Birgitta let out a tinkling laugh and motioned with an arm at the three children. "I'm glad you are here to collect yours now. Elyn has been busy all day between training the youths and settling quarrels. I think it's the first chill that gets the menfolk so prickly this time of year. She actually had to wrestle the ax from Torsten's hand to keep him from whacking a piece of Knute clean off!" She laughed and Sigrid wished she had been there to witness her woman in action.

"Mama!" The three-year-old ran over and threw her arms around Sigrid's neck, greeting her with a sloppy wet kiss. Sigrid scooped her up, swinging herself to a standing position. With a grin she tossed the child into the air with a twist, spinning her around before Sigrid caught her.

"Ingrid! What have you been up to all day while Mamas were working?"

"I've been working, too," the girl with rosy cheeks and honey hair announced. Then a mischievous gleam lit in her big, brown eyes. "Working on catching Olaf!" Wiggling free with a squeal of delight, Ingrid darted after the little boy, who looked just like a miniature Sigurd, and the two chased each other around until they ended up in a heap of giggles on the floor.

Girrid and Siegfried's oldest son had married the spring after Sigurd and Birgitta and had enjoyed a blessed year together before misfortune struck. The delivery of their child had been a difficult one, but the baby girl arrived healthy and sound, and they named her after her great-grand-mother, Gudred's mother Ingrid. Birgitta had given birth to Olaf during the long dark of winter and the two sisters-in-law were excited about raising their children jointly. But something went wrong, and Girrid couldn't stop bleeding. The healers did all they could for her, trying various herbal teas and stuffing wool balls in her cavity, attempting to stop the blood from flowing, but nothing worked.

Everyone understood childbirth was risky. It was not uncommon for a mother or child or both to perish in the process, but the possibility never stopped couples from planning and having children. Depressed over the loss of his wife, Ingrid's father had set out on a whaling expedition, but his ship was lost at sea. Elyn suggested the two of them adopting Ingrid was the best and most natural course of action. When the babe started imitating Olaf and calling both the women who cared for her "Mama", they didn't correct her. Sigrid would tell Ingrid the story when she got older.

Sigrid's attention was drawn to the doorway when Elyn entered with a sassy stride and her hairline damp with perspiration. Seeing her still stirred a tingle in Sigrid's deep parts, and the heat of her desire had not cooled a bit. Elyn took her turn to greet their little girl with a hug, kiss, and tickle before sliding onto the bench beside Sigrid.

"Is Gustav making any progress?" she asked, mostly because suggesting they skip dinner so she could join Elyn in a hot bath was not appropriate to say in front of Birgitta. "He's all legs. I'm surprised he doesn't trip over his own feet with every step."

Elyn laughed as her adoring gaze caught Sigrid's. "He's doing just fine. We won't take him on any outings where we expect real fighting will occur, but he tries hard. Once he stops getting taller, his coordination will catch up."

"Come get your food, you sorry lot!" Gudred called to the hall. "Or I'll eat it all myself."

Sigurd hopped up from the gameboard he and Odo and been scrutinizing and trotted over to them, swinging little Olaf onto his shoulders as the boy howled in delight. "Did someone say food? Don't worry, Mother, I'm coming."

Sigrid had been worried about their mother for a long while after they lost Girrid, but eventually her grandchildren spurred joy to return to her life. "Hey Sigurd, you big oaf—leave something for the rest of us!" Sigrid called after him in a teasing laugh. "You are already getting fat from your slothful living."

"Fat?" he countered with feigned shock. Wrenching one hand away from his tot's, he motioned to his toned midsection. "Feast your eyes on perfection, and talk about slothful? All you do every day is ride around inspecting grain and overseeing other people's labor while Elyn, here, does all the difficult and dangerous tasks. You should have seen her put Torsten and Knute in their places!"

Turning an amused expression to Elyn, she agreed. "I would have enjoyed that immensely." Taking Elyn's hand, they stood together, but when Ingrid bounded over, she squeezed between them, grabbing hold of both their hands.

"You are getting fat, brother," Odo joked as he jabbed an elbow in Sigurd's ribs and pushed past him to the head of the food line.

"I want pudding!" Ingrid chanted with glee.

"After your meat and vegetables," Elyn promised. Ingrid poked out her bottom lip until they all broke into laughter.

AFTER DINNER, Elyn, Sigrid, and Ingrid retired to their room where Sigrid stirred their fire back to life and Elyn helped their little girl change into her warm, woolen nightgown. "Tell me a story."

The bedtime ritual always began with a story, followed by the singing of lullabies while Ingrid fell asleep in their bed. Then carefully, one of them would move the sleeping child to her own small bed with wooden railings to keep her from rolling out onto the floor during the night. They would tuck blankets around her and place soft kisses to her head before snuggling close as Elyn had spent the day anticipating.

Life with Sigrid was more magical than she could have ever imagined, and each day and season, every year that passed, had woven them closer together. Their first winter had been the shortest and brightest of Elyn's life as she and Sigrid played games, making up a few, and entertained guests at their hearth. They had ventured out on calm days to go hunting, bringing their game home on a little sleigh. Elyn shared Sigrid's responsibilities as they had visited the sick and brought food to the elderly. And with as much time as they spent warming each other beneath Sigrid's bear skin, the dark season flew by. In the spring, Elyn learned about plowing, planting, and replacing thatch in roofs. Then her training sessions with the young warriors began.

The summer of their first anniversary, Sigrid took her on a trading expedition to Jutland, then on through the Baltic to the revered holy site of Upsala in the land of the Svíar. Sleeping on a rocking longboat full of crewmen and supplies had been a challenge, but the rewards of the experience far outweighed any discomforts incurred. They ran across Grimolf and Tortryggr at Upsala as they also attended the Nine-Year gathering and enjoyed catching up with them.

Near the end of their second year together, Ingrid had come into their lives and a lot of their attention revolved around her, but that, too, was a joy and delight.

"A story?" Elyn asked, as if the request surprised her. Ingrid nodded and climbed into her lap.

"Shall I tell the one about the time Elyn ended a war and brought two kingdoms together?" Sigrid suggested as she beamed adoringly at Elyn.

"No, the tale about how Sigrid rode the whale is much more exciting," Elyn recommended with a kiss to Ingrid's curls.

"Tell the one about Gudbrand and the cow," she requested, and giggled. "It's so funny."

"Whichever story you want is the perfect one," Elyn replied with a smile.

Sigrid let out a laugh. "You are no different than Gudbrand's wife, ever agreeable and looking on the bright side."

"Given the choice, I'll always take the bright side," Elyn proclaimed with a wink, and told the story with as much animation as she could.

Then Sigrid lay the little girl down on the bed and blew out the lamp, so the only light glowed from the fire. She sang soothing songs until Ingrid fell asleep, then moved her to her bed. Elyn welcomed her return by enfolding Sigrid in her arms. "I missed you today."

"I missed you too, my love." Sigrid sealed her words with a kiss. "But soon enough, winter storms will keep us indoors for days and you will be itching to get rid of me."

"Never!" Elyn quipped, and gently bit Sigrid's lower lip for emphasis. She flashed an inviting gaze. "I want your hands on me, Jarl Sigrid the Valiant, unless you fear losing control."

"I fear nothing, Elyn the Peacemaker," she teased, sliding artistic caresses across Elyn's skin, arousing her passion like a storm churns the swells of the ocean. "You should be careful what you ask for, or you'll find me riding you until dawn."

"Bring your best efforts, shieldmaiden," Elyn challenged. "You will be spent long before the sun rises, I promise." She guided her own hands with tantalizing precision up and down the length of her fabulous warrior, claiming each peak and slope with her mouth, drawing magic runes with her tongue until Sigrid moaned in pleasure.

"Keep it up, Elyn," she purred. "No matter which of us succumbs first, I still win."

Arching to Sigrid, Elyn met her lips in a driving kiss, ripe with hunger yet generous in its demand. "Nay, fair Sigrid, for with you in my arms, I cannot lose."

Their eyes met in an exchange that could only have originated from the deep waters of Mimir's Well which lay at the base of Yggdrasill. A dreamy look passed over Sigrid's face as she concluded, "I proclaim we both win."

"Skol," Elyn responded with a crooked smile.

In confusion, Sigrid asked, "Where is your drink?"

"Right here," Elyn answered with a grin, and delved into another kiss. *You are mine, and I am yours. You were right, Sigrid. Who needs titles or lands, armies or ships? When you have love, you have gained the secret of life, a treasure far more precious than silver.*

NAVIGATING THE NOVEL

PLACES, PEOPLE, AND THINGS IN THE LAND OF
NORVEGR

Since this story transpired almost fourteen hundred years ago, many of the names of people, places and things will be unfamiliar to readers. While most are actual historical terminology, some of the place names I made up, because the oral histories of the culture could not have possibly passed on to us every town, village, and even kingdom as they were established in 649 CE. Following is a way to organize the places, characters, and terms with definitions and pronunciations where applicable.

GEOGRAPHY

The kingdom of Norway was established in 872 as a merger of many minor kingdoms, but was previously known by an ancient place name, Norvegr (NOR-way-gr), which means "north way". Historians can verify little from the seventh century, but one well-documented historical event is referenced in the story: a great disaster which occurred over a hundred years prior. Tree ring research and written accounts from the Mediterranean have helped historians conclude two massive volcanic eruptions, one in 535 or 536 in the northern hemisphere and another in 539 or 540 in the tropics, pumped tremendous volumes of ash into the atmosphere, clouding the sun and dropping temperatures in until around 550. The event some call a mini-ice-age precipitated a pandemic, food shortages, and a migration period as people sought better conditions.

Sigrid and Elyn includes three Fylki (FILL-ky), or petty kingdoms, from within the territory. The kingdoms of Firdafylke (FIR-da-FILK-ah), Svithjod (SWITH-yod), and Sogn (Sawn) lay on the south-central coastal region of Norvegr. During some periods, oral histories indicate Svithjod and possibly Firdafylke were encompassed by Sogn or were in some way interchangeable, but accounts differ. Suffice it to say, all represent actual petty kingdoms of the pre-Viking era. Gudbrandsdalir (Goud-BRAUN-DS'-daul-ir) was a region (possibly a kingdom, but with a much smaller population) to the east of Sogn in the Fille Fiell (FIL-la Fell) Mountains. Raumsdal (ROMS-dal) was the kingdom lying to the north of Firdafylke which is referred to in the story.

The names of the villages, however, were my creations, based on old Norse words and patterns in place names. Gimelfjord (GIM-el fi-yord) is the principal town in Firdafylke where the king lives and Kaldrlogr (KAL-der-log'-er) is the village Elyn and Jarl Njord live in. To the south in Svithjod, I have included the capital, Sochabrot (SO-ka-brot), Sigrid and Sigurd's village of Gnóttdalr (G-NOT-daul-ir), and Siegfried's town of

Hafrafell (HAUF-ra-fell). In Gudbrandsdalir, the only village mentioned is the one where the king resides, Bjornhellir (Be-YORN-hell-ir).

PEOPLE

This novel includes many character names and here I will organize them to assist the reader in keeping track of them all. Each is arranged by kingdom and relationship.

From Firdafylke

King: Tortryggr the Navigator; Erling, his adult son; Erica, his grand-daughter; Karr, a guard in his hall

Jarls: Njord, Torban, Gudbrand, and Stefnir War Tooth

Njord's family: Hilda, his deceased first wife; Aslaug, Hilda's mother; Bjorn, his son; Yrsa, his daughter

Elyn's family: Unnulf, uncle; Liv, aunt; Geir and Frigga, cousins; Ingvar, best friend

Other warriors in Elyn's band: Frode, Horik, Ulfinn, and Gustav

Other people from Firdafylke: Halvar, Unnulf's apprentice; Krum, envoy from Gudbrandsdalir; Astrid, the Völva; Halfdan, the healer; Helga and Tyrdis, two shieldmaidens

From Svithjod

King: Grimolf the Wolf; Tori, his wife; Tyrulf, his oldest son; other unnamed children; Gyda, his house manager

Jarls: Sigrid the Valiant, Sigurd Olafson, Siegfried Strongarm, Arkyn, Brynjar, and Trygve

Sigrid's family: Sigurd, twin brother; Odo, younger brother, Girrid, younger sister; Gudred, mother; Olaf, deceased father; family servants/slaves: Sveina, Asmund, and Thora

Siegfried's family: Birgitta, sister; Frida, Birgitta's mother, his stepmother; four unnamed children; Sweyn, a warrior

Friends: Gunnlief and his wife Brenn, Rangvoldr the Black

Other people from Svithjod: Hroald, envoy from Gudbrandsdalir; Finn, a shepherd; Estrid the Revivor, the healer; Trygg the Sightless, the priest; Skelkollr, an old warrior, Arne Ragnarsson, a fisher; Skarde, a newcomer; Cnut, a tanner; Eric, former warrior with one arm; Bragi and Runa, young couple who get married; Gunne Flokisson, a farmer; Bard the Beardless, a goatherd; Thorgeir, a skald; Leiknir, a warrior killed in battle; Hallbrandr, a man who tries to murder Siegfried

From Gudbrandsdalir

King: Hemingr the Unwashed; Brunhildr, his wife; five children including Ulfvar

Other people from Gudbrandsdalir: Hroald and Krum, the ambassadors/spy-conspirators; Sune, an attendant in the king's service; Gunnar, a scout

GLOSSARY

Æsir: Odin's family

Alfheim: elven homeland

Ard: a farming implement, forerunner to the iron plow, used in Europe during the Vendel Period.

Ásgarðr: the land of the gods.

Blót: an important public or private ritual usually involving a sacrifice.

Broe: a style of Vendel helmet with a faceguard

Fylgja: a guardian spirit usually taking the form of an animal but may be invisible.

Gothi: a religious leader (not a full-time priest) who would oversee rites and ceremonies

Grædari: a healer

Holmgang: a legal duel practiced by early medieval Scandinavians recognized to settle disputes.

Hnefatafl: a Norse strategy board game similar to chess

Jötnar: giants of Norse mythology described as having powers to rival those of the gods.

Landvættir ("land wights"): spirits of the land in Norse mythology

Ljósálfar: light elves

Mare: a monster which gave people bad dreams at night by sitting on them in their sleep.

Miðgarðr: the land of men.

Norns: the three Fates of Norse mythology

Ratatoskr: a mischievous squirrel who runs up and down the tree of life, delivering the messages of the gods.

Rönd: a round wooden shield reinforced with a metal rim and center hub

Seiðr: Norse magic or shamanism, with the practitioner's intended task typically involving a prophecy, a blessing, or a curse.

Skald: a bard, storyteller, or singer of songs

Skol: a drinking salute to friends called out like "cheers"

Svartalfheim; land of the dwarves

Svíar: old Norse word for Swedes

The Thing, or Althing: a Norse meeting of freemen to discuss and vote on matters of importance, similar to a congress and jury rolled into one.

Thrall: a slave. Slavery was an accepted part of life in Norse society, but it was not based on race. Slaves were captured from unfriendly kingdoms in raids and battles or purchased from slave traders. Most farms and many wealthy households employed a few slaves to help with the workload. The practice, while still objectional to modern society, vastly differed from how it operated centuries later in the New World.

Ulfberht sword: an expensive, high-quality sword most associated with Norse warriors

Vanir: the Goddess Freya's family

Völva: a seer or prophetess who may also serve as a healer and perform magic. She was always a woman who had the ability to communicate with the spirit world and realms of the gods.

Viking curse words:

Helsike – heck, or what the hell

Sorðinn – fuck, fucking

Skitr – shit

By Thor's death – an oath only evoked in a whisper and under the direst of circumstances

THE STORY OF GUDBRAND OF THE HILLSIDE, A SCANDINAVIAN FOLKTALE

THE BEDTIME STORY ELYN TELLS LITTLE INGRID

There was once upon a time a man who was called Gudbrand. He had a farm which lay far away on a hill, and he was therefore known as Gudbrand of the Hillside. He and his wife lived so happily together, and were so well matched, that do what the man would his wife was well pleased, thinking nothing in the world could be better. Whatever he did she was satisfied. The farm was their own, and they had a hundred ounces of silver which lay in a box, and in the stall, they had two cows.

One day the woman said to Gudbrand, "I think it would be well to take one of the cows to town and sell it, and so we shall have some money at hand. We are such fine folk, we ought to have a little ready money, as other people have. As for the hundred dollars which lie in the chest, we must not make a hole in them, but I do not see why we should keep more than one cow. We shall, too, gain something, for I shall then have only to look after one cow, instead of having to litter and feed two."

This Gudbrand thought was right and reasonable, so he took the cow, and set off to town to sell it. When he arrived there, he could find no one who would buy the beast.

"Well, well," said he, "I can go home again with the cow. I have stall and litter for her, and the road home is no longer than the road here."

So he began to go homeward again.

When he had gone a little distance, he met a man who had a horse he wanted to sell. So Gudbrand thought it was better to have a horse than a cow and exchanged with him. He went on a bit further and met a man

277

walking along driving a fat pig before him, and he thought it would be better to have a fat pig than a horse. So he exchanged with the man. He went on a bit further and met a man with a goat. A goat, he thought, was better than a pig. So he exchanged with him. He went on a good bit further till he met a man who had a sheep, and he exchanged with him, for he thought a sheep was always better than a goat. He went on again and met a man with a goose. So he exchanged the sheep for the goose. Then he went a long, long way, and met a man with a cock. So he gave the goose for the cock, for he thought to himself, "It is better to have a cock than a goose."

He walked on till late in the day, and then as he was getting hungry. He sold the cock for twelve shillings, and bought something to eat, for, thought Gudbrand of the Hillside, "It is better to save one's life than have a cock."

Then he walked on homeward till he came to the house of his nearest neighbor, and there he looked in.

"Well, how did you get on at the town?" asked the neighbor.

"Only so and so," said the man. "I cannot say I have had good or bad luck," and then he began and told them all which had happened.

"Well," said the neighbor, "you will catch it when you get home to your wife. Heaven help you! I would not stand in your shoes."

"I think things might have been much worse," said Gudbrand of the Hillside; "but whether things have gone well or badly, I have such a gentle wife that she never says anything, do what I will."

"Ah," said the neighbor, "I hear what you say, but I don't believe it."

"Shall we make a bet?" said Gudbrand. "I have a hundred ounces of silver lying at home in a chest; will you lay as much?"

The neighbor was willing, so the bet was made. They waited till evening, and then set out for Gudbrand's house. The neighbor stood outside the door, while Gudbrand went inside to his wife.

"Good evening," said Gudbrand when he was inside.

"Good evening," said his wife. "Heaven be praised. Is it you?"

Yes, it was he. His wife then asked him how things went at the town.

"Oh, but so-so," said Gudbrand, "not much to boast of. When I came to the town, I could find no one to buy the cow, so I exchanged it for a horse."

"Thanks for that!" said the wife; "we are such fine folk we can ride to town the same as other people, and as we can keep a horse we might as well have one. Go and put the horse up, children."

"But," said Gudbrand, "I have not got the horse. After I had gone a bit further, I exchanged it for a pig."

"Well, well," said his wife, "that was good. I should have done the same. Thanks for it! now I shall have meat in the house to put before folk when they come to see me. What could we do with a horse? People would only have said we had got too proud to walk to church. Go along, children, and put the pig in the sty."

"But I have not got the pig either," said Gudbrand. "When I had gone on a bit further, I exchanged it for a milk goat."

"Bless me," said the wife, "you do everything well! When I think of it, what could we have done with a pig? Folk would only have said we eat up all we had. Now we have a goat we shall have milk and cheese, and we shall have the goat too. Run, children, and put up the goat."

"But I have not got the goat," said Gudbrand. "I went on a bit and exchanged it for a fine sheep."

"Well," said the wife, "you have done just what I should have wished—just as if I had done it myself. What did we want a goat for? I should have had to go over hill and dale after it. Now we have a sheep I shall have wool and clothes in the house, and food as well. Go, children, and put up the sheep."

"But I have not got the sheep either," said Gudbrand. "I went on a while, and then I exchanged it for a goose."

"You shall have thanks for that," said the wife, "many thanks! What would we have done with a sheep? I have no spinning-wheel nor distaff, and I should not care to bother about making clothes. We can buy clothes, as we have always done. Now we shall have roast goose, which I have so often wished for, and I shall be able to stuff my little pillow with the down. Go and bring in the goose, children."

"But," said Gudbrand, "I have not got the goose either. When I had gone a bit further I gave it in exchange for a cock."

"Heaven knows," said his wife, "how you thought all this out so well! It is just what I should have done myself. A cock! why it is just the same as if you had bought an eight-day clock, for the cock crows at four o'clock every morning, so we shall be able to get up in good time. What could we have done with a goose? I don't know how to cook it, and I can stuff my pillow with moss. Run and fetch the cock in, children."

"But," said Gudbrand, "I have not got the cock either. When I had gone a bit further, I got hungry, and so I sold the cock for twelve shillings so I might live."

"Thank God you did so," said his wife; "whatever you do you do it just as I should have wished. What could we have done with a cock? We are our own masters and can lie in bed in the morning as late as we please. Thank Heaven you have come back again safe. You do everything so well, we can well spare the cock, the goose, the pig, and the cow."

Then Gudbrand opened the door.

"Have I won the hundred ounces of silver?" said he, and the neighbor was obliged to own that he had.

A classic Scandinavian folk tale in common domain

MORE BOOKS BY EDALE LANE

The Lessons in Murder Series

Meeting over Murder

My Book

Skimming around Murder

My Book

New Year in Murder

My Book

Heart of Murder

My Book

Reprise in Murder

My Book

Homecoming in Murder

My Book

Queen of Murder

My Book

Cold in Murder

My Book

Foreseen in Murder

My Book

Matrimony in Murder

My Book

The Wellington Mysteries

Daring Duplicity: The Wellington Mysteries, Vol.1

My Book

Perilous Passages: The Wellington Mysteries, Vol. 2

My Book

Daunting Dilemmas: The Wellington Mysteries, Vol. 3

My Book

Atlantis, Land of Dreams

My Book

Heart of Sherwood

My Book

Viking Quest

My Book

Tales from Norvegr

Sigrid and Elyn: A Tale from Norvegr

My Book

Legacy of the Valiant: A Tale from Norvegr

My Book

War and Solace: A Tale from Norvegr

My Book

Walks with Spirits

My Book

The Night Flyer Series

Merchants of Milan, book one

My Book

Secrets of Milan, book two

My Book

Chaos in Milan, book three

My Book

Missing in Milan, book four

My Book

Shadows over Milan, book five

My Book

Visit My Website:

https://www.authoredalelane.com

Follow me on Goodreads (Don't forget to leave a quick review!)

https://www.goodreads.com/author/show/15264354.Edale_Lane

Follow me on BookBub:

https://www.bookbub.com/profile/edale-lane

Newsletter sign-up link:

https://bit.ly/3qkGn95

ABOUT THE AUTHOR

Edale Lane is an Amazon Best-selling author and winner of Rainbow, Lesfic Bard, and Imaginarium Awards. Her sapphic historical fiction and mystery stories feature women leading the action and entice readers with likeable characters, engaging storytelling, and vivid world-creation.

Lane (whose legal name is Melodie Romeo) holds a bachelor's degree in Music Education, a master's in history, and taught school for 24 years before embarking on an adventure driving an 18-wheeler over-the-road. She is a mother of two, Grammy of three, and doggy mom to Australian Shepherds. A native of Vicksburg, MS, Lane now lives her dream of being a full-time author in beautiful Chilliwack, BC with her long-time life-partner.

Enjoy free e-books and other promotional offerings while staying up to date with what Edale Lane is writing next when you sign up for her newsletter. https://bit.ly/3qkGn95